THE DEALMAKERS

Charles Dennis

VINGSBO PRESS

LOS ANGELES

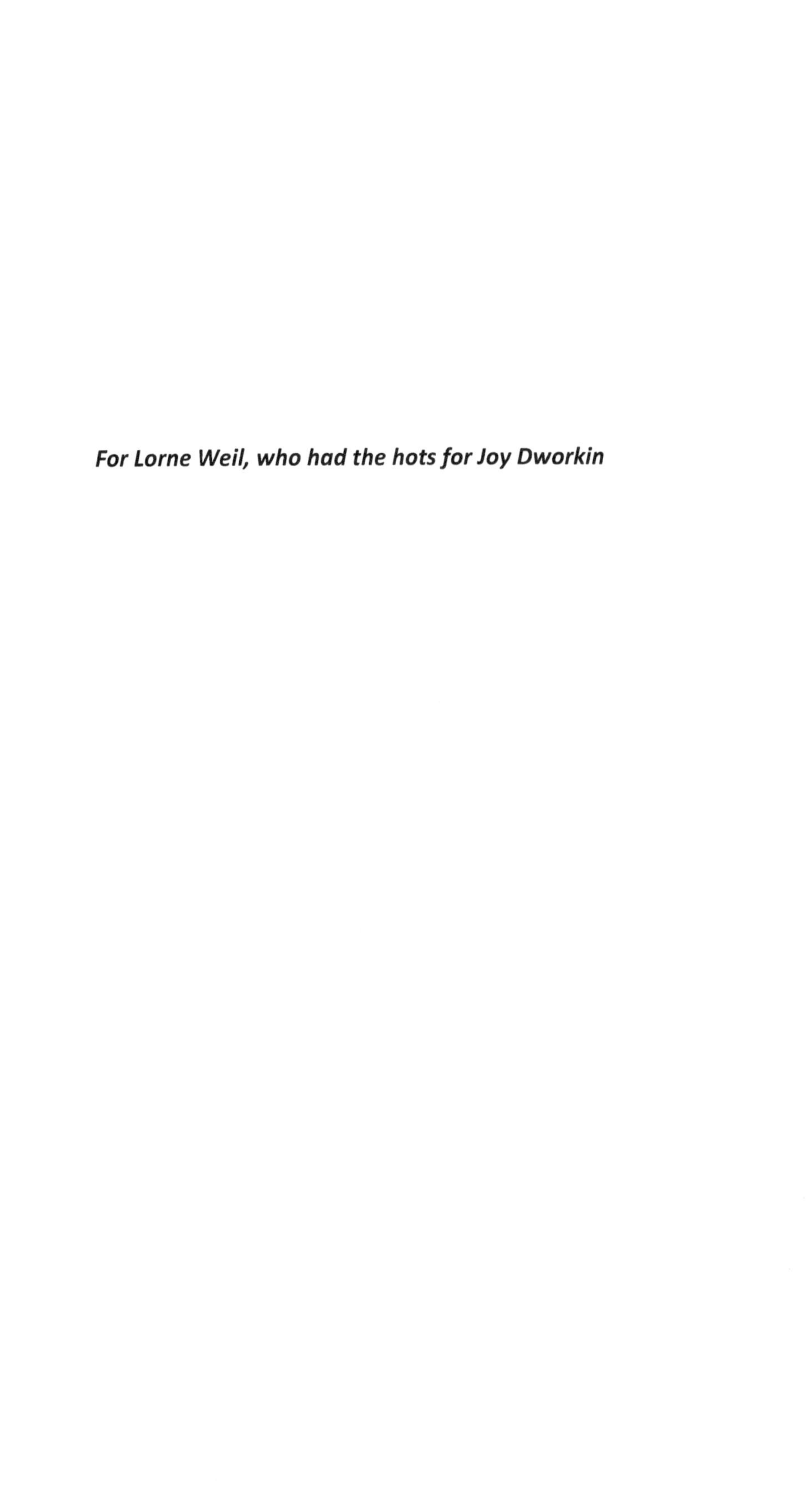

For Lorne Weil, who had the hots for Joy Dworkin

The author wishes to make it clear that all the characters depicted in this book are fictional and creations of the author's imagination. Any resemblance to persons living or dead is purely coincidental. There is no International Artists Agency at the corner of Rodeo Drive and Charleville in Beverly Hills, California. There is no IAA in New York, Chicago, or London either. Paramount, Universal, and United Artists studios do exist but the executives of these companies depicted in this book are wholly creations of the author's and in no way reflect the policies of these companies.

The author is also grateful to the following people for their contributions to this book: Emile Riley Abdelnour, for his unbridled enthusiasm; Tom Barad, for his early years in St. Louis; the late Edward Astrin, for his knowledge of show-business finance; the late Robert Littman, who longed to be Jimmy Steerforth; the late Charles Bennett, who inspired Roley Draycott; Dabney Goldman, who does the best Gary Cooper; Sarah Roger and Brian Cutler for making this book available again; Shawn and Brent Huff, who know more than their share about glamour; and my publisher and muse, Ulrika Vingsbo.

Here we stand between two eternities of darkness. What are we to do with this glory while it is still ours?

—Gilbert Murray

Table of Contents

ST. LOUIS

What is it that inspires a dream?

The question ran through Matthew Garber's mind as he stood in his old room at his parents' house in St. Louis packing for his 'great adventure'. It had been strange staying in his old bedroom again after so many years. The walls were still covered with framed photographs and awards from his high school days. Best Actor Award from a collegiate drama festival in 1969. A picture of himself as Riff in the Country Day-Mary Institute production of *West Side Story*. The linotype from his first film review for the *St. Louis Post-Dispatch.*

They had all been part of the dream and Garber was now pondering whether or not he wanted to take any of this memorabilia with him to Los Angeles the next day.

"Did you want your raincoat, dear?" his mother called from downstairs.

"It hasn't rained there in two years, Mother. They've got a drought out there, you know," he shouted down to her.

"Well, I was only asking! You don't have to bite my head off."

"Sorry."

For a moment he thought of phoning Trisha. But their marriage was over: legally and emotionally. A new life would be beginning the next day in California.

His father wandered into the bedroom at that moment. "Sure you don't want me to drive you to the airport tomorrow morning?" he asked. "Save you a couple of bucks."

"I'll take a limousine," answered Matty. "It'll be easier."

"Know where you'll be staying?"

"No. But Bobcaygeon said the job comes with an apartment."

"I still can't believe it," said his father sitting next to him on the bed. "A man walks into your life like that and bingo! You're off to Hollywood. It's like a movie."

"Everything I ever dreamed of, Dad. Everything I thought I'd lost."

"Did you pack your raincoat?"

"Don't need one out there—"

"Big shot! What if it rains?"

"It hasn't rained for two years."

"Did you phone Trisha?"

"Of course not!"

"Just asking," replied his father, holding his hands up in mock surrender. "Does she know you're going?"

"St Louis is a small town, Dad. I'm sure she's heard—"

"Not so small it didn't produce a Matthew Garber."

Matthew stared curiously at his father not knowing if he was being facetious or not. His father grabbed him and hugged him.

"I'm proud of you, Matty. Make sure you write your mother."

"I will."

His father left the bedroom. Matty rose from the bed to make certain there was nothing he'd left behind. He checked through the drawers of his dresser. Nothing. He walked over to his old study desk and went through those drawers. Nothing. He spotted the copy of the telegram he had sent the week before.

GILBOB
BEVERLY HILLS
CALIFORNIA

HAVE CONSIDERED YOUR OFFER CAREFULLY. DECIDED TO ACCEPT. WILL ARRIVE IN LOS ANGELES JANUARY 15. LOOKING FORWARD TO AN EXCITING CAREER WITH IAA.

MATTHEW GARBER

"God bless you, Gilbert Bobcaygeon!" said Matty, closing the lid on his suitcase.

RANKOFF

The man stepped out onto the patio of Inez Sanchez's sprawling Bel Air mansion and stared up at the January night sky dotted with stars.

Aging bobbysoxers, who had thrilled to his singing years before, would not be disappointed by his appearance years later. His was still the head one might find on an ancient Roman coin. A boy warrior grown old, salt-and-pepper hair, deep blue eyes, a mouth both cruel and loving, Robert Rankoff remained an enigma to all who knew him.

Rankoff's attention was distracted by a light going on at the bottom of the terraced hill sloping down from Inez's estate. A tiny cottage became visible down below.

Curious, thought Rankoff. I never noticed that cottage before. Where did it come from?

Maybe it isn't there at all. Maybe I'm not here. Could it be I'm back in Cleveland and none of this ever happened?

Rankoff turned his head around and stared through the French windows at the living room. Rock music was blaring from inside the party. Rankoff could make out the gigantic form of Geoffrey Holder dancing with Diahann Carroll.

I did not invent Geoffrey Holder, decided Rankoff. Nor did I imagine the cottage down there. I am here. Unfortunately. Trapped in the daytime soap of my life. I'm carrying the whole series! It started off as a cameo. Who made this deal? *Mea culpa*. The master dealmaker can't get his own act together.

I should send myself a memo, he thought.

R. RANKOFF TO R. RANKOFF
C.C.: NOBODY

BOBBY BABY: JUST A NOTE TO REMIND YOU YOU'LL BE 53 NEXT MONTH. YOU'RE STILL THE BEST AGENT IN TOWN. YOU WERE ONCE A DYNAMITE SINGER. YOUR WIFE CONTINUES TO CUCKOLD YOU WITH THAT MANIAC. YOU GO TO BED TERRIFIED EVERY NIGHT DESPITE CURE ONE AND CURE TWO. . . . DO YOU WISH TO COMMENT?

"No way," Rankoff sighed aloud. He turned around to gaze at the Bel Air mansion serving as a backdrop for his introspective moment. Where is our errant hostess, Senorita Sanchez? Rankoff stared up at her bedroom window. Ten o'clock at night and she still can't decide on Giorgio or Holly's Harp. Insecurity, thy name is Inez.

Rankoff stepped through the parted French windows and contemplated the assembled throng. The office never closes. Never. We are on twenty-four-hour call. Even now, staring out at a living room filled with rock, talk, and punk stars; hairdressers-turned-producers; directors both macho and ethereal; bull-dyke casting ladies; bionic heroes, heroines, and their all-too-mortal representatives gathering ten percent of their roses while they may.

"You're Mr. Rankoff, aren't you?" How old are you, vision? wondered Rankoff, staring down at the deeply tanned girl with the perfect teeth and ironed-flat blond hair. Are you a gift from the gods, or somebody else out to hustle me? If the phrase "looking for representation" escapes your lips I will feel most—

"You probably don't remember me." Here it comes! "I met you on Visitors Day ten years ago." Visitors Day? "Martine was my counselor at Palmhurst"

"Oh. You . . . must have grown up since then. Forgive my not recognizing you."

"Yeah," shrugged the girl. "I was only eight"

"Now you're . . . ?"

"Seventeen."

"What's your name?"

"Kate."

"Are you an actress, Kate?"

"Dunno. I just hang out. You know."

"You're very pretty."

"Thank you. How is Martine? Is she still . . . ?"

"She's fine."

"I really loved her. She was real neat. I sort of had a crush on her. You know, the way little girls get crushes on people."

"I do, indeed. What year was that? When you were both at camp?"

"1970."

"Think I took pictures that summer," said Rankoff, feeling familiar but forbidden stirrings overtaking him. "Yes, I'm sure I did. Bet you're in some of them. Would you like to see them sometime?"

"Gosh, Mr. Rankoff! I'd love to."

"You must come over to the house. In Trousdale—"

"I remember. I went to visit Martine once. Before her—"

"Do come over, Kate. You can use the pool."

"Thanks, Mr. Rankoff."

The crowd was beginning to boogie to Donna Summer's latest hit as Kate disappeared into the throng of gyrating bodies. Rankoff watched her vanish then picked up on a female Gallic harangue.

Who on earth was speaking French at Inez Sanchez's party? And using colloquial abuse that would have raised embarrassed heads on the toughest Marseilles dock? Staring past the celebrated names that would doubtless dot Jody Jacobs's gossip column the next morning, Rankoff spotted two of the William Morris agency's killer elite putting the managerial make on a tiny, elfin lady with huge eyes, short-cropped hair, and a tongue with the firing power of a primitive Gatling gun. The woman looked familiar although Rankoff was certain he'd never met her before. He ventured closer to see what the opposition was up to.

"I can't understand a fucking word she's saying," lamented one of the Morris men.

"Maybe she's coked out," replied his colleague. *"Excusez-moi. We, uh, we don't comprende—non comprende—"*

"That's Spanish, Mitch."

"It's better than nothing."

"Hey, man! How do we represent a fucking chick who doesn't speak the language to begin with? Come on."

Rankoff grinned as the two representatives from El Camino Drive beat a hasty retreat from the lady's hostile Maginot line. The woman noticed Rankoff's gaze and extended her range of attack.

"Vous aussi?" she demanded.

"Pas moi," replied Rankoff, holding his hands up in surrender. *"Je n'ai absolument rien a faire dans cette histoire."*

"Vous parlez francais?" Hers was the undisguised delight of a lady missionary sharing a pot with a fellow brother in Christ while chanting heathens encircled the fire licking their chops at the meal to come.

"Un petit peu. Ma femme etait francaise. Mon ancienne femme."

"You are Rankoff," announced the woman abruptly in heavily accented English. "You were married to Yvonne Corday. She made two films with Robert Mitchum. Do you know Robert Mitchum?"

"I know Bob."

"Do you think he would play a transvestite?"

"I doubt it."

"Why? He is afraid?"

"No. He just thinks this whole business is a crock of shit . . . And he's right."

The woman stared at Rankoff with a new sense of interest and asked: "You are no longer an agent?"

"Who says?"

"You are not trying to hustle me," the Frenchwoman replied, pronouncing the second to last word without an "h."

Rankoff realized at that moment the identity of the tiny, intense woman: Violette-Claire Desgouilles, a rabidly Marxist filmmaker, the darling of New York film critics, and a prestigious new arrival to the film colony—without American representation. The new girl in town. And hot. Very hot.

"I'm too old to hustle you, Madame Desgouilles. Too old and too rich."

"You are an avowed capitalist, you have the smile of a little boy, and I am mademoiselle. I do not marry."

"Why do you make so many movies about marriage?"

"The films are not about marriage. They are about crime. Marriage is a social crime. *Et le cinema n'est que le tableau des crimes et des malheurs.*"

"Thought Voltaire was referring to history when he said that."

"You know Voltaire?" asked an increasingly amazed Violette-Claire Desgouilles.

"He was never a client," shrugged Rankoff. "But we did have drinks at the Polo Lounge once. That's when he told me, *'Si California n'existait pas, il faudrait l'inventer.'* "

Violette-Claire clapped her hands together, threw her head back theatrically, and let loose a raucous laugh.

"I like you, Rankoff. Would you like to represent me?"

"Now who's hustling who? *Je ne suis qu'un vieux chanteur.* A broken-down saloon singer, lady. I don't understand your movies. You need an agent who falls somewhere between Albert Camus and Che Guevara."

"I don't need Mitchum for my movie," she replied caustically. "I've got you."

"Not for a transvestite. And not as an actor."

"But you made a movie. At RKO in 1947. With Jane Greer. Or was it Barbara Hale?"

"What are you? A walking encyclopedia?"

"Even the worst films are part of history. You sang a song. I remember:

> *The stars have lost their glitter*
> *In my trapeze of pain*
> *Wandering in the darkness—*"

"I think it's lost something in the translation," laughed Rankoff, moving to a nearby piano. "The line was 'I try to please in vain.' "

"I learned it phonetically," shrugged Violette-Claire.

"The song should have been a hit," said Rankoff, sitting down at the piano and fingering a long-forgotten Forties ballad called 'Why Can't We Be There Again.' The words were coming back to him and, much to his surprise, he found himself singing aloud for the first time in years. The buzz of conversation began to peter out in the room as the chic guests began to surround the piano. To the younger ones in the crowd, Rankoff's singing was a revelation; for those over forty, it was a happy-sad remembrance of a time and a world that would never be again. Rankoff was aware of everyone's eyes on him but, like the old pro he was deep in his heavily mined heart, he never removed his eyes from Violette-Claire, his leading lady for this scene. Even as he sang, he made a mental note to casually throw out Violette-Claire's name as a new client at the morning meeting.

The song's conclusion was greeted by tumultuous applause from the surprised guests. Unfortunately the tribute coincided with Inez Sanchez's long-awaited descent down the stairs. Inez began to blush modestly until she realized the applause wasn't for her. She began hyperventilating, ran back up the stairs, and desperately sought yet another outfit with which to dazzle her guests.

Rankoff was moved by the applause but politely demurred at the cries of encore. It was strictly a one shot. Yet another jewel for the crown of his ever-burgeoning legend. You can't follow your own act, he decided, and was resolved to make his exit from the party when a heavily tanned hand fell on his shoulder.

"You're still the best, Magic Man."

Rankoff turned around to face Stan Feingold. Slippery Stan. Once Bobby's partner in the office and a successful independent producer for the past five years despite a string of continuous box office disasters. ("Irwin Allen makes disaster movies," somebody once said. "But Stan Feingold really makes *disaster* movies.")

"Thanks, buddy," replied Rankoff, staring at his ex-partner with a mix of fond familiarity and wariness at Feingold's grasp on reality that evening. Slippery Stan was heavily into 'coconut snow' and Rankoff was always checking Feingold's Zapata moustache for telltale traces of cocaine.

"Did you get the check today?" Feingold grinned, raising his eyebrows provocatively.

"Are you completely insane?" murmured Rankoff.

"It's cool, it's cool, Magic Man," Feingold replied, taking a deep breath that lasted almost a minute.

"They're going to lock you up, Stanley."

"I'm straight, Magic Man."

"You are in the land of coconut snow, amigo."

"Negative. Nary a line. It's all cut these days. When's Bazzo going to—"

The two were silenced by the appearance of the Painted Lady in their midst.

No one at the agency could remember when Ara Whalen was dubbed the Painted Lady or by whom. But the name had stuck. Tall, flaming-red hair, late forties, with a bustline that qualified as a concealed weapon, the high-powered Ara never appeared in public without full operatic makeup and scarlet lips outlined in black. Over thirty years she had worked her way up in the company from Abe Keller's secretary back in New York to her position of power—second only to Rankoff—on the West Coast.

"You missed the Magic Man's comeback appearance," Feingold announced heartily.

"I've got to speak to you," Ara told Rankoff, ignoring Slippery Stan totally. "Alone."

"I used to be family," lamented Feingold.

"Sorry, Stan," Ara replied, remembering her manners. "It is serious."

"Well," shrugged Feingold, "I'll read about it in the trades tomorrow."

"Afraid you will," intoned Ara.

"What's up?" asked Rankoff, after Feingold had latched on to Sue Mengers and began teasing her mercilessly.

"Meet me on the patio in two minutes," whispered Ara.

"Are you kidding?" Rankoff wondered whether his distaff colleague was in her cups for a change. But there wasn't a taint of liquor on her breath. This was serious. "Okay."

California and the Pacific coast had been in the grip of a record-breaking drought for two years. The night was dry and parched as Rankoff made his rendezvous with the Painted Lady.

"We're in trouble," said Ara, staring down at the tiny cottage below Inez's estate.

"What is it?"

"Darlene English can't start the picture tomorrow."

"The hell she can't!"

"She has second-degree burns, Bobby. I just left her in the hospital."

"Does anyone know?"

Ara shook her head. "Somebody checked her into Hollywood Presbyterian as Darlene Bernstein."

"What happened?" asked Rankoff, sickened by the thought of the lovely Darlene wrapped up in bandages. "Did she o.d.?"

"Nobody knows," replied Ara. ''There's something very strange going on, Bobby. I had a call from Nurse Horton at the hospital telling me that Darlene was there. When I arrived, there was no Nurse Horton. No one had ever heard of her. Why would someone pretend to be a nurse? Why did they phone me and not her family?"

"Did you see her? Darlene?"

"Yes," said Ara, conveying in that monosyllable that she wished she hadn't. "Somebody must have poured kerosene on her. Her whole body was burned. Her hair, too."

"Jesus Christ! That's an absolute horror story."

"You're telling me," replied Ara, lighting up one of her ever-present cigarettes. "She starts shooting at Universal tomorrow morning. She's in every scene. They'll have to close down the picture. She'll lose a $250,000 role—"

"I got it up to $275,000."

"When?"

"When she got the *People* cover story."

"When was that?"

"I was promoting it. Hasn't happened yet."

"And never will now," sighed Ara, continuing to stare at the tiny cottage below.

The two agents remained silent on the patio until Rankoff cursed under his breath and pounded his fist down on the balustrade.

"It's the drought. I swear it's the drought."

"Bobby, what are we going to do about an actress for tomorrow morning?" Ara lit another cigarette. "We have three other clients involved in the deal. The entire package could—"

The Vietnamese houseboy in the white mess suit appeared silently behind them and caused the high-strung Ara to jump ten feet in the air.

"Excuse, please, but Miss Inez—"

"Don't! Don't ever sneak up on people like that!" Ara gasped.

"So solly. But Miss Inez wants—"

"He must have been with the Vietcong," muttered Ara, desperately trying to get her heart back to a pace resembling normal. She turned back to the offending servant. "Would you be a sweet little assassin and get me a drink? A double anything."

The Vietnamese feigned deafness at Ara's request and addressed Rankoff for the third time.

"Miss Inez want you hully upstairs. She say very urgent"

"Oh-oh," warned Ara. "Check her wrists, Bobby."

"That's good, Ara. That's all I need tonight"

"The lady *is* prone to accidents."

"But I'm no good at this. Steerforth is the one—"

"Jimmy's still in New York. And you *are* the boss."

"Yeah," sighed Rankoff wearily. "I'm the only thing that's holding this old paddle wheeler together."

"Did you really sing tonight?"

"Yeah. Felt good. Didn't miss a note."

"Maybe Inez wants you to open with her in Vegas next month."

"Funny."

"Sorry I missed you singing. This whole thing with Darlene—"

"Let me take care of Inez first. Okay? When does Jimmy get back from New York?"

"Soon," shrugged Ara. "Still don't know why he went"

Yes, wondered Rankoff as he followed the Vietnamese houseboy up the great winding staircase. Why did Steerforth go to New York? A red herring? Steerforth was a master of the unpredictable move. The man was sheer enigma. Built like a rugby player, dark shaggy hair, wild flashing eyes, his accent still bore traces of his native Derbyshire and set him apart from anyone else in the business out here. It made him a master *schmoozer*, the king of charm, and the only person capable of handling the agency's stable of beautiful women and all the female neurotic insecurities that went with the territory. But Steerforth was in New York that night so the boss was going to have to pinch hit with crazy Inez.

"Who is it?" the voice on the other side of the door demanded in response to Rankoff's knock.

"Bobby."

"Oh, yes, Bobby. Please, come in."

What the hell game is she playing, wondered Rankoff at these tones which would have done justice to the Duchess of Kent. *It's me, Irma. I know who you are.*

Rankoff opened the door and walked into a bedroom which might have caused Madame DuBarry to blush. The agent was momentarily startled by the site of the famed Vegas entertainer sitting cross-legged in the middle of her awesome four-poster bed, tooting cocaine as if she were feeding the snow machine at Warner Brothers—though the studio grips tended to wear clothes, which Inez wasn't doing at all. "It was kind of you to come up, Bobby." "It was kind of you to invite me, Inez. We were missing you downstairs. Do you want to put some clothes on or would you like me to take mine off?" Rankoff smiled, not minding at all this little dialogue with his extremely nude, incredibly shapely client.

"You're making fun of me, aren't you?"

"Inez, don't be ridiculous."

"You think I'm a joke, don't you, Bobby? You think I'm a fraud 'cause I didn't sing with Glenn Miller or the Dorseys or Xavier Cugat or whoever you used to sing with."

"It was a different time, babe. The business has changed." Rankoff could sense one of Inez's infamous bummer trips coming over her, and he wanted to avoid one of those at all costs. Unfortunately the coke only made Inez more verbose and perversely egomaniacal. The beautiful blonde was a sight to behold but she talked and talked and talked destroying her mystery with every whining, persecuted word. The problem was that Inez was right.

Rankoff *did* think her a joke. She had a great body; cosmetic surgery had transformed an uninteresting face from El Segundo, California, into this breathtaking goddess; her voice was incredibly sultry; but her singing was a melodic whisper, and her dancing would have brought "Thank you very much, we'll let you know" from any summer stock choreographer. But they'd hyped her: the agency, the network, the media. They had sold Inez Sanchez to the public, made her a star, two hundred grand a week at Vegas, and they had failed to notice the terrified Irma Sandowsky who still lived inside her and asked every morning: "What if they find out? What if they catch on to me?"

She had surrounded and surrendered herself to countless 'service' lovers who would take care of the outside Inez while attempting—futilely—to comfort the inside Irma.

The affairs had begun with hairdresser Paul Cassidy; dress designer Raymond Vale; cosmetician Amos Shea; jeweler B. Montaigne. Having exhausted all her vanity service men, Inez switched over to medicine and began an endless carnal conga line with some of Century City's top ear, nose, and throat men. Even these adherents to the Hippocratic Oath couldn't keep up with Irma's emotional demands, and most recently, Senorita Sanchez had to make do with the company of a bestselling dentist, whose tome *In Touch with Your Teeth* had made him a minor talk-show celebrity.

"Yes!" announced Inez breathlessly, interrupting Rankoff's rumination. "The business has changed. It's bigger. It's better! There are still stars, Bobby. Inez is a star. Inez is loved. Inez is magic."

"That'd make a helluva billboard."

"You're making fun of me again!" shrilled Inez.

"I'm serious. Talk to your manager. It should be at the corner of Sunset and Horn. Opposite Tower Records."

"I have no manager!" She spat the words out bitterly like some long-wronged orphan wailing for the parents she never knew. "I am alone in this world. Everyone's jealous of me. Everyone hates me. Jimmy hates me."

"No, he doesn't."

"Then where is he? Why isn't he here tonight?"

"He had to go to New York."

"I hate him. I hate him. I hate him. Every man in the world wants me—except Jimmy Steerforth."

"He's not a stay-around guy, Irma."

"What did you call me?"

"It was a slip."

"But I am Irma. I'm still Irma. Inside. Why can't people see that? Why can't they love me for Irma?"

"They don't know Irma exists. Remember? You wanted to destroy Irma. Didn't want anyone to know you were born in Valparaiso, Indiana and grew up in El Segundo."

"You told me to change the name. Said it wasn't commercial."

"You picked Inez Sanchez," retorted Rankoff. "You wanted to be the new South American bombshell."

"What's wrong with this stuff lately?" demanded Inez, staring down at the fleeting remnants of white powder scattered on her black onyx coke tray. "It has no kick. When's Bazzo going to get some decent—"

"That's a sideline with Bazzo. Your agency contract doesn't cover coconut snow."

"Bobby, I'm unhappy."

"I know you are, Inez."

"I can't go downstairs."

"It's a helluva party."

"Bobby, I'm scared."

"Of what?"

"I haven't got a dress to wear," she wailed.

"Everything at the cleaners?" Rankoff asked, wryly staring at the two hundred evening frocks lying in hurricane-style debris all over the bedroom floor.

"Help me, please, help me. Jimmy always helps me." Bullshit, thought Rankoff. Steerforth is an absolute sadist with women. That's why they love him. He treats them like dirt once he gets them in his power. Very English, our Jim.

"What do you want me to do?" asked Rankoff.

"Dress me. Please."

Rankoff sighed, sifted through the mess on the floor, and seized hold of a suitably stunning number.

"It's almost midnight, Cinderella. Put this on."

"You're a pro, Bobby," she breathed gratefully.

Not long after that a radiant Inez Sanchez, superstar, sailed down the sweeping staircase on the arm of Robert Rankoff, the head of the International Artists Agency.

They were greeted at the bottom of the stairs by an acceptable number of gushing, lower-echelon guests, who needed to stay in tight with the unpredictable Inez for various selfish reasons. This impromptu homage to Inez was interrupted by the front door being flung open and a short, chunky Italian with freaked-out hair and tinted sunglasses bursting into the vestibule with all the naughty glee of a junkie Robin Goodfellow owned by the Mafia. This was Larry Bazzo.

"Ladies and gentlemen," announced an obviously sky-high Bazzo, "the International Artists Agency proudly introduces its own star, its very own from deep inside its corporate bosom, a power to be reckoned with . . . ladies and gentlemen, and stunning hostess, I give you . . . Ms. Joy Dworkin!"

Inez breathed a sigh of relief. It was only Joy. Not another star.

Most of the guests were not aware of the identity of the junior IAA agent whose arrival Bazzo was heralding. They gave their momentarily distracted attention back to Inez, who had relinquished Rankoff's hand and was now making full sail into the living room. Rankoff, however, remained at the foot of the stairs wondering what the office's two Katzenjammer kids were up to.

Joy Dworkin swaggered into the house a second later wearing an Annie Hall outfit and puffing away on a huge Havana cigar. Ms. Dworkin was cute but calculating, twenty-eight years old and determined to be running IAA by the time she was thirty. Her blatant ambition amused Bobby, but also made him feel slightly uncomfortable in the girl's presence.

"Hello, boss," grinned Joy, delivering the line like a top girl friday in some old thirties newspaper movie.

"Good evening, Joyous. What mischief have you two been up to? I can tell by the look in your eyes that the boat arrived safely from Colombia."

Bazzo doubled over with laughter at Rankoff's last remark.

"You were cool before there was cool," chuckled Bazzo.

"Aren't you going to tell him?" asked Joy impatiently.

"Oh, no, Princess Leah. It's all yours."

"Saved our ass, boss."

"Didn't know our ass needed saving, Joyous," Rankoff replied, wondering how much the tough little girl knew and what her involvement was.

"You'll read about it in the trades tomorrow morning but figured I'd drop by to tell you in person. . . . I made a deal tonight, boss. A r-r-really big deal."

"Where?" asked Ara Whalen suspiciously as she floated over to join the trio at the bottom of the stairs.

"Ohh, Painted Lady!" crooned Joy, with undisguised resentment at Ara's presence. "How nice to see you again. Mommy let you out tonight?"

Bazzo doubled up again at Joy's blatant attack on IAA's Painted Lady.

"Where have you been?" repeated Ara, coldly ignoring Joy's digs.

"The Black Tower. They love me at the Black Tower. I saved their asses, too."

By now Rankoff was extremely curious about Joy's late night visit to Universal's executive offices. The kid was in cocaine heaven and Bobby had serious doubts as to whether she had done anything or merely imagined she had.

"No more titillation, Joyous. Just talk."

"They were very upset at the Black Tower about poor Darlene's accident."

"How did you—?"

"Told them there was no problem," replied Joy. "We'd replace Darlene with Sally Mitchell."

"We don't represent Sally Mitchell," said Ara.

"We do now," announced Joy, triumphantly withdrawing signed agency papers in triplicate from her Israeli officer's bag.

"Sally's with the Morris Agency," retorted Ara.

"They hadn't obtained work for her in ninety days. She's very unhappy with them."

"When did you do this?" asked Rankoff.

"Tonight," replied Joy proudly, adding the postscript: "Beat your deal, boss. I got Sally three hundred thousand. She's thrilled to death. I phoned the story in to the *Reporter* and *Variety*. They both think they've got it exclusive. Are you impressed, boss?"

"More than impressed," replied Rankoff, realizing for the first time just how dangerous Ms. Dworkin was.

"Does this get me into the big meetings now?"

"We'll see."

"Helluva coup, wasn't it?"

"We'll see, Joyous."

"Okay," replied Joy, slightly deflated by Rankoff's cool reaction. "Gotta get some sleep. I've had a busy night."

"I'll bet you have," replied Ara with little attempt to disguise her contempt for the young upstart "One thing, Joy—before your well-deserved sleep—how did you know about Darlene's accident?"

"Painted Lady, you know I can't divulge my sources."

"You are an agent, Miss Dworkin. Not a reporter for *The New York Times.* There is no such thing as privileged information in this business."

"You're an agent, too, Miss Whalen," Joy retorted with equal venom. "Not the Grand Inquisitor at Torquemada's court. Good night, boss."

Joy stormed out the front door. Ara wheeled on Bobby immediately after the younger woman's departure and demanded, "What are you going to do about her?"

"She'll probably get a raise and she'll sit in on the big meetings."

"Over my dead body!"

"She saved our asses, Ara."

"The girl is a monster, Bobby. I told you so from the first day—"

"She's ambitious."

"Like Lucrezia Borgia! Get rid of her!"

"The kid just beat *my* price on that deal. How can I get rid of her? Every other office in town will grab her."

"Let them! We don't need her."

"I'll be the person to decide on that, Ara."

The two locked glances for a moment. Then Ara drew her shoulders back, thrust out her incredible chest, and headed straight for the bar. Within fifteen minutes, thought Rankoff, the Painted Lady will be down in the depths, slurring her words, features moving slightly out of place across her face, and making enemies anew of all the people who were determined to give her one more chance. But Bobby would be long-gone by then. Back to Trousdale.

"Sweet dreams, boss," grinned Larry Bazzo, bidding the agency boss adieu and slipping something into Rankoff's lefthand pocket. "I may be a little late for the meeting tomorrow. There's this—"

"I don't want to know—"

"Hey, man, a deal! Records! There's this new group—"

"You're the daddy, kid. Sign 'em and sell 'em. Later."

"Later," nodded Bazzo.

How does the kid do it? Rankoff wondered as he waited outside for valet parking to fetch his chocolate brown Mercedes. Perpetually stoned, spaced out, yet annually responsible for twenty million dollars gross business for the agency from his rock clients. ("I feel guilty taking money from that degenerate's deals," Abe Keller, the agency's founding father, would announce, perusing the yearly balance sheet with his one good eye. "That a dago doper like that should be a wheeler-dealer! I don't understand the business anymore.")

Who does? Rankoff wondered as he drove his Mercedes east along Sunset. A few years earlier Rankoff might have shrugged away Keller's lamentations with a facile "It's what the public wants." But did the public really want all the crap they were being served? Or had they convinced the public that they *should* want it. Corporate collusion: agencies plus networks plus studios plus records equals HYPE! Accessories after the fact with a smart lawyer—but guilty in your hearts, guys. What little gem had the sardonic Steerforth come up with the other week? "We are the hollow men, we are the stuffed men, propping each other up at Ma Maison, Chasen's, and the like." Yeah, Jimmy! Rankoff would love to lock the Englishman in a room with Violette-Claire Desgouilles. A change of pace, Jimmy lad. Let me see you put the make on this urban guerrilla.

"God! I'm coming apart!" Rankoff muttered aloud. And why not? The whole fucking agency is out of sync. Steerforth is up to something flying off mysteriously to New York. Why? To see Keller? To get the old man's blessing? How sick is Abe? Is Steerforth attempting a coup? Never mind Jimmy. Little Joy Dworkin was a fifth column on her own.

"It ain't all gravy, Pop," Rankoff concluded as he swung the Mercedes up the driveway of his enormous Tudor-style home.

He slammed the car door closed in the garage and started toward the front of the house when he heard a sound from behind the rose bushes. His body flinched. Where the hell was the security patrol? How many of them were there? Should he call out for Ames? Or would they be on him, a knife in his guts, before the butler would hear his cries?

"Mr. Rankoff?"

He knew that voice. Earlier in the evening . . . The girl stepped out from behind the rose bush, her ironed-flat blond hair glowing in the moonlight and giving her the appearance of some ethereal creature straight out of James M. Barrie.

"Kate?" There was great relief in Rankoff's voice.

"Did I frighten you?"

"No. I just didn't expect you—"

"You told me I could come over."

"I didn't expect you this soon."

"I heard you sing."

"Afraid I'm not Neil Diamond."

"You were wonderful."

He stared into the child's eyes. She meant it. Could it be the kid understood? That he wouldn't have to go through his usual . . .

"Would you like to come in?" he asked. She nodded silently.

He reached into his right-hand pocket for his house keys and found the tiny amber vial Bazzo had slipped in earlier. He made a mental note to thank the rock agent in the morning and inserted his key into the front door.

"Is that you, sir?" a proper English voice called out from a room off the kitchen.

"It's okay, Ames!" he called out. "Just going to bed." He didn't want his butler to see Kate.

"Very good, sir. There's a package for you on the hall table. A present, I believe."

"Thanks, Ames. See you in the morning."

Rankoff walked over to the hall table and found the large gift-wrapped box his butler was referring to.

"Is it your birthday?" asked Kate.

"Not till next month," answered Rankoff, removing the bow and silver paper.

"How gross!" gasped Kate, staring at the contents of the box.

"That's sick."

"Yes, it is," murmured Rankoff, who read the card scrawled in bold letters: "WHAT ARE YOU GOING TO DO ABOUT IT?" He stared again into the box with the bloodied, unplucked chicken lying in a pathetic posture with its broken neck.

Not tonight, he swore to himself. I won't let him get at me tonight.

"Who did that?" asked Kate innocently.

"Never mind," snapped Rankoff. Then he stroked her beautiful blond hair hastily. "Sorry." He replaced the lid on the box and put it back on the hall table.

"I'm . . . not sure where those pictures are. The ones from camp."

"I can see them another time," shrugged Kate.

There was an awkward pause.

Kate moved to him and hugged him. Like a daughter. Like a lover.

She was making it easy for him and he was grateful to her for that.

"Will you sing some more?" she asked as they walked up the stairs together.

"You like those old songs?" he asked, staring at her in his bedroom.

"They're romantic."

The stars have lost their glitter.

She removed her clothes. A child's body surrendering to the inevitability of womanhood.

I try to please in vain.

He held her against his naked body. Cure One. Then he reached for his jacket and withdrew the amber vial filled with cocaine fresh from Colombia. The girl's eyes lit up with delight. Cure Two.

Wandering in the darkness.

She lay beside him on the bed holding on for dear life.

"I never forgot you," she whispered. "From Visitor's Day. You were the handsomest man I'd ever seen. I told Martine—"

"Shhh. Be still."

"What's that?" the girl asked abruptly. "Is it rain?"

A clap of thunder.

"It's rain! It's rain!" she sang.

"The drought's over," he murmured.

Why Can't We Be There Again?

MATTY

The rain was relentless, pouring down ceaselessly on Los Angeles as if in apology for its two-year neglect of the Pacific coast.

Angelenos cannot cope with rain at the best of times. The biblical deluge now overtaking the city was creating havoc on the roads: rear-end collisions were occurring at every intersection; mud slides were threatening homes from Glendale to Malibu; the various canyons ribboning the city resembled wild South American rivers, so fierce were the streams of water rushing down them; and clouds of steam billowed forth from the tops of the newly watered vegetation evoking the mystic beauty of Green Mansions.

This was the primeval vision of the City of Angels that greeted Matthew Garber as he stood dripping wet in the reception area of the International Artists Agency clutching his suitcases and creating a small puddle on the expensive patterned carpet.

"Can I help you?" asked the shapely black receptionist staring up at the tall, broad-shouldered young man in horn-rimmed glasses.

"I'd like to see Mr. Bobcaygeon," said Matty, shivering at the large drop of rain that had trickled down his spine from his water-logged head of hair.

"I don't think he's in town," frowned the receptionist, whose name was Seattle. "Why don't you have a seat while I check?"

Matty nodded gratefully and heard his shoes squish soggily as he retreated in the direction of a row of handsome cream-suede sofas lining the far wall of the reception area. He had no raincoat and his tweed sports jacket was soaked right through to the lining. He was hesitant to stain the suede and decided to remove his jacket when he became aware that he was still clutching the handles of his bags. He put them down, removed his jacket, turned it inside out and discovered, to his discomfort, that his shirt was soaking as well. He perched himself gingerly on the edge of the sofa and ran his hands nervously through his soggy hair.

"Sure is pouring," the receptionist offered consolingly while waiting for someone to answer in Bobcaygeon's office.

"Thought it never rained in California," replied the young man, forcing a smile as he thought of the 'I-told you-so' looks his parents would give him now if they could only see him.

"Started last night—Oh, hi. It's Seattle in reception." The black woman was talking into the phone now. "Is Mr. Bobcaygeon in town? . . . I didn't think so. There's someone out here waiting to see him . . What's your name?"

"Matthew Garber. From St. Louis."

Seattle repeated Matty's name into the telephone, waited for a reply, then hung up and said: "Mr. Bobcaygeon is out of town and isn't expected back for a few days."

"That's it?" asked Matty after a lengthy pause.

"Sorry?"

"Nothing else?"

"I don't understand."

"Neither do I," replied Matty, feeling a degree of anger surging up in him. "I sent Mr. Bobcaygeon a telegram. He's expecting me. I'm supposed to start work here."

The receptionist shrugged her shoulders helplessly.

"Don't know anything about it."

"Who else can I speak to? Who's in charge when Mr. Bobcaygeon isn't here?"

"Mr. Rankoff's the head of the agency—"

"I'll speak to him."

"—but he's in a meeting now."

"Who else is there?" asked Matty. "I just arrived from St. Louis."

"All the senior agents are in the Wednesday meeting. Won't be out till noon."

Matty stared at his watch. It was only ten and he was beginning to feel extremely foolish. He was about to make some inane protestation when an enormous black man in a tapioca suit darted through the reception area, took an impressive sideways lunge to kiss the receptionist, then without breaking stride continued past her and up a row of stairs next to the elegant antique cage elevator.

"Wasn't that Stu Jackson?" asked Matty, realizing why the black man's impressive bob and weave looked so familiar.

"Sure is," beamed Seattle. "Right on the dot"

"Is he a client?"

"Mr. Jackson's an agent," the receptionist corrected Matty proudly.

"Really?" Matty had been a big fan of Jackson's when he had been the quarterback for the St. Louis Cardinals and often wondered what had happened to the 'black Adonis' when he'd quit the game and left town.

"If you want to leave your phone number," Seattle suggested, "I'm sure Mr. Bobcaygeon will call you when he gets back."

"I have no phone number. And I'm not leaving this building until I speak to someone in charge." Matty folded his arms across his chest in a classic no-nonsense gesture. He felt like a fool but realized there was nowhere for him to go in this strange, rain-soaked city.

***

There were fifty-five agents employed by IAA's Beverly Hills office. It was physically possible to assemble them all in the agency's screening room on the fifth floor but this was only done for major policy meetings. Each department had its own daily meetings; the heads of those departments met in the third-floor conference room every Wednesday to give reports from their sections and to discuss the big deals.

Stu Jackson apologized to everyone in the Wednesday meeting for being a minute late then took his regular seat in between Ronny Liebowitz and Larry Bazzo. Big Stu was surprised to see Joy Dworkin seated opposite him at the oak antique dining table.

"Good morning," Joy chirped cockily.

Big Stu nodded.

"Joy will be joining us from now on," Rankoff announced from the head of the table.

Big Stu involuntarily turned his head to the other end of the table and noticed that the Painted Lady was not very happy about this turn of events.

"On behalf of everyone at the agency," Rankoff continued, "I'd like to congratulate Joy on her coup in signing Sally Mitchell and saving this organization from a potentially embarrassing situation.

I've sent flowers to Darlene English from all of us with best wishes for a speedy recovery."

"Will there be an investigation?" asked Ara.

"Of what?" asked Rankoff.

"Darlene's accident, of course."

"Why should there be? It's exactly what it was—an accident. We have enough on our plate this morning, Ara, without the introduction of red herrings to the proceedings. We're all sorry about Darlene. It was a bizarre fluke. But we covered ourselves and the movie is going ahead. Okay? Let's move on."

For the next hour they discussed various films in production, midseason TV replacements, record deals, Vegas appearances, new talent, and possible new clients.

"We'll be adding Violette-Claire Desgouilles to our client list," Rankoff remarked casually as he pulled on the cuffs of his imported Jermyn Street shirt.

There were murmurs of appreciation from the assembled agents upon hearing the prestigious French director's name.

"I don't think that's advisable. Tactically."

All heads turned to stare at Dwight Foley.

Foley was a huge, blond-haired giant with a bull neck and muscles that seemed to bulge out from under his avocado green sports jacket He was an ex-Green Beret and his manner of speech and methods of dealing with people on a day-to-day basis suggested someone more at home in the jungles of southeast Asia than in the sophisticated world of corporate boardrooms.

"Want to elaborate on that Dwight?" Rankoff asked.

"The woman's a Communist. Need I say more?"

Bazzo groaned and continued to play with the Stretch Armstrong doll he brought to all Wednesday meetings. (The doll, ironically, bore a remarkable resemblance to Dwight Foley. No one was sure whether the spaced-out Bazzo did that as a formal protest against the Nietzschean ex-Green Beret or simply because he liked to play with Stretch's seemingly endless arms.)

"The McCarthy era is long behind us," said Ara from the far end of the table. "A client's politics shouldn't affect whether we represent them or not."

"I didn't fight in a war, Ara, and watch my buddies fragged and booby-trapped around me to have some French cunt make movies showing the American flag being pissed on."

"Did she do that?" asked Ronny Liebowitz, who was one of the heads of the TV department and spent most nights glued to his set dutifully watching his clients prance through the usual video inanity and never went to American films—let alone French cinema.

"The woman is anti-American, Speedy. She will tarnish the image of this agency. I was in Nam for four years. I know what the French did to those people—"

"The lady is hot, Dwight. Every agency in town wants her." Rankoff enunciated every word to make it clear that the subject was no longer open to discussion. "She wants to come with us."

"Negative cant," said Dwight, pressing his powerful palms into the antique table until they almost dented the wood.

"Beg your pardon?"

"Negative cant," repeated Foley.

"What the hell does that mean?" asked Rankoff.

"More gospel according to Kislev," drawled Stu Jackson in tones of benign contempt.

"Stay out of this!" snarled Foley, pointing a thick forefinger at the ex-football player.

"Put that finger back in your pocket, boy, or it's gonna be pluggin' up the back of your pants."

A deadly silence ensued in the conference room as the two powerful men stared with unbridled hatred at each other.

Wonderful, thought Rankoff. On top of everything else I've got these two gladiators ready to kill each other at the drop of a trident.

"Think Desgouilles could do the Maude Gonne picture at Paramount?" Joy piped in, attempting to rescue the awkward moment. "I talked to Cal Chambers about it this morning."

"You have been busy," remarked Ara. "Did you sleep here last night?"

"Cal Chambers," Rankoff repeated aloud. "What were you discussing with him?"

"Nothing," replied Joy defensively. "Just introducing myself. I didn't know about Desgouilles till a minute ago. Honest, boss."

"The Maude Gonne picture is a very sensitive subject," said Rankoff simply. It was code to everyone at the table that it was not to be discussed again until Rankoff introduced the theme.

"The subject matter might make a good crossover for Desgouilles into a safe political subject," Joy continued, unacquainted with procedure at Wednesday meetings and wholly ignorant of a 'sensitive subject's' significance. "A woman's picture with a message that doesn't piss on the American flag and-"

"There are rules in here, Joyous, that are different from the ones in the typing pool." Rankoff's tone was ominous and carried the threat of returning the ambitious girl from Chicago back to the lowly secretarial rank she had risen from only two years earlier. "Okay! What's happening with the Goodlys? Are they happy? Did they find a house closer to the Temple?"

The Goodlys were an extended Mormon family—twenty-six at last count—whose clean-cut, goodhearted singing (led by twenty-five-year-old brother Nolan) had eclipsed the Osmonds and consistently found a spot amid the top-ten-rated TV shows every week. The family was handled by Dwight Foley at IAA, and Rankoff's gaze was focused in the direction of the ex-Green Beret.

"They're fine," replied Foley, still breathing heavily following his contretemps with Stu Jackson. "Their contract is up for renewal in April."

"No problem about renewing? They're happy with us?"

"Ma sends her love. Nolan's getting a bit edgy lately. But he'll come around."

"Want me to talk to him?" asked Rankoff.

"I'll handle him," asserted Foley. "Solo force."

Rankoff nodded and prayed he wouldn't burst out laughing at Foley's heavy, self-realization lingo. The ex-Green Beret was a disciple of Shmuel Kislev, an Israeli hypnotherapist who had hung out his shingle in Beverly Hills six months earlier and was attracting numerous celebrity defectors from est, TM, Scientology, and other 'now' cults.

"Solo force it is," said Rankoff, clapping his hands together—an unconscious gesture in memory of the late Sid Shankman, his mentor, who had employed the gesture to convey the present matter was closed and it was time to move onto the next item on the agenda. "I spoke with Stan Feingold yesterday afternoon. Looks like both his pictures are green lit. One at UA and one at Universal. I may need your help with the UA situation, Stu."

"What is it?" asked Jackson. "The life of Jim Brown?"

"No," laughed Rankoff. *"The Brother Who Fell from Uranus. Your protege."* As an afterthought: "Think they can get away with that title?"

"Shit," groaned Big Stu. "You don't want me to babysit for Tommy again."

"He's out of the hospital. And nobody else here can handle him."

"I could handle him," interjected Foley with a deadly smile. In addition to being super-patriotic, rabidly anti-communist and "tactically vigilant" (another classic Kislev phrase), Dwight Foley was a hopeless racist. He loathed Stu Jackson and despised his erratic friend, the scathingly satirical black comic Tom Ricker, whose bizarre, paranoid peccadilloes made him a holy terror in the industry.

"They don't make sheets your size," retorted Jackson.

"Gee! Is it always this much fun?" asked Joy Dworkin.

"When is Jimmy coming back from New York?" Speedy Liebowitz asked hastily. "The network is interested in a guest shot for Inez."

"Hope he's back by the weekend," answered Rankoff.

He'd love to write Steerforth's absence off as another 'sensitive subject' for the taboo list, but the Englishman's absence was a matter that concerned everyone in the conference room.

"Why *did* Jimmy go to New York?" asked Ara. The Painted Lady put an edge to her voice to convey that the question was not rhetorical and that she wanted some discussion to generate from it

"To get a haircut," suggested Speedy Liebowitz. Everyone in the room laughed.

There were two great unanswered questions that had kept people wondering in the IAA office for years:

(1) Whether Ara Whalen had silicone injections to keep those incredible breasts up at her age.
(2) How James Steerforth kept his shaggy hair at the same length consistently without ever going for a haircut. No one in the office ever dared to ask either of the suspects their respective secrets, but the speculations and theories became more imaginative as the years went by.

Ara was not prepared to use levity as an escape from the question gnawing away constantly at all the employees in the Rodeo Drive office: What was the future of IAA?

"There have been rumors around town," said Ara, alternating her gaze meaningfully at all the assembled agents.

"We've all heard them; we've chosen not to discuss them. It's time we got them out in the open. It is not a sensitive subject, Bobby."

"Agreed," replied Rankoff. "Where do you want to start?"

"Why did Jimmy Steerforth go to New York?"

"Don't know."

"You are the head of this agency," replied Ara. "Every major decision—"

"No one is saying Steerforth went to New York on business. Part of the success of this agency has been granting senior agents a certain degree of autonomy—"

"What about Bobcaygeon?"

Everyone at the table was astonished by the last question. Not at the question itself but by the person who asked: Larry Bazzo. The spaced-out Bazzo was usually content to sit at Wednesday meetings playing with his Stretch Armstrong doll, refraining from, any political discussion.

"Jimmy's a heavy duty agent," continued Bazzo, who had now pulled one of Stretch's arms backward, through the doll's legs till his hand was now fondling Stretch's rubber crotch. "He's a daddy. He delivers. I still want to know what the hell Bobcaygeon does."

"Bobcaygeon is responsible to Abe Keller," replied Rankoff by rote.

"Then why isn't he in New York?" demanded Ara. "Instead of out here screwing up all our deals. This office spends more time mopping up his messy—"

"Dirty tricks," interjected Foley.

"What do you mean?" asked Speedy Liebowitz, who at five-foot-six was constantly intimidated by the height and bulk of his TV associate.

"We're pussyfooting around here . . . tactically. Why not say what we all think? About the takeover."

"There *is* a takeover?" blurted Joy Dworkin.

"What do you know about it?" demanded Ara.

"Thought it was a joke," replied Joy defensively. "You know, like the fourth network. Wishful thinking."

"That sort of wishful thinking could put us all out on the street and nip your brilliant career in the bud." Ara finished her sentence with a witheringly charming smile at the upstart Ms. Dworkin.

"All I meant," said Joy, turning her back intentionally on Ara and staring down the table at Rankoff, "was the rumor—a rumor—I was in the Right Bank Clothing Company—a month ago—trying on some stuff. I heard ICM was going to make a move. What the hell! CMA swallowed GAC. IFA swallowed CMA. Shankman and Keller had jaws once upon a time, too."

"For the record," said Rankoff. "Okay? If the William Morris Agency or ICM is making any attempt to absorb this outfit, it's news to me. I like to think I know what's going on in this town."

"What about CDI?" asked Stu Jackson.

"Who are they?" asked Rankoff.

"Continental Development Industries."

"The conglomerate? Randall Hatton? What the hell would he want with a talent agency?"

"Don't know, man," shrugged Jackson. "Heard it from a guy on the Lakers."

"Jesus!" groaned Rankoff. "Who the hell starts these rumors?"

"Probably Bobcaygeon," murmured Ara bitterly.

"That CDI rumor isn't so far-fetched," said Foley. "Why shouldn't a billion-dollar conglomerate want to own us? We do over $400 million gross business a year. Know what I think? Abe Keller wants to unload this company—"

"After forty years?"

"Let me finish, Bobby. It's only a possible game plan. Let's keep our factional options open. Gilbert Bobcaygeon—a man who has been out of the entertainment industry for fifteen years— is suddenly back in the business with Abe Keller's blessing. He sent him out here. With a free rein. Why? Not to increase our annual profits."

"That's for sure," snorted Ronny Liebowitz.

"Ara's right," continued Foley. "The man is destroying our credibility in this town. He lies. Constantly. Compulsively. Abe Keller sent him out here to ruin us."

"Foley, you have said some really weird shit in these meetings," said Big Stu Jackson, shaking his head in disbelief. "But even your Dr. Kislev would have trouble going along with that one. It doesn't make sense. Abe Keller is one smart old bastard. Glass eye or not. Why the hell would he want to torpedo a company that's been his whole life? The man's got more money than God. Shit! You've heard Abe say he *loans* God money. Why would he want to sell? And even if he did why create a situation where the company's reputation is so in the toilet that you couldn't give it away? I mean a disgraced company is worth zero. Ze-ro!"

Everyone waited for Foley to go berserk after Big Stu's blistering attack. Instead the ex-Green Beret stated simply: "Someone may have instructed him to bankrupt the agency."

"Like who?" demanded Jackson contemptuously.

"Why don't you ask Larry?"

Even spaced-out Bazzo registered complete surprise at this question: Stretch Armstrong slipped out of his hands.

"Hey, Dwight," muttered Bazzo, shaking his head in bewilderment "Did you o.d. on Wheaties this morning? Man, I just do my job."

"How did you get this job?"

"Dwight, what the hell are you—?'

"Let him answer me, Bobby."

"I was sent out here from the New York office," replied Bazzo, who had nervously tied Stretch Armstrong's arms into a knot "Everybody knows that"

"Who sent you?" Foley countered relentlessly as if he had a member of the Vietcong wedged up against a straw hut with Foley's M -1 wedged into his throat.

"Abe—"

"Negative! You were sent by Tony Rabaiotti. The *consigliore!*"

"She-it!" chuckled Stu Jackson. "Welcome to the club, Larry. Foley just extended the circle to niggers and wops."

"Dwight, we're getting away from—" Foley ignored Rankoff's interruption and continued with his attack:

"Tony Rabaiotti is Abe Keller's righthand man. He is also related to Salvatore Matucci. Sally Max."

"*The* Sally Max?" asked an enthralled Joy, pulling her nose with one finger and bending her ear with the other.

"For Chrissake, Dwight!" Rankoff exploded. "Are you trying to tell me the Mafia wants to take over this agency?"

"Why not? They're no stranger to the business." Rankoff said nothing. He had learned that lesson bitterly years before

"Dwight," smiled Ara patiently. "Why don't you type up that idea in two pages? We can sell it to Quinn Martin."

Everyone at the table laughed, causing Foley to crush his palms into the wood once more.

"Merely a tactical option," smoldered Foley. "What other reason would Abe want to sell?"

"He might if he were dying," said Liebowitz.

The table went silent again. The rumors of Abe Keller's declining health had been buzzing around the agency's Chicago and Beverly Hills offices for some weeks.

"Another rumor," Liebowitz added hastily.

"Might explain Jimmy going to New York," said Ara. "For the blessing."

"Think Abe would turn the business over to Steerforth?" asked Liebowitz, turning his head loyally to Rankoff. "And not Bobby or—"

"You?" Joy to her amazement had finished Speedy's question while staring at Ara.

"Thank you," replied Ara suspiciously, wondering why the younger woman had included her as a possible successor to the agency throne. "I've never considered myself as the possible replacement. Certainly not before Bobby. The choice would certainly not exclude seniority as a prime—"

"Hey!" groaned Bazzo. "Are you all ghouls? Nobody says Abe's dying. Tony tells me he's still—"

"So you *do* talk to Rabaiotti!" Foley pointed a sausage-sized finger triumphantly at the rock agent.

"Yeah," answered Bazzo. "And I brush my teeth a couple o' times a week and phone my mother when I remember. You are heavy, man, really heavy. Tony Rabaiotti's a nice guy. He's clean. Sally Max is his mother's second cousin. Like he's met the guy twice in his life."

"You people get your stories straight, don't you?" asked Foley with a grin of superiority on his face.

Bazzo got up from the conference table and started toward the door.

"Sorry, Bobby, but this freak is just too much. Like he's read too many Blackhawk comics. What are you, Foley? The Bionic Agent? I'm goin' to my office."

"Sit down, Larry. Sit down! Okay! Everybody got a chance to talk; we've heard some wild and wonderful theories; let's get back to business." Rankoff clapped his hands together as Sid Shankman had done so successfully for so many years.

***

Lindsay Fairweather sat at her desk doing what she did best: fielding Robert Rankoff's phone calls and keeping the agency head's busy life in order. She'd been at the job for two and a half years and prided herself on the indispensable position she was now in with her boss.

"Robert Rankoff's office," she announced for the twentieth time that morning as the phone lit up on her desk.

"Is he there?" It was a young girl's voice.

"I'm sorry. He's in a meeting right now. Who's calling, please?"

"Will he be long?"

"The meeting usually lasts until noon. Can I take a message?"

"Um . . . Can you tell him Kate called?"

"Any number?"

"Um . . . no, I . . . I'll try him again."

Lindsay replaced the receiver and was about to add the girl's name to the list of the other nineteen messages. Then something instinctively made her scribble the name on a separate scratch pad. There were areas of her boss's private life that Lindsay did not like to dwell on too long. She had her own image of Rankoff that she wanted to preserve and wouldn't allow her mind to wander off into the darker side of the man's character. Kate—whoever she was—was definitely not business and had no place on official IAA stationery. Lindsay knew this by some internal radar and it was this managerial sixth sense that made her so invaluable to Bobby.

A light lit up on the office intercom. It was Seattle in reception.

"Is Mr. Rankoff still in the meeting?" asked the black receptionist.

"Yes, he is."

"Could you come down to reception, Lindsay? There's a guy here been waiting for an hour and a half. Says he won't leave till he sees Mr. Rankoff."

"Is he a nut?" asked Lindsay, well acquainted with the crazies who occasionally, wandered into the Rodeo Drive office seeking representation for the strangest talents.

"No," replied Seattle. "He's just wet"

"Be right down."

Lindsay walked out of Rankoff's impressive third-floor office and made her way to the antique elevator.

Matthew Garber saw her long legs appear first as the cage descended to the ground floor. Then he saw the girl with the marmalade hair and twinkly eyes walk over to the black receptionist who nodded in his direction. The girl turned to stare at the broad-shouldered, bespectacled young man with damp, matted hair sitting impatiently in his mildewed shirt with his sports jacket folded neatly across his knees.

"Mr. Garber?" she asked, crossing the carpet toward him. "I'm Lindsay Fairweather, Mr. Rankoff's secretary. Can I help you?"

"Yes," replied Garber with an annoyed tone as he rose to his feet still clutching his wet sports jacket. "I have been waiting two hours to see Mr. Rankoff."

"I don't believe you had an appointment."

"I'm supposed to start work today," replied Garber with a trickle of self-righteousness in his voice.

"Are you an actor?"

"Of course not. I'm supposed to be an agent here. Didn't Mr. Bobcaygeon receive my telegram?"

Lindsay stared with compassion at this earnest, rain-soaked young man, then noticed the two suitcases nearby.

"Those yours?" she asked.

"Yes, I just arrived from St. Louis. This morning. Wasn't ready for rain."

"Would you like a towel?" asked Lindsay, nodding toward Matty's still damp head.

"Thanks," nodded Garber gratefully.

"Follow me. Leave your bags here. They'll be safe."

They rode back up to the third floor in silence then emerged from the elevator and walked down the expensively carpeted corridor toward Rankoff's office. Garber's eyes were fascinated by the deco decorations.

"This is like some marvelous apartment house from the thirties," he finally said.

"Good call," replied Lindsay. "It was one of the most prestigious blocks in Beverly Hills. Mr. Shankman won it in a card game in 1945 and had it converted into the agency's offices."

Garber emitted an impressed whistle at this bit of trivia, then asked: "Who is Mr. Shankman?"

"*Was.* Sid Shankman founded the agency with Abe Keller forty-five years ago. Forty-eight, actually. He died ten years ago. That's when Mr. Rankoff took over the West Coast office. You really got soaked, didn't you?"

They'd reached Lindsay's outer office by that time and she was feeling extremely sorry for this poor guy whom she knew—instinctively—was going to be the punchline for yet another improbable Gilbert Bobcaygeon story. She opened a door and revealed a beautifully tiled 1930s bathroom. She vanished inside then reappeared with a Harrod's towel as thick as a mink coat. "Here. What size shirt are you?"

"Fifteen and a half," he replied, rubbing his head furiously with the towel. "Why?"

She disappeared through another door and reappeared again this time with an exquisite Swiss voile shirt on a wooden hanger.

"Mr. Rankoff keeps about thirty shirts here all the time," she explained, unbuttoning the shirt on the hanger. "Under the circumstances, I don't think he'll mind you borrowing this one. Go on. Would you rather use the bathroom?" There was a twinkle in her voice at the last question that matched the twinkle in her eyes.

"If you don't mind," shrugged Garber, removing his damp shirt and exposing a medium hairy chest with muscular shoulders and arms.

"You lift weights?" asked Lindsay, admiring his upper torso.

"I used to. My wife made me get rid of them. I dropped them on the floor of our apartment. We had hardwood floors and they dented the—"

Garber was in the midst of buttoning the borrowed shirt when Rankoff reappeared in the office firing off instructions to Lindsay.

"Lindsay, get me Cal Chambers on the phone at Paramount and whoever represented Sally Mitchell at the Morris— Who's this?"

Rankoff stared with bemusement at the well-built young man whose face had suddenly gone scarlet.

"This is Mr. Garber," answered Lindsay hastily.

"You have excellent taste in shirts, Mr. Garber."

"I, uh, I . . ."

"I loaned him one of your shirts," blurted Lindsay. "He was absolutely soaking and—"

"You a client, Mr. Garber?"

"This is Mr. Rankoff," Lindsay announced, in case there was any doubt.

"I've been waiting to see you," Garber replied feebly. "About my job."

Rankoff turned questioningly to Lindsay.

"Mr. Bobcaygeon offered Mr. Garber a job," said Lindsay with a poker face. "In St. Louis." She waited for her boss to silently count ten after this announcement.

"When was this?" asked Rankoff softly.

"Two weeks ago," replied Garber, who had self-consciously finished buttoning the shirt and was now tucking it into his trousers. "He was very generous in his offer."

"I'm sure he was. Mr. Garber—do you have a first name?"

"Matthew. Matty. Matt."

"Which do you prefer?"

"Whatever—"

"I'll call you Matthew for now. Why don't you comb your hair in the bathroom then come see me in my office?"

Garber murmured his thanks and slipped into the bathroom as he heard Rankoff explode, "Where the fuck is Bobcaygeon?" Combing his hair, he could hear Lindsay and Rankoff engaged in a heated conversation which made very little sense to him. He emerged from the bathroom a second later and entered Rankoff's office, decorated with several David Hockney lithographs and an original drawing by Sol Steinberg.

"Let me get this story from the beginning," said Rankoff, gesturing for Garber to take a seat. "Stay, please." The last request was directed at Lindsay.

"I work for the *Post-Dispatch* in St. Louis." Garber began rubbing his hands nervously down his thighs. "Worked. Gave up my job last week. Second-string film and theater reviews. Interviews with people who came through town promoting films or appearing in national tours of shows. Also had a TV show on KPLR. That's an independent station in town. Half-hour interviews with celebrities. Show-business oriented. In depth. Quite successful. That's where I met Mr. Bobcaygeon."

"You interviewed him?"

"No. Never knew what Mr. Bobcayegon was doing at the station precisely. When I finished taping my show two weeks ago, he suddenly appeared on the set. He was highly complementary of my work. Extravagant is the word. Never knew a man to talk so quickly in my life. An incredible salesman. He took me out to dinner and . . . made me the offer."

"What *was* the offer?" asked Rankoff.

"To join the agency. He felt that someone with my knowledge of theater, films, and television would be an invaluable asset to IAA. He assured me I could learn the business end in a couple of weeks. Starting salary was thirty thousand a year with stock options in the company. My own office and . . ." Garber's voice began to wind down as he saw the pitiful look on Rankoff's face. Only then—for the first time in two weeks—did Garber begin to realize the offer was too good to be true.

"You gave up your job?" asked Rankoff. "Both jobs?"

"They didn't pay very well," explained Garber. "St. Louis was stifling. Gone as far as I could go there. Always dreamed of escape. I love the business. Always wanted to work out here. When Mr. Bobcaygeon made the offer it was . . ." Garber paused and the next phrase came out bitterly from his lips: "too good to be true. He gave me a couple of days to think it over and told me to send him a cable if I accepted and when I'd arrive. He said there'd be . . . a car at the airport."

"You sent a cable to this office?"

"No. Just his cable address. Gilbob. Beverly Hills."

"Gilbob," muttered Rankoff, shaking his head.

"Guess I should have phoned or written when he didn't acknowledge receiving it, but I was so excited and he was so . . ."

"Persuasive," offered Rankoff.

"Yeah," shrugged Garber. "Never met anyone like him before."

"Pray God you never do again," sighed Rankoff, getting up from his chair and walking around to the front of his desk. "Don't know how to tell you this, Matthew. In certain states you'd probably get off with justifiable homicide. . . . Oh, shit! . . . Bobcaygeon had no right to offer you that job."

"He's not the vice-president of the agency?"

"There is no vice-president at this agency. I'm the head of IAA's West Coast office, but there is no distinct power structure here after that. There are certain senior agents—"

"What does Bobcaygeon do?" demanded Garber.

"He's sort of a minister without portfolio," replied Rankoff weakly. "He, uh . . . I don't know what he does. But he sure did it to you, kid."

There was an awkward silence while Rankoff tried to figure out what he could tell Garber.

"What about your wife?" Lindsay asked finally. "Did you bring her with you?"

"We're divorced," said Garber. "Six months ago. Another reason for taking the job. Coming out here. Wanted a fresh start."

"Know anything about the agency business?" Rankoff finally asked.

"You take ten percent of the deals you make," replied Garber feebly. "Your office has some of the biggest stars in the business."

"Have you had any selling experience? Retail? Anything like that?"

"My father's in foundation garments. Women's underclothes. I worked for him one summer."

"Oh, yeah?" grinned Rankoff. "My old man did that in Cleveland. He wasn't the boss, mind you. He just—"

The light lit up on Rankoff's phone and Lindsay lifted the receiver.

"Robert Rankoff's office."

"Hold all my calls until—"

"It's Mr. Steerforth. Calling from New York."

Rankoff stretched his hand out and took the receiver from his secretary.

"James? Are they holding you prisoner back there? No, I'm not worried, you goddamn limey. I just miss you. When are you coming back? . . . Well, I had to fill in for you last night. Inez had a party. Hmm? Yeah, I finally got her dressed by eleven-thirty. Oh, I gather it was a great success. Your presence was sorely missed. . . . We've got a few more ladies on the roster since you left . . . Sally Mitchell. She replaced Darlene English in the Universal—you know?... Who told Rabaiotti? . . . No, I didn't do the deal. Joy Dworkin did . . . Yeah, she *is* ambitious. Watch yourself, Jimmy. What? . . . Violette-Claire Desgouilles . . . She's a fan of mine. Someone else besides you saw that old RKO movie. I'm turning her over to you, pal. Don't worry about your French. Just brush up on your Marxist dialectic. . . . Who? I thought Bobby Littman represented him. Yeah, he's brilliant but he's erratic as hell. Jimmy, we have enough trouble with Tom Ricker. What are we going to do with a demented Hungarian—he's not a Communist, is he? I couldn't care less if he's a Nazi. It's Foley. You should have heard the America First spiel he gave me this morning about Violette-Claire . . . Who'd handle him? Okay, we'll talk about it when you get back. When are you coming back? Speedy's got an offer for Inez— Okay! You want me to send a car to the airport? Whatever

. . . yeah . . . okay. . . . Oh, listen, Jimmy, how's Abe . . . Not at all? . . . Well, what is it? . . . Okay. See you on Friday."

Rankoff replaced the receiver and took a few seconds to ponder the information—or lack of it—he had obtained from Steerforth. His thoughts were interrupted by Garber's eureka-like exclamation:

"You were Bobby Rankoff!"

"Don't let anybody fool you, kid. I still am."

"No, no, no. I mean the singer. With Nat Kane's band."

"How the hell would you know that?" asked Rankoff, legitimately surprised. "You weren't even born."

"I'm a walking trivia book," grinned Garber. "We used to have this old record player in our basement in St. Louis. One of those huge mahogany monstrosities with a radio and a place to store records. My mother was one of your biggest fans. I used to play your records in the basement. When I was six I mimed 'Latin Lady' for a B'nai B'rith amateur contest. I won second prize."

"Who won first?"

"Honey Layefsky. She sang 'Little White Cloud that Cried' . . . live. Her mother was the president of the chapter. Wow! Wait till I tell my mother. Bobby Rankoff."

Rankoff stretched across the desk, punched two buttons on the interoffice phone, and said, "Could you come in here, please?" He ran his gaze down the list of messages that had accumulated during the morning. "Anything else?" Lindsay handed him the page off the scratch pad. Rankoff stared at the name for almost a minute then looked up at his secretary.

"She wouldn't leave a number," said Lindsay.

Rankoff nodded, rolled the paper into a tight ball, and sunk it neatly into a nearby pot housing a weeping fig tree.

"Ah!" he exclaimed, looking up at the doorway.

Garber turned his head as well to stare at the incredibly built lady in her late forties with flaming red hair and a ridiculous amount of makeup on her face.

"Ara," Rankoff smiled, "this is Matthew Garber."

"How do you do?" beamed Ara, wondering who this attractive young man in the expensive imported shirt was.

"Mr. Garber has put us into a most ticklish predicament this morning. He is a journalist and broadcaster who has given up, his work and his home in St. Louis to come out here and join our organization."

"Unsolicited?" asked Ara, reaching for a cigarette from the Limoges tray on Rankoff's desk. "What an admirable—"

"Would it were so, Ara! No. Mr. Garber was offered a job with us. . ."

Ara was about to put the lit match to her cigarette at that moment. Instead she shut her eyes and allowed the flame to burn down to her fingertips. Garber impulsively leaped up from his seat and blew out the match. Ara squeezed Garber's left hand gratefully and walked dramatically over to the window overlooking the office's rear patio garden.

"He has to be locked away, Bobby." Ara delivered this pronouncement without turning back to the others in the room.

"That's not the immediate problem, Ara. What are we going to do about Mr. Garber?"

"Oh." Ara turned around again and walked over to examine Garber more closely. "How old are you?"

"Twenty-eight"

"Is your ego secure?" she asked.

"Secure enough for what?"

"To work in the mailroom with boys younger than you."

"The mailroom?"

"Everyone starts in the mailroom," Rankoff added matter-of-factly.

"But I want to be an agent."

"I started in the mailroom," replied Rankoff. "And I'd already been a star."

"How long . . . would I have to stay there?"

"Until we're ready to move you," answered Ara. "If you're bright you'll move quickly."

"How much would it pay?"

"Don't know," shrugged Rankoff. He turned to Ara. "Do you know what we start people at in the mailroom these days?"

Ara shook her head.

"Lindsay, call accounting and find out what we pay mailroom beginners . . . What's wrong?"

Garber looked as if he were about to be ill.

"I feel . . . like an idiot," Garber finally said with difficulty. "How could he have done that to me? How could I have burned all my bridges and rushed out here. . .

"Because you wanted to be part of the dream," answered Ara kindly, without condescension. "This town is still the dream capital of the world, and you wanted to join the other dreamers. Nothing to be ashamed of. We're all guilty of the same crime."

"I like you," said Rankoff. "Don't know why. You're bright. Your eyes still dance when you talk. That's rare out here. Don't let them go dull, kid. You could have a future with us if you want. I've got a feeling about you. Maybe 'cause your old man sells girdles. Maybe 'cause you and I are better than Honey Layefsky. The job is yours if you want it."

Lindsay's voice rang out from her office: "A hundred and fifty dollars a week . . . gross."

"Jesus," groaned Garber.

Rankoff lit a cigarette and stared at the young man from St. Louis.

"What do you say, Matty?"

"It's better than selling girdles." He held his hand out to Rankoff.

LINDSAY

"Don't ever let anyone tell you this isn't an important job. We are the nerve center. We are the pulse. This agency cannot move without the mailroom. This is where you will train. Where you will learn names and faces. Courtesy. Courtesy is the thing you need. I cannot stress the importance of a good smile. A good smile will open any door. You must be well-liked. You are reflecting an image. You are the standard bearers of quality. I will repeat these words many times. But they are essential. You will be grateful to me in years to come. Don't ever be afraid of ignorance. That's why I'm here. Some of the biggest names in this business got where they are because of Sol Siglan. I've never stopped smiling, boys. Neither should you."

Matty stared in amazement at the balding owl with huge pop eyes who had just delivered this directive to the young men assembled in the mailroom on the ground floor of the IAA building. Had Arthur Miller ever met Sol Siglan? Had this standard bearer of quality been the inspiration for Willy Loman? Matty had noticed his younger colleagues all suppressing yawns as the mailroom boss ran through what was obviously his patented routine.

"Garber."

Matty stared down at Siglan's pop eyes and noticed the nervous twitch in them for the first time.

"You're older than the other boys, Garber. I notice things. You've obviously been in professional life. I'll look to you for leadership."

"Thank you, Mr. Siglan."

"I've been in the business many years, Garber. I know the ropes. They can't put anything over on Sol Siglan. Anything you need to know, come to me. Never be afraid of ignorance. I've been with this agency thirty years now. I was in the field myself. Bum ticker. They put me in here. Sort of an elder statesman, you know. Mr. Rankoff himself often seeks my counsel. He is a gentleman. If he's taken a shine to you . . ." Siglan's nasal-toned whine stopped abruptly and his head began bobbing up and down like a dime store dachshund's.

"Yes, sir?"

"Smile, Garber, smile. I cannot stress the importance of being well-liked. I have been in the business forty years and I have never heard a bad word spoken against me. My smile has a lot to do with that. This is your first day, Garber. I won't ask you to go to the studios. Get to meet the agents. How do you do that? You deliver letters and scripts. There are the pigeonholes. They must always be empty. How do you empty them? As soon as there is something in there for an agent, take it out and deliver it Be fast. Ronny Liebowitz started in here. I named him Speedy. He's one of Sol Siglan's boys. Good luck to you, Garber. I have faith in you."

Armed with the faith of Sol Siglan, Matty made his way upstairs to deliver the mail to Stu Jackson, Joy Dworkin, and Dwight Foley.

Big Stu was standing over his secretary's desk when Matty appeared in the corridor with the black agent's mail.

"You new?" asked Jackson.

"Yes. Just arrived from St. Louis."

"My alma mater," grinned Jackson. "Do they remember me?"

"Still a legend at Balaban's."

"No shit. What's your name?"

"Matthew Garber."

"Come on in a minute."

"I've got to deliver some other—"

"Siglan's been givin' you the rap, eh? Come on in. I'll cover for you."

The walls of Jackson's office were covered with photos of him in his greatest moments at the Super Bowl, shaking hands with Martin Luther King, arm wrestling with Rosey Grier, in a gag shot for *Sports Illustrated* with Alex Karras. Correspondence and contracts were scattered haphazardly around the room. An autographed football rested in a corner gathering dust.

"What brought you out here?"

"Gilbert Bobcaygeon."

"Oh."

Jackson's simple "oh" spoke volumes and carried with it an enormous amount of sympathy.

"What did he offer you? 50 percent of the agency?"

"Something like that."

"He's a strange cat. You gonna stick it?"

"Going to try. If the mailroom doesn't get to me. Did you start there?"

"You mean was I 'a standard bearer of quality'? I hold the record for the shortest stay in the mail room. One week."

"How?"

"Overzealous. Siglan wanted speed. I gave it to him. Also knocked four agents on their cans runnin' up and down the halls. When I dislocated Jimmy Steerforth's shoulder, they decided I better have my own office."

Two lines rang simultaneously on Jackson's desk so Garber took the opportunity to leave the office and continue his rounds. He walked down the hall and noticed there was no secretary on duty at his next stop. Stepping into the inner office, he spotted a very shapely ankle propped up on the sofa and a pair of diminutive hands lacing up the left foot of a brogue Roots shoe.

"Hi."

The girl with the heart-shaped face, thin-arched eyebrows, and doe like eyes emitted a startled, "Jesus Christ" and whipped around to confront Garber.

"What about knocking?" she demanded.

"What about it? I have no position on the subject"

"You scared the hell out of me!"

"Didn't mean to. I was looking for Miss Dworkin."

"*I'm* Miss Dworkin."

Garber was not ready for that reply. He had envisioned Joy Dworkin as a sorority sister to the flaming-haired Ara Whalen. He had not anticipated this diminutive, funky, incredibly built girl with lips like ripe fruit.

"I have . . . mail for you," Garber managed to say when he realized that the fruit was for looking and not touching.

"Aren't you a little old for the mailroom?"

"Aren't you a little young to be an agent?"

"Touché. Where do you want to go from here?"

"My appointed rounds," said Matty. "Neither rain nor snow nor—"

"What are you doing in the mailroom?"

"Learning the ropes. Starting from scratch. Similar cliches."

"Got a name?"

"Uh-huh. Garber"

"Garber what?"

"Matthew."

"Do you want to be an agent?"

"If it means I can play with you."

"Don't give me any sexist shit, Garber. I got here through hard work. Not through my ankles."

"They're very nice ankles."

"I don't want to hear this talk from you."

"Never?"

Joy laughed at the last question, then added, "Talk to me when you're an agent"

"Yes, ma'am."

They never made 'em like that in St. Louis, Matty mused, as he turned the corner on his way to Dwight Foley's office. A bovine creature with her hair in a tight bun directed her blunt fingers at the IBM electric with devastating, karate-like blows.

"What is it?" Tight Bun asked without looking up.

"Mail for Mr. Foley."

"Just leave it on the desk."

Matty was about to drop the letters and run when he recognized the grinning clean-cut face emerging from the inner office. It was Nolan Goodly, lead singer of the top rated TV Mormon family, and a young man whom Matty had interviewed successfully on his own TV show in St. Louis the previous year.

"Hi!" said Matty, thrusting out his hand to the Mormon TV star. "Nice to see you again."

Tight Bun's face registered total revulsion at this blatant familiarity and had there been a riding crop available, she would surely have brought it crashing down on Garber's palm.

Nolan Goodly's Carteresque smile grew even wider, but his eyes remained totally blank.

"Real nice seeing you," grinned Goodly, thrusting his hand out in return.

"Matt Garber. You did my show in St. Louis last year."

"Oh, yeah." Nolan remembered. "That is still the best interview I've ever—"

Garber never heard the end of the sentence. His attention had shifted to the huge, blond hulk whose immense shape now filled the door frame and stared questioningly at Garber.

"You a client?" asked Nolan.

"Uh, no . . . I'm working here."

"Fan-tastic!" grinned Nolan. The singer turned around to the blond hulk. "Dwight, this here's Matt Garber. Remember the interview I told you about last year—"

"Collated data," interrupted Dwight Foley, clapping one of his powerful palms down on the bony singer's shoulder so that the Mormon lad's body vibrated like a tuning fork. "Give my best to the family. You. Inside."

The last two words were directed at Matty, who tentatively followed the blond giant back into his office.

Compared to the other offices Matty had seen in the IAA building, Foley's lair was decorated in early Sparta.

A gigantic canvas of a circle with a triangle in the middle dominated one wall. There were no show biz pictures or photographs of any kind on the other surfaces. Just a barrage of medals and military citations that would have made the late Audie Murphy whimper.

"You saw a lot of action," observed Matty respectfully.

"You didn't"

"My eyes."

Foley abruptly tossed a heavy glass paperweight at Matty which he just managed to catch.

"Good reflexes," nodded Foley.

"Thanks," replied Matty, gingerly replacing the paperweight on Foley's desk.

"What's special about you?" asked Foley.

"Don't know."

"I asked you a question, mister."

Matty suspected Foley was a bit strange when he first entered the office. Now he was positive the blond giant was nuts.

"I . . . um—"

"What brought you out here?"

"Bobcaygeon—"

"Negative cant!"

"Sorry?"

"Gilbert Bobcaygeon is a lunatic but he's no fool. He saw something. Robert Rankoff saw something. Ara Whalen saw something. I want to see it, too, Garber. I want you to impress me. Soon."

"What would—?"

"Negative cant."

Garber had no idea what 'negative cant' meant but he knew that this little interview had been terminated.

Back in the mailroom, the avuncular, pop-eyed owl named Sol Siglan stood in a blue blazer nodding proudly in Garber's direction.

"Hearing good things about you," said the mailroom boss, triggering his neck into its peculiar dimestore dachshund rhythm. "My faith has not been misplaced. Here."

Siglan thrust a check and deposit book out to Matty. Garber examined the check. It was from Columbia Pictures for $400,000.

"That's a lot of money," whistled Garber.

"Peanuts! Wait till you handle your first million-dollar check. But never be tempted. Never swerve. Remember one of Siglan's Laws: I.O.M."

"I.O.M.?"

"It's Only Money. Be fast, Garber. The banks close at three."

Seattle gave him directions to the bank and Matty felt greatly relieved once the deposit was made. He spent the rest of the afternoon sorting and delivering mail; learning what agents covered what studios; observing the incredible ass-kissing some of his fellow mail roomers bestowed on Siglan and certain agents; overheard a babble of names that meant nothing to him; and wondered whether he shouldn't go straight from the building to the airport at the end of the day and catch the first available plane back to St. Louis.

He was slightly startled when Tight Bun appeared in the mailroom at six o'clock and presented him with a script.

"What's this?" asked Matty.

"Mr. Foley would like you to read this tonight and give him a report in the morning. First thing."

"He asked me—?"

"You should feel honored," replied Tight Bun with the semblance of a smile. She passed the film script to Matty, who noticed for the first time that she wore a ring bearing the same circle and triangle design he had noticed on the wall in Foley's office. "My name is Beatrice."

"Thanks . . . Beatrice."

"I hope we can be friends . . . Matthew."

"Sure."

He watched Beatrice walk out of the mailroom in a new light. Maybe he'd judged her harshly. And Foley, too. He'd been paranoid. The jet lag and the unexpected rain. Bobcaygeon's lie. It had triggered him the wrong way. Hadn't they tried to make it up to him? Rankoff and Miss Whalen? Sol Siglan with his interminable advice?

They were on his side. He would read that script. And write a Ph.D. thesis for a report.

By seven o'clock the mailroom was deserted. The agency had finally closed for the day. The rain continued to fall outside. Matty tucked the script under his arm and picked up his suitcases. He descended to the lobby when he realized he had no destination. Just as the elevator arrived on the ground floor and the long marmalade hair and twinkling eyes emerged and did a stage double take upon seeing Garber.

"Didn't we play this scene already?" Lindsay Fairweather emerged in her raincoat and nodded toward the script tucked under his arm. "What's that?"

"Beatrice gave it to me," he answered proudly. "I have to prepare a report on it for Mr. Foley."

"God," she groaned and removed the script from under his arm. "You really walk into things, don't you?"

"What do you mean?" he retorted angrily.

"You've been suckered. By the dreaded Beatrice. Dwight gave *her* that script to read. She passed the buck to you. She'll take *your* report, give it to Dwight and get the credit."

"That's the most Machiavellian—"

"Welcome to the agency business. Can I give you a lift?"

"Don't suppose you'd know a cheap hotel?"

"Nowhere to stay?"

"Mr. Bobcaygeon said I'd have an apartment," replied Garber sardonically. "Must have HICK written across my forehead in very large letters."

"Don't worry, Matthew. Let me be your fairy godmother." She stepped into the elevator and he followed her. "Stick with me, kid. I'll teach you the ABCs of the agency business. And a few short cuts . So you can play with Joy Dworkin a lot sooner than you'd hoped for—God help you!"

"How did you—?"

She put a finger to his lips and spoke in a thick Scots brogue. "Nary a word should cross your lips that you do nae wish to see in the trades tomorrow."

"You should be an actress. That accent—"

"Heaven forfend, laddie. The accent is from my granny. That and my marmalade hair. Like to imitate her 'cause it helps me remember her. I was eight when she died."

They walked across the deserted basement garage until they came to a battered pink Volkswagen. Lindsay unlocked the door and shrugged an apology for the state of the vehicle. "Keep promising myself a paint job." She got into the car then reached across to unlock the passenger side for Matty. "Keep promising myself a new car. But then Mr. Rankoff keeps promising me a raise. My life is a string of broken promises. Maybe that's why I've taken your case to heart. Audience identification."

"Where are we going?" asked Matty as Lindsay bombed the car up the ramp and out onto Charleville.

"My next-door neighbor's in Europe for two months. She left me her keys. If you promise to keep the place clean, you can stay there till you find something of your own. Shit! The wipers are gone. Can you stick your hand out and get them going?"

Matty managed to get the wipers working while the battered pink bug made its way north on Rodeo toward Santa Monica Boulevard.

"First thing you have to learn, Matthew, is the difference between big Santa Monica and little Santa Monica. The first major hurtle to living in LA. Earthquakes, drugs, divorce, and busing are secondary issues."

"You're nae without a sense of humor, lass," he countered with an excellent Scots brogue of his own.

"Should have been an actor yourself."

"I was. I quit"

"Smart boy. You'll go far." She brought the car to a halt at the red light at Santa Monica and Doheney. "This is the start of Boys' Town. Wouldn't advise you walking here unless you're secure in your sexuality."

"Does that give me the license to kiss you at the next red light?"

"Nothing gives you that license. We're pals, Matthew. Let's get that straight from the beginning."

They drove east in silence along Santa Monica past Robertson, then San Vicente. Matty tried to figure where he'd gone wrong with Lindsay. He liked her; he liked her marmalade hair and her dead Scots granny; he liked the kindness she had shown him. The kiss was not meant to be anything serious (not like he'd fantasized about with Joy Dworkin), but Lindsay had pulled back like a child who'd brought her hand too close to the stove.

"Where are we?" asked Garber, as she made a left on to Westbourne.

"West Hollywood. Have you never been to Los Angeles?"

"I'm a virgin."

"A vanishing species."

It was a classic West Hollywood building: three stories built around a swimming pool, a gigantic lobby with a terrifyingly ornate chandelier that looked as if it might come crashing down to decapitate one of the tenants at any moment.

"How are your neighbors?" asked Matty, carrying his bags behind her down the third-floor corridor.

"Either very single or very old. Both factions hate each other. I keep promising myself—"

"To move?" asked Matty. "That's some list you're building up."

"And I was going to take you to dinner."

"Let me take you."

"Let's quit bluffing each other and split the tab," she said. "We'll go to Dan Tana's.

"Where's that?"

"Just down the street. My favorite Italian restaurant. *The* best garlic bread in the world. People all give you the rap about La Scala. Stay away from it. Chianti is also good and the *frito misto* mare at Peppone's is sensational. The warmest spot in my heart is still for Tana's. Especially since the fire."

"How do you afford to eat out so often on a secretary's salary?"

"I have a friend."

"A friend?" repeated Matty amusedly.

"That is a sensitive subject," said Lindsay, not remembering where that convenient phrase had come from.

"Okay," shrugged Matty.

They dropped Garber's bags off in the absent neighbor's apartment then walked a few steps down the hall to Lindsay's place.

"Just want to drop these off," said Lindsay, nodding to the pile of scripts under her arm, "then we can walk over to Tana's."

"Walk? In this rain?"

"So used to the drought," shrugged Lindsay, fitting her key into the lock.

The door opened and Lindsay took a few paces into the apartment. She froze abruptly, turned around to Garber and pushed him out into the hallway.

"Wait here a second."

She closed the door in Garber's face. Matty felt a fool standing alone in the hallway. An elderly Jewish woman toddled by and stared warily at Garber.

"Nice evening," murmured Matty.

"You live here?" the old lady asked in a thick East European accent.

"No. I mean I will be. Temporarily. Yes! I'm moving in over there."

"You married?"

"Divorced," answered Matty, taken by surprise and not knowing why he had volunteered the information.

Lindsay opened the door again at that moment and the old lady glared at her with undisguised hostility then continued down the hallway.

"She's nosy," said Matty.

"She's an old bitch. Always complaining to the manager about me."

"Does she have cause for complaint?"

"Here," said Lindsay, ignoring his question and thrusting a script with an IAA cover toward him. "Read this tonight."

"What is it?"

"Mr. Rankoff needs a report. Don't read any scripts for Foley's secretary. Or anybody else. A waste of time. I don't want to see you waste your time."

"Good Scots thrift. Are you ready?"

"Can't go."

"What's wrong?"

"Nothing's wrong. Just . . . can't go. See you at the office tomorrow."

Garber returned to his apartment very confused. It wasn't jet lag, the rain, or Gilbert Bobcaygeon. It was Lindsay Fairweather. Something about her. She had been so helpful to him all day and yet he felt she was the one who needed help. He wanted to put his arms around her lithe body, stroke her marmalade hair and say: "Its okay, lass, it's all okay." But she was unreachable. Untouchable. Why?

He went to turn the lights on in when he saw the neon sign through the drapes drawn across the balcony. He walked toward the gaudy yellow light. It said TROPICANA and had a distinct 1940s flavor to its design and effect. Tropicana. How many other people had stood here before, facing east, and shared their dreams with the Tropicana sign?

Voices.

Arguing.

Next door at Lindsay's.

What was going on?

Garber continued staring at the Tropicana sign while the rain tried its best to drown out Lindsay Fairweather's pitiful sobbing in the next apartment.

INEZ

Rankoff was in a foul mood. He'd had very little sleep the night before. The phone had rung at 2:00 a.m. and then at 4:00. Each time he answered someone on the other end of the line would begin clucking like a chicken, then hang up abruptly the moment Rankoff spoke. Rankoff knew who the crank caller was. He was no crank; he was a psychotic. One of the best directors in town, he'd also stolen Rankoff's wife from him. Rankoff's problem: What was he going to do about it?

"Mrs. Rankoff on the phone for you," Lindsay announced from the intercom.

What a coincidence, thought Rankoff reaching for the phone. Or maybe it wasn't. Maybe that psychotic had put her up to this call.

"Sabina?"

"Non! Je suis desolee de te desappointer!"

"Que veux-tu?" demanded Rankoff with undisguised annoyance.

"Toujours aussi charmant!" replied Yvonne Corday Rankoff. *"T'as des problemes sexuelles ou quoi?"*

Rankoff clapped a hand over the receiver and bellowed out toward the outer office.

"Lindsay!"

A second later a distressed Lindsay appeared in the doorway.

"Do *not* refer to my ex-wife again as Mrs. Rankoff!"

"But that's who she said she was. She is, isn't she?"

"Her name is Yvonne."

"I'm not that intimate with her."

"Fuck formality, Lindsay. It's the only way I can keep my wives straight." He waved his secretary back to her desk.

Lindsay was rolling a piece of IAA stationery into her IBM self-correcting typewriter when she looked up to discover Matthew Garber hovering overhead clutching the script she had given him the night before.

"Good morning," he smiled. "Read the script. It's a real bloodbath."

"Did you do a report?"

"Uh-huh." He withdrew five typed, single-spaced pages from inside the script.

She perused the pages quickly, then said, "You're a good writer."

"Thanks . . . You okay?"

"What do you mean?"

"None of my business but I heard you crying next door last night. I thought—"

"You're right. It's none of your business . . . Have you eaten since yesterday?" The last query was intended to offset the coldness of her previous remark.

"Went to Duke's at the Tropicana."

"If you've discovered Duke's, you're an Angeleno."

"The most incredible breakfast I've ever had. The whole world crammed into that tiny—"

The phone rang on Lindsay's desk. She answered and buzzed Rankoff, who was still talking to his ex-wife.

"Kip O'Donell for you, Mr. Rankoff." She hung up, then remarked to Matty, "He's crazed this morning. God help anyone who crosses him today."

"Thought he was a pretty easygoing guy," observed Matty.

"The word is 'mercurial.' He's an Aquarian and—"

At that moment the mercurial Aquarian in question flung his door open and hissed, "That little s.o.b. He's up to something. .What's that?" Rankoff nodded at the pages in Lindsay's hand.

"Report on *Ektalon-Z*. Matty did it."

"Any good?"

"Probably make a fortune if Rees Davenport directed it," replied Matty.

Lindsay emitted an involuntary gasp at this reply and Rankoff stared coldly at the young man from St. Louis. Matty realized he'd said something wrong but had no idea what. When Rankoff finally spoke it was merely: "He's not a client."

"Does that matter?"

"Know what a package is, Mr. Garber? What this business is all about. We package movies, TV shows, miniseries. Supply a combination of writer-director-stars or producer-writer-director or any components that make up an official package. In exchange for a package, we get ten percent of the production budget. On a five million dollar movie, this agency will see a five-hundred thousand-dollar commission."

"Wow!"

"Wow, indeed. The clients are delighted as well. They don't have to pay commission on a package situation. Keep the full hundred percent of their fee. Follow? That's why we're packaging *Ektalon-Z*. We want a bit of the *Alien* action coming into LAA. With our *own* director." Rankoff flipped to the last page of Matty's report. "Next time put in cast and director recommendations on any script reports you do. Okay, Matty?"

"Sure."

Lindsay breathed a silent sigh of relief when she realized Matty had escaped her boss's wrath over his unfortunate and unwitting Rees Davenport *faux pas*. She hated the politics and intrigues of the business but (remembering her own sins of the night before) realized she was as guilty as everyone else.

"Would you ask Joy Dworkin to come in, please, Lindsay?" Rankoff turned to leave, then asked Matty, "Surviving Siglan's lectures?"

"Was he *really* an agent?" countered Matty.

"Sol? He told you that?" Rankoff shook his head in bemusement "Come inside. Got a few minutes?"

Rankoff gestured for Matty to make himself comfortable on the sofa in his office then began pacing the room like a caged animal.

"If there's one thing I cannot stand in this world," said the agency boss, "it's ingratitude. When you go out on a limb for somebody, when you give them a break. Know what I mean?"

Matty wasn't sure if he was the "ingrate" Rankoff was referring to so he replied with an extremely wary "yes."

"Classic formula in this town," Rankoff continued. "Find an agent, have the guy bust his ass for you, then the minute you make it—dump him! What I refer to as 'the upwardly mobile amnesia syndrome.' Erase all memory of friends, wives, relatives, business associates. Anyone who might painfully remind you of your mundane life before you made it

"Two years ago flew my wife to San Francisco for dinner. Over dessert she tells me she's never been to the theater in her life. Took her to the ACT. Some play with Peter Donat. There was this kid in it. Kip O'Donnell. Had a bit. Electrifying. Felt the same way when I saw Brando with Katharine Cornell. I signed him. Jimmy Steerforth thought I was crazy. Brought the kid to LA. Put him up in my guesthouse. Left him alone with my wife all day. Sent him out on interviews. Took him to parties. Put him into a couple of good packages. This kid is going to be a star."

"Hi, boss!"

Rankoff paused in his monologue to stare at the image of Joy Dworkin in her tight-fitting Calvin Klein jeans and Saint Laurent crepe-de-chine silk blouse offset by a waistcoat purchased at the Goodwill store in Van Nuys.

"Good morning, Joyous. Have you met Matthew?"

"How's it going in the mailroom?" asked Joy pointedly.

"Miss Dworkin started in the typing pool," said Rankoff, with no intention of letting Joy get away with her putdown. "We all start humbly in this business. Joyous, my little rumor monger—"

"Hey, c'mon, boss!"

"Meant it as a compliment, kid. You seem to be plugged in all over town. What have you heard about Kip O'Donnell?"

"Besides the NBC deal?"

"What NBC deal?!" erupted Rankoff.

"Dr. Kislev got him a deal at NBC."

"What, am I going crazy? Psychiatrists are making network deals? What kind of crap is this, Joy?"

"Well, first of all, boss, Shmuel Kislev isn't a psychiatrist. He's a therapist. Don't know if he has an actual medical degree. Between you and me, I think he was running a falafel stand on Fairfax before he hung his shingle up on Camden Drive. The guy's weird. But who's normal in this town, right? He's latched on to a few show biz folk and he's sort of into personal management. Cutting in on Dr. Landy's action."

"Who's Dr. Landy?" asked Matty.

"Eugene Landy," replied Joy. "A $3.50-a-minute psychiatrist. Advises some of the biggies in the business. Alice Cooper, Richard Harris, Rod Steiger, Brian Wilson from the Beach Boys. He's the guy got Brian Wilson out of bed!"

"You telling me Kip O'Donnell is managed by Shmuel Kislev?" asked Rankoff. " How long's this been going on?"

"Months. Dwight Foley took him to a meeting."

Rankoff snarled into the interoffice phone: "Dwight, get in here!"

"What's the matter, boss?" asked a concerned Joy watching Rankoff resume his pacing while waiting for Foley to make an appearance.

"He wants to be let out of his contract," fumed Rankoff. "It's got another eight months to run but he wants out. Says he's unhappy, desperately unhappy. Shouldn't have come to LA. Negative vibes. He's not in a good space. Wants to go back to the stage. Says I'm like a father to him. Begs me to let him go. Starts crying on the phone. Wants to come over and tear up his agency papers. I asked him if he's got somewhere else to go. Another agency. 'No, no, nothing like that. He just wants to go away. Maybe to Kauai. Sit on a beach for a few months. Wants to feel free again. That little prick! What's the NBC deal?"

"A mini of *Anthony Adverse*," replied Joy. "The old Fredric March role. They needed someone with classical training. Six months on location. Half a million dollars."

"Are you certain?"

"Got a friend in beautiful downtown Burbank."

"And the little *vuntz* wants out before he has to pay us commission. The greedy, ungrateful little—"

Dwight Foley loomed large in the doorway.

"Wanted to see me, Bobby?"

"Come in, Dwight."

The ex-Green Beret lurched into the room and stared with a mixture of surprise and disdain at the presence of Joy and Matty in the room. When he realized that Rankoff had no intention of dismissing them, he trained his eyes on the IAA boss and ignored the other two totally.

"Don't want to step on your toes, Dwight. Okay? I don't care what people do in their bedrooms, where they pray, who their friends are. Okay? But there comes a time when your private life and your public life don't mesh. You may think the world of your Dr. Kislev, and the triangle and the circle and that whole *megillah*. But he's interfering with the activities of this agency—"

"Dr. Kislev has nothing to do with—"

"He's trying to control the minds of our clients! He's pirating away deals—"

"Negative cant!"

"He's got you wrapped around his fingers, Dwight! Personally I think he's crazy as a shithouse rat and probably drinks his own bathwater but everyone's entitled to their own—"

"You have no right to—" Foley's huge body was bristling with rage. Matty was certain the blond giant was going to rip the arms of the Louis XIV chair he was seated in.

"I'm the head of this agency, Dwight! Never forget that. You took a client, Kip O'Donnell, to one of your goddamn Aimee Semple Macpherson meetings. Fine! However, you owe it to me to let me know your Israeli Father Divine has taken over the personal management and/or brainwashing of this poor kid."

"I attend Dr. Kislev's classes. I am not his confidant. His actions are his own. I resent your libelous descriptions of him and me. The Constitution guarantees me freedom of speech!"

"Don't confuse freedom of speech with freedom of worship, Dwight. Thy God is a jealous God."

"Can I go back to my office now?"

"Sure."

Sweat was oozing out of every pore in Foley's outraged body as he left Rankoff's office. Joy and Matty stared like two kids at a Saturday matinee who had just watched the Crimson Pirate vanquish the entire Spanish fleet.

"Can I join your fan club?" swooned Joy with undisguised hero worship.

"Y'ain't heard nothin' yet," Rankoff replied grimly, moving behind his desk and picking up the telephone. "Lindsay? Get me Mr. Keller in New York on the direct line . . . What? Hold on. Joyous, who's producing *Anthony Adverse?*"

"Warner TV. Dick Moreland."

"Lindsay, get me Dick Moreland at Burbank! Have you got Mr. Keller yet? Keep trying. What time is it in England? See if anyone's still in the London office." Rankoff put the phone down and asked Matty out of left field, "Where you living?"

"On Westbourne. Just temporarily till I—"

The intercom buzzed. "Dick Moreland for you."

"Richard!" Rankoff eased back in his swivel chair and put his feet up on his desk. "How goes the battle? Hear you've got Kip for *Anthony Adverse*. That's terrific! You got him cheap as far as I'm concerned. I'd have held you up for a million. Upset? What for? Somebody's not happy here, I let them go. It's great you don't pay any attention to rumors . . . What? Oh, all that crap about Kip being freaked out on angel dust. I don't deny the kid had a problem. Had to sit up with him a few nights myself but— Sorry? The kid's clean now, Dick. Probably why he saw Kislev to begin with. Kid's going to be a star. Always thought so. By the way, you're doing the slave trade sequence on location . . . The Virgin Islands? Lucky dog. Dick, let's have lunch next week. Okay?" Rankoff put the phone down and began to tap a staccato rhythm on his desk. He glanced up at Joy. "Did you see that production of *Pride and Prejudice* on PBS last month? The guy who played Darcy. He's with the London office."

"Julian Mowbray," piped up Matty. "He's excellent."

"He'd make a great Anthony Adverse, don't you think?" But before Garber could reply the direct line to New York rang on his desk. "Hello? . . . Abe! How are ya? Oh, come on, Abe! They'll never get you alive. What's the weather like in New York? So what do you want to freeze your *kishkes* off there for? Keep telling you to come out here and run the office. Is Steerforth driving you crazy? He left? When? He hasn't turned up here yet . . . Abe, we've got a problem. It's a little political and should be handled right from the top. NBC is doing a miniseries of *Anthony Adverse* and they're using a client in the lead. Kip O'Donnell. Terrific kid. They're shooting on location in the Virgin Islands. Big slave sequence. Maybe I'm overreacting, being oversensitive to the situation, but this kid's entire family have belonged to the Ku Klux Klan since Reconstruction. The kid himself hasn't got an anti-black bone in his body. But you can imagine the stink the natives might raise over there if anyone found out . . . I'm thinking of you, Abe. How active you've been in the civil rights movement . . . Tell me I'm being paranoid, Abe . . . Okay. Wait to hear from you." Rankoff put the phone down once more and began to whistle the first few bars of "Mood Indigo."

Lindsay stuck her head in the door at that moment

"Maggie Hardwicke on the phone from London. And Kip O'Donnell's in reception."

"Is he? Let Mr. O'Donnell wait a few minutes and get me his contract from the files. You guys can go back to work if you want."

"I'm not missing the finale," grinned Joy.

"Maggie! Bob Rankoff here. Sorry about shouting. Terrible connection. No, no, don't hang up. What's Julian Mowbray's availability? ... *Hamlet* at Stratford? Get him out of it.... What do you mean? How much are they paying him? Eighty pounds a week! What is that? Two hundred dollars. We're talking about a $600,000 deal and international stardom.... I don't care if he is a Trotskyite. Get him out of that show! Tell Nigel I'll send him a cable tomorrow with the details. Thank you"

"Fred Silverman from New York!" announced Lindsay.

"Bless his heart . . . Freddy! How ya doin'?... What? Oh, God! I didn't want Abe to call you. This is silly. No need to phone the White House and check. Just me being conservative, that's all. No sense having a race riot on the set. Remember what Dino went through on *Drum*? Okay, Freddy. Appreciate your calling." Rankoff replaced the phone gingerly then stared at it in anticipation of the next ring.

"It's Dick—"

"Moreland. Thank you, Lindsay. I was expecting his call . . . Richard! Have you called to set a lunch—what? Oh, no, it's not that drug business—Who? —Freddy himself! The Ku Klux Klan? I had no idea. Jesus, Dick! So sorry. Will that screw up your show? You start in a week! Well, who are you going to—? Funny, I just had a call from CBS about Julian Mowbray. The kid who did *Pride and Prejudice* on Masterpiece Theatre. Just turned down a fortune for a special with Ingrid. Bergman. Real May-December weepie. He'd have been perfect but the Royal Shakespeare Company has him locked up till — yes, I'm aware there's half a million in the budget but— You could go to six? *I'd* play it for six. It's not a question of money. The guy's a Trotskyite. He couldn't— 750? For the first two runs? Bonus for European theatrical release? Okay. You've got Julian Mowbray if I have to kidnap him."

Rankoff put the phone down, whipped off his jacket, marched over to the fridge, and withdrew a bottle of Moet & Chandon.

"I love making deals," he beamed. "Too early for you kids to join me in a toast? Lindsay!"

The freckle-faced, marmalade-haired secretary entered the office carrying O'Donnell's contract. Rankoff whipped it out of her hand and thrust a wine glass into it.

"Kip O'Donnell's outside," she whispered.

"Send him in."

A tall, bronze-skinned beach boy with penetrating blue eyes entered the office sheepishly and murmured to Rankoff, "Hey, man, I really don't—"

Rankoff walked over to the contrite O'Donnell and put his arm around the young bronzed god.

"It's okay, Kip. Thought it over. If it'll make you happy . . ." Rankoff lifted O'Donnell's contract up from his desk and tore it in half. "You're free, Kip."

"Gee, Bobby, I—I don't know what to—"

"No sweat, kid. How 'bout a farewell glass of champagne? For old-times' sake?"

"No, man. You've done too much for me. No hard feelings?"

"Don't be ridiculous. We'll issue a statement to the trades this afternoon. 'Kip O'Donnell asked for and received his release from the International Artists Agency.' "

"Love you, Bobby."

"So long, Kip."

After O'Donnell had left the office, Rankoff raised his glass and announced to the trio: "That asshole will never work in this town again."

***

Dwight Foley stared at the giant circle and triangle on his office wall in rapt concentration, studying the 'factional options' available to him. Nothing seemed to materialize. He was unable to draw any strength from the circle. The random thoughts ricocheting off his brain were being rejected by his mind as 'tactically inadvisable.' He needed a session desperately; he needed to see Kislev. He would have to make do - for now - with Beatrice.

He leaned his hard, hulk like body forward and buzzed his secretary. Seconds later the tight-bunned Beatrice appeared in the office.

"Have you been operative?" Foley asked in conspiratorial tones.

"Collated data," replied Beatrice proudly.

"Solo force?"

"Of course. Couldn't trust anyone else."

"Go ahead."

"Which one first?"

"Don't care," growled Foley, who had always loathed briefings despite their importance to a mission. "The little bitch. Get her out of the way."

"Joy Dworkin," Beatrice began after clearing her throat and reading from a file card. "Place of birth: Unknown. Parents unknown. Adopted by Harry and Rose Dworkin, retired vaudevillians. I think they had a magic act. I can find out more, if you want. They ran a flower shop in Chicago for years. Attended public school and high school in Chicago. Moved to New York City 1968. Attended American Academy of Dramatic Arts. Dropped out after one year. One summer in stock in New England. Married 1972. Divorced 1973. Moved to California 1976. Real estate office 1977. I think it was Mike Silverman. Yes, I'm sure. Joined IAA in 1978 as secretary. Became junior agent in spring 1979. Promoted to senior agent in—"

"I know when that was, Beatrice. Anything we can use on her?"

"She takes drugs. She and Bazzo—"

"Inoperable data. What about her ex-husband? Is he a fruit?"

"No idea. Would that help?"

"Not sure. Can we find out who her parents are?"

"Why don't you ask Ara?" demanded Beatrice, arching an eyebrow. "Settle the rumors once and for all."

"What rumors?"

"Joy Dworkin's her daughter. That's why they hate each other so much."

"Where'd you get that one from?"

"Sol Siglan."

"Siglan? He's not playing with a full deck, Beatrice."

"He's a friend of Mrs. Shankman's. Not a friend-friend. But she's the only one who's consistently kept him from being fired for years."

"I don't believe it."

"Neither do I. But it's a great piece of gossip. By the way, have you heard about the proposed CDI takeover of the agency?"

"Who'd you get that from?"

"Seattle."

"She's a coon! Probably puts out for that black fruit Jackson. Which is where she probably got that line about the takeover. I was at the same meeting."

"Is it true?"

"No," replied Foley scornfully. "But I think Abe Keller has cancer."

"No way," countered Beatrice. "I spoke to Lee, Steerforth's secretary. Her boss and Abe went to Studio 54 last night."

"Can't go to a disco if you have cancer?" sneered Foley. "What else have you got?"

"Matthew Garber," Beatrice answered, holding up another card. "Born St. Louis, Missouri. Eldest son of Michael and Marjorie Garber. Women's undergarments."

"Oh, yeah?" Foley's ears perked up. "The old man?"

"He *sells* them," explained Beatrice impatiently. "Shall I go on? Attended St. Louis Country Day School. Attended law school at Washington University. Did not graduate. Married Trisha Lokash, childhood sweetheart. Worked for *St. Louis Post-Dispatch* and KPLR. Divorced Trisha Garber in 1979. That's it."

"Thanks," Foley said in tones of dismissal. "Keep those cards up to date."

"Will you be at the session tonight?"

"Possibly," answered Foley petulantly.

Once Beatrice had left the office, he punched in a Beverly Hills number on the Touch-Tone phone.

"Shmuel? Can you talk? . . . Get ready for trouble. Rankoff knows about Kip. Shmuel, it's not funny. He's still the best agent in town. That deal may not be as secure as you'd like it to— No! This is not the time to go operative. Steerforth isn't back yet. It would be too obvious. Well, who would they suspect? That poor lush Ara Whalen? . . . My main concern for the present is Nolan Goodly. . . . No! Solo force. . .. Why? I think it's tactically inadvisable . . . Negative cant! . . . I'm sorry, Shmuel. I didn't mean to shout . . . Just let me try it my way. I will *not* botch it! . . . I think I have a new lead for us. Right inside the agency. He just joined us yesterday. If we can put him through the training, he'll be perfect. His name is Matthew Garber."

* * *

Matthew Garber sat in the mailroom of the International Artists Agency waiting for his next delivery assignment and thinking about the incredible performance he had witnessed that morning in Rankoff's office. He had never been so fascinated, impressed, appalled, mesmerized, enervated, and ultimately, hooked on an individual as he now was by Robert Rankoff. The man was an enigma, a puzzle. And Matty had always been a sucker for puzzles. Who was this guy? What was his story? *(Once a journalist, always a journalist, whispered a little voice in his brain.)* How had the guy who'd sung "Latin Lady" years ago on Decca records risen to this position of incredible power in the entertainment industry? Where was he from? Did he have any family?

There was a wife. The one he'd flown up to San Francisco for dinner. The one who'd never been to the theater in her life. The one he'd left Kip O'Donnell with all day. Poor Kip O'Donnell! Lindsay had had a premonition. "God help anyone who crosses him today." She knew her boss pretty well. How well? Who had her mysterious visitor been last night? The guy who made her cry so pitifully? Could it have been Rankoff? Wouldn't be the first time a boss and his secretary—

"Garber!"

Matty stared up from his stool at the pop-eyed face of Sol Siglan.

"Take this script over to Inez Sanchez's house. Right away."

"Inez Sanchez. *The* Inez Sanchez?"

"Our client, Inez Sanchez."

"Where does she live? How do I get there?" The words seemed to tumble out of Matty's mouth at once. He was ready to scale the Andes for a first-person peek at the South American bombshell whom he had fantasized over for so many years. Inez Sanchez was synonymous with legs and sequins. Long bare legs. He had always been a sucker for long bare legs and high kicks. God! Inez Sanchez. Maybe she'd ask him in for a drink. He could dazzle her with his encyclopedic knowledge of her film career. Maybe she'd ask him to stay for dinner. Intimate. *A deux.* They'd go for a swim afterward. "I have no suit," he'd protest. She'd giggle obligingly and step out of her dress (as she'd done in that film with Michael Caine), then murmur, "I don't have one either." All right!! South America, take me away!

Armed with a map of Bel Air and the screenplay tucked safely under his arm, Matty strode toward the elevator while humming Rod Stewart's "Do You Think I'm Sexy?" He stepped into the elevator and pressed the button for the underground garage. So engrossed was he in his erotic Inez Sanchez fantasy he failed to notice the lean, hard Mediterranean-looking man riding down with him. Matty spotted the scar on the man's right cheek and recognized Yael Shomrim.

Shomrim had gained international notoriety when he had walked off the set of a very expensive Hollywood movie at the outbreak of the Six-Day War in 1967 to re-enlist with his old regiment. The studio threatened to sue him until Shomrim single-handedly captured an Egyptian installation (receiving his famous scar) and made the cover of every news magazine in the world. He'd been an idol of Matty's ever since. But now—standing inches away from him—Garber was totally tongue-tied.

The elevator door opened on the garage level. Shomrim stepped out and marched briskly toward his car.

Matty finally blurted out: "Shalom!"

The Israeli star stopped in midstride, turned around, sized Matty up and down, and in his patented growl returned the greeting: "Shalom."

"Are you, uh, making a film here?"

"In the garage?" countered Shomrim playfully.

"Anywhere," shrugged Matty, feeling like a jerk in the presence of his hero. "My name's Matthew Garber. I'm with the agency."

"Oh, yes!" Shomrim's eyes lit up. "Mr. Garber. I've heard about you."

"You have?"

"You must be more confident, Mr. Garber. Of course, I've heard of you. Please excuse me. I have a pressing engagement. Shalom."

Matty watched with fascination as the Israeli got behind the wheel of an old Austin-Healey and roared out of the garage. How did Yael Shomrim know who he was?

Garber pondered the question as he drove his car north to Sunset, turning left toward Bel Air. The rain continued to come down on the city. Matty was convinced that the song about it never raining in California was all a hoax. The weather in the two days he'd been there approximated monsoon conditions.

The IAA delivery Volkswagen continued its climb up the fabled hills of Bel Air past some of the most spectacular homes Matty had ever seen. Finally he pulled into the driveway of Inez Sanchez's sprawling Mediterranean villa. Matty checked himself out in the mirror, ran a comb through his hair, sniffed his breath, then removed his glasses and tucked them into his breast pocket. He hadn't gone through an inspection like this since the junior prom at Mary Institute the first year he'd gone steady with Trisha.

The front door was opened by a diminutive Vietnamese male in a white mess jacket.

"Please?" asked the houseboy.

"Is Miss Sanchez in?" Matty inquired in his best 'cool' tones. "I'm Matt Garber from IAA."

"Who is it?" a female voice called out from within the villa.

"Boy from agency!" the Vietnamese called back.

Matty's heart sank. Boy? Me no boy. Me twenty-eight.

"Have him come in," the voice called back.

The Vietnamese led Matty into the living room where Inez Sanchez stood in a pair of skin-tight, black-satin disco pants, a yellow halter top, and huge gold hoop earrings peeping out from her manelike, streaked-blond hair. She was tinier than Matty had imagined but had an incredible figure for a woman of—what? thirty-five? And she was even sultrier looking than her usual highly sexy screen persona. Garber's eyes were so riveted on her that he failed to notice the large, shaggy-haired man seated at the Steinway grand picking out Gershwin's "He Loves and She Loves" with considerable cocktail piano flair.

"Can I help you?" asked Inez, stepping toward Matty and knocking him dead with her aphrodisiacal perfume.

Matty desperately wanted to come up with a line—a wonderful Cary Grant line—that might sweep this incredible goddess off her feet and make her realize that he, Matthew Garber, was the one she'd been waiting for all those years. What the hell! Younger men were in. He'd be good for her, he'd shower her with affection, he'd take over her career, get her into more serious parts and better directors. If Ann-Margret could do it, why not Inez? *His* Inez.

"Something wrong?" asked Inez.

Matty had so fallen into his daydream under the spell of this celluloid goddess that he had failed to realize that that great Cary Grant line had managed to elude him and the best he could come up with was: "I brought you a script."

"How sweet," purred Inez. "Was it your own idea or did somebody put you up to it?"

"No, it's, uh . . . from the agency. I'm with IAA."

"Are you?" asked the big, shaggy-haired man at the piano. "Fancy that. . . . Is it true what they say about show business, Mister . . . ?"

"Garber," he replied, wondering who this guy with the English accent and insufferably arrogant manner was. "Matt Garber."

"Matt Garber," repeated the Englishman. "You're not related to Greta Garber, are you?"

Inez burst into peals of laughter and Matty wanted to belt the Englishman in the mouth.

"What is the script about?" asked Inez, curling up on the green velvet sofa and tucking her legs underneath her. She patted a spot next to herself on the sofa. "Tell me all about it. I never have time to read scripts."

Oh, God! Matty groaned inside himself. He'd blown it. He knew nothing of the screenplay inside the IAA envelope. Why hadn't he scanned it inside the garage? Done a quick mental precis and then dazzled beautiful Inez with his incisive analysis and dry, Midwestern wit. She'd have been impressed with him. She'd send that English sheepdog for a walk and spend the rest of the day getting into Matty. Oh, fate!

"Haven't you read it?" asked a disappointed Senorita Sanchez.

"Normally I do," blurted Matty, "but I've had an incredible load since joining the agency."

"How long have you been with them?" asked the Englishman, switching his repetoire from Gershwin to Coward.

"Are you in the business?" asked Matty.

"Good heavens, no! My mother would die of shame."

"Two weeks," lied Matty, feeling that the truth of his two-day tenure would make him a callow neophyte in Inez's large green eyes (to match the sofa? or vice versa?).

"A fortnight," murmured the Englishman. "A veritable fortnight Do you know Robert Rankoff?"

"He hired me," replied Matty breezily.

"Did he? Fascinating man, Rankoff. Don't you think?"

The Englishman spoke in choppy, staccato sentences with traces of an accent from somewhere in Great Britain's industrial north. The overall effect was of some misplaced character from a Harold Pinter play. Fascinating on stage, Matty had always felt. But definitely murder in someone's living room.

"Would you excuse me?" Inez leaned her whole body toward Matty upon this request and brought her lips maddeningly close to his. She leaped up abruptly from the sofa, dashed into the hallway and up the great sweeping staircase. At the top of the stairs she turned right at an alcove then vanished through a doorway. Matty never removed his eyes from her for a moment.

"Well?" The Englishman broke the silence of Matty's hypnotic trance. "What do you think?"

"Sorry?"

"Of her."

A second later the Englishman had abandoned the piano and was next to Matty on the green sofa.

"Do you find her . . . attractive?"

"She's Inez Sanchez," answered Matty, feeling no other reply was necessary.

"She's mortal. She breathes, she walks, she's insecure . . . like us all. She is subject to whims, flights of fancy . . . infatuations." On this last word the Englishman stared meaningfully into Matty's eyes. Garber had never felt so uncomfortable in someone's presence.

"I . . . don't understand," said Matty awkwardly.

"Do you want me to spell it out for you?"

"Is she coming back?"

"Tell me about your work with IAA," the Englishman said abruptly.

"Just a junior position at the moment"

"Ah! But you look the sort of chap who can rise quickly. Can you rise quickly, Mr. Gerber?"

"Garber."

"So you're not the baby food heir?"

"Huh? No. It's a whole different spelling."

"I surmised. Which brings us back to Miss Sanchez. You *would* like to come back to Miss Sanchez, I take it. Nervous sort to be in the business you're in. What made you become an agent?"

"Always been hooked on show business," shrugged Matty, wondering why on earth he was even having a conversation with this total stranger. "I was a film and theater critic in St. Louis for several years. Met a great many actors and actresses and felt an affinity—"

"An affinity? How refreshing to find someone in the agency world acquainted with the English language. . . . She adores educated men."

"She?"

The Englishman nodded toward the door at the top of the stairs.

"Been there myself, you know. I know where of I speak. . . . She fancies you."

"Oh, come on," replied Matty with considerable embarrassment.

"No need to play the fool with me, Mr. Gerber. You've been round the maypole a few times yourself. Sly dog!" He nudged Matty in the ribs with this last line.

"I'd better get going."

"What will I tell her when she finds you gone? That reverse psychology rubbish is passé, mate. She's a dead cert for the basic approach. Real he-man stuff."

"Been nice meeting you," said Matty, getting to his feet and heading toward the tiled hallway.

"Suppose I misunderstood that gleam in your eye," said the Englishman, following closely behind him. "As did she. More's the pity. Have to cope with her tantrums alone when you're gone."

"There's been a mistake—"

"More like a lost opportunity. Have you been to South America, Mr. Gerber?"

"Garber. No. Never."

"Obviously. Spent most of my life there. I am her uncle."

Matty didn't believe a word of it for a minute and yet . . .

"Know what she's like. Her blood. Why she had to leave Valparaiso. She . . . is insatiable. Knew you'd be trouble the minute you entered the sitting room. I was right. Do you know why she left the room?"

"I have no—"

"She can't endure the gringo civilities this society enforces upon her. She's a child of the jungle. Didn't know clothes until she was twelve. Get my drift?"

Matty stared up at the top of the stairs. This guy had to be putting him on. Either that or he, Matthew Garber, was about to blow the chance of a lifetime.

"She's really up there . . . waiting . . .?"

"Doesn't *all* happen in the movies, Mr. Garber. Ask your Mr. Rankoff. He'll think you a fool if you walk out the front door. That's Inez Sanchez up there, boy."

"But you're her uncle!"

"Does that make me a priest? Where is the boundary between sin and pleasure? Never been defined for me. This is California, Garber. Still a Spanish country. A different code than you're used to. I shall remove myself. You needn't worry. She's waiting. At the top of the stairs and through that door. Go to her. Or accept the fact that you're old before your time."

What the hell! thought Matty. This was L.A. God knows he'd heard enough stories about encounter groups, hot tubs, and cocaine mountains. Maybe Inez Sanchez really was what he'd always fantasized her to be: a raving nymphomaniac, who could only be satisfied—was waiting desperately for years—for Matty Garber.

Matty ascended the stairs as if directed by some unknown power. He paused on the upper landing and stared down at the "uncle" waiting at the foot of the staircase. The uncle pointed to the door on the right then waved a comradely salute.

"Adios," said the Englishman, who vanished from the hallway.

Matty's heart was pounding as he paused in front of the magnificently carved oak door. Resolutely placed his hand on the gold handle, he burst inside.

"What the hell do you want?" shrieked Inez Sanchez, who was planted firmly on the toilet seat with her disco pants down at her ankles. Her black onyx coke tray was balanced in one hand and her silver tooter in the other. "Get out of here! Jimmy, get him out of here!"

Blinded by humiliation, Matty raced down the length of the winding staircase accompanied by the raucous laughter of the Englishman, who had set him up for this bizarre practical joke. Matty ripped open the front door and raced across the lawn to his car when insult was added to injury: the timed lawn sprinklers went on and totally drenched him. He barely made it to the agency Volkswagen praying that the motor would start. He had to get out of there as soon as possible. And as far away from the sound of the Englishman's cruel laughter as his memory would allow.

He decided to go back to Westbourne first and change his damp clothes before returning to the office. He pulled into the garage, and was surprised to see Lindsay's battered pink Volkswagen in its familiar parking spot. Had she taken ill since that morning?

Walking along the third floor, Matty decided to knock at her door and see if she was all right The door was open a good half inch. Matty eased the door open.

"Lindsay?"

No reply.

He stepped farther into the living room.

"Lindsay?"

He heard her groan from the bedroom.

Was she sick? She'd probably caught the flu from all the recent downpour.

"Lindsay, you okay?"

The moaning increased.

Matty was alarmed now and raced into her bedroom.

"What the hell do you want?" demanded Lindsay, covering her nakedness with a sheet. "How dare you! Get the hell out of here!"

Matty stumbled backward out of the bedroom, babbling profuse, inadequate apologies. The second time in one day a woman had said that to him. Like a bad movie.

He was breathing heavily once he'd reached the apartment next door. What had he done? Why had he done it? He felt like a child who'd wandered into his parents' bedroom and seen them making love for the first time. Only this time Mommy was Lindsay Fairweather. And, if his eyes hadn't deceived him, Daddy was Yael Shomrim.

A pressing engagement, indeed.

ROLEY

It was six o'clock in the morning. Sabina Rankoff was wide awake and staring out at the rain pouring down on the Pacific Ocean. Was it never going to end? Granted she had prayed two years for the drought to vanish. But the rain was a real bummer.

She stared over at the man in the bed beside her. Funny how childlike he looked when he was asleep. All the incredible anger seemed to dissipate from him. That's when she loved him most: when she could still see the little boy in him. She tried not to think of the other times: the terrible rages, the bizarre games, and the sadistic tests of strength. She had overlooked them all in the four months they had been together because deep inside herself she knew he needed her. Truly needed her. Bobby had never done that. To Bobby she had merely been a charm on the bracelet of his life. Something that looked good; went well with his cuff links and dinner jacket at premieres; mixed the drinks for his friends and looked fabulous carrying them out to the pool; didn't have to do anything but lie around all day watching old movies and leave the running of the house to that old maid, Ames.

She had tried to love Bobby—but he couldn't accept love. So many walls, so many unspoken pains, so many sensitive subjects. She'd never forget the first time she'd asked him something about his daughter. "That's a sensitive subject." Period-boom-finished. He had not allowed her to breathe Martine's name in the house again. And then his thing about young girls. She'd try to understand; she said they should talk about it; but he'd merely fly into a rage at the suggestion that the problem even existed.

After one of his incredible silences, he'd turn around and buy her something at Tiffany's, or take her to La Scala or Perrino's. They even flew up to San Francisco for dinner once. She just couldn't handle it—like living with a time bomb.

Not that her present sleeping partner was all there. At least his bombs went off regularly, daily, sometimes hourly. But with him it was different. He was an artist. A great man. Bobby used to say *he'd* been an artist once. Singing in a band? Those old cornball tunes! Her parents used to dance to Bobby's records, for crying out loud! Yet the age thing had had nothing to do with it. Again she stared at the man in the bed. He was the same age as Bobby. But they were so different One was a man, a real man. And the other was—

"What the hell you doin' up?" asked the man squinting at the beautiful, blond girl sitting naked on her knees staring out at the morning Malibu sky.

"Go back to sleep, darling."

"Ain't tired no more," he said with the look of a greedy child staring at a delectable lollipop.

"That's good, lover," she replied, running her tongue down the length of his chest and tracing the circumference of his navel.

He grabbed her violently, threw her over on her back, and began to devour her greedily.

Another morning had begun for Sabina Rankoff and Rees Davenport.

***

"Let me apologize for yesterday. Never done anything like that before. I'm not a weirdo. It's just—You've been so kind to me. Thought maybe you were sick. When I heard you moan—"

"Would you shut up, for God's sake!" Lindsay Fairweather lifted the last page of the contract from the Xerox machine and stared with unbridled hostility at Matthew Garber. "People walk in and out of this room all the time. Want to get me fired?"

"For what?"

Lindsay heaved a sigh, walked over to the door of the IAA Telex and Xerox room, and shut it firmly.

"You *did* notice I wasn't alone," she whispered.

"That's what I came to apologize for. It's none of my business if you're in the sack with—"

"Would you keep your voice down! I accept your contrition, Matthew. That's not what's at issue. If anyone here found out about yesterday, I'd lose my job for sure."

"Because you played hookey?"

"Did you recognize the man?" she asked.

"Am I under oath?"

"One cardinal rule at IAA for secretaries. We are never, ever to date clients. It's like a filing clerk at the Pentagon dating someone from the Russian consulate. We know too much. We have influence with our bosses. In some cases, we can fuck them up. We type the deal memos, the contracts, everything. Yael is a very important—"

"Is that who he was?" asked Matty in fake astonishment. "Thought he looked familiar."

"It's not funny. Said he saw you in the garage."

"Is that how he knew me? . . . He the friend who takes you to all those restaurants?"

"Yael and I are lovers. We have been for two years."

"Aren't you the brazen lass," Matty commented in his best Scots brogue. "How does Mrs. Shomrim feel about all this? Recall seeing him arm in arm with some lovely *sabra* in People magazine last year. Kids, too, aren't there?"

"She doesn't know. He only sees me when he comes to town."

"How often is that?"

"A couple of times a year. Why do you want to know?"

"Hate to think of you sitting home ten months of the year waiting for some married man to turn up and throw you a bone when his schedule allows it."

"You're out of Victorian times, Garber. You know that? I have a life of my own. The world doesn't come to a stop the minute Yael leaves town. I lead a very happy—"

"That why you were bawling your eyes out the other night?"

"Do you get your kicks out of listening? How do you do it? A glass tumbler against the wall or do you have your own stethoscope?"

"I care about you!"

"You don't know anything about me."

"You were kind to me," he replied, "Just trying to return the favor. Don't want to see you get screwed up. My sister had an affair with a married man and—"

"I'm not your sister, okay? Just somebody who was stupid enough to feel sorry for some soaking wet sucker from St. Louis—"

"A great piece of alliteration!"

"I am asking you to keep your nose out of my business from now on. Leave me alone. That's asking a lot 'cause you've got the goods on me now to—"

"Goods on you? What am I? Some sleazy blackmailer? Who burned you, Lindsay? Who made you so cynical? Has Los Angeles turned a nice—"

"I was born in Glendale, jerk! Save your fantasy about some poor victim from the farm for your ex-wife."

"How did my ex-wife get into this?"

"As far as I'm concerned, the discussion is over. I will be civil to you. I'll try and help you. In exchange, you are never to mention this incident again."

"Don't behave like a child, Lindsay!"

"Goddamn you!" she hissed. "Leave me alone!" She pushed the marmalade hair that had tumbled down onto her angry face back above her forehead. "Mr. Rankoff wants to see you."

"Why didn't you-—?

"I forgot. I'm human. Do you know what that means, you pious, supercilious, Midwest ayatollah!"

Garber made his way upstairs to Rankoff's office feeling the same bitter aftertaste he'd always felt when he and Trisha had quarreled. How could a girl he'd only known for two days do that to him? Had he learned nothing from his marriage?

Rankoff was leaning against his desk with his jacket off chatting to someone on the other side of the office when Matty entered.

"Need you to run an errand for me," Rankoff announced in his most businesslike manner. "Take this envelope and run it up to Mulholland. Know where Benedict Canyon is?"

"On the west side of the Beverly Hills Hotel."

"Go straight up Benedict and turn left. Don't leave it with anyone except Yvonne. Okay? Take my car." He held the keys to the Mercedes out to Garber. "This is *not* company business. Take it easy in that rain. The canyons are murder. Oh! I don't think you've met James Steerforth yet. Mr. Steerforth is one of our senior agents."

Matty turned around with his hand outstretched and found himself staring into the face of the Englishman, the 'uncle' from Inez Sanchez's house the day before.

"Gerber, isn't it?" asked a deadpan Steerforth.

"Garber."

"Have you two met?"

"Indeed," grinned Steerforth, putting an avuncular arm around Matty's shoulder. "Mr. Garber and I discovered a common affinity yesterday afternoon. Didn't we, Mr. Garber? He's a modest chap, Bobby. Hardly says a word. Have you noticed? Understand you hired him two weeks ago."

"Two *days*," corrected Rankoff.

"Is that all? Two days. And suffering from an 'incredible load' in so short a time? You do plunge in, Garber, I daresay. He made an impression on our Inez. She was quite taken with him." Steerforth jolted him in the ribs as he had done the day before. "Sly dog."

Matty wanted to die. No, he wanted to haul back and deck Steerforth totally. But there was little likelihood of that with the shaggy-haired agent's powerful grip on his shoulders and the fact that the sadistic bastard was built like the center forward on England's World Cup team.

"Where did all this happen?" asked Rankoff, oblivious to the incredibly obvious undercurrent in his office.

"Better get going," said Matty, breaking loose from Steerforth's grip. "Nice meeting you again."

"Adios." Steerforth shot him another comradely salute.

Garber was beet red and homicidal by the time he reached the empty mailroom to fetch his sports jacket.

The telephone was ringing incessantly. Matty picked up the receiver.

"Sol there?" The crackle of long distance accompanied the voice.

"No, I'm sorry. He's not around," replied Matty politely.

"Damn!" snapped the voice on the other end. "I was expecting a script in the mail. Think you could have a look in my box? The name's Bobcaygeon."

Bobcaygeon! That was all Matty needed today. That lying, two-faced, double-crossing—

"I thought your voice sounded familiar," said Garber.

"Who's this?" asked Bobcaygeon.

"Matthew Garber."

"Sorry. The name doesn't ring a bell. Do I know you?"

"You hired me!" blurted Matty, fighting every desire to add 'you bastard' to the end of the sentence. "You offered me this 'fabulous' job. In St. Louis. Two weeks ago. KPLR. I had the interview show. Remember?"

"Oh, yeah! So you joined the agency, eh? Good for you!"

"You lied to me, Mr. Bobcaygeon! No one knew about me. There was no job, no office, no $30,000 salary, and no stock options. It was all a lie, wasn't it?"

"Of course," answered Bobcaygeon.

Matty was dumbfounded. He'd expected stammering, stuttering, fervent denial, claims of misinterpretation. Not bald-faced admission of guilt.

"But why?" asked Matty pathetically. "Why did you do that to me? I believed you. Gave up everything to come out here."

"I'm proud of you, Matty," boomed Bobcaygeon from the other end of the line. "Knew you had the stuff in you, Junior. The minute I saw you at the station. I said, 'Gilbert, that kid's got it. He is a born agent.' Don't mind telling you, Junior. You reminded me a helluva lot of me at your age. And I was nowhere near where you are now."

"I'm in the mailroom!" wailed Matty. "A twenty-eight-year-old messenger boy. I haven't phoned my parents. Ashamed to tell them the truth. They think I'm a success."

"*I* think you're a success. Took courage to do what you did, Matty. Give up everything like that. I couldn't have done it."

"Then why did you con me?"

"Something had to get you off your ass. You were dying there in St. Louis. You told me so. Just come out of a dead-end marriage. Barely making ends meet with two jobs. I saved your life. Made you follow the dream. Nothing's easy in this world, Junior. Have to do it yourself. No one else can do it for you. When I was twenty-one my dad gave me a map of the United States, a handshake, and said good luck. That was all. Been grateful to him ever since. Don't get mad, kid. Get even." Bobcaygeon burst into a Goofy type laugh at this last line. "That's a good one, huh? 'Don't get mad. Get even'. Remember that, Matty. It helps out there. You can be a big help to me. I'm on to some really big deals, and don't mind sharing them with you. You won't find anyone else in the office who will. Steerforth won't. Believe me. Watch out for Ara Whalen. She hates men. She's like a scorpion— she'll eat you and spit you out. I'm going to take care of you, Matty. Just like I promised. We're going to the top together. Got a deal cooking here—"

"Where are you?"

"Can't tell you right now. When I get out there, we'll go to Chasen's for dinner and I'll give you the lowdown. Been to Universal yet?"

"Not yet."

"Go see Lew Wasserman. Tell him you're a friend of Gilbob's. Lew'll take care of you. Got to run. Good talking to you."

The phone clicked at the other end and Matty found himself staring in amazement at the receiver in his hand. What had happened? It had been his intention to verbally blast Gilbert Bobcaygeon off the face of the globe. Instead he found that all his animosity toward the man had vanished. He actually liked him again. He felt that Bobcaygeon was looking out for his interests. Giving him advice. Introducing him to Lew Wasserman. Cutting him in on his deals. What deals?

Wait a minute! He was walking right into it again. The old Bobcaygeon con. That was when Matty realized the secret of Bobcaygeon's survival: it was impossible to hate the man. There was something about him despite his lies and deceits that made him lovable. Totally untrustworthy but lovable.

How many more "Gilbobs" are out there in Tinseltown, wondered Matty as he picked up Rankoff's envelope and keys and set out for the garage.

***

Joy Dworkin was having a terrific day. By noon she had managed to place two clients in a TV pilot at Paramount, signed a director for a feature at AIP, and (unbeknownst to Bobby Rankoff) was secretly putting a package together for the *Ektalon-Z* science-fiction epic. If only she could pirate Rees Davenport away from his agents. No one could shoot that film the way he could.

How could she get to Rees Davenport? What was the method of beguiling the most macho director to ever come out of Spotted Horse, Wyoming? Maybe Sabina Rankoff could. Was she crazy? Joy thought. There was no way IAA would represent the man who'd stolen Bobby's wife away from him. And no way Joy intended to alienate her boss. Not professionally or emotionally. One day she would have to decide which of her two fantasy men she'd rather end up with: Bobby Rankoff or Jimmy Steerforth. Both impossible objects, natch. Totally neurotic obsessions. But that's what happens when you're an orphan. Oh, no! she thought. Not my orphan bit. Not right now. I've got hustling to do. Deals to make. Just like the big boys do it. Beautiful Bobby Rankoff and Jimmy—speak of the devil!

"We must have words, you and I," announced Steerforth, leaning against the doorframe of her office.

"Sure," replied Joy, trying to reduce her nervousness into something resembling cool. She wondered if her hair looked all right. How the hell did Jimmy keep his hair the same shaggy length without ever going to a barber?

"I understand that congratulations are in order," said Steerforth, stepping pantherlike into her office and closing the door behind him. "You've been a busy girl in my absence."

"Just luck," shrugged Joy, loving that the Englishman was drawing closer to her every second but fearing all the while the turns she knew his Machiavellian mind could take.

"Luck? Or a touch of your Samantha Glicks?" He put a hand to Joy's cheek and the girl shivered under his touch. A second later his hand had slipped to the back of her neck and was clutching the roots of her jet black hair in a painful knot. "What the hell were you doing signing Sally Mitchell? Only eunuchs and Steerforth are allowed near the harem, my darling."

"The deal! The deal was in jeopardy!" gasped Joy. "The picture would have been postponed after Darlene's accident. Probably canceled. You weren't here. Somebody had to do something."

"That somebody was our little Joy?"

"Want your name on the booking slip?" hissed the frightened orphan from Chicago. "Are you that insecure, mystery man?"

"What are you talking about?"

"Let go of me!"

"Tell me about the accident!"

"How come you get all your mail at the post office?" asked Joy despite her discomfort. "How come no one's ever been to your place? What's your secret, Jimmy?"

"Tell me about the accident!"

"I don't know what—"

"You know what happened to Darlene. I've kept bloody Ara from opening a police investigation. Hope I've good enough reason for saving your beautifully sculpted ass."

"You . . . stopped her?"

"Yes." Steerforth finally released his grip.

Joy - shaking like a leaf - collapsed into a chair. She looked around the room for her bag.

"Here," said Steerforth, lighting a cigarette and popping it into her tense mouth. "It's not your regular brand."

"I hate your guts," said Joy, gulping down the smoke gratefully. "Never hated any man as much as I do you."

"If one more woman says that to me," sighed Steerforth. "Get on with your story, Scheherazade." Steerforth lit a cigarette for himself and stared down at the deflated Ms. Dworkin crumpled in her chair.

"Darlene joined the agency when I was working as Speedy's secretary. Used to speak to her on the phone a lot. Tip her off about jobs, things like that. Then she got her own series and I became a junior agent. We never saw each other anymore. Then Ara got her the feature deal at Universal. Thought I'd buy her a gift for her first day's shooting. For old-times' sake."

"And put you in her good books in case the film took off," suggested Steerforth.

"What's wrong with that? You know half this business is based on *schmoozing*—"

"Ah, yes! It's not who you know, it's who you blow."

"Bought her this toiletry set. Never heard of the brand but it smelled terrific. Took it over to her place in Silver Lake. She lives in this really crummy little house across the road from a bunch of Mexicans. Scared shitless getting out of the car. But I knocked at the door. Darlene answered it sweating bullets in a purple Danskin—the girl has a definite weight problem. Anyhow, she was touched, genuinely touched by my gift. She asked me in, gave me a Diet Dr. Pepper, and went to take a shower. She was chatting with me from the bathroom after she'd finished. Shouting really. I went in to talk to her. She was swabbing herself with the *apres le bain* I bought her and she was really uptight. I offered her a joint. She took it, lit a match, and bingo! I was terrified, Jimmy. Her whole body went up in flames. The moisturizer must have had a kerosene base. Everything.

Her hair, her eyebrows. It was horrible. I grabbed a bath towel and wrapped it around her. Then I phoned the ambulance and emergency at Hollywood Pres and told them to expect Darlene Bernstein. That was her real name before Ara invented Darlene English. They'd know who Darlene English was right away, and the papers would have a field day with that freak show. Planned to ride with her in the ambulance when I remembered the picture. Knew I had to move fast. So I phoned Ara."

"You phoned Ara?"

"Not as me. As Nurse Horton." Joy switched to a perfect reading of a concerned but professional night nurse. "'Miss Whalen? Good evening, this is Hollywood Presbyterian Hospital. We've just admitted a young woman.' Knew the Painted Lady would rush to the rescue. That would give me time to figure out a plan of action. I'd gotten stoned with Sally Mitchell a couple of times at parties with Bazzo and I knew she was pissed off at the Morris agency. I also knew this baby mogul at Universal—Steve Goodbaum—had the hots for her. So a couple of phone calls, a few frantic hops over the hill and back and . . ."

"A coup Robert Rankoff himself would be proud of," concluded Steerforth, most impressed by her tale.

"What about you?"

"My style is less flamboyant, more byzantine. You're a power to be reckoned with, Joy. I shall have to watch out for you in future."

"You won't let her call the cops, will you?"

"It was an accident. You said so yourself. Just wanted to make sure you weren't cutting in on my territory. I'd present you with the *Legion d'Honneur*, if it were at my disposal. So this must suffice." He planted a kiss on both of Miss Dworkin's lovely apple cheeks.

"That the best you can do?" asked Joy, getting some of her old cockiness back.

"You *are* ambitious." Steerforth walked toward the closed door.

"Jimmy?"

"Hmm?"

"Do I really have a beautifully sculpted ass?"

***

The rain had abated temporarily as Garber drove the chocolate brown Mercedes north on Benedict Canyon. He glanced at the envelope lying on the passenger seat with the name "Yvonne" scrawled across the front of it. Who was she? Not company business. Rankoff had made that point clear. The man was a maze of intrigues. Matty returned his attention to the road and slammed on the brakes. A car was stalled in front of him and an elderly man with snow-white hair was moving around the uplifted hood in futile arcs hurling Shakespearean cadences at the offending motor.

Matty pulled the Mercedes over to the side of the road, tugged on the emergency brake, and got out to stare in awe at an immaculately preserved 1937 blue Cord 810 automobile.

"That's a beauty!" gushed Matty.

"If it was a horse, I'd shoot it," boomed the stocky old man in distinct English tones that might well have been heard at the Old Vic half a century earlier. "This wretched machine's been nothing but a bother to me for the past forty years."

"That's the original?"

"Both car and driver, young man. Don't suppose you know anything about motors?"

"A bit. Mind if I have a look?"

"I'd have called the auto club," the old boy said as Matty proceeded to poke around with the machinery, "but I'm not a member. Have to have a driver's license, you know. Lost mine in 1960. Don't see why you have to have a damned license anyhow. Hardly drive the damned thing what with all this petrol nonsense. 'Even and odd days'. They're all odd days to me, you know. Any luck?"

The old man's face was peering hopefully into Matty's. Garber did a double take. He'd thought the voice was familiar . . .

"Aren't you Roland Draycott?"

"Good Lord! How would you know that?" asked the white-haired Englishman, touched and astonished at the same time.

"Your voice. Your face. I didn't realize you were—"

"Still alive?" asked the actor, who had been a familiar face in films throughout the thirties and forties along with the likes of Claude Rains, Edmund Gwenn, Herbert Marshall, Cedric Hardwicke, and Basil Rathbone.

"I didn't mean that," said Matty, who had thought precisely that.

"It's all right, young man. I went through that 'aren't you-dead' phase about ten years ago. Anyone I meet today —and there aren't many, I can assure you—is convinced that I am a double for the late Roland Draycott. But I promise you, young man, I am alive. Only my career is dead. How on earth did you know who I was? I haven't made a film in twenty years."

"Television," shrugged Matty. "You seem to be in one movie or another every week."

"And no residuals. Wish I had my career now. All I've got is this great monstrosity to show for thirty years in the cinema. They gave me this car. The Cord people. I posed for an advertisement in 1937. Saturday Evening Post. 'The car that Roland Draycott drives.' Now we're both dinosaurs."

"The car's making a comeback."

"Good for the car," replied Draycott sardonically.

"Would you be interested in working again?" Matty offered, in amends for any pain he might have caused the old actor with his tactless 'comeback' remark.

"Are you in the magic wand business?" The last line was delivered with the classic Roland Draycott wryness that had characterized his many upper-class snobs with hearts of gold. "I shall be eighty in August, which makes me far too old to be trifled with."

"I'm with the International Artists Agency. My name is Matthew Garber." Matty held his hand out to Draycott and was impressed by the vigorous and strong grasp that greeted it.

"Didn't that used to be the Keller-Shankman agency?"

"Still is. Different name."

"They represented me for twenty years. Sid Shankman himself you know. Signed me in 1933. Huge mistake. Sid thought I was Claude Rains. Claude had just done *Invisible Man*. No one had seen him. Dear Sid heard me in a booth in the Brown Derby. Thought I was Claude, signed me on the spot. Lived in Claude's shadow for years. Got all his leftovers. We were the same height, you know. Is that boy still at the agency?"

"Who's that, sir?"

"Don't call me 'sir'. Please. Makes me think of the knighthood I missed. Call me Roley. What was that boy's name? Got himself in trouble with the Mafia. He was a client at the time. Sid made him an agent. He was a singer."

"Bobby Rankoff?"

"That's the chap. Studio had dropped my contract. Wasn't getting much work. Sid made him my agent. That was the beginning of my decline."

"He's the head of the agency now."

"Is he indeed? Didn't do much for me. Surprised he did so well for himself. Quite a naughty boy in those days. Was married to that French actress. Did a film with her. Yvonne. Yvonne . . . Corday, I think."

The name reminded Matty of the envelope and that he was late to deliver it.

"Shall we try the engine again, sir—Roley? I'm a bit late."

"Of course. Didn't mean to natter on like this. Don't talk to many people these days, you know." Draycott walked around to the driver's, side, placed one foot on the running board, and climbed in behind the wheel. "Once more unto the breach, dear friends, and all that tosh." The motor wheezed slightly then kicked over. "You're a marvel, Mr. Garber! Would you mind popping the bonnet down? There's a good chap. Have to get back to my little cottage before this wretched monsoon washes it away."

"Meant what I said before," said Matty, resting one foot on the Cord's running board and leaning his head through the open window. "About trying to get you work again."

"Very kind of you. Don't think I'll see a camera again till I get up there." Draycott nodded his head toward the overcast sky. "Good Lord, it's going to rain again! Got some decent sherry at my place if you fancy a glass."

"Can I take a raincheck?"

"Don't know if I'll live long enough to see a clear day again, my boy."

"I can come over after work. Today."

"Got a pen?"

Draycott gave Garber an address in Bel Air, then tooted his horn jauntily and plowed his vintage Cord up the hill.

Matty got behind the wheel of the Mercedes once more and mused on his meeting with Roland Draycott. Roley. A great character. He looked forward to that glass of sherry and more stories of the old days. Maybe he'd learn a little more about Bobby Rankoff and the Mafia. The Mafia! The plot was definitely thickening.

Yvonne Corday Rankoff stood in front of the mirror applying her lipstick for the third time that morning. It gave her something to do while waiting for the taxi. Perhaps she'd change her sweater. What for? She was only having lunch with Ara and Evelyn. She could be herself with them. Well, *almost* herself. She'd known them for thirty years. Lunched with them once a week for the past ten. They traded gossip and swapped observations on the passage of time. Each one had known tragedy of sorts. But still Yvonne knew she couldn't discuss everything. There were other ladies one talked about those things with. Usually late at night. With the lights off.

Yvonne laughed aloud. *Quelle scandale!* When had she stopped thinking in French? Before Martine? No. Perhaps. Strange. There was a time in her life when everything was before or after America. Then it was before or after Bobby. But for years now it had been before or after Martine. Martine's accident had changed both their lives. Hers and Bobby's. *Pauvre* Robert. She still loved him. How could you not love Bobby? That bastard! He was a week late with the check again. Did he think they'd let Martine stay there on credit? She'd begged him to pay them a yearly lump. But not Bobby. He could never be tied down that easily. "Don't they trust me?" These were doctors. Not producers. Did he really think he could make deals with everyone?

Did he never learn? Wasn't it enough that that little blond tramp of a wife had run off with Rees Davenport and the whole town laughed at him behind his back?

She checked her own white-blond hair in the mirror, then the large full breasts under the yellow cashmere sweater. She'd never had them lifted. Not bad for forty-nine. She ran her hands over her breasts soothingly, then fondled her nipples unencumbered by a brassiere. What the hell was she arousing herself like this for? She was going to lunch, not an affair. That was if the stupid taxi ever turned up.

"You must be telepathic!" Yvonne announced aloud as the doorbell rang a second later. She grabbed her Alan Austin blazer from the banister, tucked her Vuitton envelope purse under her arm, and whipped the door open. "I have been waiting an hour for you to arrive."

"I'm sorry," said the broad-shouldered, good-looking, bespectacled young man holding an envelope out to her.

"What's this?"

"Mr. Rankoff said I was to give this to you personally. Are you Yvonne?"

"I am Madame Rankoff," Yvonne corrected with distinct French hauteur in the face of the young man's unwarranted intimacy. Damn, he was attractive. And her nipples were still throbbing from her attention a few moments ago. "And you are *not* my taxi."

"Uh, no. I'm from the office."

Yvonne stared past him and out to the driveway where the chocolate-brown Mercedes was parked.

"You're driving his car. He must trust you. Does he trust you, Mister . . . ?"

"Garber. Matthew Garber."

"Would you like to come in, Mr. Garber?"

She took the envelope from Matty and led him into the sitting room with a huge picture window commanding an impressive view of the sprawling San Fernando Valley below. Yvonne opened the envelope and withdrew a check from inside it, while Matty gazed around the large stone-walled room dominated by a cavernous six-foot-high fireplace. Beside the fireplace was a pine table with a framed photograph of Rankoff, Yvonne, and a beautiful teen-aged girl.

"Is that a recent photograph?" asked Matty, wondering who the girl was.

"No," replied Yvonne, tucking the check into her Vuitton bag. "Are you going back to the office?"

"Yes, I—"

"Good. You can give me a lift to the Brown Derby. My car's stuck in the garage, and I've been waiting all morning for a taxi to take me to lunch."

"Sure. It'd be my—"

"Let's go."

The rain was falling again as Matty steered the Mercedes back down Benedict Canyon. He didn't know what to make of Madame Rankoff. Dismissing her as a French bitch was too facile. After all, she was part of the Rankoff mystery. She was his wife. Or was she his ex-wife?

"Ran into an old co-star of yours on the way here," said Matty, not quite certain of his motives for wanting to make conversation.

"Oh, yes?"

"Roland Draycott."

"Is he still alive!?"

"He's alive and in great shape for eighty."

"Sweet little Roley," murmured Yvonne. "He was very kind to me. We did a film with Burt Lancaster. It was chaotic. I was crying all the time and Roley would take me in his dressing room and give me sherry. Hated sherry but I drank it. If you ever see that film on the late show, I'm drunk the whole picture. He was married to a terrible bitch, Roley. She took everything from him. Haven't thought about him in years. It was a hard time in my life. Bobby was crazy in those days. He was still on top. He'd made a film; his records sold millions; and he had the radio show. He was an egomaniac. I remember once a stagehand dropped a prop in the middle of Bobby's number. It was an accident. Bobby had him fired during the commercial. It was horrible."

"Was this before he got in trouble . . . with the mob?"

"Who told you that?" demanded Yvonne.

"Heard a lot of stories about him," shrugged Matty.

"Have you known him long?"

"Two days."

"And you're caught up already," laughed Yvonne. "He has that effect on the very young."

"Were you his first wife?"

"Are you writing his biography? Is there a Boswell running around Rodeo Drive? Bobby hates people prying into his private life. Haven't you been warned about 'sensitive subjects'? This is a warning, Mr. Garber. Bobby Rankoff is an Indian-giver. He giveth and he taketh away."

"Were you his first wife?" grinned Matty.

"When did you learn that your smile would get you anything, Mr. Garber? Were you very little?"

"I was a very tenacious journalist, Madame Rankoff."

"I was his second wife. You'll have to ask him about the first. One clue: He suffered incredible guilt about her for years."

"How can you do this to me?" wailed Matty. "It's . . . it's gossip interruptus."

"Will you give me an acknowledgment in your book if I tell you more?"

"I'll dedicate it to you," he replied, thrusting his arms out to her dramatically.

"Please, keep your hands on the wheel. You're a fascinating young man, Mr. Garber. What made you become an agent?"

"Gilbert Bobcaygeon."

Yvonne threw her head back and laughed. "Oh, no! You must tell Ara. Have you met Ara Whalen?"

"Just briefly."

"You've stumbled into an incredible mosaic of incest and coincidence, Matthew. X-rated Dickens. You must come to lunch with me. I know Mrs. Shankman will want to meet you. But you must ask no questions. Just listen and observe. Agreed?"

"Sure," shrugged Matty.

It was exceedingly difficult to distinguish between Sol Siglan annoyed and Sol Siglan enthusiastic. The popeyed, balding owl's penchant for bobbing his head like a dime-store dachshund was present in both humors. However Matty could tell by the excessive twitching in Siglan's eyes that the mailroom boss was annoyed and Matty was the object of his anger.

"I feel betrayed, Garber," Siglan announced in his nasal whine. "I feel a trust has been betrayed."

"What's wrong, Mr. Siglan?"

"You went on a delivery. A simple delivery at eleven-thirty this morning and it is now three in the afternoon. Where have you been? Mr. Rankoff needed his car. He couldn't remember where it was. He was going to call the police. I had to step in, Garber."

"I was with Mrs. Rankoff. Her car was in the garage. I then went to lunch with her and Mrs. Shankman."

"Ah! You met Evelyn?" The twitching in Siglan's eyes stopped abruptly. "She's a beautiful woman, isn't she?"

"Incredibly. She's over seventy, I believe."

"Is she? She's a few years younger than me, I know. And I'm seventy-four so—"

"You're *not*, Mr. Siglan! You don't look it."

"Oh, that's kind of you, Garber. California, you know. Keeps us all young. No winter here. Beautiful woman, Evelyn. Evelyn Hughes she used to be. On the New York stage. With Louis Calhern. Don't suppose you remember Mr. Calhern?"

"Only from his later films—"

"Marvelous stage actor. Mrs. Shankman was his leading lady back in the thirties. Then she married Mr. Shankman and came out here. Retired. She's always been kind to me, Mrs. Shankman. Thought she was a double for Barbara Stanwyck."

"There is a resemblance. Does she have any children?"

"No. They never had any kids. She's been ill for many years. Since the early fifties. Always seeing one doctor or another."

"Seemed in great shape to me. But now that you mention it, she was on her way to the doctor's after lunch."

"See what I mean?" asked Siglan. "It's all front. Still a great actress. That woman's in pain, Garber. She won't let anyone see it. Bravery. Bravery, Garber. I'll take Mr. Rankoff's keys now. And Miss Dworkin wants to see you right away."

A buoyant Matty took the fire stairs two at a time up to Joy's office and found the possessor of those incredible doe-like eyes combing out her jet black hair.

"The little prince has arrived," she remarked as Matty stuck his head in the door.

"What's that supposed to mean?"

"You made a big hit at lunch, I understand. With the dowager duchess. Mrs. Shankman. She just floated through the office telling everyone you had the manners of a little prince. What did you do, Garber?"

"Nothing. I gave Mrs. Rankoff a lift to the Brown Derby and—"

"You know Sabina Rankoff?" Joy's tones were a mix of jealousy and blatant opportunism.

"Yvonne."

"Oh. The ex-Mrs. Rankoff. You had my heart going there for a minute. What the hell were you doing with her?"

"Look, Miss Dworkin, I don't think I have to—"

"Close the door, will you. Want a Tab? Perrier? A little toot?"

"Little toot? Like in the tugboat?"

"Like in coconut snow. Close the door, please. Beatrice is across the hall and reports everything to Foley. Everything!"

Matty closed the door and returned to the sofa where Joy was tucked up with her lovely legs underneath her Maxfield Bleu skirt. Unscrewing the cap of a tiny amber vial, she withdrew a miniature spoon and scooped up some chunky white powder.

"What is that?" asked Matty.

"Cocaine."

"Jesus Christ!"

"You don't snort?"

"No!"

"We're not talking about devil worship, Garber. It's the Eighties now. Welcome aboard. Going to have to get with it out here, Matty." She made the white powder vanish from the spoon up her left nostril. "Don't mind me calling you Matty, do you?"

"Is it like grass?" he asked warily.

"Better. Come on. It's good stuff. Bazzo only gets the best."

Garber felt like one of Dracula's victims yielding to the inevitable as he sat beside Joy on the sofa. She had a devilish gleam in her eye as she held the spoon up to his right nostril.

"Breathe! Go on! Deep! Get a good hit! That's it!"

"It hurts!"

"It doesn't hurt! Don't be such a baby. Come on! Put some in your other nostril."

She was right. It didn't hurt. It just made him feel up. High. But not trippy. And extremely gregarious.

"I feel very chatty," laughed Matty.

"Terrific! Let's have a little chat. You're hot, Matty. Don't know how you did it. Here for two days and everybody's on your side. Mrs. Shankman loves you. You had lunch with the Painted Lady."

"Who?"

"Ara."

"Why do you call her the Painted— oh! That's funny. You're very funny. Did I tell you that?"

"You told me about my ankles."

"Oh, yeah. You have great ankles. And incredible eyes. And lips that— God! This stuff makes you horny, doesn't it?"

"Horny guy, aren't you, Matty?"

"It's been a long time. Got divorced and haven't really dated since—"

"You're not breaking your fast in my office. Not during the day anyhow. I want a truce with you, Matty."

"A truce?"

"Don't want to fight you. Okay? You're ambitious. I'm ambitious. We could be running this office together."

"I'm in the mailroom!"

"For how long? A couple of weeks? Rankoff likes you. The Painted Lady—"

"Steerforth hates my guts!"

"He can be made inoperative," she replied, taking another toot.

"You sound like Foley."

"He's the one to worry about," gasped Joy, holding the coke deep in her lungs. "Him and his goddamn guru."

"Dr. Kislev?"

"Shmuel the Shmendrick. Tell me about lunch."

"They just gossiped," shrugged Matty.

"What did they say?" Joy brought the spoon up to Matty's nose again.

"They all seem worried about Abe Keller. His health."

"We're all worried, Matty. If anything happens to Abe Keller, this agency is up for grabs. He's the last surviving partner. Mrs. Shankman still has a controlling interest as Sid's widow but—"

"She's something, isn't she? Do you know she's seventy?"

"She was Louis Calhern's mistress."

"Is that true?"

"That's the rumor."

"Everything's rumor. Do you know Stan Feingold?"

"He's Abe Keller's son-in-law. When Sid Shankman died, he and Bobby Rankoff took over the agency. Stan left the business five years ago and became an independent producer. He's doing *Ektalon-Z* and *The Brother Who Fell from Uranus.*"

"What's that?" asked Matty. "Sounds gross."

"Crazy Tom Ricker. The first black sci-fi comedy."

"First-class *schmoozer*, that Feingold. And a very funny storyteller. He came over to our table at lunch. Apparently a Brinks truck pulled up in front of the black tower at Universal this morning and a dozen guerrillas in battle fatigues jumped out carrying Israeli machine guns and captured the lobby. They were led by Rees Davenport."

"He's so sick!" exclaimed Joy.

"That's what Ara said. Apparently she was married to him once. Is that true?"

"Oh, yeah. But that was before he was *the* Rees Davenport. When Ara was married to him he was directing *Bonanza* and *High Chaparral.*"

"They don't seem like a very likely couple to be together."

"I guess she was going to the opposite pole after Bobcaygeon."

"Gilbert Bobcaygeon? She was married to—?"

"It's the embarrassment of her life. She'd been living it down for years. Then he dropped out of the business and no one remembered him. When he came back to work here, she was ready to commit sepuku."

"Poor woman."

"Poor woman, my ass. She's a monster! A man-eater. She deserves everything she gets. Watch out for her, Matty. She'll try and eat you alive."

"That's what Bobcaygeon said."

"He ought to know. When did you speak to him, busy boy?"

"He phoned this morning. Do you think he's all there?"

"Definitely not. He's a nutjob. Totally amoral. You know what his problem is? He mistakes tolerance for affection. Just because no one's ever had him put away he thinks everyone loves him."

"Did you make that up?"

"No," she replied begrudgingly. "It's the Painted Lady's."

"Why do you hate her so much?"

"Why shouldn't I? She's been against me from the moment I came to work here. She's fought every promotion of mine. She's the one who hates me."

"Why?"

"Cuz I'm young. I'm pretty. I'm everything she used to be that ended up at the bottom of a bottle of J&B. Have you ever been near her when she's blotto? 'I used to be a great beauty once. Now I'm merely handsome.' She has no pride anymore, no dignity."

"You sound ashamed of her. What is she? Your mother?"

"Don't you ever say that!" shrilled Joy. "Ever!"

"Hey, come on! I'm just joking."

"It's not funny. You're not funny. What are you doing up here anyhow? Aren't you supposed to be delivering mail?"

"Thought we had a truce. We were going to run the office together."

"Leave me alone, will you!" As a pathetic postscript she added the hopeless explanation: "I'm neurotic."

Matty leaned forward and kissed her briefly on the lips.

"I'll be your friend," he offered.

"I grew up on charity. You just want to fuck me anyhow."

"No, I don't."

"Why not?"

"Because we're friends now."

"You can't fuck your friends?" she asked. "Boy, are you screwed up! You should meet Sabina Rankoff."

"Who is this Sabina Rankoff?"

"She's Bobby's child bride. But she dumped him and moved in with Rees Davenport."

"Oh, God! A sensitive subject. I really blew it"

"What?"

"I suggested to Mr. Rankoff that Rees Davenport direct *Ektalon-Z.* He looked at me like I'd shat on the carpet."

"That was a smart move, Matty. You'll go far."

"Oh, Jesus! Yvonne was right. This is a mosaic of incest and coincidence."

"Do you like Yvonne?"

"Yeah. Thought she was a bit cold at first. But once she loosened up, she was a lot of fun."

"She's a dyke."

"Beg your pardon?"

"Yvonne Corday's a lesbian. Has been for years."

"You know this from experience?"

"No, dahling," she drawled in an impressive impersonation of Tallulah Bankhead. "She never sucked my cock."

"Another rumor."

"Welcome to the business. Stay in touch, Matty."

"Thanks, pal. I love you, too." He started toward the door.

"Hey!" interjected Joy, stopping him before he vanished into the corridor. "Hear you've got a crush on Rankoffs' secretary."

"Jesus! This place is worse than high school."

"She's cute," shrugged Joy. "Bye-eee!"

Matty spent the rest of the afternoon traveling back and forth between Culver City picking up and delivering packages at United Artists and M-G-M. To combat the boredom of the drive and the endless downpour he constructed a mental graph of the Rankoff-Keller-Shankman-Whalen-Bobcaygeon-Davenport mosaic, trying to figure out where the overlaps (if any) fitted in. Margaret Mead would have had a field day trying to analyze this extended family.

It was seven o'clock before Matty finished his final delivery of the day, and he was most surprised to see Lindsay staring at him quizzically from the doorway of the mailroom.

"Did you have a nice visit with Joy Dworkin?"

"Is the whole place bugged?"

"Warned you, didn't I?"

"That's when we were friends."

"Can't we still be?" asked Lindsay holding her hand out to him. "Truce?"

"Don't think I can handle another truce today," replied Matty warily.

"I was a total bitch this morning. Sorry. Give you a lift home?"

"Thanks. But I've been invited somewhere for a drink."

"Joy or Ara?"

"Neither."

"You don't have to bite my head off, Matthew. Said I was sorry. What more do you want?" She seemed quite disturbed about something other than the apology and looked up beseechingly into his eyes. "Can you nae forgive a lass, Matty?"

"How'd you like to meet a friend of mine?" asked Garber. "Well, he's not exactly a friend yet. But I think he will be."

Twenty minutes later Lindsay pulled her battered pink Volkswagen to a stop in front of a thatched-roof cottage in Bel Air.

"Is this a set?" asked Lindsay, totally captivated by the little bit of rural England in the middle of Los Angeles. "Someone really lives here? Oh, my God!"

"What's wrong?"

Before she could answer Matty, she'd raced toward the 1937 Cord parked next to the cottage and touched it as if it held the mystic power of the Moonstone itself.

"It's a miracle," sighed Lindsay.

"Are you into old cars?"

"My grandfather went bankrupt buying them. He had a 1919 Pierce Arrow. A 1931 Chrysler CG Le Baron— he traded a 1931 Franklin Speedster for that. Then he bought a Packard and swapped both of them for a 1925 Bugatti."

"Where did he keep them all?"

"That was the problem. My grandmother put her foot down when he put the Bugatti in the dining room."

"He put the car in the dining room?"

"There was no space in the garage . . . I come from an eccentric background. Glendale is James M. Cain territory, you know."

"Yeah. I read *Mildred Pierce.*"

"What's going on out there?" a stentorian English voice boomed from inside. "What do you want?"

"It's Matthew Garber, Mr. Draycott We met in the rain this morning. You invited me for a drink."

Draycott opened the front door. His snow-white hair was disheveled and the young couple obviously had woken him from a nap.

"Oh, my dear boy!" boomed Draycott. "Quite given up on you. Who is this lovely creature?"

"My friend, Lindsay Fairweather. Didn't think you'd mind my bringing her along."

"Not at all, not at all. What beautiful hair you have, my dear. Trust you don't mind my pointing it out."

"Not at all," blushed Lindsay.

"I was in love with a girl once with hair like yours. She was Scots."

"My grandmother was Scots."

"Was she indeed? Perhaps it was her. Don't just stand there on the threshold. Come in, you two. Where's that sherry bottle gone to?"

The inside of the cottage was as charming as the exterior. The walls were adorned with posters from 1920s London stage productions Draycott had appeared in.

"Forgive the disarray," Roley chirped as he poured sherry into three Waterford crystal glasses and passed them to his visitors. "Had to let the cleaning lady go last year. Too many things missing after her visits. A silver cigar case which Gerald du Maurier gave to me. Gone! Ah, well. Came into this world with nothing, go out the same way. Would you like to see my garden?"

Draycott walked over to a slightly tattered red-and-gold brocaded curtain, pulled it to one side, and revealed a pair of French doors.

"Haven't opened these in years," explained Draycott as he struggled with the bolts at the top of the doors.

"Let me," said Matty, passing his glass to Lindsay, and pulled the rusted bolt down from the top of the door letting in the evening air.

Lindsay and Matty followed their host out into the garden. It was twenty feet deep and ten feet wide, surrounded by a stone wall five feet high. The ground had been paved with brick and imported Italian tiles now covered with dirt and dust. A beautiful marble and alabaster fountain stood alone at the far end of the garden encased in cobwebs. The soil between the brick and the walls contained only weeds that had long since choked to death the luxuriant flowers that had once bloomed there.

Matty imagined what the garden must have looked like in its heyday when Roley all but read his thoughts.

"Do you know Barrie's *Dear Brutus*?" asked the old actor. "It's about a magical garden that only appeared every hundred years. If one went into the garden on midsummer's night, one found out what they might have been. Often wondered what happened to the garden the other ninety-nine years."

"Now I know," said Matty reverentially, despite the garden's obvious decay.

"Precisely," replied Roley. "Of course, it needs a gardener desperately. Far too impecunious, as it were, to do much about it. Still, I'm quite fond of this little patch. Reminds me of home."

"It's beautiful," whispered Lindsay. "So still. I love it."

"Thank you, my dear. Built it for myself years ago to escape all the hubbub at the big place." He nodded toward a sprawling Mediterranean villa dominating the hillside above.

"That was . . . yours?" asked Matty.

"From 1940 until 1950. When my wife divorced me, lost everything except the cottage. The big house has been sold several times since then. Fortune's fool, eh what? Shall I get you some cheese and biscuits?"

"Please, don't bother," said Lindsay.

"No bother at all. Just hope I have some after all that. Please, enjoy the garden. Shan't be long."

"He's very sweet," Lindsay said after Roley had departed. "Reminds me of this actor in old movies."

"Probably him," commented Matty sadly and he filled Lindsay in on Roley's credits from his heyday.

"He worked with all those people!" she gasped. "And he can't get a job. Terrible. I'll speak to Mr. Rankoff."

"He was his agent. Years ago. Suspect it might be a 'sensitive subject.' "

"You're learning quickly," she replied proudly. "I knew you would."

"How's your friend?"

"Went back to Tel Aviv this morning."

"Oh."

"Oh what?"

"That why I got my head bit off?"

"Let's not talk about it."

"When's he coming back?"

"Don't know."

"Waiting for him again?" He stepped toward her on this question.

"Please, Matty, don't . . ."

"'Full many a flower is born to blush unseen—'"

"Please!"

He had her in his arms by this time and was kissing her tenderly on the lips. She resisted him at first but then . . .

"It's nicer when you help," he announced when they broke their embrace.

"I'm confused."

"Who isn't? Let's just enjoy the garden. Okay? Isn't that house incredible up there?"

"Oh, my gosh!" said Lindsay.

"What's up?"

"That's Inez Sanchez's house!"

"You're kidding. I was there yesterday."

"I know," giggled Lindsay. "I got the story from Mr. Steerforth's secretary."

"He told her! That bastard told her? I'll kill him!"

"Matty."

"What?"

"Would you kiss me again?"

"My pleasure."

He took her in his arms once more, oblivious to Inez Sanchez's house above and James Steerforth standing on the balcony staring down at him.

RABAIOTTI

March 14
St. Louis

Dearest Matthew,

Thank you so much for your long overdue letter. Your father and I were growing quite worried about you. But you have landed on your feet once again. How proud your grandfather would have been of you! You were always the apple of his eye, Matty, and I think he would be thrilled to know you are now a junior executive with the International Artists Agency.

What a stroke of luck your finding that "Latin Lady" record in the basement all those years ago! Who would have thought you'd be working with Bobby Rankoff one day? By the way, I ran into Honey Layefsky's mother the other week. Honey is still in the mountains in India living with that guru. What a disappointment she's been to her family.

What is a "negative pickup deal"? It seems you have acquired an entirely new vocabulary since joining the agency. Aunt Helen keeps asking me if you've met any big stars yet. Also if you can get discount tickets for Disneyland or the Universal tour. Can you?

Your father says you should ask Stu Jackson if he remembers meeting him at the B'nai Brith dinner at the Chase Hotel four years ago. Your father says he told him a joke that really cracked him up. Your father and his jokes!

Your colleagues all sound like fascinating people. There were some Foleys who had a hardware store next to our old store about twenty years ago. I don't suppose you'd remember them but perhaps your friend Dwight is a relative. Wasn't James Steerforth a character in *David Copperfield*? See? I do remember a few things from my high school days. Certainly an unusual name.

And what's happened to your benefactor Mr. Bobcaygeon? You made no mention of him whatsoever in your letter. I hope he's keeping an eye out there for you. You being his protégé and all.

How temporary is this "temporary" address of yours? Have you found a new place yet? Your father and I would love to come and visit but not before you have enough space. Thank goodness, it finally stopped raining out there! You Californians certainly go to extremes, don't you?

It must be very exciting for you—finally living and working in the place you've dreamed of all your life. I ran into Trisha last week—I wasn't sure whether to mention it or not but we can't pretend you two weren't married, can we? It was at the hairdresser's and she asked about you. Well, I told her about you being an agent and having drinks at Inez Sanchez's house. She turned green, Matthew. Positively green. I don't think she had much faith in you. No! Let me correct myself. She never had faith in your dreams. She always felt you could be whatever she wanted you to be. I'm glad you followed your own course. Don't be surprised if she phones you one of these days!

I'm sure you're busy making deals and hobnobbing with your film star friends. We are so proud of you back in little old St. Louis. Please let us hear from you soon. Love from us all.

xxx Mother

"I'm a fucking fraud, Mother!" Matthew Garber bellowed out from his bed that mid-March morning. He let the letter slip down from his fingers onto the sheets as he swung himself out of his bed in preparation for another day in the IAA mailroom.

He'd been with the agency for two months and he was still a messenger boy. But he didn't have the nerve to tell his parents. No! For them, he would have to be a "junior executive." And where did his mother get the idea that Dwight Foley was his "friend." What had he written to his parents? Had he embellished on the Inez Sanchez encounter or had they? Oh, well, if it made Trisha envious . . . So what! You're divorced, buddy. And Honey Layefsky is still freaked out in the Himalayas. So much for the little white cloud that cried. But where does it all leave me?

On the positive side: Speedy Liebowitz and Stu Jackson have been terrific to me. Taking the time to teach me the ins and outs of dealmaking . . . Making deliveries all over town has given me a crash course in Los Angeles geography. . . . I've made a friend in Roland Draycott . . . I own a 1968 Camaro outright.

On the negative side: That same Camaro cost me every bit of my savings. James Steerforth is continually on my back with his snide remarks. Dwight Foley is openly hostile about—what? Ara Whalen has made it clear I can be out of the mailroom in a flash if I let her take me under her wing—and right into her nest. No way! Joy Dworkin and Bobby Rankoff are competing for schizophrenia honors regarding their day-to-day attitudes toward me. Gilbert Bobcaygeon continues to phone me long distance with absolutely outlandish proposals and promises. And Lindsay Fairweather is giving me the worst case of blue balls I have had since high school. ("Board her, woo her, assail her!" Roley would urge when Matty would lament his unrequited love for the girl with the marmalade hair. But she was hopelessly hung up on Yael Shomrim and her relationship with Matty had never gone beyond that magical bit of necking in Roley's garden.)

To make matters worse—or the worst—Lindsay's next door neighbor is due to return from her European vacation in a week and

I have to vacate the apartment. Where can I go? At eight hundred dollars, the Camaro absorbed every penny I've brought with me from St. Louis. My take-home pay from the mailroom (after withholding) just covers gas, food, and cleaning bills. Jesus! Want to know how temporary this address is, Mother? Let's put it this way. If I can get a suite at the Beverly Hills "Y," you and Dad should fly out tomorrow. What the hell am I going to do?

The sound of the phone ringing startled Matty out of his depression. Who was phoning at eight in the morning? If he was quick enough he could get to Duke's for breakfast before the line started forming down Santa Monica.

"Hello."

"My dear boy!"

"Oh, hello, Roley. I'm really late and I've got to—"

"You sound positively dreadful, Matthew. Death in the family?"

"No. I'm in a bind, Roley. Lindsay's neighbor is coming back next week and I've got to find somewhere else to live. But the rents are sky-high in a ten-mile radius from the office, and I've a premonition I'm going to be in the mailroom for a few more years. They're probably grooming me to replace Sol Siglan."

"Oh, dear. Can't be as bad as that, old boy."

"Think it is, Roley. What's that line from *Antony* and *Cleopatra*? 'The land bids me tread no more upon't.' Afraid I'll have to swallow my pride and go back to St. Louis."

"Nonsense! You have a promising career ahead of you. Shan't let you go back. The town needs someone like you with taste, sensitivity, a grounding in the classics—"

"No luck with women," added Matty

"Lindsay still leading you a merry chase?" chuckled the old actor.

"She isn't leading me anywhere. I keep telling you that, Roley. She is totally mesmerized by that Israeli s.o.b. I haven't got a chance. I'm her best friend. We go to screenings. Sometimes we hold hands. She makes me cocoa at night—"

"Board her, woo her—"

"Assail her. I know. It doesn't work."

"I'm a great believer in attrition, Matthew. Many years ago I had an affair with an actress in England as famed for her frigidity as her histrionic talent. Naturally I was inspired by the challenge of it all. I cornered her in her dressing room. We were doing *Trelawny of the Wells* or some Pinero piece. I began to remove her garments while showering her with kisses and sweet nothings. Actually they were sweet somethings. Never understood that phrase. I was murmuring the thousand-and one delights that were waiting in store for her. And throughout it all, this celebrated daughter of Thespis began to moan, 'Don't! Don't!' Naturally I didn't heed her warning being quite absorbed in my own ardor. Her moans became cries, then shouts. Quite deafening. 'DON'T! DONT! DON'T!' They finally pierced the membrane of my lust and I withdrew at once clutching my head in shame. What had I done? I, a mere lad of twenty, and she, a great lady and long past her fortieth year. I looked meekly into her eyes and was about to recite a litany of my humblest apologies when, with great annoyance, she demanded to know why I had retreated from my line of attack. 'You—you—said don't,' I faltered. She looked down at me—I shall never forget that look and I'll be eighty in August—she looked down at me and said, 'I meant don't stop.' With that remark, she stepped over my prostrate body and left the theater. Never taken no for an answer since."

"Roley, I love you!" laughed Matty. "You just made my day."

"Did I? How clever of me! Now, Matthew, what you should do is throw all of your things into a suitcase and come straight round here after work."

"What do you mean?"

"That little study of mine. Really not more than a glorified, linen closet, but I can clean it out for you and we can fit a little bed in there. If you don't mind sharing digs with me."

"Roley—"

"Can well appreciate if you don't want to live with an old fossil like me. Tend to talk too much, but I shan't charge you any rent—"

"I'll buy the groceries!" announced Matty delightedly. "And do the gardening! How's that?"

"Capital."

"You've saved my life, Roley."

***

Tony Rabaiotti took out his Dunhill lighter and lit the Winston dangling from his mouth as he watched the plane circle over Vegas for the fifth time in half an hour. LAX was heavily stacked with incoming traffic and the American Airline's 707 carrying the IAA New York office's number-two man was in a holding pattern over the Nevada desert waiting for clearance to cross the line back into California.

There goes lunch with Bobby, he thought Oh, well! He hated all those Beverly Hills clip joints. Poor Bobby, always trying to come up with new Italian restaurants to impress him. When was Rankoff going to learn? The town had no soul. How could it possibly have a decent restaurant?

Rabaiotti hated Los Angeles. His idea of hell would be taking over the Rodeo Drive office. But he would never tell Bobby that. Or Ara or Jimmy. He loved watching them squirm every time he arrived on business. Wondering what he was *really* on the Coast for. To take over? Send reports back to Abe? Tony stared at the inscription on his Dunhill: TONY . . .THE ONLY WOP IN MY LIFE . . . ABE. The only person at the agency he allowed to call him a wop was Abe. He'd been Abe's boy for a long time. Despite the old gag at Sardi's: "You know why Abe Keller hired Rabaiotti? He had to have someone in the office at Yom Kippur in case an offer came through." He knew this wasn't true even though there were times when he felt himself used by the diminutive, one-eyed patriarch of IAA. But it was like a joke after all those years. The dialogue was always the same.

Old Abe would say: "How long have you been with me, boychik?"

The emotional blackmail would begin. How Abe had brought him all the way up from the mailroom. Over the heads of the Jewish boys in the agency. He had used it that famous time when Pamela Cassidy had attempted suicide at the Plaza in the middle of the night and Tony was dispatched to pay off the house dick. Poor Pammie! What a hard luck case. Her husband had been two-timing her with Inez Sanchez and Pamela's career was going down the tubes in perfect synch with the affair. The agency found her a picture in Miami. Soft-porn. Only poor Pammie never made it to Florida. The plane was skyjacked by terrorists and eventually blew up. A long time ago.

That was when Abe begged Tony to phone Sally Max. The Mafia. Not to rescue Pamela—Keller's beloved Pammie—but to save the package deal Pamela was flying to participate in. What *chutzpah*! Thinking his mother's second cousin could have influence over deranged terrorists. Just because he happened to be a don in the Mafia.

"Have I ever asked a favor of you, Tony?" Rabaiotti remembered Keller's pleading voice as if it had been yesterday. "Not the little requests from day to day. I mean a real favor."

Now Tony was flying out to California as another favor for Abe. Ostensibly it was for discussions with Orion regarding the film rights to David Maxwell's new book *Brother Billy Meets Brother Rat.* The talks were a smokescreen for Tony to find out how Wheezer was really doing.

Wheezer was the family name for Louise Keller Feingold, Abe's only child, married for a quarter of a century to "Slippery" Stan Feingold. Something was wrong with the marriage. Abe knew it instinctively. For years, Wheezer had been best friends with his old secretary, Ara Whalen. He could always rely on Ara for reports of life on the West Coast; Ara was incredibly discreet (God knows the two of them had kept a precious secret for almost thirty years). But Ara had fallen apart in recent years. What was it they called her now? The Painted Lady? That such a beautiful girl should end up like that. She must have had trouble before this. Look at all the losers she married. The first husband turned out to be a *faygel*; Bobcaygeon, the golem of stupidity; and that redneck Davenport. She certainly liked variety in her life.

No, the reports from Ara had stopped long ago. As had her friendship with Wheezer. All Abe had to go by these days was gossip. What did Woody Allen call it? The "new pornography." People shouldn't know the truth about movie stars. Really want to know how normal they are, folks? Or abnormal.

Which was Wheezer? Was she making it with young boys or old girls? (Keller had heard reports of both.) And Stanley. A failed actor but a great agent. Was he really over his head with the gambling? The drugs? And the deals the IRS should never find out about? These were just stories about the parents! God only knew what Abe and Babe Keller's grandchildren were up to in the Hills of Beverly. *This* was Rabaiotti's mission. To discover how freaked out the Feingolds really were.

The trip West also had a third purpose for Rabaiotti: to try and put a few pieces of the IAA puzzle together for himself.

Question: What had been the purpose of Jimmy Steerforth's recent trip to New York and why had he been locked away with Abe for so many hours?

Question: What was Gilbert Bobcaygeon doing flying all over the United States? What the hell was he doing on the IAA payroll to begin with?

Question: What was the 'grand scheme' of Dwight Foley's and Shmuel Kislev's that Bazzo kept referring to in his coded messages dropped in the agency's eastbound pouch every night?

Question: Why had Abe Keller flown off for a week's vacation with the mysterious Randall Hatton? Was Abe really going to sell the agency to Hatton's conglomerate? And why had he had lunch with Marvin Josephson twice the previous week? Was ICM finally going to swallow them? Why was Abe constantly going to the doctor despite his heartfelt assurances to Tony that there was nothing wrong with him? What time does war break out?

One last Question: Who was the incredibly well-preserved woman of fifty? Fifty-five? Sitting across the aisle in first class staring with terminal boredom at the bleak Nevada desert below.

She was no spring chicken, decided Rabaiotti. Probably had the world's most expensive bolt at the back of her neck under that pinned-up honey-blond hair. But the legs were incredible under the tasteful Italian-knit traveling suit and the breasts were high and firm. Tony wouldn't kick her out of bed on a cold night.

Who the hell was she? She looked so familiar. Must have been an actress. Movies or stage? Jesus! Maybe she'd been a client once. Heyyyyy, Tony! Mister Charm. Never forget a face. Flash the caps, kid. It never failed. You're forty-two. A career diplomat in show biz. You're allowed a couple of slips. Go on. Ask her.

"Excuse me," said Rabaiotti leaning across the aisle and giving her the fullness of his capped flash. "Did I ever handle you?"

"I . . . I beg your pardon?" replied Sylvia Nardino haltingly in polished tones that still had traces of the street in them. She looked like she was about to faint. "You must have me mixed up with—"

Rabaiotti realized who this beautiful, seemingly ageless woman was. "Of course!" he grinned, pouring on all the famous Rabaiotti charm. "Mrs. Nardino! I stayed at your hotel on the Jersey shore with my wife and kids. Your portrait was hanging in the lobby. I looked at you every day for a week. It didn't do you justice."

"What's your name?" purred Sylvia, finding herself turned on by the handsome man with the incredible smile.

"Anthony Rabaiotti. Call me Tony."

"Will you be in Los Angeles long, Tony?"

"Couple o' days." He couldn't believe it but he was starting to get a not unpleasant, very familiar tingle in his loins.

"Only going to be in Los Angeles briefly," sighed Sylvia. "I have to go to Vegas and check up on our hotel there."

"Will your husband be joining you?"

"Mr. Nardino died four years ago. He'd been ill for some time."

"I'm sorry," replied Rabaiotti, feeling an incredible hard-on overtaking him. "Have you been lonely?"

"It has been difficult," she answered, staring into his eyes and wishing they had a king-sized bed on these flights. "What do you do, Tony?"

"I'm with IAA. The agency."

"Do you know Bobby Rankoff?"

"Very well. As a matter of fact, we were supposed to have lunch today, but I think it will have to be high tea."

"Very high," smiled Sylvia, nodding toward the clouds below. ""Haven't seen Bobby in years. Would you please remember me to him?"

"I'm sure he'd never forget someone as lovely as you, Mrs. Nardino."

"Call me Sylvia."

"We'll be going down now, Mrs. Nardino."

Sylvia looked up at the flight attendant hovering over her not quite certain what the young woman meant by that crack. Did she know? Impossible. It was all so long ago. Almost thirty years . . .

She was twenty-four when she first went to bed with Ed Nardino in 1950. He was just a rich john to her. Forty, fat, bald. But he was crazy about her. He'd buy her services for days, and then weeks. Finally he asked her to marry him. He'd never been married; he always bought it. Lived with his mother. No girl pleased her. When Mama finally died, Ed was on the loose. And he had the hots for Sylvia.

Sylvia added up the pluses and the minuses. She'd been tricking for three years and hated it She was scared of losing her looks, too. She didn't like taking orders, so she could never get a normal job. But the damned pimps were taking sixty percent of her action. What the hell! Why not marry Ed? He owned a big hotel in New Jersey and he was loaded. She'd have her own floor at the hotel and anything she wanted; she just rang room service. He owned two other hotels in Ohio and Pennsylvania so he traveled a bit. He was older than Sylvia. And fat. So fat. The way he huffed and puffed after they made love, he'd be dead of a heart attack within a year and the hotels would be hers.

But three years later Mr. Nardino was not dead—just fatter—and Mrs. Nardino was going out of her pretty little skull with boredom as the first lady of the Driftwood Hotel 'with a great tradition of dining and dancing for over twenty years.'

When Bobby came to sing at the Driftwood, none of their lives was the same after that.

She'd been a fan of his for years. Since he was a kid (she always thought of him as a kid even though she was only two years older). She loved the way he sang "Latin Lady," "Our Last Embrace," and "Why Can't We Be There Again." His voice was like velvet. He turned out to be a cocky bastard in person and she had taken an instant dislike to him. But he was booked into the hotel for two weeks, a huge draw for the customers. Ed was thrilled to death.

Sylvia would stand at the back of the room those first few nights watching Bobby sing and watching the eyes of all the women devouring him from their tables. What makes you so big, she wondered.

Two days later she discovered that she could make him very big, indeed. Ed had gone to Ohio to fire the manager of the hotel there. He left Sylvia in charge of the Driftwood with specific instructions to make sure Bobby was happy.

Bobby and Sylvia stalked each other for two days. He complained about the waiters making too much noise during his act; she retorted about the rudeness he showed to guests who only wanted his autograph. Little things, picky things that were masking the incredible undercurrent between them.

Late that second night, Sylvia went for a midnight swim and discovered she wasn't alone on the beach. She resisted him at first but he unleashed an incredible force inside her: something she'd buried through three years with Fat Ed and the hundreds of johns she had faked it with before him. Bobby uncorked the real passion within Sylvia and it frightened her. When the sun came up Bobby lay asleep on the beach in Sylvia Nardino's arms, while she lay awake in terror, wondering how she could ever get the genie back into the bottle.

They couldn't keep their hands off each other after that. Bobby would come into Ed's office while Sylvia was on the phone to the linen company and crawl playfully under the desk. Poor Sylvia would end up ordering twice as many sheets while approaching orgasm. They would rush up to his room between shows and make frenetic, fabulous love. Ed called from Ohio. Might as well check up on Pennsylvania while he was in the neighborhood. How was it all going? Fine, fine, fine.

Sylvia and Bobby were falling in love with each other. Caution and discretion were not part of their amorous lexicon. When Ed came home and found out the truth, he beat Sylvia senseless. He'd have slashed Bobby's throat if the singer's engagement hadn't ended and Rankoff had already returned to California.

Ed Nardino swore revenge. He would make sure Bobby never sang in another hotel, never made another radio or TV appearance, and never cut another record. All it took was one phone call and Bobby Rankoff's career was finished.

***

Matty Garber was growing annoyed. He'd missed his lunch break when Siglan dispatched him to the airport to pick up Tony Rabaiotti. The plane from New York was late and no one at the airport would tell him when it was finally going to land. On top of all this, two lumpy Hari Krishna members kept driving him crazy trying to get a contribution from him.

"Love off!" said Matty when the two overzealous Krishnas began pawing at his jacket.

The flight from New York finally arrived and the elegant Rabaiotti appeared at the gate with a stunning, middle-aged woman on his arm. Seconds later, a small cadre of men in dark blue suits surrounded the woman and whisked her away (not before she had kissed Rabaiotti on the cheek and they'd exchanged murmured ciaos). Matty stepped forward and introduced himself to the New York honcho.

"Serving with our armed forces in the mailroom?" asked Rabaiotti, giving the broad-shouldered, bespectacled young man the once over.

"Yes, sir."

"Spare me the 'sir'. Just kiss my ring and genuflect."

Matty laughed and escorted Rabaiotti to the baggage area.

On the drive back to Beverly Hills, Rabaiotti cleverly picked Garber's brain about recent events in the office. Under the guise of friendly gossip, the New York honcho was able to learn of Bobcaygeon's most recent lies, Joy's blatant ambition, and Bazzo's outside activities in the drug trade. By the time they reached the Rodeo Drive office, Garber was in the thrall of Rabaiotti's considerable charm and Tony had taken a shine to the amiable young man from St. Louis.

The senior agents were all out to lunch on the third floor and even the steadfast Lindsay was absent from her desk. A note was planted prominently in her typewriter.

Matty:
    Mr. Rankoff called away suddenly. Should be back by 2:30. Please apologize to Mr. Rabaiotti. Just popped out for a sandwich. Shouldn't be long in case you finally get here.

                         Thanx.
                       Lindsay 1:25 P.M.

Garber showed Rabaiotti into Rankoff's office then proceeded to play host.

"Just a Perrier," grinned Rabaiotti. "They feed you about eight times on that flight. Have you heard from old Gilbob recently?"

"He called from Louisville the other day," replied Matty, handing Rabaiotti a glass of the French soda water.

"Can't figure him out," said Rabaiotti, shaking his head. "Years ago at staff meetings, we all agreed as soon as Gil started telling a lie we'd snap our fingers over our heads. It was a riot. Gilbert would sit there droning on and on about some mythical deal he had on the hopper and twenty people would start snapping their fingers."

"What did he do?"

"He'd laugh. You know that Goofy laugh of his. Thought everyone loved him. Why else would they go to all that trouble? He does it all for attention. To be a storm center."

"But what does he *do* for the agency?"

"Damned if I know."

The telephone rang on Rankoff's desk. Matty figured Seattle would pick it up in reception, but it continued to ring and ring. Garber finally picked it up.

"Robert Rankoff's office," he announced.

"Is he there?" The voice was abrupt and Midwestern in sound.

"No, I'm sorry but—"

"Godammit! This is Cal Chambers at Paramount."

"Oh, hello—" Matty was about to say "Mr. Chambers" but something about his new rapport with Rabaiotti made him assume the more chummy—"Cal. This is Matt Garber. Can I help you?"

"Yeah. Tell me where the hell Gilbert Bobcaygeon is."

Oh-oh. What had everybody's favorite psycho done now?

"Don't think he's in town, Cal—"

"Oh, I'm sure he's not. He's past his deadline to make the deal for *Shoes*. He promised me Minden Prescott."

Shoes was in its fourth year on Broadway and was the definitive musical of the Me-Decade. Productions were also running in London, Paris, Amsterdam, Stockholm, and Tokyo. No fewer than three touring companies were playing throughout North America. Paramount had purchased the motion picture rights three years earlier for the equivalent of the gross national product of Luxembourg. Two different Academy Award winners had failed (expensively) to transform this very theatrical piece into a workable screenplay.

Perhaps Minden Prescott could be the one to finally crack the project. One of the survivors of television's golden age along with Chayefsky, Serling, and Costigan, Prescott had written some of the most memorable episodes of *Playhouse 90, Studio One, and Philco Playhouse.* The three-time Emmy winner had moved to Broadway when live television died and won the Tony award his first time at bat. Despairing of the American theater by the mid-seventies, Prescott moved out to Malibu "to enjoy his twilight years as a high-priced literary whore of the silver screen."

To the best of Matty's knowledge Minden Prescott was not represented by IAA and—seven-to-one on the morning line—had probably never met Gilbert Bobcaygeon. However, Garber was not about to admit this to Cal Chambers. Not with Tony Rabaiotti beaming at him across the room. Matty had prayed for a miracle that morning. He'd found it in Roland Draycott's generous offer. Why not parlay it into the trifecta?

"Had you discussed any terms yet?" asked Matty, sitting in Rankoff's chair for the first time. "Ballpark figures?"

"Ballpark figures?" shouted Chambers from his office. "Old motor-mouth phoned me in the middle of the night last week from Waco, Texas to ask if I wanted Minden Prescott to rescue *Shoes*. I said I was interested. What the hell! I'm not going to start jumping up and down at three in the morning. Not with a hiatus hernia and a twenty-six-year-old wife. Know what I mean? Haven't heard boo from Bobcaygeon since."

"All right," said Matty, taking a deep breath. "Let me be up front with you, Cal. We do represent Minden Prescott. He just hasn't signed his agency papers yet. But I'm expecting them literally any minute by messenger."

"That's your problem. I'm willing to negotiate now."

Here it goes, thought Matty. Jumping in at the deep end for his first deal. A deal he had no right to make. But one he knew instinctively would be blown if he didn't move on it immediately. Besides Bobcaygeon owed it to him whether it had originated as just another Gilbob lie or not. How would Rankoff handle this? "Go for the jugular." That was Bobby's credo for the big deals. So the jugular it is.

"Okay, Cal. It's $750,000."

"What!?"

"That's $750,000 fixed compensation for the first draft. Only."

"Are you out of your—?"

"Let me finish, please . . . For two succeeding drafts and a polish, you'll pay another $250,000.

"That's a million dollars!" exploded Chambers on the other end of the phone. "It's unprecedented! No writer ever got that kind of money!"

Matty Garber of St. Louis, Missouri, had long since left the body of the young man seated behind Robert Rankoff's desk. *That* Matty was now floating somewhere on the ceiling watching Matt Garber, Dealmaker, at work on the phone.

"We're not talking about *any* writer, Cal. This is Minden Prescott. Emmy-winner. Tony-winner. Oscar-winner. We're also talking about a musical that was the hottest show—"

"What do you mean 'was'?"

"Come on, Cal. You guys bought *Shoes* three years ago. Made eighteen different announcements about the project that came to nothing. Everyone from Fred Astaire to Travolta was locked into it. You spent God knows how much on rights and five hundred different drafts and where's the picture? No one believes you're going to make it. *Now*, if you suddenly pump new money into a prestigious writer like Minden Prescott, you've got a hot item again. Got a news story, something you can hype. Are you with me, Cal? See where I'm going?"

Rabaiotti had long ago put down his glass of Perrier and was staring in awe at this overage mailroom kid wheeling and dealing on the phone.

"That's a helluva price," Chambers finally answered.

"Heyyyy, Cal! We're in an age of never-ending inflation. Our grandchildren will pay a million dollars for a hamburger. That's the deal, Cal."

"What's your name again?"

"Garber. Matt Garber."

"Are you authorized to make this deal, Garber? I never heard of you before."

Matty's heart sank. He clapped his hand over the mouthpiece and looked beseechingly at Rabaiotti.

"He wants to know if I'm authorized to make this deal."

"Gimme the phone!" said Rabaiotti rising from his chair. "Hello? Cal? Tony Rabaiotti here. How are ya? . . . Nope, just got in this afternoon. Little business, little pleasure . . . Hmm? Oh, Abe's fine. You know him. They'll never take him alive. Now, on this Prescott deal, I think Matt's made our position clear. You want to check with your people? . . . Okay, let's have this wrapped up by the close of business today. Okay, guy? . . . Speak to ya."

Rabaiotti replaced the receiver delicately on its cradle, let out a slow whistle, then turned to Matty admiringly.

"I think you got a deal."

"Don't know what came over me," replied Garber, feeling faint suddenly.

"Obviously a case of reincarnation," shrugged Rabaiotti. "You were either Leland Hayward or Charlie Feldman in another life. But you're a born dealmaker, kid. Why are they hiding you in the mailroom?"

"Think Mr. Rankoff will be angry? I mean I had no right to—"

"What? Net a hundred-thousand-dollar commission for the agency? Bobby's a shareholder. He'll love you. Ole Massa Bobby might even give you yo' freedom, Matthew."

"Or fire me."

"Why?"

"We don't represent Minden Prescott. It's another of Bobcaygeon's lies."

"And the one to finally put the nail in his coffin," grinned Rabaiotti. "Been after Bobcaygeon for a long time and I think I've finally got him. He's been jumping all over the country on our money, and he wasn't even here for the biggest deal of his career. It's poetic justice that you made it."

"Yeah. What I thought at the time. Except his lie made the deal happen."

"Please, don't feel sorry for Bobcaygeon. Want to see his 1963 memo to Abe Keller why we shouldn't sign the Beatles."

"Oh, no!"

"The man is a show business Jonah, Matthew. He'd have refused to represent Bogart for having a speech impediment. He's Rip van Winkle, totally ignorant of any major entertainment trend in the past twenty-five years. His only talent - if you want to call it that - is being able to speak for half an hour without thinking. In short, he is in a category with the Elephant Man, Christine Jorgenson, and Spyro Agnew."

A breathless Lindsay ran into the office and apologized profusely to Rabaiotti for her boss's absence and her own tardiness in getting back from lunch.

"It's all right, Lindsay," beamed Rabaiotti. "Matt and I have been keeping ourselves amused."

Lindsay stared curiously at Matty but Garber maintained a straight face.

"Lindsay, do you have any agency papers handy?"

"Sure."

"Would you get them for me, please? Three copies." After Lindsay left the room, Rabaiotti turned conspiratorially to Garber. "Okay. Find Minden Prescott, sign him, and we'll put both our names on his agency papers. Then you'll deliver the deal to Paramount."

"Won't they think I'm out of line? Mr. Rankoff and Miss Whalen? There are rules around here—"

"Hey, Garber! Luck and timing are the only rules in this business. Just watch yourself with Little Miss Mindy."

"Who?"

"Prescott. He's queer as a three-dollar bill."

***

Matty had never been out to Malibu before let alone the highly guarded compound known as Malibu Colony, a security patroled ghetto of show business's upper echelon. It is one of the highest priced stretches of beach in the United States and on a day as beautiful, bright, and smog clear as it was, Matty decided it was worth every penny.

The guard at the security gate phoned Prescott's house and waved Matty through. Garber was greeted at the door by the tallest, thinnest man he had ever seen. No meat on him whatsoever. His hair was pewter-colored, long, and came to a fifties-style d.a. at the back of his head. He wore a powder blue safari suit cut extremely tight to emphasize his rake-like figure and rose-tinted glasses through which he was now peering at an extremely apprehensive Matthew Garber.

"Well, you needn't stare at me as if I were the illegitimate son of Laird Cregar and Carmen Miranda begat in Ty Power's dressing room," drawled Prescott in a marked New England accent. "Imagine what I'm thinking of you. Would you like to come in or should I pack a box lunch?"

The only reply Matty could think of was: "Thank you for seeing me."

"I don't see you at all, Mr. Garber. It is Garber, isn't it? Please, come in. The neighbors, you know. I'm still living down all those stories about Ryan O'Neal."

Matty followed Prescott down the hallway whose walls were plastered with framed photographs of Little Miss Mindy posing with various stage and film luminaries. The only photo Prescott didn't feature in was an 8 X 10 studio publicity shot of Lowell Sherman, a mustachioed actor-director, who died in the Thirties. Matty was fascinated by this picture, isolated from the rest like a shrine.

Seconds later Matty found himself standing on an outdoor patio commanding a majestic view of the endless Pacific.

"China's out there somewhere," said Prescott, sitting down at an elegantly laid table and tucking into a crisp *salade nicoise.*

Matty hadn't eaten since breakfast but realized that this was not the time (nor the best person) to ask for a little nibble.

"Phoned the Writers Guild, Mr. Prescott. They told me you're not represented by anyone at the present time."

"Haven't been for two years, twig. Don't need an agent anymore. I have a lawyer who peruses those standard contracts in less than an hour for a reasonable sum thus saving me from the tithe I used to pay you mercenary sycophants."

"Well, if you feel that way, why did you agree to see me?"

"Wanted to see what a Matthew Garber looked like. Those earnest Midwestern voices always turn me on. Relax, twig. I never bite on the first date. Actually, I was a trifle curious to see what 'the highest fee ever paid to any writer in history' was. Bill Goldman and I have a little friendly rivalry going."

Matty stared intently into Prescott's rose-tinted spectacles and announced: "One million dollars."

"Please, leave my home, Mr. Garber," replied Prescott, daintily daubing his lips with an Irish linen napkin. "You are the worst kind of cockteaser: a demented agent. Not since the days of Gilbert Bobcaygeon—"

"You know him? You actually know him?"

"I sang at his wedding, twig. For joy. Where is old motor-mouth these days? I always thought it was a pity Jack Carson died before he could star in the life of Gilbob."

"How long has it been since you've seen him?"

"Eons. Does he still laugh like Goofy?"

"Let me clarify something: Bobcaygeon never spoke to you about doing the screenplay of *Shoes*? Ever?"

"Wasn't aware Gilbob was back in the agency business. Thought he'd been banished by Lew Wasserman under penalty of death."

"I thought Lew Wasserman was his friend."

"As close as Joan and Olivia. The man's a terrible liar, you know. Don't think he means to be. Clearly somewhere in Gilbert Bobcaygeon's life he decided every day had to be a triumph. No one's been that lucky since Alexander the Great. So Gilbert makes up triumphs. On the hour. If Huck Finn were to come back today, he'd do so in the guise of Gilbert Bobcaygeon. Now, what about *Shoes*? You know it's the story of my life. I saw it six nights in a row in New York. It is the only show other than *Streetcar* I wished I'd written. God would never ever allow me to write it and be paid a million dollars. Certainly no executive in this dermoid cyst, *Hollywoodus in latrina*, would—"

"That's John Barrymore's line."

"Never said it wasn't, twig. I was about to give him credit. I've been ripped off enough times in my career to acknowledge the wit of others properly."

"Didn't mean you'd stolen it. Just figured you being a Lowell Sherman man you'd—"

Minden Prescott removed his glasses and stared at Matty as if for the first time.

"You recognized his photo?"

"Sure. I've seen *What Price Hollywood* six times. Lowell Sherman's performance is probably one of the funniest bitterest *tours de force* in movie history. He's light years ahead of Fredric March and James Mason in *Star Is Born.* It's also a brilliant impersonation of Barrymore."

"They were brothers-in-law, you know. Both married to the Costello sisters. How they loathed each other! Barrymore and Sherman. Did you ever see *General Crack*? Sherman stole it from Barrymore. He was a director, too, you know."

"Yes. *She Done Him Wrong.*"

"He died of cancer in his fifties. We have the same birthday. Both Librans. I'd loved to have known him. A neglected talent. I used to tell people I was his illegitimate son. They didn't know who he was. Funny, you knowing. Would you like some salad?"

It was close to five before Matty got up from the patio with Minden Prescott's signed agency papers in his hand and the writer's insistence that only Matty would handle him at IAA. (Matty hadn't breathed a word of his official mailroom status.)

The two paused once more in front of the framed photo of Lowell Sherman. Matty noticed the photograph next to it showing a much younger Minden with brushed-cut black hair embracing a beautiful young woman. Circa 1950.

"Don't you love it?" asked Minden. "Before I came out of the closet. Out? I had no idea I was in."

"Who is she?" asked Matty with undisguised admiration.

"She was my wife. A whole other life, twig."

"She looks like a young Ara Whalen."

"That's exactly who it is."

"You . . . were married to Ara?"

"Yes, I'm an exclusive member of that club along with Gilbob and Red Meat Rees Davenport."

"He's the only part of the puzzle missing now."

"What puzzle?"

"Don't know," shrugged Matty. "There's an incredible something at IAA. Some untold story. I just feel it."

"You're a hopeless romantic, twig. Probably why I like you. Oh! I have a little piece for your puzzle. Remember when we were having lunch? That blond *Charlie's Angel* reject in the bikini who jogged by on the beach? The one you almost came in your pants staring at—"

"I didn't—"

"She's your boss's wife. Sabina Rankoff. She lives down the beach with Red Meat. I can't tell you the mischief those two get up to."

"Why did you and Ara get divorced?" asked Matty abruptly.

"Male ego," replied Minden, after a considered pause. "I was fresh out of college. Hopelessly in love with her. Woefully inadequate in the sack being unaware of my predilection. She was so very beautiful then and I just couldn't satisfy her. She found it elsewhere and got herself pregnant. I called her a slut, a whore. Wanted a divorce. I was the one in pain. Never thought about her for a moment. She agreed to the divorce and vanished for a year. I guess to have the child."

"When was this?"

"In 1951. Before you were born."

"Just a year. What happened to the child?"

"Guess she gave it up for adoption . . . She's had a lousy life, Ara. Do they still call her the Painted Lady? How did she let herself go like that? It must have been Davenport. The man is evil . . . Traffic's going to be murder going into Bev Hills now. Sure you don't want to hop in the sack with me?"

Matty's face went scarlet.

"Oh, twig, you are a delight! Give me a shout when I can start typing."

As Matty drove east on Wilshire a snippet of dialogue continued to run through his mind like a scratched recording. "

When was this?

In 1951. Before you were born.

Just a year.

Just a year. Just a year. Just a year. That wonderful year: 1952. Which would make Ara's child 28 years old. The same age as Joy Dworkin.

Maybe it was true. Maybe Joy was Ara's illegitimate child.

So who was her father? Who was Ara making it with in 1951 when she was still Abe Keller's secretary in New York? Maybe it was Abe Keller himself. Wow! Talk about X-rated Dickens!

Sol Siglan's eyes were twitching furiously when Matty finally turned up in the mailroom at half past five.

"Garber, I feel you've done this once too often," droned the mailroom boss. "I have spoken to you and spoken to you and spoken to you. I had hoped you would be a standard bearer of quality but your attitude—"

"I was on company business, Mr. Siglan—"

"Mr. Rankoff has phoned down here at least six times in the past two hours. He is furious—"

"But didn't Mr. Rabaiotti—?"

"You'd better get upstairs. I'm sorry, Garber. I had great hopes for you."

Matty was hopelessly confused as he rode up in the antique elevator. He'd expected a hero's welcome. Garlands. A terrible thought flashed through his mind. Actually, it was a line from *I, Claudius*: "Trust no one, Caesar." When in Rome etc. And you couldn't get much closer to Rome than Tony Rabaiotti. What reason had Matty to put his faith in that cap-toothed *schmoozer*? Why should he let the credit for an incredible million-dollar deal—a $100,000 commission—go to some up start from the mailroom? A yahoo from St. Louis? A 'protégé' of Gilbert Bobcaygeon's? Who'd believe Matthew Garber could summon up the expertise after only two months at the agency?

Matty felt ill as he stepped off the elevator and walked down the corridor toward Rankoff's office. Lindsay was away from her desk so

Matty had absolutely no barometer to go by. He knocked at the door of Rankoff's inner office.

"Come in."

Garber stepped into the office and was immediately confronted by the image of Rankoff on the phone. The agency boss put the phone down upon seeing Garber without saying good-bye.

"What did you do?" Rankoff asked slowly, rising from behind his desk and advancing toward Garber. "Better yet: How did you do it?"

Before Matty had a chance to figure out what Rankoff meant the agency boss clapped one hand behind the young man's neck and drew him into his chest in a fraternal embrace.

"I'm proud of you, kid," beamed Rankoff. "Tony told me what you did."

Matty's sigh of relief coincided with a voice saying congratulations behind him. He turned around to see Ara Whalen and Tony Rabaiotti seated on the sofa against the wall. Ara came forward a second later and kissed Matty on both cheeks. Matty, looking at her in a new light since meeting Minden, saw a still beautiful woman obscured by all that war paint and sadness.

"I signed Minden Prescott," said Garber, removing the agency papers from his inside jacket pocket. "He . . . wants me to represent him personally."

"You can't do that from the mailroom," replied Rankoff.

Matty's heart sank again and he hoped that Rabaiotti would rise to his defense. He couldn't go back to the mailroom after what he'd done.

"Did you think you'd become an agent?" asked Rankoff, seeing the disappointment in Matty's face. "It's unprecedented to leave the mailroom after two months."

"Stu Jackson did it after one week!" Matty was close to tears as he blurted this.

"Bobby, stop it!" said Ara. "Don't tease him anymore."

"Okay," laughed Rankoff. "Didn't want him getting a swelled head. You're an incredible success story, Matthew. Never known anyone to pick up the business so quickly."

"I had the best teachers," replied Matty, looking around the room.

"Better watch your step, Bobby," advised Rabaiotti. "This kid's hot"

"Not making him a partner yet. You're just a junior agent, Matty—"

"That's okay—"

"Hold on, fleet foot. Let me tell you what you won today. Thirty thousand a year, your own office, a secretary, but no stock options. Basically what Bobcaygeon promised you."

"Hard to believe I owe him so much," commented Matty wryly.

"Please!" said Ara, rolling her eyes up to the ceiling. "Mr. Bobcaygeon is a sensitive subject."

"So I understand," replied Matty.

"You're part of the family now," laughed Ara. "You know all our secrets."

More than you think, thought Matty.

"You can afford to move out of Westbourne," said Rankoff.

"I'd already made arrangements for a new place this morning."

"Where?"

"Bel Air," answered Matty with a mix of pride and embarrassment.

"You're either the luckiest bastard in the world," said Rankoff, staring intently at the young man from St. Louis. "Or the biggest con."

"Or both," said Rabaiotti.

"Or neither," said Ara.

Matty bounced along the third-floor corridor of the apartment building on Westbourne carrying a brown paper bag under his arm. He paused in front of Lindsay Fairweather's door and rang the bell. She answered the door a second later in a peasant skirt, bare feet, and a Ferrari T-shirt.

"Looked all over the building for you," he said. "You never came back."

"Had to pick up my car at five," she answered. "Mr. Rankoff told me I could go home."

"I'm an agent," he announced proudly.

"Mr. Rankoff told me."

"You know? That's all you can say?"

"Congratulations."

"Hoping for a little more than that."

"Many happy returns. Or is that just for weddings?"

"Lindsay—"

"What do you want me to do? You got what you came out here for. You don't need me anymore."

"Can we discuss this inside?" asked Matty. "I feel silly standing out here."

Lindsay turned around and Matty followed her into the apartment.

"I do need you," he said, closing the door behind himself and walking over to the sofa with her.

"I'm just a secretary, Mr. Garber," she said, sitting on the sofa and staring up at him.

"Stop it, Lindsay! I want to celebrate tonight. There's no one in the world I want to share my jubilation with than you." He withdrew a chilled bottle of Piper-Heidsieck from the paper bag.

"Do you really mean that?" she asked.

"Don't be an idiot."

"Oh, thanks a lot! You tell me you need me then you—"

"I'm in love with you, Miss Fairweather. Have been for some time. I know you cannot reciprocate. But I'm not giving up. I'm a great believer in attrition."

"I'm glad," she said with tears in her eyes.

He brought his head down to hers and kissed her yielding lips. She brought her arms up to his neck and coaxed him down to the sofa.

He wrapped his arms around her and began to kiss her passionately, ferociously. She returned his kisses with equal energy and their hands soon began to explore each other's bodies.

"I wanted you to care," she breathed into his ear. "Afraid you wouldn't anymore—"

"Because of Yael?"

"Don't talk about him." She sealed her mouth over his to silence his words. She began to take little bites out of his neck. Then deeper ones.

He stretched out next to her. It had been so long . . .

She continued to kiss him as he ran his hands soothingly up and down her long legs, feeling their smoothness.

"I love your touch," she sighed.

He grinned and began to explore farther up her legs until he reached the naked warmth between her thighs.

"I don't wear my underwear at home," she blurted hastily but shyly.

"I hope you never will."

He moved his fingers gently, rhythmically against her, and a tiny gasp escaped her lips. She reached out to stroke him, hugging him closer.

"I feel as if I've known you all my life," she said.

"Do you mean that, lass? Truly?"

"Aye."

"This couch is a little bit—"

"Let's go in the bedroom," she whispered. "Don't forget the champagne."

"Where are the glasses?"

"We don't need them," she said, leading him into the next room.

They stood on opposite sides of the bed suddenly wary of each other.

"It's been a long time for me," he finally said.

"Me, too," she replied, unbuttoning her skirt.

"How long?"

"Six weeks." She pulled her T-shirt over her head.

"I've been six months," he replied, feasting on the nakedness of her tall, slim body.

"How wonderful! I'm flattered." She walked across the bed on her knees and began undoing his trousers. Sliding them over his hips, Lindsay leaned back on the bed, her arms outstretched. Looking into her sparkling eyes, Matty caught her hands and sank down on top of her. She wrapped her legs up around his back as he began to thrust inside her slowly, then faster and faster and faster. They were both too excited to explore each other, to take their time. Instead their lovemaking was fierce, almost desperate—and it was over all too soon.

Matty looked sheepishly at Lindsay. There was a twinkle in his eye and she knew he had no intention of lying still as he slid down the length of her body, planting kisses along the way until he arrived at her legs locked together.

"Open up."

"No," she teased.

"Must I take you by force?"

"If you must," she sighed.

He began to kiss her gently and she giggled at the tickling sensation. He used his tongue and she arched toward him, surrendering to pleasure.

She lay still for the longest time afterward, then turned to Matty propped up on one arm next to her.

"Don't know how you feel about me," she said, "but I'd like to put you under exclusive contract."

"Think we can work something out," he grinned, reaching for the neglected bottle of Piper-Heidsieck next to the bed. "When did you change your mind?"

"When I opened the front door tonight." She reached her hand out to explore his face. "So glad you didn't give up."

"Bless your heart, Roland Draycott!" cheered Matty as he popped the cork. "May you live to be a hundred!"

The two drank their champagne and made love through the night under the glow of the Tropicana sign.

STEERFORTH

The announcement of Paramount signing Minden Prescott to write *Shoes* was front-page news in the trades two days later. The Hollywood grapevine soon spread the word there was a hot new agent in town named Matt Garber. Matty's phones were constantly ringing with calls from writers both unknown and established seeking representation.

Stu Jackson bought Matty lunch at The Saloon and got his nondrinking colleague from St. Louis blasted on margaritas; Speedy Liebowitz passed onto him a pair of cuff links that Sid Shankman had presented him when Speedy had become an agent; Dwight Foley grunted his congratulations and rumbled something about always remaining tactically vigilant; Ara Whalen insisted Matty come to her house for a home-cooked meal. Matty had visions of himself reduced to tiny morsels in her sexual Cuisinart; Larry Bazzo stealthily slipped a gift-wrapped gram of coke into Garber's jacket; Joy Dworkin suggested a platonic weekend at Two Bunch Palms in Desert Hot Springs to prepare a feasible two-year game plan for taking over the agency.

Matty realized he had finally arrived when James Steerforth stuck his head into Garber's office three days after the *Shoes* coup and magnanimously asked Matty to accompany him to Las Vegas for Inez Sanchez's opening at the new Scheherazade Hotel.

"I do appreciate your coming with me, old son," said Steerforth, undoing his seat belt after the Hughes Air West flight had taken off from Burbank Airport. "It's not an event I am greatly looking forward to. In fact, I think it will be a total fiasco."

"Thought Inez's Vegas act is a smash hit," said Matty, still uncertain of Steerforth's motives for asking Matty to go with him and his own for accepting.

"Has been in the past. Due to my omniscient supervision. Not that I'm trying to set myself up as a Svengali, mind. Just that the woman is so tacky. Her choice of numbers, her costumes. You know Bob Mackie turned her down for this show? Bob bloody Mackie! She's got herself nine-inch spikes she can't walk in—let alone dance. She's singing songs Tina Turner would have second thoughts about. She can't sing a note, our Irma."

"Irma?"

"Not wishing to burst your bubble, old son. But she's not from South America. The only Valparaiso she's ever seen is the one in Indiana. Where she was born."

"But what about the South American bombshell?" asked Matty, whose bubble had indeed been burst.

"We made that up. She and I. She had drive, she had guts, she'd kill to be a bloody star. When you've got those three things, talent can prove inconsequential. Hell! She wasn't going to be Zoe Gail."

"Who's that?"

"My boyhood pinup. She climbed to the top of the statue of Eros in Piccadilly Circus and sang 'I'm Gonna Get Lit Up When the Lights Go Up in London.' She lives in Vegas now, dear Zoe. I'll take you to meet her."

"Are you her uncle, too?" asked Matty pointedly.

"You're not still angry about that, are you?"

"Let's just say we're not even yet."

"Oh, Garber! You're not spurning my friendship, are you?"

"Examining my factional options," Matty replied coldly.

"Good Christ! You're not one of that Kislev lot!"

Steerforth appeared considerably alarmed when he said this and Matty burst out laughing—delighted at scoring a direct hit.

"Okay, James. We're even."

"Little bastard! Oh, well, suppose I deserved it. Which is probably Inez's attitude. She's getting back at me for some transgression or another. Probably my little trip to New York."

"What did you do there?"

"That's a loaded question, Garber, and we both know it. Is my answer for the record? Or Rabaiotti? Or Rankoff? Whose man are you, Garber?"

"Do I have to be anyone's?"

"Not at all, old son. Which puts you in a separate category with the delectable Miss Dworkin. By the way, have you had her yet? Or has she had you? Little barracuda."

"What is this power struggle at the agency?"

"Oh, thank God!" sighed Steerforth. "You still haven't chosen sides."

"Just trying to do my job. Took me long enough to get it. I don't want to know about office politics."

"Pull the other one," said Steerforth, pointing to his left leg. "Bells will ring. Come on, old son. You're a candidate like the rest of us—whether you know it or not."

"Candidate for what?"

"The crown. The agency's up for grabs. The natives are restless. Abe Keller's days are numbered."

"He *is* dying?"

"We're all dying, Garber. When is another question. I have no secret information regarding Abe's mortality. But what is dead is the business he knew about. Tin Pan Alley. Rodgers and Hart. Irving Berlin. Jerome Kern. The Gershwins. The Barrymores. Jolson. Eddie Cantor. Earl Carroll. Bojangles. Glenn Miller. The Dorseys. Vaudeville. Flo Ziegfeld. They're all gone. Taste, quality, imagination. They're gone. And that's just the East Coast. Sid Shankman's Hollywood died before he did."

"So what's left?"

"The deal. That's the new glamour, old son. The romance is the deal. Sweating out the price and the points we want. I love it! I bloody love it! What comes afterward's a flaming bore. I mean if I had to think about *what* I was selling, I'd puke. Got five different producers right now desperate for me to package Richard Gere and Amy Irving in a tale of bisexual sharks from distant galaxies. Double the price if Sly Stallone does a cameo. What price art now, Mr. Garber?"

"It's the packaging that's ruined the business."

"Rubbish! Didn't the studios used to 'package' years ago? With contract players and directors? Miscast talent 'cause they were all on the payroll and had to do something. Would *you* have cast Katharine Hepburn in *Dragon Seed*? And what about Norma Shearer as Juliet? Don't blame packaging. Look at the larger decay of society. We've been anesthetized. The only thing that'll wake us up is a dollop of horror or a bit of titillation. Like our Irma. Bloody woman! She's doing the first 'hi-tech' nightclub act."

"What does that mean?"

"I don't know. 'The industrial look,' she said. She's totally beyond my control these days. Won't listen to me anymore. She's found some bizarre Latvian émigré. I suppose he's the only one left who'll touch her. Actually, Garber, this could be a minor footnote in history tonight: the return of Irma Sandowsky to the anonymity she sprang from."

The main room of the Scheherazade was packed for the eight o'clock show. The entrance to the room was dominated by a twenty-foot-high cutout of Irma and the patrons had to walk between her incredible legs to reach their tables. Steerforth and Matty were led toward a roped-off reserved table at ringside where complimentary champagne and kewpie dolls of Inez awaited them.

"Someone else joining us?" asked Matty, noticing two more kewpie dolls at the table.

"Rabaiotti's in town," answered Steerforth, glancing about the packed room to see who else he knew. "Hmmm. Don't suppose you're wearing any garlic around your neck? Wolfbane? Anything like that?"

"Frank Langella in the audience?"

"No. Dr. Kislev."

"Where? Where?"

Steerforth nodded to a far corner of the room. Matty could vaguely make out a pear-shaped man with a large hooked nose and tiny, glassy eyes one usually found on teddy bears.

"Who are those people with him?" asked Matty, staring at the earnest cadre of anonymous patrons squeezed into the table with the notorious Israeli therapist.

"Acolytes. Kislevians. What-you-will. Poor demented sods giving up their identities to his every whim. Ah! The curtain riseth."

Inez was preceded by a nervous, fat young man who paced about the stage in an extreme degree of agitation telling what were meant to be jokes. It might as well have been his laundry list for the dead silence from the audience.

"He's terrible," whispered Matty.

"Of course," nodded Steerforth. "Inez's insurance policy. They've got to love her after this nonentity. It's why she picked him."

"Poor schmuck."

"Why? He'll get on the Carson show after this. Someone will write a new act for him. Two years from now he'll be headlining and poor Irma will be lucky to share the bill."

"Really think she's going to bomb?"

"She's never been good, Garber. Haven't you picked up on that yet? All done with mirrors, old son."

The comic mercifully finished his act to a charitable smattering of applause. Matty noticed Tony Rabaiotti wading his way between the tightly packed tables followed by the beautiful woman the New York honcho had been with at the airport.

"There's Tony! He's with Mrs. Nardino."

"Who?"

"That stunning blond woman. He flew in with her from New York. She owns some hotels or—"

Steerforth stood up abruptly from the table with a pleading look in his eyes.

"Cover for me, Matty. Can't explain. You'll have to go back and see Inez—"

"But where are you—?"

"Please!"

Steerforth vanished from the table. Matty knew instinctively this was no prank like the uncle routine at Inez's. Jimmy Steerforth was scared shitless of something or someone in the room.

"Matt, this is Mrs. Nardino."

"Please," she gushed, extending her hand to Garber, "Call me Sylvia. Tony tells me you are the wonder man of the office."

"He's very kind," replied Matty, nodding gratefully in Rabaiotti's direction.

"Where's Jimmy?" Rabaiotti asked as he pulled out Sylvia's chair for her.

"He . . . had some business," lied Matty, not knowing why he was sticking his neck out for Steerforth but aware that some force was compelling him to protect the Englishman.

"Goddamn Jimmy," chuckled Rabaiotti. "He's the dealmaker of dealmakers. You know that? He once told me, 'I'd shoot me old mom in the middle of the Rose Bowl if I could get the right price plus world cassette rights.' He's a character."

"Is he coming back?" asked Sylvia.

"He'd better," growled Rabaiotti, "or Inez will have a fit. She can't go to the can without Jimmy. Jesus! This is the longest overture in history."

"Relax," cooed Sylvia, placing her hand on Tony's thigh.

"You've got an electric touch," murmured Rabaiotti.

The curtain finally went up to reveal a mass of steel girders piled up on stage.

"What the hell is that?" asked Rabaiotti.

"Hi-tech," replied Matty in shocked disbelief. "Inez wanted an industrial look."

"What's she gonna do? Build a new theater?"

The band switched into a disco beat of "Let Me Entertain You" and seconds later someone appeared on stage in gold lame coveralls wearing a glitter welder's cap and carrying a neon pile driver. The welder began to dance about the stage—a beat or two behind the band—applying the neon pile driver to various rivets in the superstructure. Upon contact each rivet was illuminated in a different neon color. Eventually the rivets began to spell out I-N-E-Z!

Once the name was spelled out, the welder's coveralls begin to break away—one leg at a time—then one sleeve. Eventually the welder was down to nothing but a bikini of iridescent rivets. The welder ripped off her mask and the crowd went berserk. Inez Sanchez had just performed the most bizarrely effective number since Carmen Miranda's 'acid' banana sequence in *The Gang's All Here*.

The rest of the act continued in this vein for fifty-five minutes— a monument to bad taste—with the audience loving every minute of it. For a moment Matty was convinced Steerforth had bolted merely to avoid having to watch. When the show finally ended and the houselights came up, the audience hustled themselves back to the gambling tables. Steerforth had still not returned.

By two in the morning the Inez Suite of the Scheherazade was overflowing with hundreds of guests from various walks of life. Inez herself was brimming with the milk of ego aggrandizement and had overcome her mid-show hysteria at not having Steerforth appear.

Matty garnered considerable points with La Sanchez in her dressing room by citing her long list of credits and triumphs for the benefit of all the well-wishers who had flocked backstage after the first show. She was posing for pictures with various stars of the Strip's other hotels. Matty watched as Inez planted a sisterly kiss on the cheek of Nolan Goodly, who was packing them in at the Stardust with his extended family.

"They can't stand each other," muttered a pretty blond girl with ironed-flat hair and the kind of tan that can only come from a lifetime at the beach.

"What makes you say that?" asked Matty.

"I'm his fiancée."

"Oh, congratulations. I wasn't aware Nolan was engaged."

"We're keeping it a secret. 'Cause I'm not a Mormon yet. I really shouldn't have said anything but I'm a little high. The champagne."

"Thought Mormons don't drink."

"I'm not a Mormon yet," she giggled.

"Gather ye roses while ye may."

"Huh?"

"Enjoy it while you can."

"Oh, yeah. He's neat, Nolan. A lot more cool than they let him be on television."

"Yes," replied Matty. "I interviewed him on my show last year."

"You're in TV? Far out!"

"Not anymore. I'm an agent now. We represent Nolan. IAA."

"Do you know Mr. Rankoff?" she asked with a curious mix of hope and reverence in her voice.

"Sure. He's my boss. He hired me."

"Is he a nice guy?"

"Terrific. A little moody but—"

"Could you say hi to him for me? My name's Kate Baker."

"He'll probably be at your wedding, Kate."

"Dunno," she shrugged. "Sometimes I get the worst vibes about— Do you believe in things like that?"

"Psychic phenomenon?"

"How old are you?" she laughed.

"Twenty-eight."

"You talk older. I'm seventeen. Don't think I'm too young to get married, do you?"

"What do your parents say?"

"They think it's terrific. Nolan Goodly's gonna be their son-in-law. Guess they think I'm set for life."

"Do you love him? Nolan?"

"Does he remind you of Mr. Rankoff?" she asked abruptly.

"Gee, I don't know. There's an age difference and Nolan's quite a bit taller. And he's got red hair."

"But when he sings, it's like Mr. Rankoff."

"When did you hear Bobby sing?" Matty asked, amusingly wondering if he'd stumbled across another "Latin Lady" freak.

"At a party," she answered nervously. "He was really nice to me. I used to know his daughter."

"Martine?"

"Do you know her?"

"I've never met her."

"You probably won't."

"What do you mean?"

"Don't you know about Martine?"

"What? What about her, Kate?"

"She's in the hospital. Has been for almost ten years."

"What's wrong with her?"

"Would you tell Mr. Rankoff that you saw me? I phoned him a couple of times but—" A big plastic smile suddenly flashed across Kate's face as Nolan arrived at her side.

"Good to see you again, Matt," grinned the singing Mormon, pumping Garber's hand enthusiastically. "Hear you've shot right up like a rocket since I last saw you. Having a chat with Kate, eh?" Nolan flashed his Carteresque smile.

"I told him about us," murmured Kate.

"Oh?"

"It's okay, Nolan. I can keep a secret. Congratulations."

"'Preciate that Matt." Nolan took Kate's hand and led her across the room to meet some people.

Is there no end to this mystery? wondered Matty as Kate Baker floated across the floor. What was this spooky beach child to Rankoff? And what was wrong with Martine? Why was she hospitalized?

"I've been hoping to have a talk with you," a voice rumbled behind Matty (although the actual way the sentence came out in a heavy Israeli accent was "I've been hewping to have a toke with you").

Garber turned around and confronted the pear-shaped body and glassy teddy-bear eyes of Dr. Shmuel Kislev.

"Good morning, doctor."

"You know who I am?"

"You're quite famous," smiled Matty, noticing that the doctor's fingernails had all been bitten off. How secure could the great guru be with nails like that?

"You're not unknown yourself, Mr. Gerber."

"Garber."

"That's what I said." He had. The problem was his Israeli accent mangled all vowels into totally unrecognizable forms. "Mr. Foley thinks very highly of you."

"Who? I don't know anyone named Fewley."

"Dwight!"

"Foley! Yes. Sorry. It must be the noise in here. Some party, eh?"

"Could we take a few minutes to chat? Would that be possible?" Before Matty could stop him, Dr. Kislev grabbed his elbow with his pudgy fist and steered the agent out to the balcony.

"Have you been to the desert before, Mr. Garber?"

"No, this is my first visit to Las Vegas. Although I haven't seen much except the hotel lobby and—"

"I draw my strength from the desert," rumbled Kislev. "My childhood was spent on the desert. My first revelation was in the desert."

"You and Moses," smiled Matty good-naturedly.

"And Christ," intoned Kislev. "All great movements began in the desert. Do you know about the circle and the triangle?"

Oh-oh, thought Matty. I think he's trying to sell me something.

"The circle is infinity and the triangle forms—"

"Could you excuse me a moment, please, Doctor?"

"What's wrong?"

"I have to speak to Miss Sanchez."

"I'll only be a few more minutes. Surely you can—"

"Just remember where you were, doctor. Be right back."

Matty left an annoyed Kislev on the balcony overlooking his beloved desert and scurried straight back to his room. He picked up the phone and dialed Los Angeles.

"Hello," groaned Lindsay, after dropping the receiver on the floor beside her bed and retrieving it.

"This is a conscious to unconscious call from Matthew Garber. Will you accept?"

"Wha' time is it, Matty?"

"You don't want to know. I do want you to know I love you. Go back to sleep."

"No, no. More, more," she grinned, still keeping her eyes closed. "How was the opening?"

"Insane. Steerforth vanished."

"What!?"

"Thirty seconds before the curtain went up, he vanished."

"The mystery deepens."

"Which mystery?" asked Matty. "The Joy Dworkin mystery? The Bobcaygeon mystery? Or—"

"No one knows where James Steerforth lives."

"What?"

"He picks his mail up at the Beverly Hills post office every morning. He has no phone number. You have to leave any messages for him with an answering service. Mr. Rankoff tried to reach him once and went crazy—"

"Why do you think he does that?"

"That's what Mr. Rankoff wanted to know. You know about Steerforth's hair?"

"You mean that mop's a wig?"

"Oh, no. It's just he never seems to get it cut. It mysteriously stays the same. Every secretary in this office goes crazy making and canceling hair appointments for their bosses. Lee has never made one appointment for Mr. Steerforth."

"Maybe Inez does it."

"There's something weird about him, Matty."

"Not any weirder than Shmuel Kislev. He just hit on me at the party."

"He *is* weird, isn't he?"

"Bites his fingernails. Or his 'fangernails' as he calls them. Don't know how he manages to have any followers. Who can understand a word he says?"

"I love you," she laughed. "You don't take any of them seriously."

"I take my work seriously."

"Oh, we know that, Mr. Sobersides!"

"Quit teasing me."

"I love teasing you. You're such a great target"

"Do you know who Kate Baker is?"

"No. Who's Kate Baker? Haven't met another woman have you?"

"Oh, for Chrissake! She's only seventeen."

"You and Mr. Rankoff— Forget I said that, Matty."

"Said what? Kate says she knows Rankoff. She was kind of funny about him."

"That's a sensitive subject, Matthew."

"Does Rankoff have a thing for young girls?"

"Not on the phone, Matty. When are you coming home?"

"Noon."

"Want to have lunch at my place?"

"Or something."

"I love you, Matty."

"I love you, Lindsay. Go back to sleep."

"You, too."

By the time Matty climbed aboard the plane the next morning, Steerforth was already in his seat and staring blankly out the window at the tarmac.

"What happened to you last night?" asked Matty.

Steerforth did not reply.

"The show was even worse than you predicted," Garber continued. "But the audience ate it up. That proves another one of your theories . . . James? . . . You okay?"

"I don't trust many people in this world, Matthew." Steerforth continued to stare out the window as he spoke, even as the plane left the ground. "For reasons that I may someday impart to you. But, for some reason my black hearted soul cannot fathom, I trust you. And I am putting my fate in your hands. Here."

Steerforth withdrew an envelope from his inside jacket pocket and handed it to Matty. There was a small lumpy object inside.

"Hold on to this for me, Matthew. I feel better knowing it's in your hands. Will you keep it for me?"

"Sure."

"I'd appreciate you not mentioning my behavior last night to Rankoff or any of the others. Do I have your word?"

"Of course," replied Matty, already regretting having spilled the beans to Lindsay.

"Make it worth your while one day."

"You don't have to—"

Steerforth had turned away once more and was staring out the window. But he did not see the billowing clouds. For him they were waves and the infinite blue was not sky but ocean. His mind had returned to innocence and a fifteen-year-old named Willie Stubbs, who looked much older than his age and dreamed of the States from the moment he had first set foot in the cinema at Bakewell. He'd fallen in love with Hollywood's America and the women who populated it. He'd run off to sea to get closer to it.

There he met a woman straight out of those films. Beautiful, voluptuous, insatiable. She persuaded him to break the law. He had paid for it ever since with his nightmares.

FEINGOLD

"Wheezer?"

Silence.

"Wheezer?"

More silence.

"Wheezer, where the hell are you?"

Louise Feingold lay flaked out on her canopied bed feeling the rivulets of perspiration running down her delicate little plastic surgery. It was incredibly hot for May and her heart was threatening to pound right through her chest. She felt so goddamn empty despite five rousing sets of tennis capped by an even more rousing orgasm in her private cabana at the club courtesy of the junior pro. The boy was most complimentary of her body, her backhand, and her lovemaking but it meant nothing to Wheezer. In five days she would be forty-six years old and, if she was not such a goddamn coward, she'd kill herself.

She had never felt so alone in her life. Her parents were thousands of miles and generations removed from her; her children might as well be Martians for her ability to communicate with them; her best friend, Ara, had long ago sunk into drunken self-pity and a denigrating public spectacle; and there was her husband.

Wheezer knew in her heart of hearts that it was Stanley, who caused her so much pain. She could endure age and the agonizingly rapid passage of time if she had Stan's love to support her. But somewhere along the line he had ceased to be the boy she loved. Where was that young Garfield she had dragged her father to watch in a Greenwich Village basement so many years ago? What had happened to "Steve Fairley," the earnest young actor she had urged Ara to put up for any TV role going? When had he given it all up to become Slippery Stan Feingold, the most devious agent in Hollywood? King of the bottom line.

Her father, Abe Keller, had been delighted when his prospective son-in-law had accepted his offer to become an agent. Keller had never been thrilled at the notion of having an actor in the family. When Stan had taken to dealmaking like a duck to water, Abe overcame his own sense of personal loss when Wheezer went west with her husband to join the Beverly Hills office.

They bought a beautiful home; had two kids; were the prince regent and consort of the Sixties social scene. They were liberally chic; entertained blacks; didn't eat grapes; clutched each other for mutual reassurance at the Ambassador the night Bobby Kennedy was shot; they protested against the war.

Then came the Seventies: the decade of Me. Self-exploration; self-examination; self-absorption. No one got into it more than Stan Feingold. Always egocentric, Stan Feingold was born to shine in the Me Decade. He tried est, TM, Scientology. He spent weekends at Essalen and shed his clothes at Sandstone. He got his bantam weight body back into fighting trim, jogged every morning with the kids at UCLA and grew a Zapata moustache. He graduated from grass to coke. He began to gamble: cards, crap, the market. His expenses rose with his hedonism quotient. Cash flow was a problem. There was no longer enough money in being an agent. He became a producer. And a stranger to his once-adoring wife.

"Why aren't you getting dressed?" asked Feingold, standing in the doorway of his wife's bedroom and staring at her prostrate body sprawled across the four-poster still in her tennis skirt and clutching her racquet for dear life.

"Why?" she murmured, opening one eye and watching him remove his sweat-stained shirt. How ironic! His body had never been so firm and muscular since their courtship and they hadn't touched each other in almost two years.

"Cause we're going to Bobby's for dinner," he answered, starting out of the bedroom for the privacy of his own quarters.

"Bobby who?"

"How many Bobbys are there in our life? The Magic Man. Don Roberto."

"Was that tonight?" she asked, managing to force her body into an upright position. "What's the date today?"

"May the second," he replied.

She hoped he would add: "Five more days till your birthday." But it didn't happen.

"I'm really tired, Stan."

"Get dressed, Louise!"

"I just finished five sets of tennis—"

"I want you there."

"Why? You always ignore me when we go anywhere. You're always off hustling or schmoozing or putting the make on some Farrah Fawcett look-alike."

"Negative cant!" bellowed Feingold.

Wheezer paused for a moment not knowing what her husband was talking about. Then she remembered his latest cult of self-absorption and shook her head sadly.

"How much did you have to pay for that decoder ring?" she asked, nodding toward the circle and triangle he wore on his right hand.

"I've asked you not to make fun of things you don't understand," smoldered Feingold, staring at his petite, short-haired wife as she met his gaze with mocking eyes.

"What's not to understand? You are a selfish bastard, Stanley. I've always known that but tried to overlook it. Made excuses: you came from Brooklyn, didn't have a father, all that Harold Robbins shit. But you survived, Stanley. You became successful. Married a rich Jewish princess. Your childhood pain should have been compensated. For ten years it was. You were a *mensch*, Steve. You really were. Along came L. Ron Hubbard, Werner Erhardt and Shmuel Kislev and you went right back to the womb. Right back to the corner of Flatbush and Self-Pity."

"Get dressed, Louise."

"What do you do at those meetings with Kislev? I'm really curious. What kind of rap does he lay on you? Does he tell you it's all right to ignore your children becoming invisible in front of your eyes? To drive your wife into other men's arms? To steal from your associates—"

He was on her in a flash and his fingers were around her throat. Forcing her back on the bed, his grip grew tighter and tighter. When he saw the terror in her eyes, he released his grasp.

"Sorry," he whispered breathlessly, still lying on top of her. "You know I got a temper. You've always known that. Why do you start with me?"

"Cause at least I get some kind of reaction," she said, staring up into his eyes with tears in her own. "For a few seconds you're the old Steve. Even if it's the crazy one. . . . Hey! What's that?"

"What?"

"That hardness."

"Sorry—" He started to roll off her, but she pulled him back with the strength that usually went into her backhand.

"No use wasting it, Steve."

"You haven't called me that in a long time."

"You haven't had one of those in a long time."

"I was saving it for the seventh," he replied, nibbling her ear.

"You remembered my birthday."

"Collated data," he replied and began to remove his trousers.

***

Robert Rankoff had hired Ames as his butler, chef, and general factotum shortly after his divorce from Yvonne in 1972. The prim and proper Englishman had proven invaluable to the agency boss and he was besieged by lucrative offers to lure him away from his employer. But Ames was incredibly loyal and considerably overpaid by Rankoff and, where three marriages had failed hopelessly, this was one relationship Bobby could never dream of severing.

The guests arrived promptly at seven thirty: Stan Feingold and his wife Louise; Paramount VP Cal Chambers accompanied by his twenty-six-year-old wife Norrine and his celebrated hiatus hernia; Violette-Claire Desgouilles in exquisitely tailored military fatigues; and the ever young Evelyn Shankman on the arm of Matthew Garber to whom she had taken a considerable fancy and interest.

The chitchat over sherry was about 'the business' as usual, although Rankoff made a few aborted attempts to steer it off toward other subjects. Norrine Chambers, however, put a damper on serious discussion by innocently inquiring when exactly World War II had taken place.

Violette-Claire Desgouilles burst into peals of derisive laughter at this question and shook her head in disbelief, muttering phrases in French which Rankoff chose not to translate.

"What's she saying?" growled Chambers, who on the one hand was used to the inanities of his incredibly stacked, incredibly stupid wife and on the other hand felt a proprietorial need to rise to her defense.

The moment was rescued by Ames's appearance in the sitting room to announce that dinner was ready.

"What's on the menu tonight, Ames?" asked Feingold, who, Brooklyn-born and bred, never ceased to get a kick out of Bobby's butler.

"As this is Mile. Desgouilles's first visit to Mr. Rankoff's home, Mr. Rankoff and I planned a suitable meal in her honor." Ames nodded politely to Violette-Claire and announced his choice. "I thought, mademoiselle, you might appreciate *truite de mer sauce verte, noisettes d'agneau aux pointes d'asperges* with a refreshing *fraises et framboises Chantilly* for dessert."

"Where did you find this man?" demanded a duly impressed Violette-Claire.

"What the hell are we eating?" asked Feingold.

"Salmon trout with green sauce," replied Louise. "Lamb chops with asparagus tips and . . . um, strawberries and raspberries with whipped cream. Right, Ames?"

"Spot on, Mrs. Feingold."

"Vous parlez français?" asked the petite Violette-Claire giving the equally petite Louise the once-over.

"Un petit peu," shrugged Louise. "It was my major in college but—"

"Nous devons parler seulement francais ce soir," ordered Violette-Claire, seizing Louise by the hand and dragging her into the dining room.

"There go our dates," shrugged Rankoff.

"Want to talk to you later," murmured Feingold as the two ex-partners walked into the dining room.

"Can't it wait till—?"

"No!"

Ames had produced a young Puligny-Montrachet to accompany the trout and a superb Bordeaux, a Château Leoville Las-Cases, to go with the lamb. Violette-Claire got hopelessly bombed on both bottles and began a denunciation of capitalism, Hollywood, and the United States - when she wasn't trying to run her hand up and down Louise Feingold's resistant leg.

"I have an allergy," Louise finally remarked pointedly. "Rather you didn't scratch my leg."

"It was yours?" asked a nonplussed Violette-Claire. "Forgive me. It must be the wine."

"Have you seen Ara lately?" Louise asked, leaning across the table to Evelyn in an attempt to avoid contact with the gung-ho Frenchwoman, who had insisted upon sitting next to her and confounding Ames's carefully planned seating arrangement.

"We had lunch together last week," replied Evelyn.

"How is she?" asked Louise. "I should phone her but it's been so long . . . You know what it's like when friends drift."

"A way of life out here," nodded Evelyn sympathetically. "The saddest phrase in the world to me is 'we used to be friends.' My greatest difficulty is the loss of contemporaries. I seem to have outlived all my old friends."

"I was going to invite Ara tonight," announced Rankoff from the other end of the table. "But there's a big network affiliates' dinner at the Century Plaza and she went along to represent the agency. She and Joy. The network is presenting Nolan Goodly with some kind of award. Dwight was thinking of wearing his medals to the dinner."

"How are Joy and Ara getting along?" asked Evelyn with, what Matty thought to be, more than a casual interest.

"Ask your escort," replied Rankoff, nodding toward Garber. "He's in contact with them all day."

"We all have our own clients," shrugged Matty, wishing Rankoff hadn't put him on the spot like this. "Pretty busy with my own deals so I don't . . ."

"Don't get along, do they?" asked Evelyn.

"They tend to take little bites out of each other," admitted Matty.

"That's tragic," commented Evelyn.

"Has anyone here read *Mommie Dearest*?" Norrine Chambers was ignorant of the Ara-Joy rumors but determined to take part in the discussion no matter what.

Both Matty and Evelyn froze upon hearing this classically tactless but innocent question from Mrs. Chambers. Mrs. Shankman's eyes met Garber's and they knew that their thoughts were identical.

"I'd like a word with you after dinner," said Evelyn as she raised the napkin to her lips.

"Sure."

The subject of plumbing came up and all the guests leaped in with names and numbers of discount plumbers, electricians, carpenters, pool men, gardeners, landscapers, exterminators, and so on. Matty couldn't believe it. His first formal Hollywood dinner party and the most passionate subject of discussion was the cheapest way to get Japanese beetles out of your oleander bush and how to buy an Advent screen without paying sales tax.

After dinner Ames switched on the lights in the garden. Cal Chambers took Violette-Claire for a promenade around the swimming pool in a futile attempt to interest the French director in the studio's Maude Gonne project. Matty was left to amuse Mesdames Feingold, Shankman and Chambers, all perched like a singing trio in a yellow and-white-striped swing next to the cabana while Bobby and Stan talked business in the library.

Rankoff was rattled. He had never recovered from the regards that Rabaiotti had brought him from Sylvia Nardino a month earlier. Sylvia! Talk about the ghost of Hamlet's father! Bobby didn't think of himself as superstitious but her turning up again after all those years—even via a second party—was enough to give him the shakes for a week.

Over dinner Matty had mentioned Nolan Goodly's fiancée Kate. She was still trying to get in touch with him. Why had he allowed her into the house that evening? And the others? Get her out of your mind, Bobby. It'll only trigger you off onto Martine again and all that guilt. And your father. And Murray. Fucking Murray dead thirty-six years and you can't get rid of him!

What about Davenport? He'd phoned again before dinner. How was all that going to end?

"Magic Man."

"What is it?" asked Rankoff, staring at Feingold stretched out on his leather sofa under an original Remington roundup, puffing away on the Havana cigar his ex-partner had just given him.

"What do you think about the French broad directing *Brother Who Fell from Uranus*?"

"Violette-Claire directing Tom Ricker? You must be crazy, Stanley. They'd kill each other. They'll never bring the picture in."

"Exactly what I figured. I could insure it for twice the budget and make a killing."

"UA would never go for it."

"Wanna bet? They love me over there."

"That's 'cause you never made a picture for them. You never lost them any money."

"My pictures have never lost money, Magic Man. Wanna toot?"

"No."

"What's the matter, buddy?" Feingold took two big hits of cocaine then put the vial back in his pocket. "Goddamn! Ames knows how to cook, doesn't he? But can he make *kneidlach*?"

"Better than my mother's. How's your mother, Stan?"

"Losing her marbles. She thinks I'm my father. Must be the moustache. They take good care of her in that home but it's such a goddamn depressing place. Always smells like dirty diapers."

"Did you ever think of moving her into your place?" asked Rankoff.

"What are you? On the rib? Got enough heat at home without— Did Rabaiotti talk to you about me last month?"

"Just wanted to know how you were," shrugged Rankoff.

"He's a fucking spy for my father-in-law. Goddamn mafioso! I really resent him coming out here snooping around trying to get the dope on me and Wheezer to take back to Abe. And he's so smooth. With those capped teeth. He came over for dinner oozing charm and asking every loaded question in the book."

"How are things with you guys?"

"Fine!" exploded Feingold. "*Shtupped* my wife this evening for the first time in two years."

"Congratulations."

"She's better than she was twenty-five years ago," reflected Slippery Stan.

"I should hope so."

"She's picked up a few fancy moves elsewhere."

"People with glass jockstraps shouldn't throw—"

"I know."

The two old friends burst out laughing having relieved the air of tension.

"What's happening with *Ektalon-Z?*" asked Feingold after the laughter had subsided. "Have we got a picture yet?"

"Everyone in the office is running around trying to package it. The problem is finding a director we represent to—"

"*Don't* . . . package it," interrupted Feingold emphatically.

"Why not?"

"Been thinking about this for weeks, Magic Man. Sometimes I wake in the middle of the night with the sweats thinking about it."

"Stanley, what are you—?"

"Don't use one of your directors," repeated Feingold. "Charge the talent their normal ten-percent commission. Then take a packaging commission and put it into the IAA number-two account."

"Charge a double commission? That's a felony, Stanley. It may even be grand larceny—"

"Magic Man, we're talking a fifteen-million-dollar budget on this picture. One and a half million dollar commission. 750 K each. You can't walk away from that, Bobby. *I* can't. Not with the markers I got spread all over town and Vegas. Plus the money I owe the Jones men. Not to mention Wheezer's charge accounts, the gardeners, the servants— I'm over my head, buddy, and I'm sinking. You can't be doing much better than me what with the mortgage on this joint the alimony you pay Yvonne. You giving Sabina money?"

"No, she—"

"Okay. What does it cost you for Martine's treatment?"

"Three thousand a month."

"Right. I hear Ames gets more than Carroll O'Connor does for *All in the Family.*"

"Not that much," replied Rankoff wryly.

"Okay. But you're laying out 150 large a year easily before you can shit and before taxes. Got to be feeling the squeeze, too."

"Not saying I'm not—"

"Not like we've never dabbled in the number two account—"

"That was peanuts, Stan. It's not the same as—"

"Negative cant!!"

"What. . . did you say?"

Rankoff noticed the ring on Feingold's finger. The circle with the triangle in the middle.

"Oh, Stanley! Not you. Don't tell me Kislev's got to you, too, with his mumbo-jumbo."

"This is the real thing, Bobby. I've futzed around in the past with the est and the pest and TM. But this works for me, you know. It's a concept I can relate to as a human being, as a Jew—"

"Oh, come on, Stanley!"

"Have you ever driven into the desert, Bobby? Right into the middle of the desert and stared up at the stars? Until you find *your* star."

"I sang this song, for Chrissake! With Tommy Dorsey."

"Dr. Kislev has a concept. It's called 'becoming operative.' I'm not supposed to discuss it with anyone outside the circle but you're like a brother to me, Bobby. I want to share this thing with you. Becoming operative is the final release. It's performing any act without feeling the slightest pang of guilt. Can you imagine the limits a human being can stretch to?"

"This is Kislev's theory?"

"Yeah. Exciting, isn't it?"

"It's Machiavelli, Stan! It's only five hundred years old!"

"There are no new concepts, Bobby. Everything is collated data. Under our present financial circumstances, it is tactically advisable to go with a director outside the agency."

"Who'd you have in mind?"

"Rees Davenport."

"No way!"

"He's shacked up with Sabina and that's got to be a sore point with you but—"

"It's more than that, Stanley. The guy is nuts. He's psychotic—"

"He's a director," shrugged Feingold.

"More than that. The man phones me in the middle of the night and clucks. He sends me dead chickens—with their necks broken—gift wrapped!"

"Jesus! What does he want from you? He's got Sabina."

"I've been saying that for weeks. He phoned me tonight. First time he's actually spoken to me. He . . . wants me to fight a duel."

"Huh?"

"Says I can choose any weapons I want. He's 'stolen my woman' and he wants me to call him out on it. Man to man."

"He's nuts," nodded Feingold.

"What am I going to do, Stan?"

"Postpone the duel till we get the picture made."

***

It was close to midnight when Matty pulled the Camaro into the drive next to the '37 Cord. He was surprised to see the light still on in the sitting room and Roley sitting up in his favorite chair reading Wordsworth.

"How was your dinner?" asked Roley, looking up from his book. "Did you enjoy your glimpse of life amid the nabobs and potentates?"

"Those people are all millionaires," said Matty, removing his jacket and draping it over the back of a chair, "and all they could talk about was how to save fifty bucks here or twenty bucks there. I couldn't believe it!"

"Those people were not *born* millionaires, old boy. This town is notorious for the fortunes made and lost. You have only to look at myself."

"Did you really do that well?"

"I was loaded. Used to buy sweaters by the dozens. At one time, Matthew, I owned six hundred sweaters. What on earth does one do in southern California with six hundred sweaters?"

"Find six hundred Lana Turners to fill them," grinned Matty.

"Tried that for a while. Until I picked the winner of that unofficial competition. She's the one who cleaned me out. Left me skint."

"Skint?"

"Penniless."

"Why didn't you go back to England?"

"In 1950? The Germans may have surrendered in '45, dear boy, but the country was still under wartime conditions. I shipped a trunk full of bananas to my sister in Plymouth. She apparently made a fortune in the banana black market there. Can I interest you in a brandy? I know you don't drink but . . ."

"Hey, let me tell you. For a guy who doesn't drink I sure got into it tonight. Anon, anon, mine host of the garter."

Roley pulled himself up from his chair and crossed over to the Victorian writing desk which served as the bar.

"Another reason I never went back," continued Roley as he poured two snifters full of Remy Martin, "was Wordsworth. The passage I was reading tonight:

Earth has not anything to show more fair:

Dull would he be of soul who could pass by

A sight so touching in its majesty:

This City now doth, like a garment, wear

The beauty of the morning.

"That 'garment' was not meant to be a kaftan and a sheik's headdress. No, the London I remember is dead. I want to live out these remaining—what? Months? Days? Never presume to say years—shall we say, 'the time which remains to me'? I'll live with my memories, Matthew. Cheers!"

The two touched glasses and sipped their brandies.

"Ever know Evelyn Shankman?" asked Matty, settling comfortably into a chair opposite Draycott.

"Evelyn Hughes? Oh, indeed. Fancied her like mad when I was a young actor in New York. She only had eyes for Louis Calhern. Louis didn't know she existed. Is she still beautiful?"

"She looks incredible, Roley. Whenever I see her. Which is what bothers me. Everyone tells me how ill she is. For the past twenty-five years. Yet she looks better than Ara Whalen and Ara's twenty years younger than her. Why would a woman pretend to be sick for twenty-five years when she's not? And I don't mean hypochondria."

"Do you have delusions of being Arthur Conan Doyle? If so, I refuse to play Dr. Watson to your Sherlock Garber."

"She asked me to do a very strange thing this evening."

"Don't think I want to hear this," said Roley after clearing his throat. "Like to keep my illusions of Evelyn intact."

"Nothing like that, you incorrigible satyr. No. She took me aside after dinner and asked me to try and affect some sort of entente between Ara and Joy. She asked me to use my 'good offices.' "

"Sure you're not creating this entire climate of intrigue, old boy? Rather like Dickens strutting down Rodeo Drive with a Gucci bag and a Hermes scarf."

"You're the second person to mention Dickens. What am I supposed to think when one of the character's names is James Steerforth? Oh! I spoke to Jimmy about representing you. I don't handle actors at all, Roley. Just writers. But Jimmy promised if the right part came along he'd—"

"Dear boy, please! You don't have to go through this charade with me. My career ended a great many years ago. Don't even know if I'd want it back. Grateful to you, more than anything, for your companionship this past month. Now, dear boy, I'm going to bed."

Must have been the brandy. Matty had no other explanation for the incredible dream he experienced that night. He was watching an old movie starring John Barrymore, Lowell Sherman, Louis Calhern, and Roland Draycott. He couldn't identify any of the women although one of them was undoubtedly a young Evelyn Shankman. All were dressed in formal wear of the twenties and bantering away in the style of that period's drawing room comedies. They were gathered together in a cottage not unlike Roley's when the lights began to dim and a beautiful garden magically appeared outside the French windows. Everyone exited to the garden and the dream began to follow the plot of Barrie's *Dear Brutus*. Everyone got to see what they might have been. The cast changed abruptly. Barrymore, Sherman, and Calhern vanished and were replaced by Rankoff, Minden Prescott, and Jimmy Steerforth. Steerforth was a painter and Joy was his daughter. A beggar woman came by played by Ara. Steerforth chased her away. Joy burst into tears. "Why did you chase her away? She was my mother, wasn't she?" Then Sol Siglan rode by on a tandem bicycle—and someone began tapping at the window.

Tap-tap-tap-tap-tap.

"Matty! Matty!"

It wasn't the dream.

Someone was really tapping at the window.

Matty bolted upright out of his dream and saw Joy Dworkin's face at the leaded glass of his bedroom window. He reached for the brass handle and pushed the window open.

"Lemme in, will you?" Joy sounded desperate.

"What time is it?" asked Matty, still asleep.

"Five to seven. Come on. Let me in."

Joy held her arms up to him and Matty pulled her through the window onto his bed. She looked around the tiny room then asked: "Where do Grumpy and Dopey sleep?"

"Are you stoned, Joy?"

"God! I wish I were!"

"What's the matter?"

"The police have been at my place for the last hour. Know what it's like being rousted by the cops at five-thirty?"

"What did they want?"

"She must have done it! That bitch! She steered them onto me."

"Who?"

"Ara. She's out to get me. She really is. The cops knew about Darlene's accident. How could they have known that if the goddamn Painted Lady didn't tell them?"

"What are you talking about?"

"Have you got a joint? I'd really like a joint."

"Got some brandy."

"At this hour? I'll puke. Give me a minute to catch my breath, okay? Oh, Jesus! Never been so scared in my life. How could they think I did it?"

"Did what?"

"It was on the radio in the car on the way over. Guess it'll be in the final edition of the *Times* this morning."

"What will?"

"Nolan Goodly killed himself."

"What?!"

"He murdered his girlfriend, then killed himself."

"Kate's dead?"

"Was that her name?" asked Joy. "Little Miss Suntan with the long blond hair. They sat with us at the dinner last night and had a wonderful time. Why the hell would they go home and do something like that?"

"Is this a gag, Joy?"

"Who do you think I am? Steerforth? I don't play games like that, Garber."

"Sorry. It's just— Why did the police question you?"

"Don't know. Maybe 'cause I gave them a lift home from the affiliates dinner. Supposed to have been the last person to see them alive. Me and the killer."

"What killer? Thought you said it was a murder-suicide?"

"That's the official story. But you knew Nolan. Mr. Goody-Goody. Think he could do something sick like that?"

"Why did you drive them home? ... Joy?"

"Oh, God!"

"Joy, why did you drive them home?"

"Cause I was sucking up. Okay? Goddamn it! You know I'm ambitious, Matty. . . . They said they found drugs."

"Who found what drugs where?"

"The cops said they found drugs in Nolan's apartment. Somebody must have planted them there. Mormons don't—"

"She wasn't a Mormon."

"How do you know?" asked Joy.

"I met her. She was probably a freak. She was cleaning up her act for Nolan. Maybe she got him to try them when they came home and he wigged out. What did you mean before about Darlene's accident? Did you mean Darlene English? Do you know something about—"

"There's more to this than they're saying," interrupted Joy, purposely avoiding Matty's questions. "Why else would they want to know about the jade?"

"What jade?"

"The cops showed me a piece of black jade,'' said Joy. "Said it might have fallen off a cuff link or an earring. It was found near the bodies in the apartment."

The telephone rang in the sitting room. Matty heard Roley answer it. A few seconds later there was a knock at the bedroom door and Roley stuck his head in.

"It's Lindsay, old boy. She wants a word with—"

Roley stared in amazement at Joy sitting cross-legged on Matty's bed and wondered how on earth she had managed to materialize there in the middle of the night.

"Hi!" Joy waved to Roley. "Wouldn't have a joint, would you?"

"It's not Sunday," replied Roley.

"One of us is not understanding the other," said Joy, shaking her head.

"Miss Dworkin, this is my roommate Mr. Draycott"

"No need to be formal, Matthew. Who is this lovely apparition? You look very familiar, my dear. Did I know your mother?"

Joy was startled for a moment then burst out laughing.

"Are you going to be my long lost father after all these years, Mr. Draycott?"

"Do call me Roley. Would you like some coffee?"

All three left the bedroom: Matty to answer the phone; Joy and Roley to prepare breakfast in the kitchen.

"Good morning," Matty said into the phone. "Have you heard the news about Nolan?"

"Mr. Rankoff phoned me half an hour ago," replied Lindsay. "He was very upset."

"Understandably. It was a helluva shock—"

"The network's freaked. After they gave Nolan Goodly a humanitarian award last night, he went home, murdered his fiancée and bumped himself off."

"Hadn't really examined that aspect of it."

"The network did. They canceled the show an hour ago. Mr. Rankoff has called an emergency breakfast meeting for eight o'clock sharp at his house. All senior agents. Have to call everyone and tell them. I've left three messages with Mr. Steerforth's service. Of all times for him to be elusive."

"Better get off the phone if you have to call everyone. See you later at the office."

"See you at Mr. Rankoff's."

"But he wants to see the senior agents," replied Matty.

"He specifically asked I include you. Guess you've been promoted to the big meetings. Congratulations. Now all I've got to do is find Joy Dworkin—"

"She's here."

"What is she doing there?" An Arctic chill had attached itself to Lindsay's question.

"She came over this morning to tell me about the murder—the suicide—whatever it was. She's in the kitchen with Roley. Nothing happened!"

"I believe you . . . this time! Getting tired of hearing how cute and adorable you are from other women, Matthew."

"I'm yours! I'm yours!"

"I missed you last night."

"See you at Bobby's!"

Matty put the phone down and told Joy about the emergency meeting at Rankoff's. Then he showered, shaved, got dressed, and was starting out of the cottage with Joy when the phone rang once more. Matty answered it.

"Good morning, Matthew." It was Steerforth.

"Thank goodness you phoned," replied Garber. "Just heading out the door. Lindsay's been trying to reach you—"

"My service gave me the message. Dreadful business about poor Nolan."

"Yeah."

"Recall that envelope I gave you last month when we flew back from Las Vegas, old son? Obliged if you could return it to me this morning."

"Sure. I'll bring it to the meeting."

"Excellent. Don't make a fuss when you return it. Just slip it into my pocket when nobody's looking. All right? See you in Trousdale."

Matty hung up the phone with a strange gnawing feeling in his gut.

"Who was that?" asked Joy, standing in the open doorway.

Matty marched briskly back to his bedroom and opened the drawer where he had buried the envelope under a pile of socks and underwear. It was Scheherazade Hotel stationery and Matty double-checked he had an identical envelope before he tore this one open.

Inside the envelope was a cuff link. A gold cuff link. Mounted in the center of it was a piece of black jade.

Matty closed his fist over the cuff link to hide it from the world. He opened his hand once more and stared at the black jade.

It was then Matthew Garber realized that Nolan and Kate's deaths were not as the police had reported. This was no murder-suicide, no lovers' quarrel. Someone else had murdered both of them.

Matty was terrified to put the next piece of the puzzle together.

IVOR

"Never been here before," said Joy as Matty pulled his humble Camaro up behind the Mercedes, BMWs, and Bentleys parked in the driveway of Rankoff's Tudor mansion. "It's a knockout. The boss really knows how to live, doesn't he?"

"Come on," answered Matty, getting out of the car. "We're late."

"Will you sit beside me, Matty? I'm shit scared of Ara. She's got the evil eye on me."

Matty found himself seated in Rankoff's dining room for the second time in twelve hours. Gone was the carnival atmosphere of the previous evening when Violette-Claire had tried to put the make on Louise Feingold, and Norrine Chambers had everyone biting their lips to keep from guffawing at her endless stream of inanities. This was business.

Deadly serious business. Accent deadly. Rankoff sat at the head of the table with Steerforth facing him at the other end. Ara sat on Bobby's right with Speedy Liebowitz on the left. Dwight, Stu, and Bazzo (sans Stretch Armstrong) sat in between with Ames and Lindsay hovering nearby with coffee and croissants. Matty and Joy found seats at Steerforth's end of the table.

"Okay," Rankoff announced clapping his hands together.

"We all know what happened; we don't know why. Can't get into that now. I'm still in shock, as you all are, but that doesn't change the fact that we have a problem."

"Is the network definite about the cancellation?" asked Speedy. "They're not just reacting in light of the bad publicity?"

"Goodly has become a non-word," replied Rankoff. "Imagine contagious cancer, that's what happened between here and New York at four o'clock this morning. Lot of people went without sleep, Ronny. But it's over. The Goodlys are deader than Nolan. It's Fatty Arbuckle all over again. Sunday night has a big hole and we've got to plug it before somebody else gets that spot. Any ideas?"

The agents around the table went silent. Matty took advantage of the quiet to study them all. Was there a murderer in their midst? Who? Little Joy? Ambitious Joy? What motive could she have for bumping off Nolan? How might his death propel her further up the IAA ladder? Big Stu Jackson? Lindsay told him he'd once thought of joining the Mormon church and how Nolan had laughed at the idea. Stu was a sensitive guy under all that élan. Maybe he harbored a grudge that finally exploded into senseless violence.

Freaked-out Larry Bazzo never disguised his contempt for the singing Mormon family. Maybe he'd taken one toot too many or did a little windowpane that set him off into a Manson mood? Talk about moody! The Painted Lady had been walking a thin line between reality and madness for some time. Maybe she'd had a thing for Nolan and couldn't handle his fondling Kate all night at the awards dinner.

Dwight had the expertise, the training, the killer's instinct to do the deadly deed. But why? Nolan was his meal ticket, his number-one client. What about you, Speedy? Tired of living in Dwight's shadow as the number two man in TV? Maybe you wanted to handle the Goodlys?

Matty's eyes darted back and forth between both ends of the table. Those were the two he *really* didn't want to think about. Rankoff. Mysterious, moody, enigmatic Bobby Rankoff, who had obviously had a fling with Kate Baker (one of many such "lemon-haired ladies" as he had subsequently learned from Lindsay). Had it been jealous rage? Male menopause? A *crime passionelle?*

Steerforth. How about it, James? What the hell is this piece of black jade in my pocket? What does it all mean . . . sly dog?

"Think we've examined all our factional options?" asked Foley, breaking the silence. "I resent the network dumping the Goodlys after this accident. The years spent bringing that family along, watching them grow—"

"It's no accident," sneered Jackson. "That was an ugly goddamn murder. Nobody's gonna forget it overnight."

"Their image is shot," shrugged Bazzo. "Lucky to book them into a county fair in Newfoundland after this, Dwight."

"Gloating, aren't you?" snarled Foley. "Where the hell were you last night, Bazzo?"

The dam had burst. What Rankoff had feared most was unleashed in the dining room. Accusations. Threats. Insults. Joy accused Ara of squealing to the cops; Ara all but called Joy a murderess. Bazzo denounced Foley as a zombie and hit man; Foley reiterated his firm belief that Bazzo was a quisling planted among them by the Mafia. The subject switched somehow to Rabaiotti's visit and more paranoia poured forth: What was happening to the agency? Was it up for grabs? How secure were their jobs? And, just for good measure, did anyone have any idea what Gilbert Bobcaygeon was up to?

The manic bickering continued for a good twenty minutes. James Steerforth remained silent through it all. Only when everyone seemed to have run out of spleen and steam did the shaggy-haired Englishman finally speak.

"Everyone quite done?" asked Steerforth, his eyes closed and his chin perched on his clasped hands. "Have we solved the problems of the world? Did we finally find out who killed Jimmy Hoffa?"

"Negative cant," sneered Foley.

"What was that, Dwight? Another bit of your Hari Kislev gibberish, old son? Please, don't dent the table, lad. Bobby paid a king's ransom for it."

Joy giggled with delight. She adored Steerforth. His tones of benign contempt were a welcome respite after everyone else's unleashed fury. The room seemed to relax and everyone knew Steerforth was onto something.

"What have you got?" asked Rankoff.

"First, let me tell you what I don't have. I don't have the ghost of Paul Robeson coming back as a concerned black policeman cleaning up the dope scene and singing, 'Water Boy.' I don't have Laverne and Shirley teaming up with Starsky and Hutch to do a sitcom based on *Private Lives*. I don't have Mork from Ork, Flash Gordon, Mr. Spock, and Buck Rogers teaming up against the Jeffersons on 'Battle of the Network Stars.' I have something strange called entertainment in mind.

"Those poor Mormons had something. Only they and Brigham Young ever knew what it was. I certainly didn't. But they filled a vacuum. Good old-fashioned variety. Don't think that hour ought to vanish."

"Who would you replace them with?" asked Ara.

"Not 'replace,' luv. A phoenix will rise from the ashes of the Goodly hour. A musical series that television has not seen since the golden days of the Fifties. Stars, real-honest-to-God stars will guest every week. Not the talentless cretins who appear on other network shows. We're talking about event television."

Everyone was sitting on the edge of their seats. Old Jimmy could be a spellbinder when he wanted to be.

"At least poor Nolan had the good taste to do himself in during hiatus," continued Steerforth. "His series wouldn't have resumed until July. That gives us six weeks to get this thing off the ground. Everyone is going to have to break their backsides to pull it off. Not just the telly people. All of you." He turned to Foley and asked: "What was the budget on the show?"

"$250,000 an episode," Dwight grunted begrudgingly.

"We made a $25,000 packaging fee. Times twenty-six a season. How much is that?"

"$650,000 a year," answered Matty a second later.

"Alright," said Steerforth. "I propose a show with a $400,000 budget. That would bring the annual packaging fee alone to . . ."

Everyone at the table began scribbling numbers on their yellow legal pads.

"One million and forty thousand dollars!" exclaimed Joy with the delight of a victorious bingo player.

"Give the girl a kewpie doll," purred Steerforth.

"How 'bout another kiss?"

"Cheeky thing."

"Network would never go for that," scoffed Foley. "That kind of budget for a variety series? Who'd star in it? God?"

Steerforth shook his head and replied: "A goddess."

Matty finally broke the puzzled silence. "Inez?"

"She'd never do a TV series," said Rankoff.

"With all due respect, Robert, I know the lady better than you do. Between you and me, old son, her film career's over. Can't sell her anymore. She's not worth the bother. Haven't laid that trip on her yet. But I will. And as she sinks into the depths of despair—as only our Irma can—she will be raised from the dead, lissome Lazarus that she is. She will respond and she will comply. Particularly to the first show with Bette Midler, Barbra Streisand, and Donna Summer. Just the four of them. Singing."

"You'll never get them!" shouted Foley.

"We will. People owe us favors. Old favors." Steerforth stared meaningfully at Rankoff on this line. Rankoff nodded in understanding. Matty was absolutely mystified.

"The caliber will never drop. She'll dance with Baryshnikov, Astaire, and Travolta one week. Sing with Paul McCartney, Bruce Springsteen, and Bob Dylan. She'll do sketches with Danny Kaye, Dudley Moore, and Johnny Carson."

"Can we really get them?" asked Joy.

"Scheherazade, there was a time in this business—before you were born, I fear—when people were judged on talent. Not what a bloody computer printed out. This show is going to be a weekly event. Everyone in the business will be fighting to get on it. We're going to give TV back to the audience in the Eighties."

"Bravo!" cried Matty, leaping to his feet with childlike enthusiasm. He slumped embarrassedly back into his seat when he found his colleagues staring at him curiously.

The assembled agents waited for Rankoff's pronouncement. "I love it. You ought to be running a goddamn network, James."

"I'm just a humble agent."

"You're a fucking genius," countered Joy with unabashed devotion.

"Praise from Caesar," answered Steerforth, returning her service.

The meeting bubbled along for the next hour as the agents discussed possible writers, directors, and producers for the Inez Sanchez show. By the time they were ready to leave for the office, Nolan Goodly's tragedy had been forgotten.

Rankoff added a postscript to the meeting.

"I asked Matty to sit in on the meeting this morning. We've all watched his incredible grasp of the business in the five months he's been with us and admired—sometimes begrudgingly—some of the incredible deals he had no business making in so short a time. Matty will be joining us from now on. Now, let's get back to the office before the clients start negotiating our release."

The agents filed out of the dining room and outside to their cars. Matty remained behind in stunned silence. Why had Rankoff chosen that morning to make him a senior agent? Why was he being rewarded so quickly? Or was it a payoff? For what? His silence? What did Matty know? What did Rankoff *think* he knew?

"Congratulations, old son."

"I thought you left."

"Not without my envelope." Steerforth held his hand out.

"How about some answers first?"

"Stop acting like an agent, Matthew. Give me the envelope."

"I know what's inside it."

"Do you?"

"The police found a piece of black jade next to Nolan's body."

"Fancy that."

"Don't fuck me around, Jimmy. I don't want to be an accessory to—"

"To what? What the hell are you accusing me of?"

"I don't know. Everything's been happening so quickly to me—"

"Too much too soon?"

"It's not funny, James. What's to stop me from going to the police with this?"

"Don't think you will."

"Why not?"

"Because I have something to offer you in exchange."

"What?"

"My secret."

They drove in silence in Steerforth's car down the hill from the Trousdale Estates and onto Doheny Road. At Sunset they made a right onto Doheny Drive and drove south past Santa Monica, past Wilshire until they arrived at Pico. Steerforth turned west for a few blocks until he found a parking spot. He got out of the car and a confused Matty followed him as he crossed the street and walked into a small barber shop.

The tiny shop was deserted except for the barber seated in one of the two chairs reading the air-mail edition of the *News of the World*. The barber turned around at the sound of the footsteps, folded his newspaper, and rose from the chair. Matty was amazed. The man was ramrod tall, well over six feet, with the bearing and moustache of a colonel in the British Infantry. A monocle dangled from a gold chain around his neck and he popped it into his right eye to take a better look at his visitors.

"Wondered what had become of you," remarked the handsome elderly barber with the clipped tones of a West End British theater star. "Not like you to be late."

"Sorry," replied Steerforth with marked deference. Matty had never heard Steerforth apologize to anyone in all the time he'd known him.

"This, I take it, is Mr. Garber. Wondered when he'd bring you along. Willie doesn't often speak of people from the office with admiration."

The barber held his hand out and Matty shook it. The man had a powerful grip. Who was Willie?

"Have a seat, Mr. Garber," said the barber, gesturing to the chair closest to the street. "While I take care of this boy. Come on, lad. Warmed it up for you." He patted the seat he'd just been sitting in. Steerforth sat down and, with considerable dramatic flourish, the barber tossed a sheet out into the air, spread it out over Steerforth's seated frame and fastened it round his neck. Picking up his scissors and comb, the barber began snipping gingerly at the agent's hair.

"Gather from the radio you had a spot of bother last night"

"That's putting it mildly, Uncle."

Matty leaned across the chair hoping his mouth wasn't open.

"Are you his uncle? His real uncle?"

"Didn't you tell him?" asked the barber. "Sly dog." The barber shifted around to stare at Matty. "He's my sister's boy. Ivor Manning is my name."

"How do you do, sir?" That was all Matty could say as he let it all sink in. He burst out laughing. "Your secret is out. Your uncle cuts your hair."

"Rather you didn't tell anyone," said Steerforth, staring at Matty in the large mirror hanging on the wall.

"But why? What a crazy thing to keep secret!"

"That's not the secret," murmured Steerforth.

"How long has this been going on?"

"Been cutting Willie's hair for fifteen years," replied Uncle Ivor. "Must admit he's the best-groomed man in Hollywood. For the present period, of course. Cary Grant, naturally, is my all-time favorite. Willie does run a close second, even if he is my nephew."

"Willie?"

Ivor bent forward toward his nephew's ear. "What have you told him?"

"Nothing."

"You are a strange boy. Ahhh! You've brought him here so I should tell him. Is that it? Want me to tell him everything?"

"Six of one, half a dozen of the other."

"You are a scamp, Willie. Truly. Well, Mr. Garber! Where to begin? It's like something out of Dickens. It *is* out of Dickens. His name."

"You're not James Steerforth," Matty stated flatly, as if it was the first line in a typed confession.

"Give us the paper, Uncle," said Steerforth, hoping to avoid any participation in the story. Ivor passed him the *News of the World*.

"Found another bishop in a wardrobe with a member of the Boys' Brigade."

"Be quiet, Willie. He's from Derbyshire, this one. Bakewell. Famous for its tarts. The edible variety. Pastry edible. His name is Willie Stubbs. Of course, I never knew him as Willie Stubbs. The only Stubbs I ever knew was Archie Stubbs, his father. Married my little sister. Beautiful girl, she was. Poor old Archie never forgave God for not making him an American. Worse. Not making him an American gangster. His father was absolutely besotted with the films. Lived in the cinema at Bakewell! My poor sister. What do you do when your husband comes home late at night pretending to be Edward G. Robinson or Cagney or Bogart? Course it didn't make matters any easier that I was living out here. Old Archie was waiting for me to become a star in films so he could come out and manage me or something."

"Were you an actor?"

"Not really. I was tall and I was handsome. Shed my Northern accent along the way. Everyone said I ought to be in films. Was, too, for a while. Ever seen *Lives of a Bengal Lancer?*"

"Sure! What did you play?"

"I was in the third row of mounted horsemen behind Gary Cooper and Franchot Tone. Practically invisible when you see it on television. They showed it at the Vagabond last year and I popped along to have a peek. Still invisible. Best part I ever had was in *Gunga Din*. Speared through the heart standing next to Cary Grant. Actually it was Cary, who suggested giving up my dreams of stardom and becoming his barber. Cut his hair for a lark when we were shooting up at Lone Pine. Ended up cutting all their hair. Fairbanks, MacLaglen, Olivier, Niven, Aherne, Rathbone, Rains, Draycott—"

"You were Roley Draycott's barber?"

"For years. A dear man. Dead now, you know."

"No, he's not! I live with him!"

"You never told me that," said Ivor, admonishing his nephew, who was critically assessing a scantily clad bit of crumpet on page three of Britain's most famous scandal sheet

"Must have slipped my mind."

"Humph! Now where were we? Oh, yes. They were all my customers. The entire British colony. Roland Young, Nigel Bruce, Edmund Gwenn, George Sanders. He was my favorite. Of course he wasn't really British. Russian, you know. He was always filled with advice, old George. He once told me in that gorgeous baritone: 'Ivor, three things you must never take to a Hollywood party: a hat, a coat or a date. Thus, if the occasion proves an insufferable bore one can make one's way toward the bathroom and climb out the window sans impedimenta.' Poor George. Did hate being bored. Am I rambling? Happens when you get to be seventy-four."

"You're not!" exclaimed Matty in astonishment, thinking Ivor must have been a child in the Thirties.

"He is," piped up Steerforth.

"Cheeky sod!" said Ivor, rapping his nephew on the head with his knuckles. "Old Archie, his father, started dragging him off to the cinema soon as he was old enough to keep quiet and not fidget in his seat. Well, Willie here fell in love with the films as well. But not the gangsters. Oh, no! Not this little chap. Fell in love with the beautiful ladies. Lana Turner, Hedy Lamarr, Rita Hayworth, and Ann Sheridan. All those sultry sirens of the Forties. Used to steal movie magazines for fear the lads in the village would see him buying them. Old Archie thought him a raging poof for a while there. Then he thought it rather quaint. A ten-year-old walking around Bakewell like Tyrone Power. That's when Archie started writing to me. Begging me to adopt him so he could come to Hollywood and live like a film star."

Steerforth remained silent throughout all this tale, burying himself deeper and deeper into the *News of the World*. Matty stared at him throughout, trying to imagine this self-assured Machiavelli ever having been Willie Stubbs of Bakewell.

"I couldn't adopt him. Out of the question. He had parents. And I was a bachelor. Quite happy to remain so. Came close to marrying a few times. Always thought I'd wait a few more years. Waited too long now. I'm very vain. Bit of a peacock. Can't go and marry one of those little bunnies on the beach. Be dead in a fortnight. Where am I going to find a beautiful woman close to my age? Find her for me, Mr. Garber, and you'll have a match."

"How did Willie finally get out here?"

"On the *Queen Mary,*" replied his uncle.

"How did you manage that?"

"As a steward," replied Steerforth, his nose still buried in the paper. "Fifteen but I looked older."

"All those films that did it."

Steerforth, folded up the paper and took up the rest of the story himself. "Wanted to get out of that town so badly. That country. Ran off to London and lied about my age. They sent me down to Southampton. Can't tell you the thrill when we left the harbor knowing the next thing we'd see would be the Statue of bloody Liberty. Seen her in so many films, I was shaking at the prospect. Even though I couldn't go ashore for more than an afternoon.

"We'd been out to sea for about two days when I had to deliver a tray to a first-class cabin in. Been busy chatting up all the passengers. Trying out the old Hollywood charm. Bit of your Cary Grant. Touch of your Ray Milland. Good tips. Knew all their room numbers, too. When I rapped on this door it was someone who'd never been out of their cabin. A woman's voice said: 'Come in.' My life's been a nightmare ever since."

Steerforth was staring blankly into space as he had done on the flight back from Vegas. Matty was uncertain if he'd continue with the story or not.

"She was sitting up in bed in a negligee." Steerforth had finally resumed his tale. "Looked just like Virginia Mayo. I went all hard and she must have noticed. Next thing she had me in bed with her. Hardly got out of that bed the rest of the voyage. I'd only known tarts till then. The Bakewell variety and others. Usually in doorways. Standing up. None of them had ever smelled like her. Or knew the tricks she did. She was Hollywood to me. Must have been water after some sexual drought to her. She'd ring room service every hour. Always ask for me. At nights I'd sneak into her cabin. She was rich, too. Married to an old man who'd been keeping her under lock and key. He finally let her go to Europe. With armed escorts. She was the randiest bitch I'd ever known. I was fifteen.

"Saw the Statue of Liberty from her porthole. Must have been tears in my eyes 'cause she asked if I'd like to go to New York with her. She smuggled me ashore in her bloody trunk. spent three hours just sniffing her underwear waiting to be unpacked."

"Wow!"

"Set me up in a little room in Greenwich Village and she'd come over every afternoon and fuck me silly. That went on for three months. I was afraid to go out in the street for fear the cops would arrest me and have me deported. Then she stopped coming. Vanished. The landlord turned up asking for the rent. Had to get out of there. She'd bought me a suit and some shirts. Packed them up and the only book that had been in the room. *David Copperfield*. Must have read it eight times. James Steerforth became my alter ego. And I became him."

"Did you ever see her again?"

"Not till the other month. When we went to Vegas."

"Sylvia Nardino?"

Steerforth nodded.

"Why did you run away?" asked a bewildered Matty.

"Because she knew who I was."

"Twenty-five years ago! More. She'd never have recognized you."

"I recognized her. Couldn't take a chance. I'm in this country illegally. Not going to give up everything. Not going to go back to being Willie Stubbs."

Matty rose and walked over to Steerforth. He rested his hands on the arms of his colleague's chair, and stared into his frightened eyes.

"You are one of the most powerful and respected men in this business. You've taken nonentities and turned them into stars. Goddesses! Yet you have lived in fear for twenty-five years since jumping ship? Afraid to tell anyone where you live, what your phone number is, where you get your hair cut. Are you crazy?"

"There!" Uncle Ivor pronounced triumphantly. "Not just me. Someone else agrees."

"But I'm illegal! Been breaking the law all these years."

"There's a statute of limitations! Get a lawyer! Christ! We've got our own immigration lawyer at the agency. You're a special talent. We can get letters from every name in the business. You could have a green card tomorrow."

"Really think so?" asked Steerforth warily.

"You can't go on living this shadow life. It's madness.."

"Grown so used to it."

"All these years, who have you besides your uncle?"

"No one."

Matty held his hand out to Steerforth.

"Here. Take it. Please. Let me be your friend. Let me help you. Be someone you can talk to. Someone you can trust. You can't go on like this, Jimmy."

"Go on," urged Ivor. "Take his hand. He wants to be your friend."

Steerforth felt trapped in the barber chair. He bolted out of it, rushed over to the window and he stared out at the traffic on Pico for the longest time. When he finally turned around, his eyes were wet and he held his hand out to Matty.

"Thank you," gasped Steerforth, pumping the younger man's hand gratefully. "Never thought I'd be doing this."

"Can't believe you've been living like this. As if the Gestapo are hunting you."

"Starts as a real fear and becomes a phobia," shrugged Steerforth. "Thought of going to see a psychiatrist ten years ago, but was certain the shrink would turn me in. Feel like a bloody hundred-pound weight's been taken off my shoulders."

"Here," said Matty and handed him the envelope containing the black jade.

"Want to tell you about this," said Steerforth.

"Not necessary."

"You're dying to know, you little snoop . . . I got it from Inez."

"What was she—"

"Someone gave it to her. Part of a set. She had nothing to do with Nolan. Believe me."

"Then who—?"

"Can't tell you that right now. It's important I handle this on my own. Will you trust me and give me that space? As a friend?"

"Sure."

"Okay. Let's go back to work and make some deals. Good-bye, Uncle."

"Cheerio. Bring him round for dinner some evening."

"I shall."

"Good-bye, Mr. Manning," said Matty, crossing to the handsome mustachioed barber and shaking his hand. "It's been a pleasure meeting you."

"Call me Ivor."

"Okay. If you call me Matty."

"Delighted we've met at last, Matty."

"Shall I say hello to Mr. Draycott for you?"

"Would you, please? Tell him I'm delighted he's still alive. So few of us left, you know."

The two agents dodged the cars racing westward in the direction of Twentieth Century-Fox studios.

"Does he make a living?" asked Matty as a sleek Porsche nearly removed his kneecap.

"Uncle Ivor? Does all right for himself. Goes over to the Hillcrest Country Club a few days a week."

"Haircuts?"

"No. Bridge. Fantastic player. Socked his money away when he was young. Never had a family to take care of. Has a lovely house in Cheviot Hills. All paid for. Probably worth half a million, my uncle."

"So we don't have to take a tag day for him?"

"No fear. Just find him a wife or a live-in. Randy old sod."

Steerforth unlocked the car doors. Matty slid into the passenger seat and began to giggle.

"What is it now?"

"In the mailroom, there were two great mysteries to be solved. One was how you managed to keep your hair the same length every day. I know the answer to that now."

"What was the other one?"

"Whether the Painted Lady's boobs were real or not."

"You're on your own with that one, old son."

DAVENPORT

The secretaries on the third floor were absolutely terrified. They had grown accustomed to Mr. Rankoff's abrupt shifts of mood through the years but the obscene shouting and rage emanating from his office that July morning was something else. His voice could be heard echoing up and down the corridor and everyone—agents, secretaries, and clients alike—were grateful they weren't on the receiving end.

"What the fuck possessed you guys to do something like that?" demanded Rankoff as shamefaced Stu Jackson and Matthew Garber stood in front of his desk like cadets at West Point being chewed out as they had never been before. "How could you have let something like this happen?"

"We didn't know it would end up this way," murmured Jackson. "Honest."

"We thought he'd get a kick out of it," said Matty.

"Jesus Christ!" Rankoff continued to rage. "Don't you have any fucking foresight? Do you know what you've done to him? You've probably ruined his marriage. Should have heard his wife on the phone shrieking at me. Harriet, who never raised her voice in all the years I've known her. The man trained under me. He's the straightest son-of-a-bitch in this town and you fucking assholes have ruined him."

"Must be something we can do," said Jackson hopefully.

"Like what? Bust him out of jail? Jail! Can't believe the fucking word is coming out my mouth. Speedy's in jail! Little Ronny Liebowitz, whose biggest worry is whether his kid is going to have an *aliyah* in *shul* on Saturday. Tell me what we're gonna do, Stu! Come on, big guy! You dreamed this one up; dream up a better one. And you, boy wonder! Can't believe you were in on this."

"It was a joke," replied Matty pathetically. "Who knew?"

"I could have told you!" thundered Rankoff from Olympian heights. "You don't take a guy like him and put him into that situation. Holy shit! What are we going to do? That's all I want to know."

"Think we should call a lawyer?" offered Matty feebly.

"Garber, I'm trying to kill this thing. Not get it into court! Ohhhh, God! Can't believe you guys did this! If you wanted to murder the poor prick intentionally, you couldn't have dreamed up a worse way of doing it."

A gentle tapping at the door and Lindsay stuck her head in.

"Sorry, Mr. Rankoff, but Mr. Feingold's on the phone and—"

"I can't talk to him!"

"He says it's urgent."

"Have to call him back."

Matty interjected, "He's probably calling about—"

The look Rankoff shot Matty made it clear he wanted the disgraced whiz kid from St. Louis to keep his mouth shut.

Matty felt five years old. He couldn't believe the whole mess had started a week earlier.

***

Matty had pulled his car into IA's underground parking garage. Stu was chatting with Speedy Liebowitz and Matty walked over to join them. Speedy was recounting his latest light-bulb joke.

The three agents laughed but went silent as an incredibly built young redhead from the typing pool wandered across the floor of the garage toward the elevator.

Speedy groaned with frustrated anguish. "It's not fair," moaned Liebowitz. 'I'm going to be forty next week and I've missed out on all of that."

"She's a moron," said Matty.

"Who cares?" wailed Speedy. "Do you know how many of them I represent? How many of them I'm Uncle Ronny to? And all I'd like one of them to do is sit on my face for a few hours. You guys are so lucky. You're bachelors. You can swing."

"Hey, man," said Stu, putting a comforting hand on the TV agent's shoulder. "You can, too. Harriet doesn't have to find out."

"Oh, come on, Stu! Where would I do it? Who would I do it *with*?"

The elevator arrived and the three got in. Matty and Stu exited on the third floor leaving the forlorn Speedy to ride up to the fourth with his unrequited fantasies.

Matty arrived at his desk and Karyn, his Australian secretary, handed him a list of phone messages that had already come in from the answering service before the agency opened.

"What time do these people get up?" mused Matty, seeing one call clocked in at seven fifteen.

"Mr. Rankoff wants to see you in his office right away."

"Thanks, Karyn. Just keep those messages piling up."

"Good morning, Mr. Garber," chirped Lindsay with correct professional detachment as he walked into Rankoff's office.

"Good morning, Miss Fairweather. Did I leave that hickey on your neck last night?"

"Where?" she asked with alarm then realized he was teasing her. "You bastard. What time did you leave?"

"One. You were sound asleep and I had to do some more reading this morning."

"I hate waking up and you're not there."

"Maybe we can do something about that"

"He's waiting for you inside," she said, trying to steer the cozy conversation back on a business plane.

Matty knocked on the door of the inner office and walked in to discover Stan Feingold sitting in a chair next to Rankoff's desk. His cowboy boots were resting atop a pile of scripts and he wore a pair of skin-tight leather pants and a purple satin cowboy shirt. He'd grown a smudge goatee since Matty had seen him last

"Whaddaya say, kid?" asked Feingold, winking at him.

"You look like John Garfield in *Juarez*."

"Oh, yeah? Thanks. I worked with him, you know. I was an understudy in the revival of *Golden Boy* just before he died."

"You were an actor?"

"Oh, yeah. Steve Fairley was my name. Did a couple of shows in New York. But *Golden Boy* was my first job. Helluva cast, too. Julie,

Lee Cobb, Joe Wiseman, Jack Warden, and Jack Klugman. Learned a lot from those guys."

"I'll bet."

"Can we cut this excursion down memory lane short?" asked Rankoff. "Your father-in-law's going to phone me any minute and I haven't got any answers for him."

"Don't worry about Abe," said Feingold, swinging his feet off the desk. "It's lunchtime in New York. He's usually shtupping that *schvartze* secretary of his. Have you met my father-in-law yet, Matty? He's a trip. Got a glass eye and when he wants to put you on the spot he makes you sit in a corner so the sunlight bounces off it and blinds you. He's also a midget with toilets custom built to his height. Sit down to take a crap, your knees go up over your head."

"Stanley, will you shut up already!" Rankoff had difficulty dealing with Feingold when he was coked that early in the morning.

"Okay, Magic Man, okay. Read us the morning line."

Rankoff lit a cigarette and got up to walk around the room. "As you are aware, Matthew, we have been unable to find a director within this agency suitable to the subject matter of *Ektalon-Z.*"

"Right."

"Ironically, your first instinct was correct when you read the script for me. Rees Davenport is . . . the only man to direct it. But we have a slight problem there." Rankoff paused. Matty wondered if the agency boss was actually going to mention that his wife was living with the controversial director.

"You see, kid," said Feingold, leaning across to Matty, "we've got the necessary components for a package already. Myself, the screenwriter, and the two women on board the space ship."

"What women?" asked Matty.

"You haven't read the revised script," explained Rankoff.

"We needed some tits and ass," interrupted Feingold.

"For reasons of a personal nature," continued Rankoff, "I can't enter into negotiations with Davenport or his agent. Stanley has his own difficulty—"

"I broke a beer bottle over his head in Durango two years ago making a Bronson movie," grinned Feingold. "He needed eight stitches. Called me a fag."

Rankoff sunk his face into his palms, shook his head, and tried to continue. "Someone has to talk to Davenport on our behalf. Someone he doesn't hate."

"Which eliminates 99 percent of the people in this town," cracked Feingold.

"Stanley, let me finish! You have a knack, Matthew, a gift of drawing people out, getting their stories. You're also a movie freak, which will appeal to Davenport. Take the script to him personally. Sit there while he reads it. Stroke him, *schmooze* him, arm wrestle with him. Just get a commitment from him."

"Do I make him an offer?" Matty asked Feingold.

"There's half a million in the budget" replied Slippery Stan. "Play with it."

***

Rees Davenport turned the last page of the *Ektalon-Z* script in his Malibu living room and gazed through the sliding glass doors at the porch where the broad-shouldered, bespectacled kid from the agency was waiting for a decision.

Not a bad script. Certainly enough potential for a visually exciting film that might break new ground in the already hackneyed genre of sci-fi movies. He could have fun with the women, too. Especially when they were stuck on the space shuttle.

Davenport chuckled at the idea floating through his mind. The image of the two women lashed to the giant gyroscope. Reminded him of an old fable his grandfather Stanislaus had told him as a child in New Hope, Pennsylvania.

New Hope. He closed the script and stared across the room at the sabers, pistols, and rifles displayed on the far wall until his eyes came to rest on the portrait of the Polish hussar charging into battle. It was not a drawing of his grandfather but since he'd first discovered the picture years before in a junk store on Western Avenue it was how he'd always imagined old Stanislaus at the turn of the century.

His grandfather had been the only bright spot in Karel Rybnik's bleak childhood in the Pennsylvania mining town. (It would not be until his twenty-first birthday that Karel would change his name to Rees Davenport to go with his new identity.) Karel's father was a slave in the mines, an immigrant who had come to America in search of a dream and only found hell on earth deep in the bowels of the New Hope colliery. His life was a caricature of hopelessness: up at dawn, slaving in the mines till the night was as dark as the shaft he went half-blind in all day. Getting drunk in the company saloon after work to erase some of the pain. Then home to his ungrateful wife, whom he usually battered about from frustration. All the while little Karel would sit at his grandfather's feet listening to tales of long ago Poland, cavalry charges, honor, and the beautiful women who were an officer's reward.

Occasionally Karel would attempt to write his impressions of his grandfather's romantic tales. His father would find the stories and tear them up out of spitefulness.

"Stop filling his head with bullshit!" his father would drunkenly threaten old Stanislaus. "He'll end up in the pit the same as me."

Karel would never go down in the pit. He vowed that to himself at the age of sixteen when he stood at the edge of his grandfather's grave. He would carry on the tradition of the hussars. He, too, would be a horseman.

He hitchhiked out to Wyoming and went to work on the Davenport Ranch near Spotted Horse. He was taken under the wing of a man named Rees Jenkins, who taught him everything about horses, roping, branding. He married a local girl when he was eighteen and had a kid by her. But the dreams of glory never died within him and drink only magnified them. The ranch was too confining. He needed adventure and his quest usually resulted in a night's stay in the Spotted Horse drunk tank.

He fought with his wife and eventually left her. He was determined to become a writer and on his twenty-first birthday he buried Karel Rybnik, became Rees Davenport, and headed south for California to follow his dreams.

It was 1950 when he arrived in Hollywood with a battered suitcase and a dozen hand-written short stories. Six months later he was unemployed and suicidal. He was about to buy a bus ticket back to Spotted Horse when he got a job as a stagehand at CBS on the "Bobby Rankoff Hour."

Davenport was nervous as a cat five minutes before air time. It was his first show and Rankoff's guests included Fred Allen, Jane Powell, and Joan Davis. The studio audience was strictly SRO as always for the popular singer's show. Rankoff turned up ten minutes before the program was scheduled to go on the air with Yvonne Corday, his beautiful wife, on his arm. He introduced her and that week's guests to the audience, who went wild with applause. Rankoff answered a few questions from his fans, took his place at the microphone, and waited for the red light to go on. The band started to play "Our Last Embrace", the show's theme song.

The show was running smoothly for the first fifteen minutes. Rankoff captivated the audience with "Latin Lady" and "Night and Day." Joan Davis was introduced and did a comic sketch with Rankoff.

After the commercial break, they returned with Jane Powell's rendition of "I Feel a Song Coming On." Following that Powell and Rankoff did a medley from *Annie Get Your Gun.*

Davenport was loving every minute of it. He felt he belonged. He was in 'the business' now, as everyone at CBS referred to it. He was preparing the prop table for the Fred Allen spot that would follow the next commercial. He was lifting a huge triangle that would punctuate one of Allen's gags when it slipped from his hands and landed on the floor with a terrible clanging sound.

Rankoff was in the middle of "The Girl That I Marry" when the crash occurred. It so startled Bobby that he jumped four notes in front of the band and screwed up the rest of the song. Mercifully the commercial followed the number and was prerecorded and transmitted from the control booth.

"I—I'm sorry," murmured Davenport, bending down to retrieve the triangle.

"Get rid of him!" Rankoff shouted to the stage manager.

"Oh, come on, Bobby," said the stage manager appeasingly, "It was just a—"

"He fucked up my number! I want him fired. I don't want to see him anymore."

Yvonne, who was a guest on the show, walked over to her husband and stroked the sleeve of his mohair jacket. "Bobee, it was an accident. The poor man didn't mean to—"

"Goddammit!" raged Rankoff. "Is this my show or not?"

The band began to play "There's No Business Like Show Business" to keep the audience from hearing the brouhaha onstage.

"Please, Mr. Rankoff." Davenport was near tears. "I really need this job. Haven't worked in six months—"

"I can see why," replied Rankoff, walking away from him. "You're a half-wit"

Davenport spent six weeks searching for another job and finally ended up as a night watchman at Bekin's Storage. It would be two years before he found work connected with show business again. He would marry once more during that two-year period and have that marriage go on the rocks as well. He would drink harder and get in worse fights. Be eaten up with self-loathing, frustration, and pain. He would blame it all on one man: Bobby Rankoff.

Someday, Davenport vowed, he would have his revenge on the man.

"Wha'd you say your name was?" asked Davenport, stepping out onto the sun deck to confront his visitor.

"Matt Garber." Matty was staring up at the creased and weather-beaten face of the director with the steel gray brush cut and thirties style moustache. He thought if Howard Hughes, John Dillinger, and G. Gordon Liddy had been tossed up and down in a paper bag they'd have come out as Rees Davenport.

"Want a beer?"

"Sure." Matty did his best to growl back at the director but just couldn't hit the sandpaper depths old Red Meat could.

Davenport bent over a tiny fridge beside the door and pulled out two cans of Foster's Lager. "Only good thing about that goddamn picture I made in Australia was discovering this stuff."

"I liked *Dingo*," said Matty, ripping the top off the can.

"You saw it?" asked Davenport through a hearty belch.

"Twice. Got the feeling it must have been chopped to pieces."

"It was mutilated. Some fag took over the studio halfway through the picture and— Aaah, shit! Same old story. Goddamn studios butcher my cuts and I'm the one gets dumped on by the critics. Bunch of fags and Jews!"

Matty felt the hairs standing up at the back of his neck and wasn't prepared to let the remark go by—deal or no deal.

"I'm Jewish myself."

"Queer, too?"

"No."

"So relax. Don't always mean what I say. Nor do I always say what I mean. Want another beer?"

"Just started this one."

"You drink like a Jew." Davenport crossed back to the fridge to get himself another Foster's Lager. "It's a hot mother-fucker today. What's that line about heat? 'I cannot praise a fugitive and cloistered virtue, unexercised and unbreathed, that never sallies out and sees her adversary, but slinks out of the race, where the immortal garland is to be run for, not without dust and heat.' Yeah . . . That's where your boss is a pussy."

Matty was stunned. He wasn't ready for a Rees Davenport who could quote Milton. He swallowed more beer then asked, "'What did you think of the script?"

"Piece of shit. But I can fix it."

"Then you'll do the picture?"

"Not so fast, sonny. Why'd they send you out to see me?"

"They thought I could talk to you."

"Those chicken shits were afraid to come out themselves, huh?"

" 'Peace hath her victories no less renowned than war.' "

"You like Milton?" asked Davenport, taken aback by Garber's quote.

"Not particularly. But it's stuck in my head. Thought you might get a kick out of the script because it reminded me of that old *Have Gun, Will Travel* you wrote about the chase across the Mojave."

"How the hell would you remember that? You weren't even born."

"Caught the tail end of all those western shows. Some of your *Gunsmokes* were classics."

"Yeah. They won't show them anymore 'cause they weren't in color. Ever see the one about Chester's fiancée getting killed? Actually had someone quoting from Spenser in that show. Try getting Elizabethan poetry on the air now!"

"Did you go to college?"

"I was my own college. Back in Wyoming. Where you from?"

"St. Louis."

"Got the show biz fever, huh? This place is a magnet for every fucked-up dreamer who ever thought he could leave his mark on a world that don't give a shit. Y'ever seen so many assholes in your life chasin' their tombstones? That pussy Rankoff's the worst of 'em. And that little sidekick of his. That gutless runt Feingold. That little cocksucker came up behind me in Mexico and hit me on the head with a lead pipe."

"Heard it was a beer bottle."

"That what it was?" grinned Davenport. "Felt like a lead pipe."

"Why would he want to do something like that to a nice guy like you?"

Davenport let loose the laugh of a wild stallion and slapped his knees.

"Goddamn! Gutsy colt, aren't you? Come on! Drink up! Got a fridge full o' beer."

Matty finished off the can and decided if it didn't work out for him at IAA he might join the diplomatic corps. All merely a question of patience and a cast-iron stomach.

"Here! Try some of this with it." Davenport passed him another can of Foster's Lager and a bottle of tequila.

"I really don't think—"

"Don't think. Drink!"

Four cans of beer and a bottle of tequila later Matty had trouble remembering what he had come out to the beach to see Rees Davenport about.

The director by this time was hanging over the railing of the sun deck staring out toward the Pacific.

"Hey, Morty—"

"Matty."

"Matty, c'mere."

Matty managed to struggle to his feet and made it to the railing before his legs gave out on him. Davenport was pointing toward the sand where a beautiful, blond-haired girl in a stunning one-piece bathing suit was rushing up out of the water like some erotic sea nymph.

"Is that a ten, boy? I'm askin' you?"

"She's lovely,"

"Don't be such a goddamn perfessor. We're talking like men here. We're lookin' at a piece of ass. Look at her! Wouldn't you want to throw her down on the sand right now and stick yer prick into her till she howled like a coyote? Wouldn't you like to spread her legs apart and stick your head in between them right up inside her and eat her like a melon? Wouldn't you? Well, wouldn't you?"

"God, yes!" intoned Matty drunkenly. 'I'd like to fuck her silly."

"That's the woman I live with, boy," said a deadpan Davenport.

Matty felt ill. What had he done? Worse: What was Davenport going to do to him? Were the pistols going to come off the living room wall? Or the rifles? Well, Garber, you drunken bum, you got yourself into this. Face it like a man.

He turned stone-faced to Davenport, who merely burst into his wild stallion laugh once again.

"Sure walked into that one, sonny." He waved to the stunning sea nymph drying herself with a beach towel.

"How ya doin', gal?"

"Hello, my darling!" called out Sabina Rankoff.

"Get yer butt up here. Someone I want you to meet."

Matty stared at the still-grinning director and asked: "Do you know Jimmy Steerforth?"

"The agent? Never met him."

"You should. The two of you would get on like a house on fire. Same sense of humor."

Sabina climbed up the steps to the deck and threw her arms around Rees, drowning him in kisses like an affectionate dog might its master. She turned to Matty and held her arm outstretched.

"Hello. I'm Sabina Rankoff."

"Matt Garber," he replied shyly, shaking her hand.

"Matt here was just admirin' you, darlin' girl. Weren't you, Matt?"

"Did he set you up?" asked Sabina. "Don't pay any attention to him."

Davenport slapped her wet behind. The sound it made caused Matty to wince. More than a playful tap.

"You hurt me, Rees."

"Did I? Didn't mean to. Whyn't you go make us something to eat? I'm starvin'."

"Please, don't bother on my account," said Matty.

"I want her to bother," replied Davenport coldly. "She's too damned spoiled. That's what came from bein' married to that pussy Rankoff. She didn't do nothin' with him? Didja ever cook? No! Didja ever clean the house? No!"

"He had a butler," she replied in a teeny-weeny voice like a frightened child. "He never let me—"

"I know. That butler did everything. Did he fuck you, too? 'Cause sure as hell Rankoff didn't."

"Please, Rees. Don't talk about this now!"

"Why not? He works for Rankoff. You know all about Bobby-baby. Don't you, Matt? Know about his little girls?"

"Maybe I'd better come back another—" Matty's head was spinning and he couln't handle another anti-Rankoff pitch.

"Scarin' you off, boy? That what's happening?"

"I came here on business."

"Then le's talk business." He turned on Sabina. "What the hell do you want?"

"Wha—what would you like me to make you?"

"Nothin'. I'll get a hamburger down the beach."

"Please, let me make something for you, Rees!"

"No! Get outta here!"

Sabina ran into the house. Matty was certain he could hear her crying as she vanished into the bedroom.

"You married?" asked Davenport after a long silence.

"Was."

"Don't do it again, boy. Ain't natural. You know Ara?"

"Just from work."

"Bet you can't believe she was once the most beautiful woman in the world. The way she looks now! Had an affair with her for two years before we got married. Then it all turned to rat shit."

"Was she married when—"

"Yeah. To my agent."

"Bobcaygeon was your agent?"

"Sure. That's how I met her. He was our link. Neither one of us could stand him. How much they want to pay me?"

"Um . . ." Matty was momentarily thrown by Davenport's abrupt shift in gears. "Not really authorized to deal with you directly but—"

"I want a million from those pussies. Non-negotiable. Tell 'em that."

"They're not going to—"

"They'll pay. 'Cause they want me. Tell them to get me that Israeli for the captain."

"Who?" Matty knew but he didn't really want to hear—

"Yael Shomrim. Need a real military man for that part. Not some goddamn Polo Lounge private. Million dollars and Shomrim or no deal."

By some minor miracle of self-control Matty managed to shake Rees Davenport's hand good-bye. He walked out of the beach house in a straight line while a cocktail of beer, tequila, and images of Lindsay thrashing about between the sheets with Yael Shomrim washed around in his mind. Putting the key in the ignition, he drove about a hundred feet down the road when he realized he was dead drunk. No way he could get the car back to town without causing murder and/or mayhem.

Fortunately, he remembered Minden Prescott's proximity to Davenport's place. Matty prayed Little Miss Mindy would come to the rescue.

"My God, twig!" drawled the writer when he finally opened his front door. "You've fallen on hard times. Any one I know?"

"Sorry to turn up here like this, Minden, but I'm not—"

"The powder room, twig! Very quickly."

Matty made it in time and was violently ill. Prescott steered him into the bedroom and left him alone with the shades drawn.

"Want to close my eyes for a minute," murmured Matty.

The dream was a lulu. Would have made a better science fiction picture than *Ektalon-Z*. Matty and Lindsay were seated behind the wheel of her grandfather's Pierce-Arrow while that old gentleman (played by Roland Draycott) cranked up the motor. Matty thought it a bit odd the car was atop the dining room table, but Lindsay reminded him that it *was* Glendale. The motor finally turned over and the car promptly flew out the dining room window and up, up into space.

They were somewhere between Saturn and Jupiter when the car got a flat. Yael Shomrim appeared in his battered Austin-Healey and offered to help change the tire. It was Matty who did all the work while Shomrim and Lindsay climbed into the back seat of the Pierce-Arrow and began going at it like thieves. Matty tried to ignore this but it was very difficult as Lindsay was screaming and shouting joyous profanities through it all. Which was when a fiery chariot appeared with a demonic Rees Davenport holding the reins. Instead of horses, the chariot was drawn by strange beasts, blood dripping from their mouths. The chariot changed direction abruptly and roared in Matty's direction with Rees howling, "Your turn next! Your turn next!" Closer and closer and closer and—

Matty screamed.

Minden was standing over the bed and reached down to touch Matty's shoulder reassuringly. "It's just a dream."

"Minden?"

"Relax and go back to sleep."

"No, no. I've got to get up. You can open the blinds now."

"They are open."

Matty stared out at the darkness of the ocean then asked: "What time is it?"

"Eight thirty. You've been out for four hours."

"Oh, my God! The office is closed. Bobby must be having a fit"

"Why should this night be different from all other nights? If one may borrow from the Hebrews. Just whipped up shrimp and scallops in garlic and ginger. Join me."

"He sent me out to see Rees Davenport. He's been waiting to hear—"

"Calm down, twig. It'll keep till morning."

"My head's killing me."

"You need food. Come and tell me what that beast Red Meat did to you. Did he use whips and chains?"

"Just tequila."

They sat on opposite sides of the bar in the open plan kitchen poking at the homemade Chinese food with ivory chop sticks while Matty recounted the events of the afternoon.

"When Ara phoned to tell me she was marrying him," said Minden. "I was still living in New York. We'd become friends again. 'What's he like?' I asked. She paused, then answered: 'A butch you.'

"Didn't know whether to be flattered or call my shrink. I must admit his early writing was almost lyrical. He really understood the

West and loved it. Graduated from TV to features and crossed over into directing. His personal life was appalling. Ara used to phone me in the middle of the night shrieking: 'He's beating me! He's beating me!' Usually five in the morning my time and I was always non compos. Once I asked: 'Is this a collect call?' She called me an insensitive queen and didn't speak to me again for two years. By that time she'd divorced him. She really hasn't had much luck with her consorts."

"What do you know about Sabina?"

"Susy? That was her real name. Susy Hepplewhite. Or something like that. Knew her when she was making obscene phone calls for Kinks Unlimited."

"What are you talking about?"

"Years ago I knew a boy named Leroy. Very pretty, he was. We shared a moment, so to speak. But he was an emotional transient. And ambitious. A combination of Horatio Alger and Havelock Ellis. He discovered by the mid-Seventies that most Angelenos—I love that name, don't you?—were ready for something adventuresome in their sexual diets. Probably the same time everyone switched from Cantonese to Szechuan. Problem was the poor little buggers—or would-be buggers —didn't know where to get it. I mean you couldn't walk into Bullocks and ask for a size-six blow job with black velvet and pearls. That's where Leroy filled the vacuum. He set up a sex agency. From home."

"What does this have to do with Sabina? Or Susy?"

"Patience, twig. Never interrupt a master storyteller. The two streams will come together and form a river eventually . . . Susy was from Palmdale. The Land of the Bulge? Poor kid grew up smack on the fault line—something that will never insure security in the young. She had dreams of stardom like us all and made her way to the Sodom and Gomorrah of the Vitamin E set. She did not find work as an actress despite an infuriatingly sexy voice and, down to her last diet pill, she ended up on Leroy's doorstep. A friend of a friend of a friend suggested she might find work.

"Leroy, being the Metternich of licentiousness, knew talent when he saw it and heard it. He started Susy—whom he redubbed Sabina—off with dirty phone calls at ten dollars a pop."

"I don't understand," interrupted a bewildered Matty.

"Oh, twig! What are we to do with you? It's not all peepies in popoes, you know. There are people who get off—you're acquainted with the term?—on hearing dirty words over the phone. They will *pay* to hear a rhapsody of smut brought into their living room by Ma Bell. That was how Sabina started. Eventually she graduated to bigger and better roles. She was particularly noted for her remarkable impersonation of a boy scout while locked in a closet with a certain senior vice-president from Lockheed. She was possibly the most beautiful boy scout I've ever seen."

"Are you making this up?"

"I have Leroy's number if you don't believe me. You can order anything you want. Parties are his specialty. That's how Sabina met your Mr. Rankoff. At a very kinky party in Trancas. I was there. She was dressed like Little Orphan Annie and Bobby fell like a ton of old records. You could hear the crash as far as Yvonne's house. I was flabbergasted when he married her a week later. Leroy lost a great deal of business after Sabina left him. But he found new talent. And he's still going great guns. From home."

Which explains how Matthew Garber managed to come up with his ill-conceived notion of a surprise birthday gift for Speedy Liebowitz.

Rankoff continued to glare in hostility at Jackson and Garber. Lindsay had returned to the outer office to inform Stan Feingold that Bobby couldn't speak to him.

"May I say something," asked Matty feebly.

"What?" demanded Rankoff.

"I'm to blame. Not Stu. It was my idea to hire her."

"Hey, man! I'm not gonna let you take the rap for this alone. We set it up; we paid for her; we picked out the motel."

"At least you guys are loyal," commented Rankoff caustically. "Hope you visit Speedy every weekend."

"Can they really put him away?" asked Matty.

"In the state of California, a little fellatio and a touch of cunnilingus can get you a quick two years inside."

"Where they holdin' him?" asked Stu.

"Van Nuys. He's lucky. Cop house is just around the corner from the motel. You know how energy-conscious Speedy is."

Rankoff's sick jokes were starting to get to Matty. He almost preferred the ranting and raving a few minutes earlier.

There was a knock at the door.

"What is it?" bellowed Rankoff.

Ara walked proprietorially into the office.

"No need to shout, Bobby. I've just been informed Ronald is in jail. Is that true?"

"Oh, it's true."

"What happened?" asked Ara.

"Which one of you Rover Boys wants to tell her about it?"

"Hey, come on, man! I don't wanna talk about this in front of a lady."

"Ara, you want to be a lady or do you want to hear the story?"

"I'm a big girl, Stu."

"We, uh . . . we hired a girl for Speedy. For his birthday. He was forty yesterday."

"Where did you get her from?" asked Ara, as if there'd been a choice between Geary's and David Orgell's.

"Someone gave me a number," murmured Matty after deciding very quickly that it would be far from politic to mention Leroy's name in front of Rankoff.

"You, Matthew? I'm surprised."

"It was a joke, Ara. Like a delayed coming-out party."

"Yeah," corroborated Jackson. "We thought he'd get a kick out of it."

"Aren't they something?" asked Rankoff, sticking the needle in once again. "Nature's noblemen. . . . Go on."

"There's this uh, motel," continued Matty. "In the valley. With waterbeds and X-rated movies on closed circuit TV. We drove Speedy over there yesterday at lunchtime."

"Blindfolded," prompted Rankoff.

"Yeah." Matty had purposely omitted this detail. "We, uh, took him to the door, opened it, and uh . . . pushed him inside. Then we left. She was supposed to drive him back afterward."

"Which didn't happen?" asked Ara.

"No. It didn't work out that way," replied Matty.

"We don't know what happened right after that. Guess they got it on. When Speedy didn't get back to the office by three we started to get worried. We phoned the motel and, uh . . . that's when they told us the police had, uh, raided their room. Speedy and the girl were in jail."

"Why did the police raid their room?" asked Ara.

"We still can't figure that out!" blurted Big Stu. "Just doesn't make sense."

"Can they be charged with simple fornication?" Ara asked Rankoff.

"No," replied the agency boss. "But I gather when the marines landed the hired help was playing *soixante* to Speedy's *neuf*."

"Oh. I see. Oh, dear."

An awkward silence followed until Rankoff started in again. "They've ruined him. Stupid bastards have ruined him. His wife'll leave him for sure. They're the scandal of Encino. She can't show her face in Gelson's."

"Where are they holding him?" asked Ara.

"Van Nuys."

"What have you done about it?" she asked Rankoff.

"What the hell am I supposed to do? They caught them red-handed. Worse! He's going to go down for going down. Little Ronny!"

"We just can't leave him there, Bobby."

"Nothing we can do!"

Ara began pacing the room then walked behind Rankoff's desk, sat in his chair, and picked up the phone. "May I?"

"Sure."

Ara punched in some numbers on Rankoff's phone and waited an inordinate length of time until someone answered.

"Rees, my darling?"

Rankoff's mouth dropped open. Matty was certain his boss was going to have a seizure.

"It's Ara . . . Ara *who?* How many Aras were you ever married to? How many Aras' beds did you put live lobsters into? . . . Yes, it has been a long time. I know you're frightfully busy, Rees, and I don't want to keep you—not that anyone could—but I have to pick your brain. . . . What? No, your brain. Oh, Rees, you're disgusting!" She clapped a hand over the mouthpiece and told the others: "I think he's drunk. Can you believe it? Ten o'clock in the morning! . . . Rees? Are you there, darling? How on earth would I know where you put your shoes? I haven't had to worry about that for fourteen years. Was it only twelve? How sweet of you to be so accurate! But you never forget anything, do you? You have the most infuriating memory of anyone I've ever known. Which is why I'm calling you. Do you remember when we went to Colorado for that Hathaway film you wrote? The one with John Wayne and Glenn Ford. . . . Yes, I know they fucked it up, darling. You can always make it again, Rees. That's not the point . . . The stunt captain. The one I called 'Camp Harry.' He doubled as one of the villains. You know the one I mean. The one who got in trouble. Something like Bottomley. Or Endicott . . . What? Rumpwell! Of course! You are brilliant . . . What? Jesse W. Rumpwell? How on earth can you remember that all these years later? . . . Oh, no particular reason. I was just reminiscing and remembered how you had to bail him out of jail when no one else would help him. There is a sweet side to you, Rees. You just never want to admit it . . Hmmmm? Oh, I don't do too badly, thank you very much. . . . Afraid it's a little late for that. But you're very dear to offer." She clapped her hand over the mouthpiece once more and turned to the others. "The man is a complete degenerate. Matthew, light me a cigarette, please?" Matty lit a cigarette and placed it between the Painted Lady's lips. She smiled her thanks and sucked in the smoke like a fire-breathing dragon. "Must run now, Rees. Truly. It's been exhilarating sharing these moments with you. Well, you're a 'sweet old shithead' yourself. Congratulations, by the way, on *Ektalon-Z*. You're going to make it a huge success. Of course, we're sorry it couldn't be a package for us. But *c'est la vie*! Or *le show biz*. Bye-bye." She replaced the telephone and drew in more smoke. "A remarkable talent ruined by liquor and self-indulgence."

Rankoff had to restrain every urge to have the pot call the kettle black. Instead, he wondered what the hell the Painted Lady was up to. He watched in silence as Ara punched in another number.

"Is Mrs. Shankman there, please? . . . Ara Whalen . . . Thank you . . . Evelyn? Good morning, dear. Trust I'm not disturbing you. Do you recall the charity fair in Van Nuys last year? Crippled Children or something. Was it multiple sclerosis? The agency had a booth. . . . That's right. Do you remember the police officer, who introduced himself to us? The one who'd been an actor. Was his name Rumpwell? *Lieutenant* Rumpwell? My God, Evelyn! What a memory you have! My mind's like a sieve. Don't know what I'd do without you. . ... Oh, please, Evelyn. You're just being kind. Lunch next week? Marvelous! No, not Scandia. All those blue-rinsed matrons who've had 'one martooni too meany.' All crashing their cars on Sunset when they leave the lot at a quarter to three. I can set my watch by them. . . . All right, we'll decide next week. Good-bye, darling." She replaced the receiver once again and asked Rankoff: "Do you have the number of the Van Nuys Police Station?"

A still mystified Rankoff crossed to his desk and pointed to a number on his pad.

"Thank you." Ara dialed the number. "Lieutenant Rumpwell, please. . . . He's *Captain* Rumpwell now?" She clapped her hand over the phone yet again: "Can't believe our luck! . . . Hello? May I speak with Captain Rumpwell, please? . . . Yes. Ara Whalen from the International Artists Agency. . . . Thank you . . . Jesse? Is that you? How marvelous to speak with you again. . . . Ara Whalen. From IAA. You came up to me at the Multiple Sclerosis Fair last year. . . . In Van Nuys . . . You *are* the Jesse Rumpwell who used to be an actor and stunt man? Remember the Henry Hathaway film in Colorado fourteen years ago? My ex-husband Rees Davenport wrote it. . . . *Now* you remember!" She turned to the others: "Turn an actor into a police captain and he thinks he's the goddamn Pope. Could I have another cigarette, please, Matthew?" Light. Cigarette. Action.

"You certainly have done well for yourself, Jesse, I must say. When did you get out of the business, dear? As long ago as that! And do you find law enforcement rewarding? You've certainly made a name for yourself. . . . Now, Jesse, why I'm calling: There seems to have been a terrible miscarriage of justice. You've been holding a man overnight. A senior agent with our company . . . Ronald Liebowitz. . . . Sorry? . . . No, I don't think it's accurate to call him a pervert. I've known Mr. Liebowitz for fifteen years and he is a fine family man and very active in community affairs. . . Jesse, there's no need for you to be graphic. I'm well aware of what he's been charged with. That's why I'm phoning you.

"I was rather hoping you might be lenient. Possibly drop it altogether. The man has a clean record and . . . Jesse, I really don't appreciate your language. Don't recall you being this coarse in Colorado. I'm not getting on my high horse. I do not have a horse. Just hoped for old times' sake . . . You don't remember? Oh. I didn't think it was something you'd forget that easily. Certainly the people in Shoshone, Colorado, haven't forgotten the man who molested those three high school boys. Not molested. Let's say seduced. . . . Jesse? Are you there? I can't hear you, darling. Get some water. Sounds like you're choking. . .. There! Much better. Did you ever see those boys again? Perhaps, you might have kept in touch—no pun intended. Ever told anyone in Van Nuys that story? Wondering how voters would feel knowing Captain Jesse W. Rumpwell is queer as Dick's hat band."

Rankoff was seated on the sofa between the glazed figures of Jackson and Garber staring in awe at his long-time colleague. She had not been Abe Keller's secretary for nothing all those years.

"Jesse, darling," she continued. "No one's trying to be nasty. Think of it as mutual backscratching. Everyone's entitled to a mistake once in their life. What I am curious about is why you sent your men in there to begin with . . . I see . . . Yes . . . I see . . . Yes . . . Fine . . . Well, keep up the good work." Ara replaced the telephone and ran her fingers through her flaming red hair.

The trio on the sofa waited with proverbial bated breath. "Unbelievable!" said the Painted Lady getting up from behind Rankoff's desk. "Someone phoned the station with a tipoff of a drug party going on at the motel. The police obtained a search warrant and raided the place. Unfortunately, they got the room numbers mixed up and walked in on poor Ronald. They couldn't go back empty-handed after all the fuss, so they arrested Ronald and the girl. Isn't that outrageous?"

Ara started across the office toward the door. Rankoff leaped up from the sofa and planted himself in front of her awesome chest.

"What's the bottom line?"

"He's releasing him," she replied matter-of-factly. "All charges are dropped. They're tearing up his rap sheet."

Rankoff dropped to his knees, grabbed her hand, and kissed it. Turning to the others, he ordered: "On your knees, gentlemen, in the presence of a great lady."

Matty and Stu followed suit.

Ara's bosom swelled with pride. She had regained her old prestige and clout. And, if need be, allies in the battle to come with Joy Dworkin.

WHEEZER

By the end of August, Los Angeles is a merciless cauldron of thick, stagnating gases with nowhere to go. The smog is the equivalent of the eleventh plague and warnings known as "first-stage alerts" are issued by the local government. Children and elderly people are advised to stay indoors and avoid any form of exercise. "Second stage alerts" are even more fun: *everyone* is advised to remain indoors. It is at times like these that the residents wonder whether Los Angeles may have been one of God's better practical jokes. "Yes," said the Lord, "I will give you perpetual sunshine and no snow or cold. But I will also give you lethargy beyond belief, debilitating chemical headaches, swollen eyes, and crippling lung disorders. So what's it going to be, children? Window A or Window B?"

It was on one of these relentless late August nights when Roland Draycott sat coughing his lungs up in Ivor Manning's sitting room in the Cheviot Hills south of Century City.

"Can I get you a glass of port, old boy?" asked Ivor. "Don't much like the sound of that cough."

"I've been living with this faulty motor for years, Ivor. Think it's leftover from being gased in '17. I will take you up on that port."

"Had no idea you were in the First War, Roley," said his host passing a glass of rare Cockburn's '47. "How old are you, old boy?"

"Turned eighty three weeks ago."

"Did you indeed? Jolly good show. Don't look a day over seventy."

"What the hell's the difference after sixty-nine? Cheers. Bible only gives us three score and ten. I'm on golden time, as we used to say at the studios. Ahhh! That went down well. Excellent dinner, Ivor. Didn't think you could get good lamb out here. Where did you find that mint sauce?"

"Made it myself. Got a batch growing in the garden. Along with a few other things."

"What sort of things?"

"Bit of marijuana."

"Good gracious, Ivor! You're not a hippie, are you?"

"Bit late for that, old boy. Save it for my dates once in a while."

"You are an old rogue," chuckled Draycott. "But you always were. Delighted we've been able to meet up again. Thought you were snipping St. Peter's hair ages ago."

"And I thought you were in residence at Forest Lawn with the other mummers. We've young Garber to thank for that. More port, old boy?"

"Very kind of you, Ivor. Yes. No sense letting it go to waste, eh? Do you have many . . . dates?"

"Not in the last little bit. But I'm always on the hunt. There you go, old boy." He passed Roley a fresh glass of port. "How is Matthew? Haven't seen him in over a fortnight."

"He's on his way to New York tonight actually. What I believe they call the red eye. I envy him getting away from this filthy weather. Perhaps the trip will cheer him up."

"What's wrong?" asked Ivor.

"He's suffering from a bad case of 'the other man'."

"Not my nephew, is it?"

"Oh, no! James is a gentleman from what I've seen of him. No, no. This chap's an Israeli. Somewhat of a bounder. He's here making a film and Lindsay, Matthew's girl friend, has taken up with him. Bit of a Svengali, the Israeli. Matthew's quite torn up about it."

"Why doesn't he do something? Give this chap a good thrashing!"

"Not that easy, Ivor. There's unfinished history between Lindsay and Mr. Shomrim. She was besotted with him for years. Matthew erroneously thought she'd got him out of her system."

"Oh, dear."

"Yes. He's taking it very badly."

"Mmm. Went through a few of those myself. Remember Madeleine Carroll?"

"I was in *Lloyds of London* with her. Ivor, you didn't—"

"No, no, no, no, no. But I was mad about her. And Evelyn Hughes."

"Ah, Evelyn! Everyone was mad about her. Sid Shankman was a lucky devil getting her."

"He treated her dreadfully," said Ivor. "Never paid any attention to her once he married her. Deals and gambling were all he ever cared about. And his looks. I used to cut his hair three times a week. At his home. He'd be on the phone the whole time. Almost took his ear off once. She was always very gracious to me. 'Mr. Manning' she'd call me. I had fantasies of carrying her off to the desert. I think she'd have gone if I'd only had the gumption to ask. Oh, well, can't mourn the lost opportunities."

Roley paused over his port to reflect then recited:

"Time, you old gypsy man,
Will you not stay,
Put up your caravan
Just for one day?"

"True," said Ivor. "Too true."

***

The sun was coming up over the East Coast as the TWA flight continued its path toward New York City. Matty had been asleep for three hours when he awoke and saw a familiar face smiling across the aisle at him in the deserted first-class section.

"Hi," said Louise Feingold, putting down her book.

"Have a nice sleep?"

"What time is it?" asked Matty, stretching.

"Six. I said hello to you three hours ago but you passed out the minute you sat down."

"Sorry," grinned Matty apologetically. "I was so wiped out. Didn't get away from the office till nine last night. Just had time to go home, pack, and get to the airport."

"Tell me about it. I was an agency widow for twenty years. An agency orphan for twenty years before that. I grew up thinking a telephone was an appendage to my father's ear."

"Meeting your father this morning. Looking forward to it."

"The man has mellowed. He's got time now. Too much time. The business is dead in New York. Why don't you join me?" she asked, nodding to the empty seat beside her.

"Don't you want to sleep?"

"I'll sleep this afternoon. This novel kept me up all night."

Matty got up from his seat and moved across the aisle to join the diminutive Mrs. Feingold.

"What takes you to New York?" he asked.

"Had to get away from the smog," she groaned. "It's murder on my sinuses. On top of which I've become a widow again. Stanley's busy night and day with *Ektalon-Z* and the Tom Ricker movie. I never see him. He probably doesn't know I'm gone. I haven't seen my mother for a couple of months. So . . ."

"How's the Ricker movie going?" Matty had absolute horror stories funneling back from the set of *The Brother Who Fell From Uranus.*

"Fun and games. Crazy Tom Ricker has chosen this vehicle to right all the wrongs perpetrated against his people for the past two hundred years. And continue his longstanding war with IAA."

"What's all that about?"

"My father, I'm afraid. Tony Rabaiotti discovered Tom Ricker in a little club in New York about twelve years ago. Flipped over him. Wanted to sign him. He brought Tom up to the office to meet Daddy. Dis-aster! 'I can't understand a word he's saying, Tony! What the hell's he saying?' Ricker stormed out of the office cursing 'the old Jew' as Daddy has remained ever since. Ricker felt Daddy humiliated him and Daddy thought he was a foul-mouthed *shvartzer*."

"Thought your father was big on civil rights."

"With his checkbook. And on the couch at lunchtime. But that's the extent of it. Thank God *Ektalon-Z's* going well! Stan says the dailies are stunning. It's finally going to make Yael Shomrim a big star in the States. Oops! I gather he's a sore spot with you."

"What do you mean?" asked Matty, trying to be cool.

"Lindsay."

"Does everybody know?" sighed Matty.

"Roderick Mann doesn't, if that helps. He only writes about it if one of the stars are British. So how are you doing otherwise? I haven't seen you since that hilarious dinner at Bobby's when Joan of Arc started looking for the lost Dauphin between my legs."

Matty burst out laughing. He liked Louise Feingold and found her acid sense of humor a breath of fresh air in the midst of the Bel Air-Brentwood-Bev Hills ladies who lunch.

"I don't know how you got through that dinner," said Matty shaking his head at the memory.

"I just didn't believe it was happening. I'm a babe in the woods, Matty, when it comes to the well of loneliness, if you follow."

"Oh, you're all girl. I can tell that."

"Some people can surprise you. I didn't believe it when Yvonne switched ball clubs after all those years. But I guess Martine wasn't the only one in that family who freaked out."

"What happened to her? Everyone tiptoes around that subject so carefully."

"Nothing so unusual for the Seventies. But it destroyed Bobby and Yvonne's marriage—shaky at the best of times—and they've never been the same since. Bobby has his own peculiar devils and Yvonne . . . promise you won't tell anyone?"

"Sure," replied Matty when he realized she wouldn't give him any further information about Martine.

"Hear she's taken up with Joan of Arc."

"Violette-Claire?!"

"Couple of hometown girls. Hope it works out"

"You're some dish!"

"Are you making a pass?" she asked.

"No, gossip. Except it's more than that. I've been obsessed with the agency's skeletons since landing here eight months ago. It's so damned byzantine."

"Borgiaesque, if you ask me. Rampantly incestuous. But all company towns are. What else do you want to know?"

"Seriously?"

"Sure. Nothing spoken on an airplane is admissible evidence in court. Wheezer's Law. I will deny all of this on the ground," she said with a twinkle in her eye.

"Who's Wheezer?"

"Me. Since I was three."

"Okay, Wheezer . . . Is Joy Dworkin Ara Whalen's daughter?"

"Nope."

"Just like that?"

"There are only two possible answers. She is not Ara's daughter. Ara has never had any children."

"But Minden Prescott told me she was pregnant—"

"Little Miss Mindy sees Fannie Hurst plots everywhere. Ara had an abortion that year. I know because I drove her to New Jersey to have it done. . . . I was sixteen years old and she was the big sister I never had. Stole my mother's car to do it. I've never told anyone that till now, Matthew Garber. Understand? I like you and I hope I can trust you."

"You can."

Matty told Wheezer the story of Ara's rescuing Speedy Liebowitz from the law seven weeks earlier. Wheezer laughed with delight.

"That's what did it! Damn! Been wondering what snapped Ara back after all these years."

"She looks great, doesn't she?" asked Matty.

"She looks fifteen years younger again. She doesn't wear that horrible makeup anymore—"

"No more Painted Lady."

"Right on! She's lost thirty pounds. She's jogging. And she's off the booze. She turned up at the house last week in a tennis outfit and challenged me to a game. Hadn't seen her for about a year. Didn't recognize her. We just laughed and laughed and hugged each other like old times. Wow!"

"She's a dynamo now," nodded Matty. "None of us can keep up with her. She and Joy have split Speedy's clients since he left the agency."

"Poor Speedy. He just fell apart after that business?"

"Still feel guilty."

"Don't. My father pulled worse gags in his day. Uncle Sid, too. It was just bad karma for Speedy."

"Harriet left him. Wouldn't forgive him. She took the kids and went back to Toledo."

"Now *that's* martyrdom!"

The two laughed and continued to chat amiably until the flight landed at JFK.

They shared a cab into town. Wheezer dropped him off at the Warwick before continuing on to her parents' town house in the exclusive Turtle Bay section on the East Side. Garber checked in, showered, ordered some breakfast, then walked down Avenue of the Americas to the IAA offices.

Tony Rabaiotti embraced him like a long-lost brother then walked him down the hall to meet the founding father.

"So! This is the new wonder man!" announced Abe Keller, getting up from behind his gigantic mahogany desk.

It took Matty a second to realize that Keller was no longer seated. The sun-tanned septuagenarian in the pin-striped suit was two pathetic inches short of five feet tall but his walk had a bounce and vigor that seemed to add the necessary inches which kept him from being tagged a midget. "I've heard a lot about you." He began pumping Matty's hand as if he expected water to come spurting out of the young man's mouth.

"Heard a lot about you," grinned Matty. "They say you, George Burns, and Jimmy Cagney are the only three buck dancers left in the United States."

"This kid does his homework," chirped Keller in a nasal Brooklyn voice while winking at Rabaiotti. "Tell you something, *boychik*. I was never that hot a dancer. Why I got out. Now Cagney! There was the dancer. We used to hang out on Panic Beach together. You know where that is?"

"No, sir."

"Corner 47th and Broadway. Where all the unemployed hoofers used to congregate and cry the blues about not working. Me and Jim and Sid—that's my late partner. Guess you never met him. I remember the day when Jim was asked to join an act called Parker, Rand, and Leach. Leach was leavin'. You know who Leach was? Cary Grant! Didn't know he was a hoofer, did you? That's what we all were: hoofers. Now, they call 'em 'gypsies.' A hoity-toity name for *faygels*, if you ask me.

"So! Welcome to New York. Bet you're glad to get away from the smog. Couldn't get me out there on a bet! If I need the sun, I fly down to Florida. Go down once a month with Mrs. Keller. Oh, by the way, we're having a party tonight. You'll come, of course. Yeah, I wouldn't live out on the Coast. My late partner and I tossed a coin to see which one of us'd take New York and which one'd go to Hollywood. It was a two-headed coin. Never told him. Poor old Sid. He never forgave me for breakin' up the act. The man never knew his limitations. Never understood the bottom line. Never understood a lot of things. But what the hell are we talking about Sid Shankman for? He's been dead ten years. Deader than radio."

"Radio's coming back," said Matty.

"Vaudeville will never come back!" said Keller, determined to top his young visitor.

"Wait till you see the new Inez Sanchez show," warned Matty good-naturedly.

"Any good?"

"They've got four shows in the can for the fall and they're all dynamite. The one with Neil Diamond and Barry Manilow is going to win an Emmy for sure."

"Listen how he talks about them!" cackled Keller, nudging Rabaiotti. "You'd think they were Jolson. There was a singer. The first pop star. And a great showman.

"Years ago. Your grandparents probably weren't born. He was doin' a show. Think it was *Sinbad*. Anyhow, he was singin' 'Swanee.' Somewhere between notes, he cut the cheese—broke wind. Embarrassing! Now, what do you do? Ignore it? It was a real boomer. They could hear it at the back of the balcony. But Jolson was a showman. He walked down to the footlights, put a hand to his mouth, and in a stage whisper told the audience, 'Joley made a *fartzel*.' They loved it! He took 'em into his confidence, and went right back into 'Swanee.' Lemme see Inez Sanchez do that in Vegas!"

"Is that true?" laughed Matty.

"I'm an old man. Got no need to lie. Besides, it's a great story."

Matty's eyes turned to an old vaudeville poster framed on the wall. The billing featured Sophie Tucker, Bums and Allen, Keller and Shankman, and a magic act called the Dworkins.

"Were those the magicians who adopted Joy?"

"Yeah," replied Keller evasively. "Wonderful people."

Abe quickly shifted gears onto a discussion of the lousy season on Broadway. Matty wondered why. Wheezer had assured him that Ara wasn't Joy's mother. But what about the rumors that Keller was the father? Maybe that was true. In which case Ara, as a dutiful secretary, might have found a foster home for the illegitimate child in Chicago with the retired vaudevillians.

Rabaiotti and Garber stayed to *schmooze* with the show biz patriarch for another fifteen minutes then returned to Tony's office to discuss east-west business.

"Steerforth really pulled a coup with that Inez Sanchez series," said Rabaiotti admiringly. "Advance hype on it is incredible. Every time I think I'm making it as an agent—discovering talent, making a deal on a show, bringing a hit over from London—that goddamn limey pulls a rabbit out of his hat and steals all our thunder. Don't get me wrong. I love him. We started in the mailroom here together. Jimmy, myself, and Ira."

"Who's Ira?"

"You don't know?" Rabaiotti flashed his legendary caps. "The Boswell of IAA missed out on some tidbit?"

"Who's Ira?"

"Ira Fogelson."

"Never heard of him."

"Ira was this tall, skinny Jewish kid who didn't know who he was or where he was going. He was the butt of all our practical jokes in the mailroom. Then Kennedy got elected and all the idealists found a new outlet: the New Frontier, the Peace Corps, the Green Berets. Ira applied for the Green Berets. We couldn't believe it. What was more astonishing, they took him. Next thing we heard, Ira'd been shipped off to Vietnam. We figured he was a goner for sure. Two years later he walked back into the office. But he wasn't skinny anymore. He was built like the Incredible Hulk and he'd changed his name to—"

"Dwight Foley! He's Jewish? I thought he was Mr. White Bread."

"He is. Ira Fogelson 'died' in the jungle. Dwight explained it to me. He had a revelation over there. An overdose of Nietzsche and Thai stick, if you want my opinion. But nary an *oy vey* has crossed his lips these past twenty years. He's just waiting for the Fourth Reich to come along. He and his pal Dr. Kislev are doing everything they can to speed up the process."

"What do you mean?"

"Can't prove anything but I think he and Kislev are trying to steal the agency."

"Steal it?"

"The clients. Kislev's already got their hearts and minds. All Dwight needs are their signatures in triplicate. Crazy Larry Bazzo was sending me regular coded messages on the subject up until May—four months ago. I haven't heard anything since. As a matter of fact, it was just before Nolan Goodly committed suicide. Did the cops ever come up with anything further on that?"

"No," answered Matty, shaking his head. "That goes onto a long list of unsolveds along with Thelma Todd, George Reeves, and Marilyn Monroe."

"Think the cops are covering up?"

"No, they just can't solve it. Easier to call it murder-suicide and leave it at that."

"Some crazy town you chose to live in," said Rabaiotti, shaking his head. "How's your love life?"

"The office didn't send you a Telex? I'm dying of a broken heart, Tony. Can't you tell?"

"Bobby's secretary? Sorry, kid. Want me to set you up while you're in town?"

"No, thanks. Yeah. Maybe. I don't know. . . . Did you ever see Mrs. Nardino again?"

Rabaiotti got up from behind his desk, went to the door, and closed it.

"Sylvia has rescued me from male menopause. I just don't know what to tell my wife when the time comes."

"Is it that serious?"

"I feel like a teen-ager again."

"Wonderful!"

"Horrible! I got three kids. My wife'll take me to the cleaners. Nah, it's not that! It's just that Tina and I have been together since we were kids. It's really gonna hurt her. . . . *Finito!* Back to business. One of our producers here has a terrific concept for . . ."

The Kellers' East Side town house was quintessential New York chic. Matty arrived at eight and was led up to the second floor where everyone in the Manhattan literary, theatrical, fashion, and political world seemed to be congregated. Drop a bomb on Abe Keller's house, Matty mused, and it would take the Western world ten years to recover.

Dorothy 'Babe' Keller was a vivacious, tiny, silver-haired lady of seventy, who took great delight in spiriting Matty around the room to meet her guests.

"You want old ones or young ones?" asked Babe with a twinkle. "I try to get a mix. 'Cause if you stick with old guests—the way everyone's dropping these days—you've got no party. Have you met Gilda?"

"Yes. Is that Lauren Bacall over there?"

"Haven't got my glasses. Tell me who you want to meet and I'll take you over."

"I'd love to meet Lauren Bacall."

"Done! Betty! Betty, darling!"

Babe took Matty's hand and waded through the guests in the library. But when she arrived in front of the tall, lanky woman with gray-blond hair wearing a stylish Halston original, she laughed aloud at Matty's mistake.

"Phyllis!" gushed Babe. "I'm sorry. He thought you were Betty Bacall."

"That's all right," replied the handsome, fiftyish woman with devastating green eyes and wide, arched eyebrows. "Better Betty than Bella. Who is this handsome, misinformed young man?"

"Matthew Garber from the Beverly Hills office. Matthew, this is Phyllis Marshak." Babe vanished back into the crowd.

"Hope I'm not a disappointment to you," said Phyllis, removing a Benson and Hedges from her gold cigarette case.

"Who needs Lauren Bacall?" asked Matty, lighting her cigarette for her.

"Wasn't aware IAA was recruiting agents from the diplomatic corps these days."

"You're very kind."

"And you are very polished for one of Bobby's lieutenants. I usually reach for the shark repellent after being introduced to one."

"Do you know Mr. Rankoff?"

"Vaguely. I was married to him. Many years ago."

Matty was stunned. He remembered Yvonne's cryptic reference to Rankoff's first wife and the 'incredible guilt' he suffered about her for years. Matty always imagined some frail, little match girl abandoned to her fate along Bobby's road to fame. Not anything like this tall, sophisticated member of New York's smart set.

"Something wrong, Mr. Garber?"

"You're nothing like I imagined you to be."

"Why would you imagine me at all? I've been one of his best best-kept secrets for years. Officially Yvonne Corday was his first wife."

"When . . . were you married to him?"

"Do you really care?"

"Actually, yes. I'm sort of his unofficial biographer."

"Does he know that?"

"No. He'd probably throw me out of the office if he ever found out. I just. . . find him fascinating. He's a total enigma."

"Don't let me spoil his image for you."

"Do you hate him?"

Phyllis thought about that before answering. "No. Not at all. Quite honestly, I haven't thought about him in years. I see his name from time to time. My husband is Edward Marshak, the attorney. He has quite a few show business clients. Many of them represented by IAA. So the name does come up. But I haven't set eyes on Bobby in over thirty years."

"Then you were married to him in Cleveland?"

"You are persistent. Yes, we were married in Cleveland. We were high school sweethearts. . . I adored him. He was very special. I was a hopeless romantic and he was an incredible dreamer. Of course, he had that voice. You were too young to have ever heard him sing, I'm sure."

"I've heard his records."

"He was incredible. Totally untrained. He'd come over to our house and sing with the radio. My mother and I were spellbound. We couldn't believe this voice was standing in our living room. My mother adored Bobby. Was there ever a woman who didn't?

"But he was desperately unhappy. His father was a widower. A bitter man. He didn't appreciate Bobby's voice. Thought it was a waste of time. Tried to get Bobby a job at the shop where he worked. A lingerie shop in Cleveland. He managed it. Strange job for a man who didn't seem to like women particularly. He was a miserable man. His only joy came from Murray, Bobby's older brother. Murray could do no wrong in Irving Rankoff's eyes. But Bobby was a bum. Used to tear Bobby apart. He wanted his father's love so desperately and received nothing but scorn. I became Bobby's emotional refuge. He adopted me and my family."

Phyllis paused in the middle of her story and lit another cigarette. She wondered why on earth she was telling this absolute stranger something she had banished from her mind so many years before. What was it about this broad shouldered, sympathetic, bespectacled young man that caused her to reopen the floodgates of memory? She couldn't explain it. At the same time, she felt compelled to continue.

"Bobby dropped out of high school and got himself a job singing in a local band. Ten dollars a week. He was thrilled to death. His father refused to come hear him. It killed Bobby. His father had no faith in him. Murray was going to be the big shot. As soon as he came back from the war. But Murray was killed at Anzio. Irving died of a broken heart a year later.

"Bobby and I were married by then. I was seventeen and he was eighteen. Living with my parents. Bobby resented his father dying before he became a success. He felt cheated. Wanted to prove he was better than Murray.

"Ironically, Bobby got the offer from Nat Kane's orchestra about a month after Irving died. Six-month tour. That's what finished us. I was young and I loved him. Didn't want him to leave me. It's an old show-business cliche. I was Doris Day and he was Frank Sinatra. He left. I got a divorce and moved to New York. And lived happily ever after. What more can I tell you?"

"That's a helluva story."

"He's still my favorite singer," she said wistfully. "It's tragic his career was . . . How did you manage to pry this out of me?"

"I asked," he shrugged. "You talked."

"Have you met Barbara Walters yet? She'll absolutely adore you. Just saw her over—"

Matty lost the tail end of Phyllis Marshak's sentence. His eyes were riveted on the library doors where Louise Feingold had just entered in a stunning black and silver-sequined sheath slit up the side. She was absolutely breathtaking and looked like a maharini as her proud mother steered her around the room to meet all the guests.

"Do you know Matthew?" asked Babe when they reached the spot where Garber stood like a statue.

"We flew out together," beamed Wheezer. "How's your day been?"

"Thought it was pretty good. Until now."

"What does that mean?"

"Now it's perfect"

"You are a little devil, Matthew."

"You're beautiful, Wheezer. If there was a band, I'd ask you to dance."

"I'm old enough to be your mother."

"Not quite."

The two stood stared into each other's eyes not quite certain where the chemistry of the moment was taking them nor what they were going to do about it.

They were rescued from the predicament by Abe Keller reaching up to touch Matty's shoulder.

"Telephone for you, *boychik*. Take it in my bedroom. Wheezer, show him where it is."

"This could be dangerous," winked Matty mischievously as they wedged themselves into the tiny elevator and rode up to the third floor.

"Behave yourself," she replied, squeezing his hand. He sat on the edge of Abe Keller's king-sized bed and picked up the telephone.

"I'll leave you," whispered Wheezer from the doorway.

"No, no, it's—" But she was gone. "Hello?"

"Hello, old son."

"James! What a delightful surprise! What time is it out there? You *are* out there?"

"A little after midnight . . . Afraid I've got some bad news for you, Matthew."

"Don't tell me. Lindsay eloped with Yael."

"Wish it was that . . . It's Roley. He's dead."

"Oh, no! Oh, God . . . When?"

"This afternoon. At Cedars. He'd been having dinner with Uncle last night. Started coughing. Terrible paroxysms. Uncle took him to the hospital. Turned out he was asthmatic."

"I . . . didn't know that"

"Poor old bugger didn't either. His lungs went into spasm and he died. The bloody smog killed him."

"Oh, Jesus!"

"Uncle and I made funeral arrangements for tomorrow. It's quick but with the heat and all . . . I know you just got there—"

"It's okay, Jimmy, I'll take the first plane out tomorrow morning."

"I'll pick you up . . . I'm so sorry."

"Thanks."

He put down the phone and began to cry. Pulling himself together, he started back down the stairs. Wheezer was waiting at the bottom.

"Have to go back to my hotel," he said with difficulty. "A friend of mine just . . . died."

"I'll get my coat," she said.

Five minutes later they were in a cab on their way over to the Warwick.

"Just spoke to him yesterday afternoon. He was a wonderful man. Did you know him?"

"My seventh birthday was in California," said Wheezer. "Roley bought me a ballerina doll. I kept it for years."

She paid the driver and steered Matty through the lobby toward the elevators.

"Have to make a plane reservation for the morning."

"I'll do it for you," she said.

She took his key and unlocked the door to his room.

"Take your clothes off," she said gently.

"Haven't felt like this since my grandfather died."

"It's okay."

"Crazy how these things happen when you least expect them to," he said, sliding between the sheets.

"Yes," she nodded, turning off the lights beside his bed. Two minutes later she removed her clothes and slipped into the bed beside him where she held him in her arms while he wept like a child.

MARTINE

"What are you wearing that dress for? Are you going to a funeral?"

"As a matter of fact, I am."

Lindsay Fairweather stood in front of the full-length mirror in a guest cottage at the Beverly Hills Hotel and stared defiantly at Yael Shomrim propped up in bed with his breakfast on a tray and a cigarette dangling idly from his lip.

"Oh, yes," nodded Shomrim. "That old man. The one who lived with your . . . friend."

"Give me a break," she said pleadingly.

"What have I said now? Go! I'm not your keeper."

"You act like you are."

"No. That's your game. I have never made any demands on you, Lindsay. Lindsay. There's no such name in Hebrew."

"You weren't looking for a nice Jewish girl when you hit on me. You had Daphna for that. Remember?"

"Can you explain something to me, Miss Fairweather?"

"What?"

"You look like my mistress but you talk like my wife. Have you been taking spousal pills?"

"Going to be late," she said, moving hastily across the room.

In a second the breakfast tray was off his lap. He shot across the length of the bed with the agility and speed of the trained assassin he'd once been to block her passage. "We should talk." It was more a command than a suggestion. She planted herself in the nearest chair upon hearing it. "You're acting most peculiarly this morning, Lindsay."

"Me? I'm not the one who shot out of bed at seven like a—"

"I had a bad dream."

"You never dream."

"Last night I dreamt. Of Bornstein."

"Who is Bornstein? Mind if I smoke?"

"Go ahead."

"Give me a cigarette first."

Yael grinned, lit two cigarettes, and slid one between her lips by prying them open ever so gently with his fingers.

"You're a frustrated gynecologist," she remarked, drawing the smoke deep into her lungs.

"I have a certain touch—"

"It's a lethal weapon. Tell me about Bornstein."

"Over twenty years ago. I was in the elite corps. We were responsible directly to Ben-Gurion. Like your Green Berets. Bornstein served with us. Pretended to. He wanted the glory but none of the danger. He was also a bedwetter. Pathetic. We crossed into Egypt one night. This was years before Sadat and Begin began the beguine. To be a Jew in Egyptian territory was . . . to be dead. The only good Jew et cetera. Our target was a small military installation. There were eight of us. I split the group up to hit the Egyptians from two sides. It was the middle of the night. I left Bornstein on a ridge as a guard and backup. He was to signal if anything went wrong and give us cover in case we were chased. As there was no warning from Bornstein, we went in. It was a trap. They knew we were coming. We didn't stand a chance. We fled under what we thought was safe cover from the ridge. There was no fire, no protection. Bornstein had deserted his post. My men were wiped out. I was the only one who survived the attack."

"What happened to Bornstein?"

"No one ever saw him again. He must have left the country. No Israeli would ever tolerate his existence after that. He's alive somewhere, cowering in fear, wetting his bed and waiting."

"Waiting for what?"

"For me. He must have heard me howl his name in the desert that night. I cursed him for God and the Devil to hear. Swore to find him one day. Last night he visited me. He does that every few years when I sleep."

"Hold me," said Lindsay when his story was done.

"Why?"

"Never been held by an angel before."

"Me? An angel?"

"An avenging angel. You've got me, Yael, and I can't get away from you."

"Do you want to?"

"In the best of all possible worlds, yes. I don't kid myself. I have no future with you. You'll never leave Daphna and the kids. You'll never leave Israel. You're a hero there. What would they make of a marmalade-haired, freckle-faced *shiksa*? From Glendale yet! With two sets of parents who are so goddamn civilized they play bridge together. What kind of divorce is that? They all think they own me. I get a combination of advice and shit from my mother, my stepmother, my father, and my stepfather. Should have been an orphan like Joy Dworkin! On top of which a wonderful person loves me. A nice Jewish boy from St Louis. Don't laugh at me, you sadistic—"

"I'm not laughing. I like Garber. He'd make a wonderful husband for you. Of course, you'd have to convert and learn how to make *kugel* and *latkes* and—"

"And get fat! No, thanks. I can't go back to Matty. I broke his heart. Humiliated him. Made him an object of pity around the office. You should see the looks everyone gives me. I make Beatrice look good!"

"Perhaps he should take up with Beatrice."

"It's not funny. We were doing all right till you came back to do *Ektalon-Z.* Why didn't you turn down the part?"

"Did Sean Connery turn down James Bond? It's a turning point in my career. This picture's going to make a fortune. And with the deal Bobby made for me—"

"Deals, deals, deals! Do you know how sick I am of deals? That's all this town eats, breathes, and sleeps."

"Like the old Israeli proverb: If you don't like beer, get out of Milwaukee."

"You've got a Milwaukee in Israel?"

"We have everything in Israel."

"Except a Lindsay." She stared meaningfully into his eyes with that last statement.

"You'll be late for the wedding."

"It's a *funeral*!"

"My mother-in-law used to tell me: *'Oz me tanzt of alleh chassenes, veint men noch alleh maissim.'*"

"I don't speak Hebrew."

"It's Yiddish. 'For every wedding you dance at, you'll weep at a funeral.' Life's a candle, life's a bullet, Lindsay. Life's a finger on a button in a silo in Montana. Bingo! We all go. What are you beating your lovely little breast for? If I make you so unhappy—"

"Not when I'm with you!" she protested, throwing her arms around him. I feel safe when I'm with you. I feel protected. I feel loved."

"Get a guard dog. You won't have the bother."

"Don't you want me to love you anymore?" She was on her knees at his feet.

"You look six years old," he replied, pulling her up to him. "I feel like a dirty old man."

"I feel like a dirty old man, too," she replied, massaging his crotch with her hand. "Going to be late for the funeral. Will you be here later?"

"Waiting to hear from Rees. We may have to reshoot what we did yesterday."

"I love you, Yael," she said from the doorway. "I could learn to make *latkes*. I just wouldn't eat them."

"Shalom!"

"I know you think I'm neurotic—"

"*Au revoir.*"

"I'm not like this with other people—"

"*Auf Wiedersehen.*"

"At the office I'm known for my clear-headed, no-nonsense manner—"

"Good-bye!"

He closed the door on her. He checked his watch, dialed the operator, and placed an overseas call to his wife in Tel Aviv.

***

It was a tiny funeral.

Matty, Ivor, and Steerforth were the only men there; Lindsay, Yvonne, and Evelyn Shankman the only women. Garber had hoped t Rankoff might make an appearance for old times' sake, but there was no sign of the IAA boss at Forest Lawn. The minister said a few words, mentioned Roley's better-known films, said the obligatory prayer, and it was over. Roland Draycott—a child of the century—was dead at eighty and only six people cared. It wasn't right.

Matty caught up with Yvonne and Evelyn as they were about to climb into the back seat of Mrs. Shankman's chauffeur-driven Rolls-Royce.

"I don't want it to end like this. Couldn't we—I mean would you like to come back to the cottage and have a drink? There's some sherry. I think Mr. Draycott would have liked that"

"Of course," replied Evelyn, squeezing Garber's hand kindly. "It's a wonderful idea. Yvonne?"

"*Bien sur*. I never think of sherry without thinking of Roley."

Matty gave the address to the chauffeur and the Rolls left the cemetery grounds.

"They're coming back for a drink," Garber told Ivor and Steerforth. "Can you guys—?"

Uncle and nephew both nodded and walked toward Steerforth's car. Matty found himself alone beside the grave with Lindsay.

"Thanks for coming," he said stiffly.

"No need to thank me," replied Lindsay with equal stiffness. "Roley was my friend, too. Used to fantasize about him being my grandmother's lover."

"He had one about being *your* lover."

"He didn't!"

"Roley loved the ladies. Just didn't have much opportunity the last few years."

The two stood and stared at each other in silence. So much they wanted to say to each other; so much that pride and pain prevented them from saying.

"I asked the others to come back to the cottage for a glass of sherry. Would you . . . ?"

"Sure."

"God! Hope there is some." He laughed. "Did that sound like Roley? Do you need a lift?"

"No. Have my—"

"Same one?"

"Oh, yeah. Pink and battered."

"Do the windshield wipers—?"

"No. Another broken promise. You know me."

"Thought I did."

"See you at your place," she said hastily.

Garber arrived at the cottage to discover the other mourners were already there and being served coffee and pastries under the supervision of the ever meticulous Ames.

"How did—when did—?" Matthew was incapable of finishing a sentence as he stared in amazement at the sterling-silver coffee urn and the incredible-looking tarts, mousses, rum bhabas, and the like displayed so beautifully on the dining room table.

"Mr. Rankoff suspected you might be having a few people back after the service," explained Ames. "He suggested I come ahead and lay out a few things. Trust you're not offended, Mr. Garber, by the intrusion. I had to let myself in and—"

"Not at all, Ames. I'm grateful for your presence." Matty always found himself returning the short, red-haired Ames ever-so-polite verbal serve whenever they spoke. "And touched by Mr. Rankoff's gesture."

"It's more than a gesture, sir. Mr. Rankoff was well aware of your fondness for the late Mr. Draycott. If I may add on a personal note, I was a great fan of Mr. Draycott's myself. We were both from Plymouth. He was someone to look up to when I was a lad."

"Is Mr. Rankoff coming?"

"Oh, no, sir. He sends his apologies and asks that you understand. Some coffee, sir?"

"Yes, thank you, Ames."

"Might I suggest a piece of the *tarte Bourdaloue*?"

"Yes," said Matty, staring ravenously at the pear and apricot cream tart. "I was admiring that. Did you get it at Michel Richard's?"

"Certainly not," answered Ames icily. "I made it myself."

"Forgive me, Ames. I wasn't thinking. Of course, you do it all. Don't know what—"

"Quite all right, Mr. Garber. May I help you, Mrs. Shankman?"

"You'd have helped me a long time ago, Ames, by keeping your pastries away from me," replied Evelyn. "They will be my downfall."

"Try the *tarte Bourdaloue!*" insisted Matty, trying to make amends. "Ames made it himself."

"When did anyone ever see Ames go into a bakery?"

"Thank you, Mrs. Shankman," replied the deeply grateful butler from Plymouth.

"That man," said Evelyn, sipping her coffee. "No, no. Don't turn around, Matthew. The older man standing with Jimmy Steerforth. Who is he?"

"His uncle."

"Didn't know Jimmy had any family."

"Oh, yes. His uncle's been out here for years."

"Was he ever a barber?"

"Still is," said Matty.

"Good heavens!"

"Do you know him?"

"Years ago. He probably wouldn't recognize me."

"Let's go see."

Ivor was in the midst of recounting a story to Lindsay and Steerforth when Matty brought Evelyn over.

"Dear old Roley. He'd have enjoyed this party, you know. Always a great one for parties. And visiting sick people. Very good that way, old Roley was. He told me how he went to visit Edmund Gwenn on his deathbed. You remember Edmund? Played Kris Kringle in that film. He'd been very helpful to Roley as a young actor. Old Edmund lay there dying with a look of extreme discomfort on his face and all Roley could think of to ask was: 'Does it hurt, Edmund? Does it hurt?' Edmund looked up from his deathbed and said, 'Not as much as comedy, my boy.' "

No one laughed louder or more appreciatively at this story than Evelyn Hughes Shankman. Ivor nodded with a gracious twinkle.

"Don't you remember me, Mr. Manning?" she finally asked.

"Upon my word, Mrs. Shankman. How on earth did you remember *me?* Wasn't bad manners on my part, I can assure you. I'd have approached you earlier but—well, it must be thirty years."

"Thirty-three," corrected Evelyn. "The last time you cut my husband's hair was 1947. I never saw you again. Did you have a fight with him?"

"Probably," replied Ivor, popping his monocle back into place. "Had fights with a great many people in those days."

"Have you mellowed?"

"Not really. Still a young wine, as it were."

"I'm rather partial to young wines," she smiled.

"Indeed?"

"Well," interjected Steerforth, clearing his throat, obviously embarrassed by his randy old uncle on the make and the dowager duchess of IAA's blatant interest. "Must head back for the office. Can I offer you a lift, Lindsay?"

"No, thanks. I have my car."

"Ta-ra then. It was a smashing funeral, Matthew."

"Yeah," nodded Matty, suddenly feeling elated. "It was nice. Roley would have liked it this way."

Steerforth reached the cottage door and collided with Joy Dworkin.

"Scheherazade!" purred Steerforth. "You look like the messenger in *Oedipus*. Good news or bad?"

"I came to pay my respects," replied Joy defensively, looking up from under a respectful black sombrero. "I didn't go to Forest Lawn 'cause I can't handle all that mass emotion, you know. But I met Mr. Draycott once and he was nice to me. Just wanted to come and say I was sorry."

"That's sweet," said Steerforth taking her fingers and kissing them. "If I'm nice to you, will you come to my funeral?"

"Why do you treat me like this?" she sighed.

"I like keeping you on your toes."

"I'd like it on my toes . . . under the right circumstances."

"Cheeky little bitch." Steerforth kissed her cheek and left the cottage.

"Think I'm too old for him?" she asked Matty after her heartthrob's departure.

"Thanks for coming," said Matty, kissing her briefly on the lips and hoping that Lindsay was watching. Really appreciate it."

"How did you get Fortnum and Mason's to cater the *shiva?*" dead-panned Joy. "How ya doin', Ames?"

"Miss Dworkin," nodded Ames perfunctorily, not being particularly enamored of the 'little barracuda's' style.

"Got any lox and cream cheese?" she countered, swaggering over to the dining room table and latching on to Lindsay's arm along the way. "Just the person I'm looking for. My secretary is the pits. Let me steal you away from Bobby? You too, Ames. I'm going to be running the place eventually. Might as well get in on the ground floor."

Matty shook his head with bemusement at Joy's *shpritz* then noticed Yvonne sitting alone in the garden and went out to join her.

"Your ex-husband's a big con," said Matty. "You know that? He hides behind that whole tough, distracted facade. And inside he's a marshmallow. Look what he did today! Sending Ames over here like this. That was a wonderful thing to do. But he wouldn't come himself. He's like Joy. Can't 'handle all that mass emotion'."

After a long pause, Yvonne turned to Matthew. "Forgive me, Matthew. I was a million miles away. What did you say?"

"Just muttering about Bobby. My pet mania."

"Dig up any more skeletons?"

"Last night. She was no skeleton, though. The mysterious first wife… Yvonne? Something wrong?"

"What time is it?"

"Two. Half past"

"I must go."

"Don't you want to hear about Phyllis?"

"Phyllis who?"

"Bobby's first wife. The one you wouldn't tell me about. I met her in New York last night."

"Some other time, Matthew. Sorry. Truly."

Yvonne rose from her seat and went back inside the cottage to find Evelyn. Matty couldn't figure out what was wrong until he remembered what Wheezer had said the day before about Yvonne and Violette-Claire. Ms. Desgouilles probably wasn't the easiest person to get along with at the best of times; to be having an affair with her had to be something short of the Tientsin Massacre.

Before Matty knew it, the party was breaking up. Yvonne wasn't so distracted that she was unaware of the chemistry bubbling between Ivor and Evelyn. Sooner than break up that amiable reunion, she drafted Lindsay into service to drive her up the hill to Mulholland. The chauffeur-driven Rolls whisked Evelyn and Ivor away shortly after that. Ames began to pack up the coffee urn and dishes he had brought with him. Soon Matty and Joy were alone in the cottage.

"So?" she asked, crossing her shapely legs in Roley's favorite chair, rolling herself a joint. "How was New York? All twenty-four hours of it?"

Good question, thought Matthew, who looked upon the past forty-eight hours as one blur of activity. What country, friends, is this? Get on a plane. Sleep. Meet the boss's middle-aged daughter, who ain't so middle-aged. Meet the boss. Joley made a fartzel. Rabaiotti's in love. Phyllis Marshak. Wheezer. Beautiful sexy Wheezer. Long distance. Death. Back to the hotel. Wheezer. With clothes. Without clothes. Beautiful love. Comforting love. Love! Onto a plane. Sleep all the way. Steerforth waiting. Straight to Forest Lawn. Death again. Pain. Joy. Both Joys. Yvonne. Lindsay. Mustn't think about Lindsay. Wheezer. Where is Wheezer? I need her here now. She's still in New York. Am I in love with you, Wheezer? I think so. Is it all right to love you? Does Slippery Stan care? I would, if you'd let me. You cared last night In New York. How was New York? Who asked me that?

"Okay," he replied blankly to Joy.

"You sound wacked."

"I just crossed the continent twice in twenty-four hours."

"No jet lag," she shrugged, sucking the marijuana deep into her chest, and passing the joint to him.

"How come?" he asked, taking it from her and drawing on it.

"It cancels itself out. Like negative ions."

"What are they?"

"Don't know. Still hung up on Lindsay?"

"I don't think so," he lied.

"Want to go to bed with me? I'm feeling very emotional."

"That's really sweet of you, Joy." He took another hit. "But I don't think—"

"Not doing it for you, shmuck. For me."

"Sorry." He shook his head regretfully. "You always catch me at the wrong times."

"God! You were hot to trot when we first met."

"Should have taken me then."

"*Shtup* a mailroom boy? You must be crazy. Who are you giving the business to these days?"

"I've been celibate."

"Bullshit, Garber. You're the horniest guy I've ever met. Can't believe you'd pass up a chance to make it with someone who's been fantasizing about you for weeks."

She had moved across the room to Matty by this time and was thrusting her incredibly compact little body against his.

"What do you say, tiger?" she asked, sliding her hand inside his suit jacket and pinching his nipple through his button-down oxford cloth shirt. "Don't you think we've waited long enough?"

He stared down into her huge, doe like eyes and saw Wheezer. And Lindsay. And Trisha.

"I'm in love!" he blurted.

"Oh, yeah! With who?"

"Whom."

"Fuck grammar!"

"Thought you wanted to fuck *me*."

"I hate a cunt-teaser."

"Who was teasing? You came over under the pretext of paying your last respects and end up trying to get into bed with me. God! I'm stoned. What is this stuff?"

"Like it? Bazzo gave it to me. I'm worried about him. He's been really weird lately."

"Got to lie down, Joy. The room is spinning."

"Sure. Let me take your pants off."

"No, no! Just leave my pants where they are. I know what you want."

"Goddamnit, Garber! Every guy in town wants to get into my drawers except you."

"And Steerforth!"

"You bastard!"

"What's the matter, Joyous?"

"Don't call me that. He calls me that."

"Who he?"

"Who he?" repeated Joy.

"Who-ha-ha. Ting-tang-walla-walla-bing-bang." Matty began dancing around the room.

"I'm not getting stoned with you anymore, Garber. You're . . . you're . . . immature!!"

"Immature! *Moi?* I use Ban. Remember those commercials?" Matty began to snap his fingers and hum the opening bars of the "Jet Song." "Did you ever see *West Side Story*? I played Riff in St. Louis. Trisha played Maria. She was terrible but she looked wholesome. Honey Layefsky cried for a week. She wanted the part so badly but they made her play Anita."

"Who are all these people?" demanded Joy.

"They were the girls from Mary I. You'd have hated them. They were so dipped in shit. They all had their noses fixed by the same doctor in Ladue. Should have seen them on May Day running around in their identical little green jackets with their identical lacrosse racquets and identical nose jobs praying it wouldn't rain."

"What was wrong with the rain?"

"Ladue is not Beverly Hills. They didn't have warranties on the nose jobs."

"How the hell did we get off onto nose jobs?"

"Did you have your nose done?" he asked abruptly.

"No! This is my nose."

"It's a cutie." He wrapped his arms around her.

"I'm leaving!"

"Are you rejecting my advances?"

"You're warped, Garber. Too weird for me."

"*I'm as horny as Kansas in August, High as a fag on the Fourth of July.* By gosh, by golly, by gum. What time's the Twentieth Century coming through?"

"How could you seriously expect me to go to bed with you?"

"Oh, I'd never go to bed with you seriously, Joyous. Spoil all the fun."

"Yeah. Guess it would." She picked up her black sombrero and placed it on her head.

"You okay to drive?" he asked with genuine concern.

"Better me than you. Give me a call if you ever come down."

She no sooner left the cottage then the telephone rang. Let it be Wheezer, he prayed.

"Hello."

"Heyyyy, Junior. What's doin'?"

"Who's this?" asked Matty.

"Your old Uncle Gilbob."

Was it the dope? Or was Bobcaygeon really phoning after months of silence?

"Gilbert? Is that you?"

"It ain't Ronald Reagan." The famous Goofy laugh came rolling through the phone wire. "Hey! Ever tell you the story when Reagan first won the governorship?" Another Goofy laugh.

"Think you did, Gil." Bobcaygeon was the last person Matty wanted to hear from at this moment in time.

"Lemme tell it to ya again. Gotta tell ya. The Colonel told me this one himself. The Colonel loved me. Covered the studio, you know."

"I don't know what you're talking about."

"Jack Warner. The Colonel! I was over in Burbank when they told him Reagan had won. He made this real sour face, then he said: 'Bad casting! Dennis Morgan for the Governor; Reagan for the best friend!' " A Vesuvial laugh was followed by the worst cigarette cough Matty had ever heard. "Jesus! Don't you love it? 'Dennis Morgan for Governor; Reagan for the best friend!' Now, let me tell ya why I'm calling, Junior. I know you think I never remember anything you tell me. Mind like a sieve, right? It's all a front. Old Gilbob never forgets a thing."

Matty had removed the phone from his ear by this time and was holding it out at arm's length as if it and the cord were some snake in the bazaar in Bombay and he was the charmer trying to get the reptile back into its basket. Being stoned and having to listen to Gilbert Bobcaygeon was the definitive concept of hell, he decided.

"Are ya there, Junior?"

"Either here or on the next asteroid."

"Huh? What's that, an in-joke? That the latest Bel Air *bon mot*? Don't get caught up in that bullshit, Matty. You're too good for that, kid. Trust your old Uncle Gilbob. It's why I picked you out back in Kansas City."

"It was St. Louis."

"Huh?"

"We met in St. Louis."

"Take your word for it," replied Bobcaygeon as if humoring a senile relative. "Fairsy-doosey. Anyhow, I'm over at Universal—"

"Does Lew Wasserman know you're on the lot?" asked Matty, trying to figure out what the hell fairsy-doosey meant and where Bobcaygeon really was. From all reports around town the dreadful

Gilbob was P.N.G. (Persona Non Grata—Sol Siglan, 1980) at MCA's sprawling studio in the San Fernando Valley.

"Why? Did he want to see me? I'll pop over to his office later. Listen, Junior. Got a pencil? Here's the deal. He starts work on Monday. Guaranteed five weeks at ten thousand a week. Five thousand a day for every day over that. Special guest-star billing. Car and driver. The whole thing."

"What are you talking about?"

"*Calcutta*! Big ten-hour miniseries they're shooting. Don't you know the book? Set in India. 1880. Sort of like *Gone With the Wind*. Hey, did I ever tell you the story about David Selznick and Hildegarde Knef? It seems—"

"Gilbert, will you stop dishing a second and talk sense? What is this deal?"

"I got your friend a job! You asked me to find him a job. Remember? He's going to play the Governor of India. They're thrilled to death to have him. Thought he'd retired years ago but I told them—"

"Are you talking about Roley?"

"Roland Draycott! Starts work on Monday. Best part of his career. He'll get an Emmy for sure."

"He's dead."

"What?"

"He's dead, Gil. He died yesterday."

"Are you sure?"

"I just buried him, for Chrissake!"

"But he can't be dead," wailed Bobcaygeon. "We got a deal memo!"

"Interesting argument, Gil. Maybe you can bring Nolan Goodly back to life on that one."

"Wouldn't that be something?" mused Bobcaygeon. "Are you sure he's dead? Draycott?"

"I'm getting off the phone, Gilbert."

"No, no, no. Wait a minute! What time did he die yesterday?"

"Why?"

"If he died before I made the deal, it's not my fault. Thing like that could make me look bad, Junior."

"Listen to me, you mendacious moron. You couldn't look any worse to the world if you tried! You're a goddamn joke, Bobcaygeon. There's not a person in this town who takes you seriously. You're a freak! An insensitive, double-talking freak. You don't listen to anything anyone tells you, you lie to everyone, you either make deals you have no right to or sign booking slips for nonexistent deals. You have no sense of personal dignity with that laugh of yours and those terrible stories nobody wants to listen to. You're a fucking disaster!"

There was a pause that seemed to last an eternity until Bobcaygeon said quietly: "I tried to help you. Tried to help your friend. Didn't know he died."

"It's okay," sighed Matty, not knowing why the hell he suddenly felt guilty over what he honestly felt. "I'm just tired and sad. I appreciate what you tried to do for Roley. He'd have been thrilled. I'll call Universal myself and get you off the hook. Okay?"

"Fairsy-doosey. I owe you one, Junior."

"You don't owe me anything, Gil."

"Yes, I do! I never forget a favor. Gilbob and the elephant . . . Ya gotta admit it was a good line."

"What?"

"'He can't be dead. We got a deal memo.'"

"Oh, yeah. You'll get a lot of mileage out of that."

"Take care, Junior."

"You bet"

Matty replaced the receiver of the phone and wondered if he hadn't missed out on a chance at sanity amid the silken undergarments in his father's shop back in St. Louis. Fairsy-doosey.

Under the terms of Roland Draycott's will, he left his cottage and his 1937 Cord to his 'dear friend Matthew Garber'. Matty had never been so touched by any gesture in his life as the bequest constituted the bulk of Roley's estate.

By the middle of September, Garber had set about redecorating the cottage and having some long-neglected new plumbing installed. Ara had been very helpful in having him select carpeting and drapes; Bazzo got him a deal on a client's old road show speakers (Eventually they were placed in the garden as they were almost as tall as the cottage's tiny walls); Ivor and Evelyn—the new couple around town—brought over a bottle of Mumm's to toast the new owner and drink a cup of remembrance to his late benefactor; Rankoff kept muttering vague promises of coming to see the place, but never did. Inez Sanchez, his neighbor up above, had an orange tree transplanted from her estate and sent down via her gardener to be relocated in Matty's front yard; Minden Prescott presented his agent with a framed photograph of Lowell Sherman directing Miriam Hopkins on the set of *Becky Sharpe* the day he died; Joy Dworkin—in an attempt to shock her colleague—had the UPS deliver a life-size cutout of her in the nude. Matty proudly hung it in his newly restored bathroom and would drag all visitors in to see it until a scandalized Joy finally came to reclaim it herself.

The one person who didn't turn up at Matty's newly renovated cottage was the one person he most wanted to see: Wheezer.

Matty wondered whether Slippery Stan had grown suspicious when he would phone his office every day to see how *Ektalon-Z* was progressing. Somewhere in the midst of this idle chat, Matty would casually inquire whether Mrs. Feingold was still in New York. Matty was certain she was never coming back again when, on a Sunday afternoon in late September, Louise Keller Feingold appeared on his doorstep.

"May I come in?" she asked shyly.

"Just sent the red carpet off to the cleaners," apologized Matty with a huge grin as he ushered Wheezer over the threshold and onto the sofa he recently exchanged his soul for at Sloane's.

"Sorry not contacting you sooner," she said.

"That's okay," replied Matty, squeezing her hand warmly. "You're here now. God, Louise! I've been thinking about you every day since I got back here. That night in New York was so beautiful; you were so beautiful."

"Thank you." She put a hand to his cheek. He seized the hand and kissed her palm. "Matty—"

"I was going to write you a poem but it's tough to find anything romantic that rhymes with Wheezer. Cole Porter could have done it, I'm sure, but—"

"Matty, please!"

"Am I babbling? You make me babble. What were you doing in New York so long? I called Stan's office every day. He must have thought I was nuts ringing up—"

"I haven't been in New York all this time," said Wheezer.

"You haven't?"

"I came back two weeks ago."

"You've been in town? But where—I mean why—were you hiding? Why didn't you phone me? You knew I couldn't phone your father's house in New York. I'd never jeopardize you that way."

"Oh, Matthew, you are the sweetest boy I've ever known."

"I'm not a boy. I'm a man. I'll be twenty-nine in November. Almost thirty!"

"No." She shook her head kindly. "You're a boy the way I'm a girl. We make each other feel like high school again: holding hands at the prom; graduation night; slow dancing in the gym; wearing each other's pin."

"Are you giving me my pin back, Wheezer?"

"I never really took it from you. We shared a moment, Matty. A beautiful, precious moment. I knew the next morning you'd probably make it more than it was."

"How do you dismiss tenderness and passion?"

"Compassion, Matty. There's a difference."

"You mean pity? You felt sorry for me that night?"

"You're really going to make it difficult for me, aren't you? I came here to share something with you as a friend. I don't want to hear from a jilted teen-ager. Love me as a friend, Matty. Not as a fantasy. And not as a substitute."

"For what?"

"For Lindsay."

"Wow! You go right for the heart, don't you?"

"Hit the bull's-eye, didn't I?"

"Yeah."

She held her arms out to Matty and he knelt beside her on the carpet while she pulled his head to her breast and stroked his hair.

He finally spoke. "Hi, pal."

"Sure you've made the transition?"

"Uh-huh."

"I'm in love," she announced after a long silence.

Matty looked up at her. "Who is it?"

"Can't tell you. That's where I've been the last two weeks. My whole life's turned around, Matty. It's crazy and it's wonderful and it's so right."

"In New York? Did you meet him in New York? It *is* a guy?"

"Yes, you bastard," she laughed. "It's an honest-to-God Mary Martin-Wonderful-Wonderful-Guy."

"Does Stan know?"

"No."

"Oh."

"Stanley and I . . . I don't want to get into that right now. That shit will hit the fan soon enough. Just wanted you to know where I'm at, not screw your head up and hope that you'll be happy for me."

"I am. You're a smart woman, a nice lady and a wonderful lover—if you don't mind me mentioning it—and whoever he is, he's a lucky guy."

"So much for the speeches," she laughed. "I like your place."

"It's got a great garden. Want to—?"

"No. Have to make my 'official' return home now. Call you soon."

Wheezer left and Matty floated out to the garden accompanied by a recording of Faure's "Requiem" piping out of the Tower of Babel speakers he had placed there a week earlier. He sat in a chair and remembered the first time he'd visited the garden. When it cast its James M. Barrie enchantment over him as he held Lindsay in his arms.

I'm confused.

Who isn't? Let's just enjoy the garden. Okay? Isn't that house incredible up there?

Oh, my gosh! That's Inez Sanchez's house.

Matty turned his head up toward the hilltop for a glimpse of his neighbor's fabled— What the hell was that? He stood up and walked farther down the garden toward the stone wall that enclosed it from Inez's estate. Was he losing his marbles altogether or did he just see Inez Sanchez standing stark naked on her balcony flailing her arms like a banshee and screaming like a chorus of those same beasties? What the hell was she up to now?

He saw a pair of arms reach out from inside the living room and yank her violently back into the house.

What was going on?

The screams continued—more hysterical and terror stricken in nature. Matty was concerned. This was no game. She was in trouble.

He raced out to the front of the house and climbed behind the wheel of the Cord. He had given the Camaro to Sol Siglan when he discovered the mailroom boss was still driving a 1960 Pontiac that the Sheriif's office had condemned. Matty tried to turn the motor over. No luck. He found himself hurling the same Shakespearean cadences at the ancient vehicle Roley had used on their first meeting. The car just wouldn't start.

Matty realized he had no other option. He ran back into the cottage and out into the garden. Climbing over the stone wall, he clawed his way through the thick ivy blanketing the steep hillside two hundred yards between his place and Inez's sprawling villa. He lost his footing a few times and slid back down the hill. By the time he reached the edge of the patio, Matty looked like a battle-grimed Marine who had just captured Iwo Jima.

Inez's cries were ear-piercing at close range. Matty had to pummel the French doors with his fists in order for her to hear him.

Inez stood stark naked in the living room pointing in terror at Matty on the other side of the doors as if he were the Creature from the Black Lagoon. Under any other circumstances, Matty would have relished this privileged glimpse at one of the world's most incredible bodies. His concern was getting into the house and helping her. When Matty finally realized Inez was beyond being of any assistance, he kicked out a pane of glass next to the door handle, reached through and let himself in.

No sooner was he inside when he heard the front door slam shut and a car screech into reverse in the driveway. Should he go after whomever it was or try and calm Inez down? He opted out for the latter. Her screams only increased as Matty drew nearer.

"Inez! Miss Sanche! It's Matt Garber. Don't you recognize me? I'm your neighbor. You sent me the orange tree when I—"

She lashed out at Matty with her nails and, if he hadn't dodged her claws in time, he was certain she'd have scarred him for life. She turned and ran out of the living room, up the stairs, and locked herself in the lavatory where Matty had first encountered her what seemed centuries ago.

Matty was scared. He was out of his depth and realized only one person could handle the situation. He prayed Steerforth was home. That's if he wasn't the mysterious visitor who had bolted from the place minutes ago. A phone call would tell.

"Hello, old son. To what do I owe the honor of—?"

"I'm at Inez's house, Jimmy. Better get over here. She's lost it completely."

"Be right there."

Ten minutes later, Steerforth was at the top of the stairs trying to calm Inez down as she continued to wail on the other side of the door. All the while Matty filled his colleague in on the events of the past half hour.

"Didn't see who it was?" asked Steerforth.

"No. Didn't want to leave her alone. Who knows what she might—"

"God only knows what she's doing in there," muttered Steerforth. "What with razor blades, pills— Have you got a belt on?"

"No. These pants aren't—"

"Don't need a fashion report, Matthew. Go into her bedroom. Go through the cupboards. Find the longest belts you can get your hands on. Go!"

"Which way is—?"

"Down the corridor!"

Matty took off down the hall as Steerforth walked over to the door.

"Inez! Get away from the door, luv. I don't want to hurt you. Can you hear me? Get back from the door."

With one powerful kick, Steerforth forced the door open. A hysterical Inez was on him a second later clawing, biting, and scratching him with demonic fury. Matty was on the scene a second later holding half a dozen leather and metallic belts and staring mesmerized at the wrestling match going on at his feet.

"For God's sake, Garber! Quit staring at her pussy and help me hold her down. Might be turning you on, but it's bloody hard work for me."

It took them another fifteen minutes before they had successfully managed to manacle her ankles and wrists with the belts and carry her downstairs to the living room. She was now spouting obscenities. Steerforth had to gag her with the sash from one of her dressing gowns. Only then did he notice the blood dripping down his face.

"Matthew, get me a cold compress or a damp towel or something appropriate to the boy scout in you."

"Jesus, Jimmy! Think we should call a doctor?"

"No doctors! And no cops! Go on!"

By the time Matty returned with a soaking wet towel, Inez had calmed down. Steerforth was staring intently at a brown half-smoked cigarette he had picked up from the Mexican brass ashtray on the launching-pad-sized coffee table.

"Want a light?" asked Matty.

"Think you could handle two of us?" countered Steerforth, nodding toward the bound and gagged Inez. "Know what this is?"

"Looks like a Nat Sherman cigarette."

"There are two kinds of Shermans out here. The regular ones and the 'treated' ones."

"Treated ones?"

"PCP. Angel dust. Two tokes on this and you'd be racing for the moon faster than Vaughan Monroe."

"Jesus! Why would Inez—?"

"She didn't know what it was. I know the lady's tastes. She's too much of a snob for angel dust."

"What are we going to do with her?"

"See if she's got a cleaning bag somewhere. Preferably not transparent. We've got to get her out of here without anyone knowing."

"Where are we taking her?"

"Pasadena."

"What's in Pasadena?"

"A private clinic that specializes in drug cases. They're used to people like her. And they don't have a direct line from the admissions desk to Miss Rona's typewriter. The poor girl's name is Sandowsky. Irma Sandowsky. Remember that."

They finally settled for a serape the President of Mexico had presented to Inez on a tour she had made there early in her career. Steerforth draped this over her in the back seat and held her in a restraining position there while Matty drove. Throughout the forty-five-minute ride Inez made frantic attempts to tear off the blanket.

"PCP all right," grunted Steerforth. "They always get hot and want to tear their clothes off. If I get my hands on the bloody cur who did this—"

"Any ideas who—"

"Watch the road, lad. Time enough to play Sam Spade."

Matty leaped out of the car once they had reached the clinic. Seconds later a team of orderlies raced out with a stretcher and hustled "Miss Sandowsky" inside. Steerforth and Garber were right behind them. They were so absorbed in the problem at hand they'd failed to notice the chocolate-brown Mercedes parked in the lot with the personalized plates IAA.

***

Rankoff sat in the chair staring at his daughter curled up on the sofa. He'd been there an hour and she hadn't said a word to him. Not that she ever had for the almost ten years she'd been a patient at the clinic. Ever since the night he had brought her home from the party in Westwood. Bad acid, her friends had muttered guiltily. She hadn't come down. The doctors had no explanation, no solution. It was merely a question of waiting. And prayer.

Ten years later she remained as silent as ever. A hopeless case.

The dreamer part of Rankoff—the part the world thought had died with the Forties—continued to pray and hope for a miracle.

"Sam Goldwyn could make you talk," Rankoff told the sphinxlike Martine. "Mind if I talk, kid? I get sick of just coming here and sitting like a dummy for two hours looking real sad. You've been quiet for ten years now. Not that you missed much. It was a good decade to sleep through. We ran out of everything: honesty, love, guts, oil. Maybe you saw it coming. You always were ahead of your time, kid. Should have listened to you more. When did you start wearing beads? A year before anyone else. They don't wear beads anymore,

Marty. Remember Tom Hayden? You thought he was a god? He does, too, now. He married Jane Fonda. They're going to be the first mellow king and queen of the United States.

"We got rid of Nixon. You missed out on that. His 'honesty' drove him from office. The Christ of San Clemente. He's good for another comeback. Hell! Harry Lauder made a career of farewell performances. You don't remember him, do you? He was the Scots Don Ho. I lost a couple of good friends, too, when you were in here. Bing died. On the golf course. Which was nice. Elvis died. In the bathroom. Which wasn't nice. Groucho died. Jack Benny died. Edgar Bergen, too.

"We killed Paul Robeson years ago so everybody was amazed when he actually died. The Duke died. Both Dukes. I never met the one who used to be King but nobody played piano like Edward Ellington. Never forget the first time I heard him play 'Take the A Train.' By the way, kid, you were wrong. Jazz came back. Better than ever. I even thought about singing again. Crazy, huh? You always wanted me to sing again. I sang at a party last year. Stopped the show.

"Ethel Waters died. Louis Armstrong. Remember when he played trumpet at your fifth birthday party? Janis Joplin died, too. And that kid from the Rolling Stones. You'd have to ask Bazzo his name. Who else? John Wayne. They've turned him into a saint now. Started dragging out posters of him when the hostages were held in Teheran. Didn't know about the hostages, did you? Or Iran. Or Afghanistan. Peace and love vanished with your beads, Marty. We hate the Russians again. We love the Chinese. World politics is like Hollywood. Upwardly mobile amnesia.

"Robert Shaw dropped dead. Finally became a movie star. But I think it hurt him that the price was giving up being an incredible novelist. Peter Finch dropped dead, too. In the lobby of the Beverly Hills. They gave him an Oscar for expiring. Larry Harvey died of cancer. Poor Larushka! Uncle Gig really did it. I still get the shivers on that one. Happy-go-lucky Gig with the worst set of private devils he never told anyone about. He was always fascinated that his three best friends from the Forties did it and he was the only one left.

"Mary Pickford died. Charlie Chaplin. Adolph Zukor. And poor old Sam Goldfish. That's when I knew movies were really dead. Goldwyn knew a good story when he heard one. That's why I know he'd of made you talk. 'Bobby, Bobby. What are ya tellin' me? The girl's in a hospital for ten years and she don't say nothin'? I can't make a picture like that! We want a happy story! And look what happens to the parents: the mother becomes a lesbian and the father *shtups* girls his daughter's age. I'd never get it past the Hayes office. Even if Mary Astor was the mother. We could get Merle for the daughter. She's not too old—well lit. Could we fix the father up so Gary Cooper could play it? Maybe the mother only drinks and the father messes around with over-twenty-one's. No minors. I think we might be on to a story then. But in the last reel the daughter's got to talk. Better yet: she should sing!'

"Sorry, Sam. I'm preserving the integrity of my story. I know: 'If I want to send a message, I should do it with Western Union.' But life's not a Goldwyn movie. There is no angel named Dudley. Freddy March is dead, too. So is Merle, poor thing. How she fought it! The world's different, Sam. Nobody cares if there isn't a happy ending. Everybody's waiting for the worst: the Russians, the bomb, the big quake, the invasion of the body snatchers. Yeah. Don't tell anybody, Marty. But the invasion started long ago. We aren't the same people inside anymore.

"I loved your mother. I really did. I look at you—at your face— and see the best parts of my youth and hers. Don't know what went wrong, baby. Every day's a mystery to me. So I took up the cure. And I tried another one. And another one. I'm not a dirty old man. Don't let anybody tell you that. I see those kids and they remind me of you before you . . . went away. I mean you're not here. 'Cause if you were, you'd talk to me. Like you used to. You'd straighten me out. And your mother. Because I can't stand the pain much longer. Carried my father and my brother around with me long enough. You're dead weight now, Martine. I need some help. Please help me, baby. Help your old man."

***

Steerforth was heavily engrossed with the doctors discussing "Miss Sandowsky's" problem so Matty wandered around the Pasadena clinic in search of a coffee machine. A nurse suggested he might be more comfortable in the visitors' lounge on the second floor.

Entering the lounge with his coffee cup, he heard a man crying. He looked around the room but saw no one. Then in a far corner by the window he saw a man in silent mourning. All but spilling the hot coffee on himself, he realized it was Rankoff.

His first instinct was to leave knowing Rankoff would resent his presence. But there was something so pitiful and lonely about the racking sobs Garber's heart poured out to the man, whose life had so obsessed him the past year.

"Bobby?" He all but whispered the name as he approached the man.

Rankoff turned around, startled. Matty braced himself for one of his boss's indignant tirades. Rankoff merely stared at him like a frightened child with tears pouring down his handsome face.

Matty placed his coffee on the windowsill and stared helplessly at his employer.

"I—I—" Rankoff tried to speak but couldn't. His hands moved in futile arcs. Matty wrapped his arms around the man trying to comfort him and realized why Rankoff was at the clinic.

"It's your daughter," he whispered. "She's here."

Rankoff murmured something unintelligible into Matty's shoulder.

"Can't hear you."

"Want to get out of here," gasped Rankoff. "Please, help me."

"Sure. Sure. Give me a second."

Matty couldn't find Steerforth, but he left a message with the admissions desk explaining that an urgent family matter had come up and he'd be making his own way back into town. He returned to the visitors' lounge, took Rankoff's keys, and drove the man in silence back to Trousdale.

Ames opened the front door. His face went ashen when he saw Rankoff's condition.

"Mr. Rankoff! What is it, sir? Shall I telephone the doctor?"

"No, no. Just get me a brandy. Two of them. Like you to stay, Matty. Please?"

"Sure."

"Where would you like them, sir?"

"In the library. Thanks, Ames."

"Not at all, sir."

Rankoff belted the brandy back in one go, and asked Ames for a refill.

"Another piece of the puzzle, huh, kid?" asked Rankoff after Ames had brought him the refill and left the library.

"Don't really understand," Matty replied weakly.

"I was pissed off when I heard about you checking up on me. Then I was flattered. Never thought I was that fascinating. Now you know everything."

"I didn't follow you to the clinic today," blurted Matty. "That was a coincidence." He quickly recounted the story of Inez freaking out that afternoon. "I was completely thrown when I saw you in the visitors' lounge."

"Want a cigarette?" He tossed one to Matty. "What am I, Matthew? What conclusions have you drawn about Robert Rankoff?"

"I've never judged you."

"You're the only person in my life who hasn't. Seem to have been on trial for fifty-three years. Still waiting for the verdict."

Rankoff began to talk. He spoke about Cleveland, his father and his brother Murray. And Phyllis.

"I met Phyllis."

"Where?" Rankoff sounded genuinely amazed.

"In New York. At Abe Keller's house. She . . . told me the story."

"Bitterly, I'm sure."

"No. She said you're still her favorite singer."

"Yeah? How'd she look?"

"Terrific. She's married to this guy Edward Marshak. He's a big corporation lawyer—"

"I know. She was a great kid. Deserved better than me."

"Why are you so down on yourself?"

"Because I live a lie, Matthew. I was something once upon a time. I was an artist once. My old man used to snort and call me an *artiste* when I suggested it. But god damn it! I was good. You read, those books now. Sinatra, Haymes, and Rankoff. We were the sound of the

Forties. How did I end up a pimp? A rich, famous pimp. But still a pimp. A ten-percenter. A dealmaker. Living off the talent of others. My father wouldn't believe it if he could see me now. A big success. Famous. Don't return calls for days at a time. You wouldn't recognize me, Pop." Rankoff stared up at the ceiling then finished his brandy.

"Why did you give up singing?"

"What kind of biographer are you?" asked Rankoff sarcastically. "That's the major turning point of the story."

"You got into trouble with the Mafia."

"So you know. Or do you want the sordid details?"

"No."

"It was James M. Cain time," said Rankoff, who couldn't seem to turn off the faucet of memory. "Working a hotel back east. 1951, Had an affair with the owner's wife. He found out and made a phone call. One lousy phone call and I was blacklisted. . . . What are you staring at me like that for?"

"It wasn't Sylvia Nardino, was it?"

"Matthew, when I decided to make you an agent I didn't mean a secret agent. This is IAA. Not the CIA! How did you know about Sylvia?"

"Sylvia? The woman's name should be Circe! Luring men to their doom."

"What are you talking about?" asked Rankoff, lighting another cigarette. "Come on, kid. Give and take."

"How well do you know Jimmy Steerforth?"

"There's a family named Stubbs in Bakewell."

"You knew that?"

"Everybody out here changes their name. So what?"

"He came ashore in Sylvia Nardino's trunk. He was a . . . a gigolo till she dumped him."

"When the hell was this?"

"Early Fifties."

"When Ed Nardino sent her to Europe to get over me! Son-of-a-bitch! Life really is a mosaic, isn't it?"

"You don't understand! He's been living like a fugitive ever since. He's been living here illegally!"

"No, he hasn't," replied Rankoff matter-of-factly.

"What do you mean?"

"I found out about that Stubbs business a long time ago. Didn't want him to get into trouble. So I arranged for his papers. In case he ran into any difficulties down the line."

"Did you tell him?"

"Of course not. Jimmy's a private guy. I respect that."

"He's a private guy because he's been terrified for twenty-five years someone would find out his secret."

"Are you serious?"

"My God, Bobby! Why do you think you could never phone him? Mail a letter to him?"

"Jeez. I should tell him."

Matty burst into laughter at the sheer simplicity of Rankoff's statement.

"Had no idea," shrugged the agency boss embarrassedly.

"You're amazing! You really are the most amazing human being I've ever met."

"Really think so?"

"How did you get him an alien residency without his knowing?"

"Good connections. Do me a favor. Call and tell him. Okay? I'm really embarrassed now. . . . Jimmy and Sylvia! Can't believe it. She sure got around."

There was a long silence before Garber summoned the courage to take advantage of this newfound intimacy with the formerly secretive Rankoff to ask: "How's your daughter?"

"That's a sensitive— No change. She just sits there and stares into space. I'd give up everything—really would— just to have her say, 'Hello, Daddy' again." Rankoff sank into a moment of introspection then reached for the telephone on the coffee table and held it out to Garber. "Here. Phone Jimmy. Ask him how Inez is and tell him about this immigration thing. It's going to drive me nuts now."

Garber dialed the formerly secret telephone number but there was no reply.

"Where else could he be?" asked Rankoff.

"Maybe his uncle's."

"What's he like?"

"Who? Ivor? Terrific."

"Is he a *mensch*?"

"Why?"

"Cause he's dating a friend of mine and I wouldn't like to see her get hurt. She's had enough shit in her life."

"If you're worried he's after Evelyn's money, forget it. Ivor's loaded. Not like Evelyn. There's old unfinished business between them and they're just catching up on lost time."

"So he's okay?"

"He's a wonderful man. He's been Jimmy's guardian all these years."

"That's good. I don't like to stick my nose in. You may have gathered that. She sounds happier than I've heard her in years. Just wanted to make sure. . . . She's very special to me. She saved my life."

"How?"

"After that business with Sylvia. Couldn't get arrested. Didn't know what to do. All my life I only wanted to be a singer. Then I couldn't sing. I was suicidal. Evelyn came to the rescue. She suggested becoming an agent. Abe rejected the idea. Didn't think I was tough enough. But Abe was in New York and Sid was out here. She drove Sid nuts till he agreed to give me a chance. Been at the corner of Rodeo and Charleville ever since. And in Evelyn's debt. . . So now you really do know everything."

"Almost."

"What else?"

"Why does Rees Davenport hate you?"

"That's your assignment, Matthew. Find out, would you? Get that maniac off my back once and for all. And get the hell out of here. I'm exhausted."

By the time Ames drove Matty home, it was close to seven and Garber dreaded the pile of scripts he still had to plow through before Monday morning. The red light was on Matty's Record-a-Call machine. He hoped it was a message from Steerforth with news of Inez's condition.

"Hello, twig," said the recorded voice of Minden Prescott. "Trust you're not doing anything that'll damage your eyesight. Just wanted to let you know I've almost finished the first draft of *Shoes*. I'm already preparing my acceptance speech for the Oscar. Tell Cal Chambers to put on his best truss and get ready to read." . . . BEEP . . . "Matthew? It's Ara. I wonder if you could call me, darling. I have a bit of a problem and—never mind. I'll have to deal with it myself. See you at the office tomorrow." . . . BEEP . . . "Heyyyy, Junior! It's your old Uncle Gilbob. In Biloxi, Mississippi. Just came up with the most fabulous— What's that? No, I'll be off in a second. No! Don't go 'way. I've got the rest of my life available for you, you little poopsie— Hey, Junior. Got to run. There's a little spinner out here looks ripe for the picking. I'll call you later this week." . . . BEEP . . . "Hello? Uh, Garber . . . Matt. Dwight Foley here. How's it going, guy? It's a nice afternoon. Good day. Good conditions. Thought we might take a little jog together. Shape up for the week. Keep physically vigilant. Yeah, uh, you're not there. Signing off." . . . BEEP . . . Silence. No Steerforth.

Matty made himself a sandwich in the kitchen, pulled out a can of Olympia from the fridge, and settled down in the living room with a script entitled *Hard Nut to Crack*. Ten pages later he tossed it across the room. He'd give it to his secretary the next day and have her prepare a report.

He picked up the next script on the pile when he heard a strange gnawing sound in the wall. Oh, no! Not rats. Roley had told him there had once been a nest of them under the floor but the exterminator had taken care of them long ago. That was before the rains. This variety of rats loved ivy and the monsoon conditions at the beginning of the year had caused an explosion of growth on the hillside.

"Go away!" shouted Matty with the preposterous notion of scaring the rats away.

"Sorry," replied a voice on the other side of the front door.

"No, no!" replied Matty leaping up from his seat and heading for the door.

Dwight Foley stood there in an avocado-green jogging suit.

"Didn't mean to intrude," said the hulking blond giant.

"No, no, no," said Matty nervously. "Wasn't talking to you, Dwight. It was a rat. In the wall. Come in, please."

"Phoned before—"

"Got your message. Sorry I wasn't here but. . ." Matty was about to tell Dwight about Inez but decided not to. Everyone at IAA would hear soon enough.

"Rats, huh? We had them in Nam. Followed us everywhere. Filthy vermin. Better do something about them."

"It's the ivy. They love to—"

"Got anything to drink? Just ran twenty miles."

"Twenty miles!"

"Said that."

"Heard you."

"Collated data."

"You in the reserves, Dwight?" Matty asked from the fridge, holding up another can of Olympia.

Foley shook his head: "Negative. Got any rainwater?"

"Damn! They're late this week. Will Arrowhead do?"

"Affirmative. No ice!" The last phrase came out with all the vigor and volume of Teddy Roosevelt leading his men up San Juan Hill.

"Collated data," nodded Matty, throwing caution to the wind and daring to have a little fun with the humorless ex-Green Beret/ex-Jew. "Here you go." He handed Foley the spring water in the largest glass he could find. "I'd let you have the whole bottle but I can't lift it off the cooler stand."

"You waste too much time on trivia and nonsense," said Foley, after belting down the quart of water in one swallow. "Been meaning to speak to you about that. Been meaning to have this briefing for a long time. Understand you met with Dr. Kislev in Las Vegas."

"Briefly."

"You offended him."

"In what way?"

"Kislev's a great man. I know he's an object of ridicule to many who don't appreciate him and his teachings. People like that are close-minded. They won't survive the decade."

"What'll happen to them? Internment camps in Nevada?"

"Negative cant!"

"Could you keep your voice down, Dwight?"

"Remember the first day you came to work at IAA?"

"It's emblazoned in my memory."

"I wanted you to impress me. Remember that? Wanted to know what made you special. Remember?"

"Collated data."

"See this ring?" Foley held up one gigantic hand to exhibit the ubiquitous circle and triangle design. "Dr. Kislev tried telling you about it and you rejected him."

"It was three in the morning, Dwight!"

"I'm here to offer you another chance."

"Thrice did they offer me the crown and thrice did I refuse."

"You *are* special, Garber. I've seen it this past year. But you'll dissipate it if you don't harness it properly. Examine your factional options, man. Don't hitch your wagon to these jaded, jaundiced jerkoffs. Your instincts are all solo force! Go with them. Go with us! Know the absolute euphoria that can be yours when you become operative."

"Become operative?"

"I'm telling you more than I should. But I feel I can share with you. Collated data. Ever gone out into the desert and stared up at the stars? Until you find *your* star?"

"I was only in Vegas for one night," shrugged Matty.

"NEGATIVE CANT!" bellowed Foley. "You're resisting, Garber. You're resisting. Let yourself feel the infinite power of the circle and the strength of the triangle. Look at my ring, Garber. Look at my ring. Think of the desert. Think of unlimited release. Look at my ring."

"Dwight, please don't—"

"Don't resist, Matt! You can only be greater and stronger and—"

The biggest, fattest rat Matty had ever seen ran across his living room floor at that moment. He felt his stomach do an instant flip-flop. Foley leaped to his feet in a flash and pulled something out of his pants. An explosion rocked the tiny cottage. A second later the rat lay dead on the floor. Matty shouted in alarm, turned to Foley in disbelief and gasped: "What's that!?"

"A rat. Have you got one of those green garbage bags?"

"To hell with the rat! What's *that*?" asked Matty, pointing to the still smoking snub-nosed .38 clutched in Foley's enormous paw.

"That's my American Express card," grinned Foley, tucking the gun back in his sweatpants. "Don't leave home without it."

"Do you wear it in the office?"

"I wear it in the shower. My old CO in Nam, Colonel Claypoole, used to tell us: 'A soldier should not only carry his gun but be his gun.'"

"That's fine in wartime but—"

"This *is* wartime, Garber. Don't let anyone fool you. We must be tactically vigilant at all times both in the field and in the home."

"Do you really believe all that shit you spout?"

"We're directionless in this country, Garber. We have no leaders; we have no moral code. We're like Germany in the Thirties. Decadent, immoral, self-indulgent—"

"I liked jaded, jaundiced jerkoffs myself."

"You need to be retrained. Join us! The agency is only the beginning. We can seize control of the media. The country's at the mercy of that little box. We can sell them anything. Not with fist-pounding. Soft, soft. I tried to explain this to Nolan but . . ."

The silence that followed was unbearable. The agonizing quiet of fear. Garber knew that his baiting of Foley had led the blond hulk into a labyrinth of madness, triggering off some horrible moment that might be instantly recreated. Matty flashed on the dead bodies of Nolan and Kate. No! Dwight couldn't be that crazy. And yet . . . *become operative*. What the hell did that mean? Matty didn't want to know. Not at this moment in time. How could he rescue the situation and, possibly, his own life?

"He was a Mormon," suggested Matty hastily. "His upbringing, his teachings. They would have resisted any other form of—"

"Yes, yes," nodded Foley. "Affirmative. I should go now. Monday tomorrow."

"Yeah."

They both rose from their chairs.

"You should do something about that rat."

"I will."

"Good seeing you."

"Glad you dropped by."

"Good night."

"Good night."

Matty shook uncontrollably for ten minutes after Foley had left the cottage. It was unthinkable, unimaginable. Yet his trembling body was sending him the same message over and over again: Dwight Foley had murdered Kate Baker and Nolan Goodly.

He ran into the kitchen, took a Hefty bag out from under the sink, put on an oven glove, dumped the dead rat and the glove into the plastic bag and wrapped it into a tight ball. He was still shaking as he tossed the ball into a garbage can next to the cottage.

Steerforth! He had to talk to Jimmy. The line was busy. He tried repeatedly. The operator told him the line was out of order.

Garber slid in behind the wheel of the Cord and prayed the motor would start. He had to see Steerforth. He had to get away from the cottage. The darkest part of his mind feared Foley would come back.

The Cord's motor made a few wheezing noises before it finally turned over. Matty guided the car down to Sunset then east to Benedict Canyon. Turning north on Benedict, he reached Hutton Drive then veered off the side road that led to the secluded little glade where Steerforth had lived in secret for so many years.

The lights were on and Steerforth's car was parked outside. Stereo was blaring inside. He recognized the voice of Mick Jagger singing "You Can't Always Get What You Want." He knocked at the door. No answer. He tried the bell but the Rolling Stones drowned it out.

"Jimmy! Jimmy!"

He wandered around to the back of the house where the bedroom was.

"Jimmy! Jimmy, for Chrissake!"

The pride of Bakewell had planted speakers all over the house. No way Matty's voice could be heard over the relentless rhythm. Steerforth had to be in the bedroom. It was merely a question of tapping on the window loud enough to-

Matty stood frozen for a moment watching as they made blissful and unabandoned love. He snuck away before they could see him—

his cheeks scorching with embarrassment and a perverse sense of betrayal. *My whole life's turned around. I mean it's crazy and it's wonderful and it's so right. I just hope that you'll be happy for me.*

"I will, Wheezer. Just not right now. I can't right now," he murmured to himself as the image of her and Steerforth caromed off the pockets of his brain.

He wondered if he had enough gas as he headed the Cord east toward the desert.

JOY

Now is the time to strike, thought Joy Dworkin, lying flat on her back oblivious to the furious energy she was inspiring. Definitely the time to stage a coup while everyone was crippled. Who could stop her?

Steerforth's career was in a curious holding pattern since Inez's breakdown. The network was up in arms over her series grinding to a halt. Jimmy had always been able to pull her together in the past when she'd freaked out, but this time he was powerless and his reputation was suffering as a guy who could deliver.

Rankoff was walking around in a daze as well. Something was eating away at him and he'd been unable to make any positive decisions. Matty's disappearance hadn't helped too much either. Where was Matty? Nobody seemed to know. He'd phoned the office mysteriously at the beginning of the week and said he wouldn't be in for a few days. That was four days ago and still no sign of the boy wonder from St. Louis.

Foley seemed to be cracking up as well. He had reduced the formerly unemotional Beatrice to tears Monday morning after an awesome tirade and she'd handed in her resignation.

Which only left Ara. God, how she hated her! Not because she was her mother but because she didn't have the courage to come forward and admit it. All those years as a child in Chicago seeing this beautiful woman turn up from time to time to check with Harry and Rose on how she was doing. Peeking out at her through the crack in the doorway. Why had she disowned her? Why had she given her up?

Joy spent years tracking her down. Waiting, waiting, waiting for the opportune moment to confront her. Working her way up through the agency till she was on the same level as her.

How strange it had been to watch this alcoholic woman at close quarters for two years! How tragic to watch the incredible beauty she remembered walking through a besotted haze as the Painted Lady. Then the incredible transformation of the past two months as she miraculously regained her beauty, her poise, her self-confidence.

She'll acknowledge me now! She's strong enough to admit to the world who I really am! But it never happened.

Joy had to rely on her ultimate weapon.

"I've got her!" shouted Joy, hurling Steve Goodbaum's panting body off of her and leaping out of the bed in the Chateau Marmont.

"What are you doing?" wailed the bearded baby mogul from Universal. "I was holding it so long. Just about to come!"

"Oh, Stevie!" she groaned, stepping into her panties and pulling her dress over her head. "There's more to life than an orgasm!"

"But I waited. I've never held it this long in my life."

"Then you'll be even better next time."

"When? When?" demanded Goodbaum.

"Don't know, baby," she shrugged, zipping up her Ferarri racing driver's jacket. "Got a lot of things to do."

"Can't you finish me off?" he whimpered.

"Why don't you go home and have your wife do it?"

"She thinks I'm impotent. I am with her."

"Aww, you're sweet," she said, blowing him a kiss from the door. "Let's have lunch next week. There's a client I want to talk to you about."

She walked down the corridor to the elevator, pressed the button and waited.

Can't do it alone, she thought. I need someone to help me. Bazzo's too spaced out. Big Stu? Has he got the brains to handle it? Probably. But he'd probably just want to fuck me all the time and we'd never get anything done. Probably break me in half with that black snake of his. Not that it wouldn't be a pleasant experience as a one shot. But there's a business to run here. Deals to be made. No. Matty was still the best bet. If he ever comes back.

***

Ara Whalen put down the telephone in her office and glanced at her Piaget watch. Eight o'clock? Her days were getting longer and longer in the office. Normally she didn't mind. She thrived on work lately and the new self-respect it instilled in her. She'd be late for dinner at this rate, and she had no desire to keep Sergio waiting more than a fashionable fifteen minutes.

Checking the call-back list on her desk, Ara saw there were still half a dozen names she hadn't attended to. They'd have to wait until morning. She'd get in early and—Maybe she wouldn't.

"Wouldn't that be nice for a change," she murmured to herself as she fantasized on a possible outcome for the evening.

She switched off the lights in her office and stepped out into the deserted hallway. Everyone had left half an hour before. Walking toward the elevator, Ara changed her mind and decided to take the stairs in keeping with her new regimen of physical fitness.

The sound of a piano could be heard from the music room on the fifth floor. Ara changed direction and started climbing the stairs. She was almost at the door of the music room when she recognized Rankoff's voice.

> *The stars have lost their glitter*
> *I try to please in vain*
> *Wandering in the darkness*
> *Why can't we be there again?*

"That brings back memories," she smiled from the doorway.

"You weren't supposed to hear that," said Rankoff, looking up from the keyboard.

"I saw you sing at the Paramount in New York when I was sixteen. *Saw* you. Didn't hear a word. All the girls were screaming their heads off."

"Yeah," grinned Rankoff. "Frank and I used to compare battle scars. We were lucky to get out the stage door alive."

"Do you miss it? The singing."

"I did for a long time. Then I buried it in my work. The need. But lately . . . Can't stop thinking about it. How'd it sound?"

"Terrific. Needs a little work but—"

"Yeah, yeah. Come back in a few weeks, you'll see what you can do."

The two longtime business associates laughed and stared at each other.

"Have I sent you a memo, Miss Whalen, commenting on your incredible transformation these past two months?"

"Thank you, kind sir. You okay?"

"What have you heard?"

"Nothing. Just wonder about you sometimes. We see each other eight hours a day. Discuss nothing but business and before we know it another year's gone by."

"Where'd that come from?"

"The eight o'clock blues. Summoning up the courage for my date."

"Anybody I know?" asked Rankoff.

"No. He's Italian. Textiles. Sixty. A young sixty. He thinks I'm forty-two . . . for now."

"Where'd you meet him?"

"The Wallaces. A small gathering of two hundred. He sprinted across the room. Thought he was making a beeline for Bo Derek. I was astounded when he stopped in front of me. His English is appalling but the rest of him is first class. Is there hope for me yet, Bobby?"

"You're a survivor, kid. Knew that when you worked for Abe."

"A hundred years ago."

"Yesterday," shrugged Rankoff, who began to tinkle "The Very Thought of You" on the keys.

"Do you hate getting old?"

"Not really. It's floating that gets me. I've been floating for years. Waiting for . . . something. A change. How did you do it?"

"What?"

"Change."

"I haven't changed," said Ara. "I've been eighteen all my life. That's my problem. Wouldn't mind getting old if I could just grow up."

"Don't be in such a hurry. Always felt if you don't grow up by the age of ten, you never will. Martine was grown up when she was eight. Yvonne and I always felt she was the parent. Guess she got tired of being a grownup. She missed out on being a kid. So she found her own private existence."

"That what they say at the clinic?"

"No, that's just Dr. Rankoff, the ole philosopher. Penny for your thoughts. A nickel in the gum machine . . . Have you heard from Matty yet?"

"No. What do you want to do about him?"

"He's a senior agent Has his own wings. We never sent the dogs after Jimmy."

"We always knew where Jimmy was. We just never knew what he was doing. Did you speak to Stan today?"

"Briefly."

"How does he feel about UA shelving *Brother?*"

"Relieved. Tom Ricker was over the edge. Dailies were a disaster. Firing the director didn't help."

"The big mistake was replacing him with Violette-Claire.," said Ara. "How could Stanley have done that and expected the picture to ever be finished?"

"Don't know. What time's your date?"

"Oh, God! Thanks for reminding me. Poor Sergio's cooling his heels at L'Orangerie. How do I look?"

"Eighteen."

"Thanks a lot. Swear I'm going senile. Rehab is killing me. Losing things. Turned my house upside down for two days trying to find my earrings."

"You're wearing them."

"Not these. The ones Abe gave me when I married Minden. Had them for years. They're very special. I think somebody stole them. I really do."

"What are they? Diamonds?"

"No. Jade. Black jade."

* * *

Shmuel Kislev and Dwight Foley glared at each other on opposite sides of the desk in the good doctor's Camden Drive consulting room. Gone were the days of Damon and Pythias. This was their Hitler-Stalin period and even that fragile alliance was crumbling with each passing second.

"Why did you fire Beatrice?" demanded the Israeli.

"He'll hear you out there," cautioned Foley, nodding toward the waiting room.

"Had the door soundproofed," countered Kislev scornfully. "I don't take chances, Dwight. I want an answer."

"She was a security risk. She had ceased to be tactically vigilant."

"Don't you think I should have been consulted? I sent her to you."

"Felt I should handle it solo force."

"Like you handled Nolan?"

"That was . . . an accident."

"The girl, too?"

"How many times do you want me to go through this?" roared Foley. "He was going to slip through our fingers. I realized that the night of the affiliates' dinner. Had to recruit him that night. No other factional option was open to me. When I went over to his place, he laughed at me. He shouldn't have done that. I lost my temper."

"So you killed him?"

"I *hit* him. That's all."

"You're a trained killer . . . Ira."

"What did you call me?" Foley raised one of his gigantic hands over his head.

"Calm down, you maniac. You're not in the jungle now."

"Don't talk to me like that, Shmuel. Don't ever talk to me like that. I've done a lot for you. Brought you your patients. *My* clients! Remained tactically vigilant throughout our entire—"

"Did you have to kill the girl, too? That was not an accident, Dwight. That was murder."

"I was blown away when she came out of the bedroom. Mr. Goody Two Shoes balling a little bunny like that! She saw him lying there. Had to go operative. Made it look good, don't you think? Cops thought it was a lovers' quarrel. Even got the dope from Bazzo and scattered it around the place."

"Did Bazzo ever wonder—?"

"Negative! Told him it was for a client. He's so spaced out he can't remember one day from another. Don't worry about him. A dead issue." Foley chortled at the last line.

"Proud of yourself, aren't you?" asked Kislev, mangling his vowels and glaring at the blond hulk with the most condescending look his glassy, teddy bear eyes could convey.

"What do you mean?" countered Foley warily.

"Thought of everything?"

"Collated data."

"What about the jade?"

"The jeed?"

"The black jade. The little gift you gave Inez on her opening night? She thought a great deal of it, didn't she? So much so she gave them to Nolan Goodly to spite you!"

"Insensitive bitch!"

"Stupid fool! I told you to stay away from her. She was totally in Steerforth's power. What made you think you were a lady's man?"

"I bought the jade in Saigon. Cost me a fortune setting them into gold. Went to eighteen different jewelers to get it right. Inez was touched. Said she'd keep them forever. Nolan flaunted that jade at me! That's when I blew up and—"

"What a fool you are, Dwight! She could have gone to the police any time."

"She didn't, did she? She's too dumb to put two and two together—"

"Steerforth isn't! Something had to be done."

"And you really did it, didn't you, Shmuel?" Foley's eyes had narrowed into little slits as he realized the Israeli had opened his own can of worms inadvertently. "You went operative, didn't you? A regular little Moshe Dayan last Sunday? Hmmm?"

"I examined my factional options. . . ." Kislev's speech was losing some of its old assurance. "Felt another approach to the woman might swing her round to our—"

"So you gave her a goddamn Sherman dipped in PCP. Now she's out of her mind and of no use to anyone!"

"At least she won't talk."

"'Von't toke?' She won't do anything, you stupid putz!" Foley's voice had become shrill on the last line and his whole persona reverted to the long-buried Ira Fogelson. "The prize catch for our stable. Remember? Our spokesperson once we seized control of the network. You blew it!!"

"Negative cant!"

"Horseshit with your negative cant and your tactical vigilance and your collated data. I don't know why I ever trusted you, you hook-nosed *goniff*!"

"Dwight!" The good doctor was genuinely shocked. "You're overwrought."

"'Over rut'? I've had it! The coup has failed, Shmuel. Nobody believes in us. You can't beat Rankoff."

"I will!" thundered Kislev. "He rubbed my nose in the dirt with Kip O'Donnell. Think I can forget that?"

"Whatever happened to Kip?"

"What do I care? He went back to the beach. Pain-in-the ass! After all the work I did for him! That ungrateful *shaygetz*! That blond *loksh*!'

"Wasn't his fault," shrugged Foley.

"Whose side are you on, Dwight? For crying out loud! Still say Rankoff is the key. Remove Rankoff and the agency is ours!"

"How do you plan to get rid of him?"

Kislev turned his pear-shaped body toward the and nodded toward the man waiting in reception.

"He's a flake," scoffed Foley.

"One of our most devout disciples. Ask him to come in, Dwight. Politely."

Seconds later Stan Feingold sauntered into the consulting room.

"Good evening, Stanley," chirped Kislev.

"How ya doin', doctor? Dwight?"

Foley grunted his best noncommittal greeting.

"Please sit down, Stanley." Kislev gestured to a wing-back chair. "So sorry to read about the cancellation of your film."

"What the hell!" shrugged Feingold, pulling a pack of Marlboros out of his pocket. "Mind if I smoke? Maybe it was fated. That *schvatrzer* was always crazy. Should've listened to my father-in-law years ago."

"But the film is insured?" asked Kislev.

"In where?"

"Insured."

"Insured? Yes. Oh, yeah. We're covered." Too covered, thought Feingold. He should have listened to Rankoff and abandoned the notion of hiring Violette-Claire and purposely sabotaging the picture to collect the insurance. There was bound to be an investigation. Not that he worried about collecting. But if those dicks from the insurance companies started snooping too closely they might stumble onto the IAA number-two account and all the money they were stealing from *Ektalon-Z*. Not to mention the other little scams he and Rankoff had been pulling for years under the innocent guise of packaging. The way the Magic Man was behaving lately—moodier than ever, particularly vis-a-vis Davenport and Sabina—who was to say Don Roberto might not crack and *really* start singing again.

"You look worried, Stanley."

"Huh?"

"There's great tension in your face."

"Just character," quipped Feingold.

"Everything all right at home?"

"Sure," answered Feingold when he realized "hume" wasn't Hume Cronyn.

"Good, good. *Ektalon-Z* is going well?"

"Gonna be a box-office smash. Gonna go large. Very large. Bigger than *Star Wars* and *The Empire*."

"Proud of you, Stanley. Truly. Of all the people who have come through the doors of my clinic, who have gone through the course, who have shared the mystery of the circle and the triangle, you are the shining light."

"Thank you, doctor." Slippery Stan was genuinely touched. As he'd never finished high school, this sort of academic accolade struck a nerve in his ever-deprived psyche. "You've changed my life."

"*You* changed your life, Stanley. Solo force. Never forget that. You are ready for the ultimate release."

"Really?"

"Yes, Stanley. The time has come for you to go operative."

"Doctor!"

"You seem surprised."

"Always hoped you'd let me. Just didn't think I was ready. Still got a lot of hang-ups—"

"Negative cant!" shouted Kislev.

"Negative cant!" echoed Foley.

"What do I have to do?" asked Feingold.

"You are one of us now, Stanley. Part of an elite group of human beings, who are going to help change society in the next tumultuous decade."

"I'm honored."

"Nonsense! It is we who are honored to have you with us: to share our goals, our aspirations, our dreams, and help defend us from our enemies. For we do have enemies, Stanley. Jaded, jaundiced jerkoffs who cannot see over the foam of their own hot tubs. People who would ridicule us and all we strive to achieve. You must help us to combat them."

"Where are they? Where are they?" Feingold sounded remarkably like Bert Lahr's Cowardly Lion as he asked the rhetorical question.

"Everywhere!" intoned Kislev. "But specifically in the Beverly Hills area . . . right around the corner."

Feingold stared at his guru questioningly.

"The Arabs on Rodeo Drive?"

"Further south. At the corner of Charleville."

"The agency!?!"

Kislev turned to Foley, who came forward, towering over Feingold in the wing-back chair.

"Know what it means to really become operative?" asked Foley. "To abandon fear, conscience, the bullshit moral code imposed upon us by an outdated society?"

"Sure! I'm ready, Dwight. Just tell me what to do."

"Terminate Rankoff."

"Terminate him?"

"Pull the plug on him."

"You want me to turn him in?" asked an uncomprehending Feingold.

"We want you to kill him, Stanley."

"Dead?"

"Is there another way?" snorted Foley.

"But it's Bobby! The Magic Man. Don Roberto. I love him. He was my partner."

"He stands in the way of everything we want to achieve," said Kislev solemnly.

"Can't we talk to him?" asked Slippery Stan.

"We need to make an example of him."

"Why don't you wait another week till the picture's finished? Rees Davenport will kill him!"

"Stanley, you don't understand," said Foley, sticking his face into Feingold's. "There's no tactical option here. You're under orders. Solo force!"

***

Joy kept her fingers crossed on the steering wheel as she drove her BMW up the hill toward the cottage. Let him be there! Hooray! The blue Cord 810 was parked next to the cottage. He'd finally come home.

"Where have you been?" demanded Joy as Matty opened the front door wearing his Washington University sweat shirt and a pair of drawstring pants. "Everyone in the office has been worried silly."

"There was nothing to worry about."

"Nice tan. Where'd you get it?"

"Two Bunch Palms."

"You've been in Desert Hot Springs all week? Should have thought of that. Why didn't I think of that?"

"Don't know, Joyous. Why didn't you think of that?"

"What's with you? Lose your sense of humor in the mineral baths? Mind if I come in?" She didn't wait for him to reply but merely crossed the threshold and planted herself on the couch. "So? What's the story?"

"No story. Just needed to take a break. I was overworked and needed the time to think. About a lot of things."

"The agency?"

"Partly."

"Lindsay?"

"That's a sensitive subject, Joyous."

"Jesus Christ! Have you been taking Robert Rankoff pills?"

Matty didn't reply at first. Part of him was still back in Desert Hot Springs watching the road runners scurry across the grounds of the spa where he'd gone to contemplate his life. The desert had been tranquil and solitary. Matty had struggled valiantly in the intense heat to get his act together.

Why had he freaked at the sight of Wheezer and Steerforth together? He loved them both and wished them only happiness. That's all he wished anyone. Except Lindsay.

You bastard, Garber! Can't you wish her happiness, too? You loved her once. Still do—if you can face the truth. But her relationship with Shomrim was neurotic. A dead end. There was nothing he could do about it Maybe she'd come out of it one day. Maybe. Until then he would put his love in a drawer like Peter Pan's shadow and hope she might return to him again.

Or did that only happen in the movies? Old Forties movies. And the Forties were dead. Ask Rankoff. He was a veteran. An expert on women walking out on him. And vice versa. *The stars have lost their glitter.* Bobby baby. What a bummer! You warned me that first day. Maybe Joy's right. Can she see it in my eyes? Do they still dance when I talk . . . or have I blown it?

"Been like a morgue at the office all week," said Joy, attempting to break his silence. "I really missed you. We're the only things that hold that place together."

"Steerforth wouldn't say that."

"Steerforth's not functioning anymore. Not since Irma went to Happydale. You heard about that?"

"Yeah," replied Garber vaguely. Steerforth had obviously put the lid on the real story. "What happened to her?"

"Overwork," shrugged Joy. "Guess she couldn't handle the grind of a weekly series. Who can? That little box chews up people and spits them out quicker than—"

"Ara Whalen?"

"Boy! You just saved me a lot of time."

"Glad to be of help."

"What happened to you in the desert? Did you have a vision? You're not you anymore."

"Yes, I am. Just keeping a lot more of me for myself. Not giving anything away anymore."

"Congratulations, Garber. You've finally become an agent."

"That what it is?" he asked mockingly. "Finally up there with the big boys?"

"We can be bigger than the big boys."

"Why do your eyes only twinkle when you discuss power or money, Joyous?"

"What else is there for me? I've got no family. No roots."

"What about those Dworkins in Chicago? Did they beat you?"

"They were nice, sweet. But they were old. And they weren't my parents." She undid the clasp on her shoulder bag. "I want to show you something."

She stuck her fist into the bag and pulled it out again with all the pride of a child showing her father what she'd brought home from trick or treating on Halloween.

"Where did you get those?" asked Garber warily, staring at the black jade earrings she held in her palm.

"They're Ara's!" she whispered conspiratorially.

"How did you get them?"

"Broke into her house last week and stole them."

"Are you crazy?" asked Matty.

"She's the only one stands in the way of our taking over the agency. We can blackmail her with these. Say they were *her* earrings at the murder scene. The police have a piece of jade. We only need one earring. How will they know this isn't the other one?"

Matty was tempted to blurt out: "Because Steerforth has it!" He kept his mouth shut, realizing Joy's desire to blackmail Ara had nothing to do with her dream of ascending the agency throne. Her need was far more basic than that.

"What do you want from Ara?" asked Matty. "The police will never believe a bullshit story like that."

"I want to scare her!" answered Joy. "If only for a minute. I want her to be so frightened she'll beg me to help her. And I won't lift a finger until she's ready to tell everyone the truth."

"Which is?"

"She's my mother!"

"But she's not."

"What?"

"She's not your mother."

"What are you talking about? How do you know?"

"Louise Feingold was her best friend. She told me. Ara never had a child."

"That's a lie!"

"It's not! Ara had an abortion the year before you were born and— Goddammit! You made me break my word to Wheezer! She's kept that secret all these years and I'm asking you to keep it now."

"But—but—"

"She's not your mother! Don't know how you ever got the idea. But it's not true."

"She visited my stepparents in Chicago. When I was little, she checked up on me. Didn't dream that."

"She was Abe Keller's secretary, Joy. That's all! He'd worked with your stepparents in vaudeville. Maybe he has the answer."

"Abe Keller? Are you saying he's my—?"

"I'm not saying anything. But you've got to stop hounding Ara! Get rid of this fixation."

Joy stared at the earrings in her hand, burst into tears and threw them down on the floor.

"What the hell have I done?" she wailed, huge tears running down her apple cheeks. "What kind of bitch am I?" She began sobbing pitifully.

Matty had never seen Joy cry. Never thought her capable of tears. Gone was the baby barracuda of the office, the little sex bomb, who'd use any devious means in her power to make a deal. Here was a frightened and bewildered little orphan, who'd lost the lie that had been her anthem for years. Matty's heart poured out to her.

"It's okay. It's okay," he said, wrapping his arms tenderly around her. She clung to him for dear life. Matty finally understood what Wheezer had meant by compassion the night he learned of Roley's death.

Which explains how Joy and Matty were tucked up in bed half an hour later stoned out of their minds and having a wonderful time.

"Never had Quaaludes before," grinned Matty, foolishly feeling the effects of the little white tablet Joy had given him. "They really relax you."

"Y'ain't heard nothin' yet," replied Joy in tribute to the late, great Schnozzola. She reached across the bed and pulled a neatly wrapped joint out of her bag.

"A veritable pharmacopoeia!" boomed Matty. "Tell me, little lady, what instrument of destruction are you about to set alight?"

"The Dworkin Super Special!" she replied, lighting the joint with her TeruSushi matches. "This will answer the question if there's life after death." She took a hit on it and passed it to Matty, who took a toke and promptly coughed his lungs up.

"My God!" he gasped. "What have we unleashed on the world? Whooo! Bring your kids up the way you want them to bring you down."

"What does that mean?" she asked.

"Don't know. I'm totally wiped out."

"Really?"

"Don't you feel it?"

"Got a nice buzz. Yours must be a more sensitive soul than mine." She grinned and began tracing circles on his stomach. "Why did your wife let you go? I'd lock you up in the bedroom. Didn't she like sex?"

"Messed her hair up."

"Are you serious?"

"Half. Trisha backpacked through Europe with an all-current hair dryer. She likes to mingle with her subjects occasionally but never forgets the responsibilities of the throne."

"Do you think I'm a princess?"

"You've undoubtedly tried the crown on from time to time but it's not your style, Joyous. You're a lone wolf."

"Not by choice," she said sadly.

"Don't sink into the depths again!" He felt aroused once more and pulled her towards him.

She resisted and said: "Got to tell you a couple of things."

"Right now?"

"Please?"

"Sure." He fluffed up a pillow, placed his hands behind his head, and listened.

"I've done some really shitty things since I joined the agency."

"Is this a confession?" asked Matty, who'd never been so stoned in his life.

"Guess so."

"I'm not wearing my collar."

"Your what?"

"Don't know if I can receive your confession in the nude, my child."

"You are out to lunch, Garber."

"Tell me about it. What *is* a Dworkin Super Special?"

"Grass and hashish. Actually hashish and sinsemilla."

"Ohhhh, child! What have you done to Brother Matthew? If this should come to the ears of the abbot!"

"Will you let me tell you or not?"

"Proceed, my child."

"Because of this whole Ara fixation, I really had to prove myself. Overachieve, you know? Sleeping with guys I normally wouldn't break a dollar for. Not proud of it. Pudgy little Steve Goodbaum at Universal. Took him two hours to get an erection the first time. He was terrified of premature ejaculation after all that. I tried to help him. He kept muttering under his breath: 'Walter Brennan, Joseph Schildkraut, Walter Brennan, Thomas Mitchell, Walter Brennan'—"

"What the hell was he doing?"

"Trying to remember the names of all the Oscar winners for Best Supporting Actor."

"Some guys do football players," laughed Matty.

"I lied about deals."

"I absolve you."

"This is too easy," she decided. "Let me tell you a really bad thing." She recounted the nightmare story of Darlene English and the *après le bain*.

"I absolve you," said Matty, who was really into his father-confessor trip by this time.

"Shouldn't have left her like that," protested Joy.

"No, you shouldn't have. But you did phone Ara. You made sure she got to the hospital. Your priorities are just a little screwed up, my child."

"Yeah," she nodded. "Like the drug bust in Van Nuys."

"What was that?"

"Bazzo was worried about this rock group cutting in on Dead-to-Rights. His new punk group. They'd been ripping off some of the band's material. We dreamed up a little payback for them. Larry's done me a lot of favors. Figured I'd help him out with this. This rival group was staying at a motel in Van Nuys. Really heavy dopers. Brush their teeth with coke in the morning. Never travel with less than a couple of bales of grass. I tipped off the cops. Figured the bust might put them out of circulation for a while. Only trouble was the stupid fuzz got the wrong room number and—"

"Speedy!! You did that to Speedy?"

"I didn't do it! It was a mistake. Didn't mean for him to get busted. Aren't you going to absolve me?"

"Jesus Christ!" Matty found himself recoiling from her in the bed.

"Didn't mean to—" Joy wrapped her arms around him.

With all the drugs racing through Garber's body Joy's limbs had been transformed from arms into snakes. Deadly poisonous snakes.

The baby barracuda had become Kali, the Indian goddess of stranglers.

"Where are you going?" Joy asked in bewilderment as he leaped out of bed and put his drawstring pants on backward.

"Getting out of here!"

"What's wrong? What happened?"

"You! You suckered me and I walked into your trap! With those big eyes and apple cheeks and those ankles. Ho! Almost believed you, Little Miss Penitent. You're—you're a Borgia! You got rid of Speedy! You mutilated Darlene English! You almost had me believing that story about Ara and the earrings. Jesus Christ! You probably murdered Nolan and Kate!"

"You're stoned, Garber! You don't know what you're saying."

"Don't I?!"

"Come back to bed."

"No, thanks. If I lie down in that bed again, I'll never get up. What story will you make up for the Bel Air Patrol, Lucrezia?"

"You're freaking out!"

"The hell I am! Just coming to my senses." He stormed out of the bedroom.

Joy leaped out of bed and followed him.

"Matty, where are you going?"

"Don't try and tempt me with that body! I'm not Steve Goodbaum. God! How could I have been so blind?"

"You're going to get into trouble—"

"With who?" Searching frantically around the living room for his shoes, Matty finally fled barefoot through the front door.

Steerforth had just pulled his car up outside the house when he saw Matty fleeing with a nude Joy Dworkin framed in the doorway.

"Matthew!"

Garber spun around and saw Steerforth in a light he had never seen him before: the leader of a devil cult.

"Stay away from me!" shrieked Matty.

"What the hell did you do to him?" Steerforth roared to Joy.

"Nothing," she replied defensively. "He's stoned."

Steerforth shook his head wearily and chased after Matty. Running for his life, Matty didn't get fifty yards before his drawstring pants slipped down to his ankles and sent him flying through the air.

"Come on, old son," said Steerforth, standing over him and offering his hand. "Get up."

All Matthew saw in the moonlight was an evil, powerful hand reaching down toward his throat.

"Stay away from me!" he repeated hysterically. "I know about you! You're in it with her! She takes care of the men, and you take care of the women!"

"What the hell have you been smoking?"

Matty managed to scramble to his feet and held a warning finger up to Steerforth.

"I'm onto you, Stubbs! You're the one! You and Joy. Bumped them off, didn't you? Thought I'd fallen for it. Tried to make me your confederate. I know how you work! You prey on women. Saw you with Wheezer! What are you going to do with her, you goddamn vampire?"

"Come on, old son. Calm down."

"Don't try and pacify me! Whole thing makes sense now. You're the one who's been conspiring against the agency. You're the one who—"

"Sorry, lad," sighed Steerforth.

With that advance apology, Steerforth hauled back and delivered a knockout punch to Matty's jaw. The St. Louis *wunderkind* crumbled like the proverbial sack of potatoes. Steerforth easily slung his colleague's unconscious body over his massive shoulder like the same.

By the time Steerforth had returned to the cottage, Joy had a sheet draped around herself and was staring nervously at Matty, who'd been an energetic and attentive lover only a brief half hour earlier.

"Is he . . . okay?"

"He will be, Scheherazade." Steerforth walked past her and dumped Matty back on his bed. "These your clothes?" He pointed to the dress at the foot of the bed and the underwear scattered nearby.

"Yes," she answered meekly.

"Put them on."

Joy nodded and began to dress.

"Want me to make some coffee?" she asked while she dressed.

"Go home, little girl," replied Steerforth wearily. "You've done enough for one night."

"It wasn't like you think," she offered from the doorway.

"Seldom is."

"You're not mad at me, are you?"

"Do you really care?"

"Think you're such a goddamn expert on women!" she replied tearfully and left the cottage.

It was three in the morning when Matty woke from a deep and dreamless sleep to hear a familiar North Country voice reading aloud.

He was unwilling to let me go; and stood, holding me out, with a hand on each of my shoulders, as he had done in my own room.

"Davy, if anything should ever separate us, you must think of me at my best, old boy. Come! Let us make that bargain. Think of me at my best if circumstances should ever part us!"

"You have no best to me, Steerforth, said I, and no worst. You are always equally loved and cherished in my heart."

Matty opened his eyes to see Steerforth sitting beside his bed reading from Roley's old leather-bound copy of *David Copperfield.*

"How long have you been there?" asked Matty feebly.

"Twenty-nine-chapters worth."

"Really freaked out, didn't I? Where's Joy?"

"Sent her home hours ago."

"Was she all right?"

"Dying of a broken heart."

"Not me!"

"No, Matthew. It's an older man. She's had a crush on him for some time. He's flirted with her on occasion but he never thought she took it seriously. He's only loved one woman himself. From afar. For many years. For various reasons, he never told her. Never had the nerve. Until someone—a friend—his only friend—gave him the courage to be himself again. After twenty-five years of living a lie. You did that for me, Matthew. I shall always be grateful. Both of us. I'm going to marry Louise."

"Jimmy, I—"

"It's all right, lad. I know she 'jilted' you. Can you forgive her? You can understand now why I've loved her all these years."

"Give me that, will you?" asked Matty pointing toward the book on the Englishman's lap. He began thumbing through the classic Dickens novel trying to find a specific passage. Finally finding it, he read aloud: 'No need, O Steerforth, to have said Think of me at my best! I had done that ever."

Steerforth gripped his hand gratefully.

"She wanted me to be her partner," laughed Matty. "Dworkin and Garber... Jimmy, I've got to tell you something."

"What is it, old son? Another deep, dark secret you've uncovered? Another body you've found buried somewhere? Anyone I know?"

"It's you."

Matty told him about his conversation with Rankoff the previous week: how the agency boss had discovered Steerforth's illegal immigrant status and fixed it for him.

Steerforth stared in amazement for the longest time. He rose from his chair and paced the room in circles, muttering under his breath. Finally he halted, let loose an obscene roar of rage, and exploded into helpless laughter.

"He's quite unique, our Robert. Bloody nit! I do love him."

With that out of the way, Matty proceeded to recount Joy's visit, the tale of the earrings, Foley and the rat, and his own suspicions about Kate and Nolan's fate.

"Probably right about Foley," nodded Steerforth. "He gave Inez the earrings. What he didn't know was Inez's plan to remove the jade and have them made into cuff links for me. When I didn't turn up backstage in Las Vegas after Sylvia Nardino returned from the grave, she took offense. To teach me a lesson, she gave one of the earrings to Nolan. She didn't dare give them both.

"She phoned me in hysterics the morning the murders were discovered. She was afraid the police might trace the earrings back to her. I had to get the other one back from you."

"Why did you give it to me to begin with?"

"Been onto Dwight for a while. He'd have suspected me for sure when he discovered she wasn't going to wear the damned things. Had to find a safe place to stash them."

"Thanks a lot, Jimmy! That looney might have come looking for it one night."

"Don't worry, old son. The net is closing on our Mr. Fogelson and his dear Dr. Kislev."

The phone rang at that moment. Matty stared at it weakly.

"Would you?"

"Delighted . . . Hello? . . . Hello, my love. How clever of you to track me down here at this—what? . . . When? . . . No, no, no. I'll be right over."

"Anything wrong?"

"Louise."

"Bad news?" asked Matty.

"Depends how you look at it. Stanley has vanished."

"Vanished?"

"Clothes, car, bank books. Everything."

KISLEV

By the last week of October the incidence of brush fires in the Los Angeles area had set a record high. The Santa Anas—the legendary 'winds of madness' that blow through the city annually causing millions of dollars' worth of damage—had still not abated. Firemen were working round the clock to contain the flames that erupted around the city.

Ironically, it was water and not fire creating havoc in a Beverly Hills apartment in the wee hours of that October morning.

"Ma zeh?" Shmuel Kislev demanded aloud in Hebrew, leaping to his feet and staring at the yellow puddle in his bed.

It was an omen, he decided, as a rivulet of perspiration erupted on his forehead. Sweat continued to run down the length of his hook nose, and over the contours of his huge, naked Bartlett belly. Trouble was on the way! The eleventh plague of enuresis never failed to strike whether he was in Turkey, France, or Israel.

Kislev stripped the bed as he had done on so many previous occasions and hurled the offending sheets into the laundry hamper. He wandered into the bathroom and filled the tub to cleanse the urine from his body. While waiting for the water to rise he glanced through a well-thumbed stack of *Hustler* magazines nearby. The pictures only made him hungry and hunger made him think of Inez. *Oy!* What a body! If only, if only, if only.

No use crying over spilled angel dust, he thought, standing in front of the refrigerator, listening to the sound of the distant bathwater and shoveling spoonsful of humus into his corpulent frame. She had been so gracious to him that Sunday morning. He carried the container of Israeli food back into the bathroom. Respectful. He was convinced the PCP would have made her crazy about him. Crazy *for* him. He'd never imagined she would simply go crazy.

The former Shmuel Bornstein had never known much about women. Or people for that matter. A child of the holocaust, he had lost his parents at Dachau and only survived himself by betraying other prisoners to the German guards. When the camp was liberated by the Americans, the ten-year-old boy was shipped off to a relocation center under joint Allied supervision. Here the orphan earned the epithet "Benedict Bornstein" from the Americans by offering information on both his fellow displaced persons and his English and Russian benefactors. Through lies and deceits he found himself on the first ship for Cyprus and was among the first refugees into Palestine. He was shunted from foster family to foster family over the next few years, all of whom complained of his deceits, petty thefts, and interminable bed wetting.

When the time came for his compulsory military service in the late fifties, Bornstein's perverted ego compelled him to apply for the elite corps. He cheated on his exams and was accepted. However, he couldn't lie about his courage; inside his breast ticked the slow time bomb of a coward. One fateful night—deep inside enemy territory—he allowed his comrades to walk hopelessly toward their deaths.

Bornstein fled that night to embark on his own personal diaspora, never knowing one man had survived to tell the tale and seek vengeance. Bornstein made his way to Turkey where he flourished for many years in the opium trade. Eventually chased out of Ankara by the Turkish police, he made his way to Europe where he enjoyed similar success as a pornographer in Amsterdam. Eventually the Dutch police caught up with him. Similar successes and failures dogged him through Belgium, France, and Italy.

The pear-shaped Israeli made his way to Canada in the early Seventies. He changed his name to Shmuel Kislev and found work in Toronto as a Hebrew school teacher at a parochial school on North Bathurst Street. His career as an educator of the young was cut short when one of his pupils was overheard on the telephone by his mother remarking on the incredible dope he'd scored from his teacher at *cheyder*. Kislev made it across the border to Buffalo minutes before the Mounties nabbed him.

From Buffalo he made his way to New York City where he enrolled as a night student at the New School. Here he stumbled into the world of self-realization and human potential. He developed the concept of the circle and triangle and introduced such terms as "negative cant" and "collated data" into the lexicon of his embryonic cult formed among his fellow students. Within six months 'Doctor' Kislev was a regular on the East Side cocktail party circuit. The pear-shaped con with the mangled vowels swiftly came to realize Manhattan was small potatoes compared to the West Coast. The real land of milk and honey lay in California. For a while, with the aid of Dwight Foley, his was the kingdom, the power and the glory.

"But it's all crumbling around me!" Kislev wailed aloud as he sank his pear-shaped nudity into the bathwater. Those old feelings of insecurity were returning. Just like Ankara, Amsterdam, Brussels, Paris, and Toronto. The curious sensation of rats nibbling at his toes while the distant wail of the police siren drew nearer and nearer. Like Germany as a child when the Gestapo came to take him away with his parents and sisters.

"Why don't they leave me alone just once?" he cried out in the emptiness of the bathroom. Still wincing at the memory of his visitors that afternoon, he didn't need to see their badges to know his office visitors were members of the bunco squad. They looked the same in every city in the world. Only this time, they weren't looking for him. They were asking his assistance.

"Won't keep you long, doctor," the police detective said, planting himself in a chair and flipping his pad open to scribble a few notes.

"If I can be of service," smiled Kislev, his heart threatening to pound through his chest, "it would be my pleasure."

"Did you read in the newspapers about the disappearance of Stanley Feingold three weeks ago?"

"Of course. Mr. Feingold was a student of mine. Very distressed to read about it."

"Did you know Mr. Feingold well?"

"What is the measure of knowing a man?" asked Kislev with the glassiest stare he could muster.

The detective stared at his partner then turned back to the Israeli and asked: "Did he confide in you?"

"I can't discuss my private relationship with Mr. Feingold. It's privileged—"

"Are you a *medical* doctor?" asked the other detective.

"What are the bounds of medicine?" countered Kislev, terrified they might ask to see his license.

"Dr. Kislev, were you aware Mr. Feingold's last movie was scrapped by the studio midway through production?"

"I believe he mentioned—"

"Mansioned?"

"—mentioned something to me. It was in the newspapers, too, I believe."

"How did he feel about this? Was he hurt? Disappointed? Depressed?"

"Mr. Feingold was a moody man . . ."

"Mewdy?"

"Extremely. Tremendous swings of emotion. Some days he would be so high that—"

"Did he ever discuss insurance with you?"

"Me? Why on earth would he—?"

"Do you recognize this?" The detective held up a plastic bag containing a ring with the circle and triangle design.

"Not sure . . ."

"We found it in Mr. Feingold's bedroom. All his other jewelry was gone."

"Does it have some significance?" asked Kislev.

"You tell us," said the second detective, staring at a gigantic painting of the circle and triangle hanging behind Kislev's desk.

"Oh, I see," said Kislev, swinging around to gaze at the painting and wiping the perspiration quickly from his face. "Of course! It is the symbol of our movement. The circle represents infinity and—"

"Are you acquainted with Dwight Foley?"

"I . . . know Mr. Foley."

"Is he involved in your movement?"

"Yes. He is one of the founders, actually, in the West Coast branch of—"

"What about Beatrice Kaiser?"

"The name sounds familiar—"

"She was Dwight Foley's secretary."

"Oh, yes. Beatrice!" What the hell did they want with Beatrice, he wondered. What were all these questions about anyhow? Damn that Feingold! They should never have asked him to—

"Wasn't she a member of your . . . study group?"

"She did participate in a few—"

"Do you believe her to be a rational person?"

"Gentlemen, can you explain to me what all these—?"

"Do you know Robert Rankoff, doctor?"

"Never met the gentleman."

"Did Mr. Feingold ever discuss him with you?"

"Only in the most glowing terms. They were great friends and, of course, had been partners for many—"

"Did Mr. Feingold ever discuss his business activities with you? Particularly the last two films he was working on?"

"My work, gentlemen, is not concerned with the material aspects of life but rather the—"

"Thank you very much, doctor."

The two detectives rose to their feet at the exact same moment. Kislev walked with them toward the door.

"Do you think Mr. Feingold has been the victim of foul play?" asked Kislev.

"We should all experience such foul play, doctor."

"I don't understand."

"Stanley Feingold has absconded with over three million dollars that he has systematically cheated several studios out of for the past five years. That's three million we know about. Undoubtedly our investigation will turn up a helluva lot more."

"Then you know where Mr. Feingold is?"

"Ever been to Brazil, doctor?"

"No, but I've always dreamed of—"

"We all have, doctor. Feingold did something about it. Thanks again."

Kislev raced for the telephone immediately after the police departed and dialed Foley at his office.

"Have the police been to see you?" he demanded.

"No," replied Foley. "Why?"

"They just left here."

"What did they want?" Foley's decibel and paranoia levels had risen with this question.

"They wanted to know about Feingold."

"I warned you he was a flake, didn't I? But you wouldn't listen, Mr. Shmuel Goddamn-Know-It-All! You scared him away!"

"What do you mean."

"Telling him to kill Rankoff."

"You told him, too!"

"Yeah. But you're the big brains. Remember?"

"Don't talk to me like that, Dwight."

"What're you gonna do about it? Have me terminated?"

"They asked about Beatrice."

"So what?"

"You haven't done anything to Beatrice, have you, Dwight?"

"Really think I'm a psycho, don't you?"

"Merely asking a question—"

"Cover your own ass, Shmuel. Okay? And don't phone me here again!"

Kislev's bath had grown cold as he sat remembering the conversations. He decided Foley was completely unhinged, as he turned the hot-water faucet once again. Unhinged and insubordinate. Something would have to be done. And soon. Very soon.

***

The sun was setting out over the Pacific as Davenport and Sabina walked along the sand with their arms clutching each other's waists.

"It's so beautiful this evening," she whispered. "Never seen it this beautiful."

"Can't see it," he replied.

"What do you mean?"

"You make it seem so insignificant."

"Oh, Rees. You make me shiver when you talk like that. You're the most romantic man I've ever known."

"When I'm not a bastard."

"I think you think you have to be one."

"Getting psychological on me, gal?"

"Just want you to be happy. I love it when you smile and all those crinkles in your face curl up the right way."

"I feel good these days."

"You should. The picture came in ahead of time and it's fabulous. You were incredible, Rees. If it had been anyone else under those circumstances—the producer vanishing and everything. But you were wonderful. Holding that production together. So proud of you."

"Bummed we didn't have a wrap party. That was Feingold's responsibility. What with all the scandal and trying to get the picture in on time, there was no one to organize it. Cast's all scattered to the winds. Standish went back to New York. Shomrim's leaving for Israel next week. Think it's too late to have a party?"

"No, of course not," replied Sabina. "A big party?"

"No, not too big. Maybe twenty people."

"Terrific. We could have it right here on the beach—"

"No. Got a better idea. I want a party like when I was a kid in Wyoming."

"A cowboy party?"

"Yeah. Maybe have a treasure hunt, too. Ever been to one of those?"

"No, but it sounds fabulous. Would everyone have to dress up? Like cowboys?"

"Think they'd mind?"

"Are you kidding? Saw the most fantastic cowboy shirt last week on Rodeo Drive. Wanted to buy it but it was three hundred dollars and —"

"Buy it! And get yerself the sexiest pair of jeans they ever made."

"This is so exciting! We've never given a party before. Where can we have it?"

"The old movie ranch in Agoura. One they're gonna tear down. Did a lot of TV shows there. Like to have one last visit there before it vanishes. Sound like a good idea?"

"Uh-huh. Let's go home and do the guest list"

"Can't wait, huh?"

"Nope." She threw her arms around his neck and kissed him gratefully. "I wish you could always be like this."

"Do me a favor?"

"Anything."

"Call Rankoff and invite him."

"Are you serious?" asked Sabina.

"Hell, yeah! About time he and I buried the hatchet once and for all. Call and tell him I asked him to come."

"Oh, Rees!"

She skipped off across the sand toward their beach house like an ecstatic child never suspecting his vengeful motive for a moment.

***

It was like old times at Inez Sanchez's Bel Air estate. Cars packed the driveway and an 'intimate' three hundred guests turned up for the first glimpse of the South American bombshell since her tragic breakdown weeks before. Everyone wondered how she would look after her period of intensive therapy and (most importantly) whether she would be able to regain her status as a sex symbol and superstar.

"One thing about Inez certainly hasn't changed," remarked Minden Prescott as he stood in a corner with his agent, Matt Garber, dishing like crazy as the guests floated about. "She still has the worst set of white-trash manners I have ever encountered. It's ten P.M., twig, and where is she?"

"Would you be racing down the stairs if three hundred of your 'nearest and dearest' were just dying to see you fall on your can?" asked Matty.

"My god, twig! You've become quite bitter, haven't you?"

"Bitter! Just realistic."

"That way bitchiness lies. Oh, twig! Afraid you're just another fatality in Lotusland. And I had such great hopes for you."

"None of them professional," snorted Matty.

"Matthew, this malevolence is unnerving me. Wish you'd turn to Christian Science or a massage parlor before you're consumed with self-loathing. You need a loved one, twig."

"Ain't no such animal, Minden."

Minden sang: "If happy little bluebirds fly—"

"I'm getting a drink. You want one?"

"Maybe just a triple."

"May take a while," warned Matty, staring over the heads of the guests crushed together in the living room.

"Not a problem. I'll be warming myself by that Lebanese boy over there."

Matty was greeted at the bar by a bright and bubbly Yvonne Corday Rankoff.

"*Bon soir,*" she beamed.

"Like your hair," he said, admiring her new cut then staring at her devastating outfit. "Is that for quick getaways?"

"Don't peek."

"Don't show," he laughed. "You look incredible. Not that you don't always but—"

"My life is under control again!" she boasted. "That little Marxist bitch went back to France and out of my life for good—thank heavens. One good thing about Stanley's disappearance: He destroyed her reputation totally."

"Never really thought she was your type."

"I've doubted for some time just what my type is. Things seem to be falling into place very nicely now."

"Are you in love?" he asked.

"No."

"Never seen you glowing like this—"

"Just very happy these days, Matthew. For one thing, I have my daughter at home."

"Martine?"

"Yes. I went to see another doctor. He's involved in radical therapy. Suggested removing her from the clinic. Bring her home for a while. Let her be in a family environment. Away from institutionalized surroundings."

"Is it working?"

"She still doesn't speak, but I feel she's happy. And I'm happy to have her there."

"Does Bobby know?"

"Yes."

"How does he feel about it?"

"He's been . . . distracted since Stanley vanished. I have a terrible premonition."

"What do you mean?"

"Stanley was not the most honorable of men. There's bound to be an investigation into his finances."

"Why should that bother Bobby?"

"Will you come and visit us?" asked Yvonne, changing the subject abruptly. "I'd like Martine to meet you."

"Sure. Give you a call on the weekend. Saturday morning?"

"Better make it Sunday," replied Yvonne, drifting toward a tall, muscular man in his early thirties, who had obviously been waiting for her to return from the bar. "I'm dabbling in a bit of therapy myself."

If everyone was waiting for Inez to make one of her customary dramatic appearances down the wide, sweeping staircase by ten o'clock they were shifting their attention to the front door and the incredible couples the Vietnamese houseboy was admitting.

First there was Louise Feingold, making her first public appearance since her husband's scandal-tinged disappearance a month earlier. Her fellow guests searched for signs of strain around her eyes, but Wheezer looked as if she didn't have a care in the world. Why would she when she was on the arm of James Steerforth, the most eligible bachelor in the film world? Within minutes, the room was abuzz with the fact they were obviously not friends conveniently dating but that they touched each other and exchanged the kinds of glances that usually made for big box office when projected onto the silver screen.

Following them into the house was Evelyn Shankman in a stunning silk pants suit. The former Broadway actress looked twenty years younger. Hard to believe she'd been ill for so many years. Her escort was the mysterious Ivor Manning with whom so many people had seen her having intimate tête-à-têtes in various restaurants for the past few weeks.

Matty popped over to pay his respects to the quartet.

"No date tonight?" asked Evelyn.

"I came with Minden," replied Matty. "It's safer."

"Don't pick up the soap," murmured Steerforth.

"I'm not his type," replied Matty, who turned to Wheezer and kissed her hand. "You two must be doing something right."

"It's the tea," whispered Wheezer. "I never had a man make me tea in the morning."

"You don't have to give all my bloody secrets away," scolded Steerforth.

"Sly dog," said Matty, jogging the Englishman in the ribs. "Where's your protégée? We're all waiting for her grand entrance."

"No idea, old son. Haven't set eyes on Irma since that famous Sunday when you disturbed my happy idyll. The network's been phoning me round the clock to find out when she's going to resume the series. She hasn't answered one of my calls. The little gook keeps saying: 'Miss Inez playing! Miss Inez playing!' Like to know what she's playing at."

"Hard to get," smiled Wheezer. "But what do you care?"

"Still like to think when I whistle, they answer, luv. Ah, well. Comes the revolution! By the way, Matthew, did you receive an invitation from Rees Davenport to a treasure hunt in Agoura?"

"Yeah. This weekend. Oh, shit! Told Yvonne I'd come and visit— Sorry, Jimmy. Just working out my schedule."

"Why would Rees Davenport invite me to a party?" asked Steerforth. "Never met the man in my life."

"Probably heard what a charming, stimulating, worldly wise— Actually, it's probably my fault. I once told him you guys would really hit it off. That you had the same sense of humor."

"Why on earth would you tell him that?"

"At that moment in time, it was very appropriate."

"Don't worry," said Wheezer, squeezing Seaforth's arm affectionately. "Ara's picking us up. You don't have to drive."

"That's another thing," said Steerforth. "We don't even represent the bloody man, and he's invited every senior agent in the office."

"Maybe he's looking for representation," shrugged Matty. "Bet he didn't invite Rankoff."

"You lose. I bumped into Bobby at Western Costume this afternoon."

"What were you doing there?"

"I'm not putting on a pair of jeans, old son. If it's the old West he wants, I shall give him the real thing. We've hired Kirk Douglas and Burt Lancaster's costumes from *Gunfight at the O.K. Corral.*"

"I'm going as Calamity Jane," piped up Wheezer.

"I'm going to get a drink," announced Ivor.

"Good idea, Uncle. Shall we assault the bar together? Mind the ladies, Matthew. There's a good lad."

"Don't see Joy anywhere this evening," remarked Evelyn, after her date and his nephew had vanished into the crush.

"She's been keeping a low profile the last few weeks," replied Matthew.

"She and Ara don't quarrel as much anymore, I understand."

"Guess not."

"Do we have you to thank for that?"

"Not really. Mrs. Shankman—?"

"I've asked you to call me Evelyn."

"Evelyn, I like Joy. From the first day I met her. She's my friend. And she doesn't have very many."

"Yes?"

"There's a whole dark mystery of her life that troubles her. It has something—" Matty paused until he was certain that Wheezer was out of earshot. "Think it may have something to do with Mr. Keller."

"Abe? What could Abe—?"

"Can't discuss it here, Evelyn, but perhaps we might—"

Garber's attention was distracted to the front door, which swung open dramatically to reveal Yael Shomrim with two devastating starlets on his arms.

"Is the party still on?" asked Shomrim. The two girls with him laughed hysterically.

It was all too much for Matty. Bad enough Lindsay had left him for the Israeli superstar. He'd learned to accept that bitterly. He knew Lindsay wouldn't have felt comfortable in public with Shomrim, even though most of the office seemed to know about them by now—without any of the feared reprisals. But the Israeli didn't have the decency to come alone to the party. Oh, no! He drags these two bimboes in from God-knows-where. And you, Miss Fairweather, are you sitting up there on Westbourne crying your eyes out under the Tropicana sign?

"Excuse me," Matty apologized to Evelyn and made a beeline for the bar.

The babble of all the guests reached a fevered pitch in the next few minutes as if in anticipation of the events which were about to unfold.

First came the sound of the organ. Solemn, churchlike.

All eyes turned toward the staircase and the image of Inez Sanchez in heavenly, flowing white robes floating down the steps carrying a bouquet of red roses with a beatific smile plastered on her face.

A few people tittered as if in anticipation of some riotous visual punchline. Would the dress break away? Would Inez launch into her gaudiest, bawdiest number yet? The organ music continued as Inez continued to float downward under some sort of mystical propulsion.

"My dear friends!" She finally addressed the throng grouped around the foot of the stairs. "How kind of you to come! How kind of you to truly care so much! The infinite power of Jesus can work miracles—even among the godless."

Wheezer stared up at Steerforth and saw him standing in frozen shock.

"That little gook!" hissed Steerforth, finally coming out of the ether. "Miss Inez wasn't 'playing'. She was *praying!*"

Wheezer began to giggle uncontrollably and Steerforth was forced to pinch her bottom. Precisely the moment Inez chose to float toward her agent.

"James! Dearest James! Are you happy for me?"

Before Steerforth could answer, Inez took both his hands and kissed them tenderly.

"Be happy for me, James," she continued with mounting fervor. "I want you to understand the change I've undergone. I have sinned, I have been unpure. I have wallowed in depravity. You've been called here today to bear witness that I am clean and have learned the power of the Lord."

Shmuel Kislev, who had been watching this incredible performance with amusement with some of his followers, let loose an audible snort.

Inez must have heard it for she wheeled around with righteous fury and stared with a passionate hatred in the direction of the guru.

"Never will I be swayed by false gods again," vowed Inez.

Kislev felt his Adam's apple threatening to choke him in his throat. Was she about to denounce him? Tell everyone what he did to her? He would have to take a long shot and destroy her own personal credibility before she began chipping away at his.

"So, Inez? Giving up show business for God? Is that why we're all here? Or have you signed the Mormon Tabernacle Choir as your backup group?"

Kislev's acolytes burst into supportive laughter at the doctor's contemptuous question.

"May God forgive you," sighed Inez.

"Why me?" demanded Kislev. "I'm not a sinner. I didn't bring myself to the point of insanity by smoking angel dust."

The muscles in Inez's face tightened momentarily but then the beatific smile returned to her glamourous visage.

"I forgive you that, Shmuel."

"What is there to forgive?" asked Kislev, pushing his bluff to the limit. "You came to me for help. I urged you to give up those drugs."

"That's a lie!" replied Inez shrilly. "You gave me that Sherman."

"Poor lady," said Kislev, turning to his supporters and shrugging his shoulders sadly. "The excesses of negative cant."

The Kislevians all nodded their heads sympathetically and murmured: "Collated data."

"My faith will redeem me! My faith will redeem me!" muttered Inez, closing her eyes and praying for help. The force of Kislev's lie was stronger than her prayers. She opened her eyes to confront him again. "Goddamn you! You're not going to get away with this!"

Matthew Garber was missing out on this confrontation completely. The boy wonder from St. Louis was out on the patio drowning his misery in a fifth screwdriver and staring down mournfully at his cottage below when he became aware of female giggling.

Turning around, he discovered Yael Shomrim squeezed into a chaise longue with his two dates. Matty weaved drunkenly toward them.

"Wanna talk to you!"

"Garber! How have you been?"

"Fuckin' awful! You ruined my life, you sleazeball *sabra*."

"What have I done to you?" asked Shomrim with amusement.

"Both of us!" raged Matty. "Me because I love her; and her 'cuz she loves you. What do you want from her? Why are you fucking her up? We were doin' great till you came back. I love her. I'd marry her tomorrow. Have little freckled-faced children with marmalade hair. You're ruining her life. She's addicted to you. She should be on methadone. Shame on you, Shomrim! You're a hero. People look up to you. *I* did! So did every other Jewish kid in America. You're not a *mensch*, Shomrim! You may fool everybody else but not me!"

"Do you love her that much?"

"Enough to know I'm not going to win this fight, but still going to strike the first blow." Matty drunkenly advanced on Shomrim with his fist poised.

"I don't want to fight you, Garber."

"You got no choice. I'm defending the lady's honor. Not afraid of you. War hero or no war hero."

Shomrim was no longer listening to Matty. His ears were attuned to Inez's sobbing coming from inside the house. He rose from the chaise longue despite the protests of his two shapely attendants and wandered toward the French doors.

Inside the house Inez was sobbing pathetically while Kislev continued a mounting verbal attack on her credibility in front of all her guests.

"Who do you think you are fooling with this conversion?" demanded Kislev. "We know you for what you really are, Inez Sanchez! Or should I say, Irma Sandowsky?"

"And I know you for what you are . . . Bornstein!"

All eyes turned to Yael Shomrim standing like an avenging angel at the open French windows. Inez stopped sobbing as a deadly hush fell over the room.

Kislev's back was to the French windows and his shoulders were hunched somewhere around his ears. Slowly, slowly he let them relax, wiped the perspiration from his brow, and turned around to face his accuser.

"There's been a mistake," Kislev pronounced with a painstaking effort to keep his vowels from being mangled and to keep his face from showing any signs of recognition. His old sergeant had not only returned from the dead but had been resurrected as Yael Shomrim. Both had changed their names since their army days. "My name is Shmuel Kislev and—"

"Your name is Bornstein!" thundered Shomrim. "And I have found you again after all these years. You swine! You filth! You vermin!"

With each of these three epithets, Shomrim struck the cowering Kislev blows across the face.

"Did you honestly think you could escape me?" asked Shomrim. "Run away to America, change your name, and think I wouldn't find you? Become the famous guru Kislev? Should have known it was you all along."

"Please, Sergeant!" whimpered Kislev, now on his knees clasping his hands together. "It was an accident. I thought you had been killed by the Egyptians—"

"Silence! Coward! Murderer! You set yourself up as a doctor? A healer of men? Wouldn't your patients like to know how you betrayed your fellow soldiers? Allowed them walk to their deaths?" Yael turned to the stunned faces of the guests and pointed down to the floor with contempt and loathing. "Here is your great Doctor Kislev! Look at him! Look at your guru! See how he trembles with fear. Get up, Bornstein!"

"Please, Sergeant—"

"Get up!" Shomrim seized Kislev's lapels and yanked the pathetic lump to his feet.

"I have money, Sergeant," whimpered Kislev. "A great deal of money. It's yours if you let me go. Please, please! I'm afraid of the police. There have been lies told about me. Terrible lies. I must clear my name. I can only do so if I—"

"You want me to let you go? You wish to escape?"

"Yes, Sergeant! Please!"

"Let me help you . . . to fly!" Shomrim spun the deserter around, seized him by the collar, and propelled him across the living room floor. Once outside on the patio, Shomrim hurled Kislev over the balustrade into the tangled darkness of the thick vines carpeting the hillside.

"I'm at the Beverly Hills Hotel," announced a still-smoldering Shomrim marching towards the front door, "If the police wish to question me."

It was close to a minute before anyone spoke again in a confusion akin to the Tower of Babel construction site on payday.

Matthew Garber had woven his intoxicated way on to the terrace and peered over the balustrade into the darkness. "He's probably hanging over the back of my wall."

"Maybe you should have him mounted, twig. However, I must decline my services as the mounter."

"Minden! Where the hell have you been?"

"Watching it all from an orchestra seat."

"Most incredible thing I ever saw" said Matty. "Man's a goddamn hero. Even if he did steal the only woman I'll ever love."

"Until the next one."

"Never be a next one, Mindy. My heart belongs to Lindsay Fairweather, the Rose of Glendale."

"The Rose of Glendale! I preferred your malevolent period, twig. Truly. Let's infuse caffeine in you before leaving this consecrated ground."

"Do you think Inez's career is finished now?"

"Are you mad? She'll be on *The 400 Club* the rest of her life. Praise be! Bigger than ever. When she dies, rest assured Roy and Dale will have her stuffed. More than they did for poor Marilyn."

Matty had sobered up by the time Minden dropped him off in front of the cottage.

"Better check the garbage cans," Minden called out from his Peugeot. "In case Dr. Kislev's curled up for the night"

"Very funny. G'night."

The Peugeot rolled down the hill toward Sunset as Matty put his hand on the door handle. The door was unlocked. He could have sworn he'd locked it earlier in the evening when Prescott came to fetch him.

Then he heard voices from inside.

His heart froze.

His gaze darted about in the darkness and fell upon the branch of the loquat tree he'd recently sawed off. He lifted the severed branch up from the ground, tore away the smaller branches till he had a good-sized cudgel. He kicked the front door open.

Two men he had never seen before were seated on his sofa. Their faces remained calm as though it were an everyday occurrence to have a man kick his front door open brandishing the severed limb of a loquat tree.

"Mr. Garber?"

"Yes." He felt extremely foolish and lowered the cudgel to the floor.

"Door was open."

"Is there something—?"

"We're with the Beverly Hills Police, Mr. Garber. Need you to help identify someone."

"Is this person . . . ?"

"It's a corpse, Mr. Garber. Down at the morgue. Shouldn't take long."

"Did you—did you find him in the garden?" asked Matty, staring toward the French doors.

"No, sir. In the bathroom."

"How did he get in the bathroom?" asked Matty, thinking they meant his.

"Presumably he lived there."

Garber remained silent. They weren't talking about Kislev.

Somebody else was dead.

Who?

EVELYN

"Do you know him?" asked the cop opening the drawer and pulling out the body stretched out on the tray.

Garber stared down at the dead man. Took him a few seconds to recognize the deceased. He looked so different in death. He'd also lost a great deal of weight since Garber had seen him last.

"Do you know him?" repeated the cop.

Garber stared once more at the painfully thin face, the bald head, and the penetrating pop-eyes closed forever. *Smile, Garber, smile. I cannot stress the importance of being well-liked.*

"His name was Sol Siglan," replied Matty with a degree of affection which surprised him. "He ran the mailroom at the International Artists Agency on Rodeo Drive."

"Did you know him well?"

"He trained me."

"But you weren't close?"

"Not really. . . . How did he . . . ?"

"Cut his wrists and his ankles in the bathtub. Neighbors downstairs complained of the water leaking through. They called the super and he called us."

"But why did you call me?"

"He left an envelope taped to the bathroom door. It had your name on it. Come on."

The cop walked Matty back to his office and presented him an envelope with the familiar IAA logo embossed on it. Matty opened the envelope and proceeded to read the letter inside.

October 30

Dear Garber:

By the time you read this letter, I will be dead. I have known about this cancer for some time. Thought I could beat it, but it isn't meant to be. I have chosen what I think is a dignified way of leaving this world.

Before I go I'd like to say a few things to you. Many boys have gone through my mailroom in the past thirty-five years but none I have been so proud of as you. Nor any so kind. I never thanked you properly for the car and would like to do so now. I never lost faith in you, Garber. Never for a moment. You have been a true standard bearer of quality in the past year and it has been a thrill to watch your rise in the company. You love IAA as much as I do—which is why I am leaving you this letter. The number-two account, Garber. There's something wrong there. In matters of space. You know what I mean. Have a look into it. Could be very important.

I wish you a long and happy life.

Sol Siglan

P.S. Tell Mrs. Shankman I kept her secret. Always.

Matty reread Siglan's childlike scrawl once more then replaced the letter in the envelope. He looked up at the policeman standing over him and asked: "Did you read this?"

"Yes."

"It pretty well explains why he did it"

"What's the number-two account?" asked the cop.

"Sorry?"

"He was worried about the number-two account. Said so in the letter."

"That was nothing," lied Garber. "Mr. Siglan was an old fussbudget. Always worried about enough space in the mailroom. Huge amounts of mail coming through every day and not enough room in the pigeon holes. He was a bit senile, I guess."

The cop stared at Matty for the longest time then asked if he minded hanging around a few minutes longer.

Once the policeman was gone, Matty found himself racing through the contents of the letter once more. What was the phrase he'd once heard Foley say to Beatrice? The one he chuckled over with Lindsay for hours? Forget Lindsay! *Damage Assessment Debriefing.* That was it! What do the cops know and what do I know? They know Sol's dead and he had cancer. They're after more than that. The number-two account. The number-two account. There wasn't a check that passed through IAA that didn't pass through Sol Siglan's fingers first. He received checks and mailed them out; he sent the mailroom boys off to the bank with a warning finger and that great Siglanism "I.O.M." (It's Only Money!) So none of them would be tempted to run off to Brazil. *Brazil*! Holy mackerel! *There's something wrong there. In matters of space.* Sol Siglan, thou art mighty yet, you pop-eyed cryptographer! *Ektalon-Z!* It was all falling into place. Stan Feingold had told Matty they had a package for *Ektalon-Z* the day he and Rankoff dispatched him to Malibu for the SALT talks with Rees Davenport. Something had been bothering Matty for weeks in reference to that. Something Ara had said. The day she obtained Speedy's release. She'd phoned Davenport to get Jesse Rumpwell's name. *I know you're going to make it a huge success. Of course, we're sorry it couldn't be a package for us. But c'est la vie. Or le show biz.*

That's what stuck in his mind. What made Ara think it wasn't a package? Why had they told Matty one thing and Ara another? If it wasn't a package, the clients were being charged commission. If it was a package, the agency took ten percent of the budget. *Unless they took both!* The number-one account and the number-two account. Who'd be the wiser? Rankoff made the deal; Feingold produced; they split the commission down the middle. The sweetest of sweetheart deals. Something must have gone sour. Why else would Feingold have fled to Brazil? Poor old Sol must have suspected something and was afraid to speak up. He left it for Garber to deal with it posthumously.

"Thanks a lot, Mr. Siglan," muttered Matty, staring at the letter and wondering what that most cryptic of postscripts meant. "'Tell Mrs. Shankman I kept her secret. Always.'"

The cop returned with two detectives from the bunco squad.

"How long did Mr. Siglan work at IAA?" asked one of the detectives.

"Always," shrugged Matty.

"How long you been there?"

"A year. Almost."

"What do you figure the annual gross business is?"

"Don't know. Millions."

"Did you know Stan Feingold?"

"Yes. We represented his interests at one point on the film *Ektalon-Z.* They just finished shooting the other week."

"Were they able to complete production despite Feingold's disappearance?"

"They had a very strong director," explained Matty. "He was the real muscle on the picture. Feingold—from what I saw—was never a creative producer."

"What do you mean by that?"

"He was a dealmaker. Went from agent to producer without changing his psyche. He put the elements of a movie together: scripts, stars, director, composer, cinematographer, costume, and set designers—then he walked away and pocketed his fee."

"That's not what producers do?" asked the detective.

"Unfortunately, that's what they all do these days. The David Selznicks have vanished from the planet. Excuse my editorializing." Matty's eyes darted back and forth between the stone-faced detectives. "Anything else?"

"Do you know Beatrice Kaiser?"

"No."

"She worked for your agency—"

"Oh, *Beatrice*! Never knew her last name."

"Think she's a rational person?" asked the detective.

"As much as any of Kislev's disciples," shrugged Garber.

The two bunco detectives pulled up chairs and sat down beside Matty.

"You know Kislev?"

"Anybody got a cigarette?" asked Matty.

Three packs of Camels were shoved into his face simultaneously.

"Only met him once," answered Garber after he had done eenie-meenie-mini-moe with the packages. "Twice, counting tonight."

"You saw him tonight?"

"Vaguely. I was a bit loaded. I saw him go flying over the balcony."

"Where was this?"

Matty regaled the police with as much of the Inez Sanchez coming-out party as he could remember.

"What name did he call him?" asked the cop.

"Who?"

"Shomrim. What did he call Kislev?"

"Bornstein. Shmuel Bornstein."

The cop picked up the phone and dialed a number.

"Get on to Interpol. Get them to check on a Shmuel Bornstein and use the prints we got from Kislev's office. Send a car over to— What was your address again?"

Matty told them his address and the cop ordered a car sent over immediately to search the grounds for Kislev.

"Think they could give me a lift home?" asked Garber. "I'm exhausted."

"Sure. You've been a lot of help."

"Tell me what I did."

"Did you know Beatrice well?" asked one of the detectives as he put an arm around Matty's shoulder and walked him to the door.

"We never shared the Sunday papers, if that's what you mean. One look at Beatrice and you'd know—"

"We never met her."

"Oh?"

"She phones us. A lot. Collect. From various pay phones in New Mexico. Thinks her life's in danger. Won't tell us from whom. Says if we give her immunity and a new identity, she'll tell us everything. Is the lady playing with a full deck?"

"Doesn't sound it to me," shrugged Matty.

"Garber, what the hell is going on at your agency?"

"That's what I've been trying to figure out all year. We must compare notes one day. G'night, guys."

***

Rankoff called all the agents and their secretaries together the next morning in the screening room on the fifth floor. The agency boss gave a brief but touching eulogy to Sol Siglan describing his many years of service to IAA.

"He was the butt of a lot of our jokes," concluded Rankoff, "and we probably took him for granted after a while. But I'll miss him and his advice. The mail room will never run as smoothly again. He really cared about this agency. He was a link with the past—"

Rankoff paused in the middle of his speech to see Lindsay slip into the screening room. She was late and her tardiness only reminded the agency boss that there was work to be done.

"Okay!" said Rankoff, clapping his hands together in best Sid Shankman fashion. "Let's go make some deals. Jimmy, can I have a word with you, please?"

The agents and their secretaries filed out of the screening room. Matty remained seated in the front row, his mind lost in thought. Rankoff and Steerforth were leaving together when the agency boss spotted his secretary staring blankly into space.

"Something wrong?" asked Rankoff.

"Sorry I missed your speech," replied Lindsay dully. "Didn't know you were going to—"

"It's okay. I'm not one of the world's great after-dinner speakers or eulogists."

"Sorry I'm late," repeated Lindsay.

"You said that," grinned Rankoff. "Come on. I've got calls for you to make."

"Could I have five minutes?"

Rankoff saw her staring at Matthew, nodded, then added the postscript: "Just don't turn it into a production number. Okay? I'm really behind the eight ball this morning."

"Yes, sir."

Rankoff and Steerforth left the screening room. Lindsay walked down the steps to the front row where Garber continued to stare at the empty screen.

"Hi," she said.

"Hello. Wasn't that speech something? He really is an enigma. Never does what you expect him to under any—"

"I missed the speech."

"Oh . . . Did you hear about last night?"

"Last night?"

"Your boyfriend. He was incredible. Destroyed Kislev and his stranglehold on all—"

Lindsay burst into tears and cried out: "Don't talk to me about him! I never want to hear his name again."

"But what happened? Thought you and he—"

"I'm such a fool! He came back here briefly after the party in a total rage," she wailed. "'A dumb *shiksa* from Glendale. *Trayf*!' That's what he called me. 'Forbidden fruit.' Something to play with for kicks. Wasn't good enough to meet his wife. Said whenever we made love he'd take five showers afterward to wash away the smell of me. Oh, God! I've never been so humiliated! Feel so worthless. How could I have allowed myself to— Do you think of me that way? Is that what I was to you?"

"Of course not," said Matty, rising to his feet and putting his arms around her.

"No!" she said, breaking away from him. "I don't want your pity. You're the kindest person I've ever known, Matthew. And the most loving. You're the *mitzvah* king!"

"Did you make that up?"

"No. Yael did. He threw that in my face on his way out the door. He's gone back to Israel. Isn't going to Ress Davenport's party this weekend. He was going to take me. Would have been the first time we'd ever gone anywhere in public. He just laughed at me when I reminded him. 'You didn't really believe I'd take you there?' That son-of-a-bitch! That coldhearted, arrogant, son-of-a-bitch!"

That wonderful man thought Matty. He was a *mensch* after all. He'd actually listened to me at Inez's and understood. Probably gave the most convincing performance of his life in a little apartment on

Westbourne. *Todah mi-od, Yael.* Thank you. I'll probably name our first son after you.

"Lindsay."

"What?" she sobbed.

"You're an idiot."

"Huh?" Her sobs had become sniffles.

"You're also a fool."

"What do you mean?" She was wiping the tears from her cheeks by now.

"You are a dumb *shiksa*."

"Who do you think you're talking to?" she demanded.

"Someone who doesn't know when she's well off to begin with." Matty walked up the center aisle of the screening room.

"Come back here!"

"I have work to do, Lindsay."

"Don't you dare drop a bomb like that and leave."

"See you later."

"Thought you were my friend. Matty?"

He continued climbing the stairs. She chased after him, grabbed his legs, and brought him to the ground in an impressive tackle.

"Don't leave me," she pleaded.

"Where did you learn to tackle like that?"

"I was a tomboy."

"Will you be gentle with children?" asked Matty.

"What children?"

"Our children."

"You still want me? After what he said? What you said!"

"Only said it to bring you to your senses."

"I'm brought! I'm there. How can you love me again?"

"Still," he corrected her. "Never stopped loving you." He kissed her on the mouth.

"Never stopped loving you," she replied after they came up for air. "It was that Svengali. He did it to me."

"*You* did it to you."

"You're right. The only white-bread neurotic in the office. Maybe in all of Glendale. Maybe I was Jewish in another life. I'll be Jewish in this one, if you want."

They kissed each other again.

"Just be yourself, lass," he said and rolled her over onto her back.

"I love you, Matthew."

"I adore you, Lindsay."

Their hands were all over each other—squeezing, feeling, touching.

"God! How I've missed you," he breathed into her ear.

"So many nights I wanted to phone you. Certain you'd hang up on me."

"When I saw you at the cemetery—"

"Me too! Me too!" he nodded.

"When you kissed Joy afterward, I wanted to kill you both."

"Oh, don't—"

"Did you sleep with her?"

"Not that day. I mean—"

"You *did* sleep with her!"

"Well, what the hell were you doing with Shomrim? Biofeedback?"

They both fell apart on that one. Matty nibbled at her neck and in a few seconds they were clawing at each other passionately on the floor of the screening room. Finally Lindsay broke loose from him and gasped, "Mr. Rankoff asked me not to make a production number out of this."

"We're keeping it low budget."

"I know. But we've waited this long. If we leave at six we could be home by—"

"Six? We'll take a long lunch."

"Math-ew!" she scolded.

"Lind-say!" he teased. He jumped to his feet and helped her up. "I want you to move in with me."

"Really?"

"Do you do windows?" asked Matty.

"What do you pay?"

"The barter system. A little love, a little dusting—"

"What ratio?"

"That's open to negotiation."

"I really *did* make a dealmaker out of you, didn't I?"

"You have the world to answer to now, Baroness von Frankenstein," he answered in appropriate Teutonic tones.

"Why so formal? Just call me Gertrude."

"Say good night, Gertrude." Matty flicked the ash of an invisible cigar.

"Good night," she replied in her best Gracie Allen. And they held each other in a long embrace all the way down in the elevator to the third floor. When the doors opened, Karyn, his Australian secretary, was waiting for him.

"Just coming up to find you, Mr. Garber."

"What's up?"

"Mrs. Shankman phoned. Says it's very urgent. Sending her car to pick you up."

Half an hour later the Rolls-Royce pulled into the driveway of Evelyn Shankman's sumptuous home on North Roxbury Drive. Matty was surprised when the front door was answered by Uncle Ivor in a jaunty terrycloth jump suit.

"Hello, my boy. Do come in."

"Something wrong, Ivor?"

"Wrong?" asked the handsome barber peering down at him through his monocle. "Far from it! Like a drink?"

"It's a little early for me."

"Yesss," remarked Ivor, peeking up at the sky. "Sun's not quite over the yardarm. In a few minutes, though."

"Where's Evelyn?"

"On the patio."

"Know why she wanted to see me?"

"We'd best leave that to her. Sure I can't get you that drink?" he asked as they walked through the house toward the garden.

"Is that some kind of warning?" asked Matty facetiously.

"Good gracious, Matthew! I'd have expected a remark like that from Willie. By the way, have the police found that wretch Kislev yet?"

"No. They searched my garden and the hillside till four in the morning. The man has vanished without a trace."

"Good riddance! Ah! Here she is." Ivor led Matty through the library doors out back to the pool area where Evelyn sat under an umbrella wearing an identical jump suit to Ivor's. "Isn't she lovely?" asked Ivor with undisguised affection.

"Have you told him?" she asked, staring with adoration at her long-lost love.

"Pon my word, Evelyn! Deprive you of the moment? May not have been a success as an actor but I did appreciate timing."

"Sit down, Matthew," said Evelyn, gesturing graciously toward a chair under the umbrella. "Are you comfortable?"

"Yes, thanks."

"Good." She took Ivor's hand, stared up at him with a twinkle then turned her eyes to Matty. "We're going to be married."

"How wonderful!"

"We have you to thank for bringing us together again."

"Not me!" protested Matty.

"Who then?" she asked.

"Fate. Or Roland Draycott's spirit. You were both favorites of his. He'd have been thrilled. Have you told Jimmy yet?"

"Haven't had a chance," replied Ivor. "Just came up over toast this morning."

"He asked me to pass the marmalade," said Evelyn, "then casually slipped in the proposal. I dropped the jar on the floor. When we both got on our hands and knees to pick up the pieces, I accepted."

"Course it took me five minutes to straighten up again with my bloody arthritis," snorted Ivor. "Pardon my language, Evelyn."

"I'm so flattered," said Matty. "Sending for me to announce your—"

"That's not why, Matthew." Evelyn's eyes stared directly into Garber's.

"Think I'll have that drink now, Ivor."

"Yes," purred Ivor. "Probably best. Gin and tonic?"

"Sure."

Ivor left the pool area and disappeared inside the house. Evelyn got up from the table.

"Have you seen my roses, Matthew?"

"Never been here before."

"Let me show you my garden."

Evelyn linked her arm through Matty's and proceeded to lead him around the magnificent, five-foot-high rows of multicolored roses. Walking in silence for several minutes, Evelyn finally spoke: "I was very distressed to learn of Sol Siglan's death."

"He was a nice man," nodded Matty.

"And a faithful friend. There was never anyone as loyal. Knew him for over fifty years. When I was an ingenue on Broadway, he'd be waiting outside the stage door every night. With those funny pop eyes of his and the way he used to nod when he talked. He was a messenger on Wall Street. A very humble and sweet man. Never wanted anything from me. Just a hello and to feel he could talk to me. I was very young. Only seventeen. Incredible for my ego, knowing that a man so slavishly adored me.

"His mother was ill. Sol took good care of her. When Sidney opened the office here in Beverly Hills, I suggested Sol might run the mailroom for him. Sol and his mother came out to California. She died ten years ago. No, must have been longer than that. What I'm saying is, I've lost one of the last links with my youth."

"He left me a letter," said Matty.

"Yes?" There was a wary quality in her reply.

"Said he kept your secret. Always."

"I'm sure he did." Evelyn sighed wearily. "Why is it always so difficult to tell the truth? Went through this with Ivor last night. He was marvelous about it. Know what he said? 'Telling the truth is always the easiest solution to a problem. Not necessarily for the person who hears it, but it works wonders on the teller.' Such a rogue, isn't he? I know now where Jimmy gets it from. Please, be patient with me, Matty. This would never have come to light if you hadn't become obsessed with Bobby. Too many things are coming out in the open. I'm afraid for Bobby. I don't want to see him go to prison."

"Because of Feingold?"

"Do you know about Bobby and that Nardino woman?" Evelyn ignored his question and continued to steer Matty through the rows of roses.

"Yes. He said you saved his life."

"We saved each other's lives," said Evelyn. "I'd just turned forty with a husband who had been neglecting me for ten years. A beautiful boy of twenty-five was so grateful to me for what I'd done for him. It was madness, absolute madness. I didn't care. I needed that affair so desperately. Needed to feel loved and a woman again. If only for a week. That's all it was. But the damage was done. Bobby never knew. I didn't want to tell him. He was getting his life together again. He'd patched up his marriage with Yvonne as well and she was pregnant with Martine.

"My immediate thought was an abortion. Sidney could never have children so the thought went out of my mind for years. I wondered, 'Do I dare?' Knew I'd never be able to keep the child but still wanted to have it. This was the beginning of my 'illness.' Faithful Sol Siglan would take me to the non-existent doctor every week. When the time came for me to have my 'operation', it was Sol who took me to the 'specialist' New York and stayed with me through my recuperative period."

"You kept up the pretense of illness ever since?" asked a stunned Matthew.

"Was there another choice?" said Evelyn. "Couldn't bounce back after such a serious condition. What would my husband have thought?"

"He's been dead ten years now!"

"It became a way of life," shrugged Evelyn. "Tell a lie enough times, it becomes the truth—even to the liar."

"What happened to the child?"

"Don't you know?"

"All those years she thought Ara—"

"Abe Keller and I were friends before I ever met Sid. Abe wanted to marry me but . . . he just wasn't my type. He made one of those Sidney Carton declarations to me. You know. "If ever I can do anything, . . ." Finally asked him to do something. Find a home for my daughter.

"Abe had worked in vaudeville with Harry and Rose Dworkin. They'd been great pals. The Dworkins never had a child. So faithful Ara was sent to Chicago to deliver the infant. Ara probably thought it was Abe's. She's been the fairy godmother ever since. Unfortunately Joy never appreciated her. Didn't realize how deeply troubled she was until she joined the agency. I watched helplessly for two years while those two battled with and loathed each other. Joy, because she thought Ara was me, and Ara, because this little child was so ungrateful for all the things she'd done for her. Poor Sol's death brought it all home to me. I can't live this lie any longer."

"You're going to tell her?"

"Not yet. Time isn't right. But you're not to tell her either. Or Bobby. You've been a remarkable detective, Matthew. I wanted you to hear the truth from me before you stumbled over another skeleton in the IAA closet."

"Do you really think Mr. Rankoff will go to prison?"

"If the police are half as thorough as you've been, it's a certainty. Unless . . ."

"What?"

"I'm from the old miracle school, Matthew. I pray for a miracle. But until we know the outcome of that, I don't want him to know about Joy. Or vice versa. Do I have your word?"

"Yes."

"Thank you. Hope you'll come to the wedding."

"When is it?"

"In the New Year."

"Enough time to brush up on 'Oh Promise Me.'"

"Don't you dare."

Evelyn kissed him on the cheek, removed a tiny pair of snippers from the pocket of her jump suit, and cut one of the red roses from the vine.

"There," she said, slipping the stem through his lapel. "One of the last of the season."

***

The winds were ferocious that Sunday. Matty was grateful for the ancient Cord's weight as he prepared for the long drive along Ventura Freeway to Agoura. Lindsay's stepsister was having a sweet sixteen in Glendale that afternoon. Following a bout of 'white-bread guilt',

405

she felt compelled to pass on Davenport's treasure hunt and serve as a chaperone at the party.

Matty stood alone in the cottage at noon checking out his Confederate shirt in the mirror when the telephone rang.

"Matthew?"

"Hi, Yvonne! I was meaning to phone. Won't be able to visit you today. Going to Rees Davenport's party in Agoura—"

"That's why I'm phoning. I'm worried, Matthew."

"Why?"

"Bobby is going."

"Amazing, isn't it? They're finally burying the hatchet—"

"Martine was going through some of Bobby's old scrapbooks this morning and—"

"Sounds like a big improvement," said Matty.

"A whole different person since she came home," said Yvonne with undisguised delight. "Cooking in the kitchen with me, working in the garden. Even started whistling yesterday. She still doesn't speak. Doctors say I can't expect everything at once. They feel the change so far is nothing short of miraculous,"

"I look forward to meeting her."

"You will. But listen, Matthew. She found a radio script. From thirty years ago. With the names of the cast and crew on it. Remember my telling you how Bobby fired a stagehand for dropping a triangle during one of his songs?"

"Yes."

"It was. . . . Rees Davenport"

"Oh, my God! You don't think—?"

"I know Rees's reputation. Heard enough horror stories from Ara. Wouldn't surprise me if he threw this entire party as an excuse to do something terrible to Bobby."

"What do you want me to do?" Matty asked with a helpless tone in his voice.

"*Je ne sais pas*. You could warn him but . . . Maybe Bobby's been waiting for this all along."

I seem to have been on trial for thirty-five years. And I'm waiting for the verdict.

Matty hung up the phone and dialed the Trousdale number. Ames informed him Bobby had already left for Agoura. He tried Steerforth next. No answer. Ara probably picked them up already.

Who else could he phone? Joy? Oh, perfect. "Joyous, listen I haven't got time to talk but Bobby Rankoff's your father and I have the strangest feeling Rees Davenport's going to kill him this afternoon." Terrific!

Matty got behind the wheel of the ancient Cord and drove it up the hill to Mulholland. He plowed along the ridge toward the San Diego Freeway and took it north till he connected with the westbound Ventura Freeway. All through the drive he thought of Joy and Rankoff. Of course, he was her father! They were two of a kind. When Joy told him about her incredible wheeling and dealing the night of Darlene's accident, it was exactly like Rankoff's machinations the morning he finessed Kip out of *Anthony Adverse* and put Julian Mowbray into the role. Both Bobby and Joy had the instincts for the jugular and both were incapable of dealing with emotions straight on. They'd make a helluva team. If Bobby lived past the afternoon.

By the time Matty reached the movie ranch an old-fashioned barbecue was in progress. Davenport was supervising a steer rotating over an open pit filled with hot coals.

"Given up on you," growled the director in his best sandpaper tones as Matty climbed out of the Cord. "Never seen so many damned chicken shits give up 'cause of a little wind."

"People canceled?" asked Matty as a tumbleweed rolled by.

"Bout half. Sure know who yer friends are out here. Wanna drink?"

"Sure."

"Sabina's tendin' bar inside the saloon. Just mosey inside and give her your order. Meat'll be ready anytime now."

"What about the treasure hunt?"

"After lunch. You'll need your strength." Davenport let loose his all-too-familiar wild stallion laugh.

Matty swung open the doors to the saloon and was thrown by his colleagues sitting around the tables looking like the cast of an old *Gunsmoke* episode. While a player piano tinkled a ragtime tune in the background, Matty stared in delight at the dynamic duo of Rankoff and Steerforth dressed as Wyatt Earp and Doc Holliday. Ara was impersonating Annie Oakley dressed by *Vogue*. Wheezer made the cutest Calamity Jane in her buckskins and Civil War cap. The only part of her costume that puzzled Matty was the large bandage on her right foot.

"Injuns get you?" asked Matty.

"Noooo," groaned Wheezer. "Tennis. Sprained my leg yesterday. Can't go on the treasure hunt. But there's nothing wrong with my appetite."

"Why don't you pour yourself a drink, Johnny Reb?" asked Rankoff. "And come join us."

"Sounds good to me."

Matty tugged on his belt buckle and sauntered past the table where Dwight Foley sat alone dressed in black playing a hand of solitaire.

"Whaddaya say, Dwight?"

Foley looked up and grunted.

"Collated data," murmured Matty, continuing on to the bar where Sabina was pouring out a sarsaparilla for Joy.

"What'll it be?" asked the beautiful, blond Sabina.

"Give him a double sarsaparilla," said Joy mockingly. "We don't want him losing control."

"Oh! We're on our best behavior today," observed Matty.

"Just teasing. Jesus, Garber! Can't you take a joke?"

"Something very jugular about you."

"The wind," shrugged Joy. "It's scary. Hate when it gets like this."

"Rees says they're called the 'winds of madness,' " said Sabina. "He's really hurt so many people didn't show up. Planned this thing for weeks. Oh, look!"

Sabina pointed to the two muscular stunt men carrying the steer in through the saloon doors followed by Davenport.

"Chow time!" announced the director.

The meat was delicious. Davenport regaled his guests with tales of the old movies and TV shows that had been shot on the soon-to-be demolished set. He was a master storyteller, and his audience ate up his marvelous anecdotes and incredible impersonations of the people he described.

"Do Gary Cooper again!" pleaded Joy.

"Why, ma'am," he replied in those short, jerky Montana tones of the late actor, "I don't—quite—know-what—you-mean."

Everyone applauded enthusiastically. Davenport nodded humbly in appreciation of their reaction. He had them suckered. Had them right where he wanted them. How proud grandfather Stanislaus would have been! A classic cavalry maneuver. Let the enemy think you're weakening and they will follow suit.

"How 'bout some tequila, Garber?"

"Sure," replied Matty heartily. He'd begun to relax halfway through the meal and decided his fears about Davenport had no foundation whatsoever.

Rees poured Matty a drink then wrapped his arms lovingly around Sabina, giving her a long loving kiss.

"Havin' a good time?" he asked, staring into her eyes.

"The best!" she replied.

Davenport swung around to Rankoff and asked abruptly, "How ya doin', Bobby?"

"Fine, thanks."

"That's good. It's real civilized our all sittin' here like this. My ex-wife Ara and you. Your ex-wife and me. Steerforth here and your ex-partner's ex-wife."

"I'm not his ex-wife," said Wheezer.

"Scuse me, Miss Louise. Don't know why I want to keep thinkin' of Feingold in the past tense. Sorry about any grief he may have caused you, too. But I hated that little son-bitch."

"Rees, behave yourself!" warned Ara. "We were all threatening to have a good time a moment ago. Don't spoil it."

"Damn! You still have the wickedest tongue of any woman I ever knew." Davenport lurched toward Ara and kissed her full on the mouth.

Ara slapped him across the face.

"Don't ever do that again!" she hissed.

"Wanted to see if it still tasted the same."

"Did it?" asked Joy.

Davenport turned around to stare at the baby barracuda as if he'd never seen her before.

"Wha'd you say?"

"How did it taste? Her tongue?"

"Who're you?" Davenport's eyes ran up and down Joy's body.

"Just a guest," she shrugged.

"This is Joy Dworkin," said Sabina. "She works at—"

"I know what she is!" snapped Davenport. "I want to know *who* she is." He turned and shared a private look with Ara.

"Rees, I'm warning you for the last time!"

"Ara, you don't scare me. Never did. That was your big mistake. Just want to know who everyone is. Who they *really* are. Want 'em to take off their masks. What about you, Black Bart?" His gaze was riveted on Foley sitting alone at the next table devouring a gigantic rib of beef. "Heard you were a Green Beret."

"Affirmative," grunted Foley.

"How many men you kill?"

"You're out of line," growled Foley.

"Didn't you kill any? Thought you Jews were tough fighters these days. Y'are a Jew, ain't you?"

"Negative cant!!"

"Didn't you tell me once he was a Jew?" Davenport asked Ara.

Ara shot a few thunderbolts in her ex-husband's direction. He merely let loose with his wild stallion laugh, walked behind the bar and poured himself a shot of tequila. He turned to Foley again and asked: "Wha'd yer name used to be? Don't be ashamed. I'll bet everybody here's changed their name. Well, almost everybody. S'bina here. She changed her name. You knew that Bobby, didn't you? You knew she was old Susy Applewhite when she worked for Leroy. Ain't that where you met her?"

Matty felt prickles up and down his neck. He'd become comfortable far too early and dropped his guard. The beer and tequila flowing through Davenport's veins were turning to poison and all Matty's old fears were aroused once more.

"What're you twitchin' for, Garber? You know who you are. I mean your mommy and your daddy were married, weren't they? Miss Louise, we know all about you and your lovely folks back east. Course Ara ain't what she pretends to be."

"Shut up, Rees!"

"She's a lady, ain't she? The way she dresses and walks and talks. Real Radcliffe type. Park Avenue. Silver spoon up her poop shoot. Bet you never knew her father was a goddamn dago fruit peddler in Philadelphia. And her mother—well, you never did know what your mother did, didja? Kinda suspect she was on a few mole hunts in her time. Where else did you learn, Ara? Best damned mole hunter I ever met."

"Why are you doing this?" gasped Ara.

"Want to know who everyone is," replied Davenport simply. "What's wrong with that? Don't hear no objections."

"May I object for the record, old son?"

"You?" asked Davenport, staring at Steerforth. He snorted, belted back another shot of tequila, and turned his attention to Joy. "You fascinate me, little gal. Heard a lot about you. Kind of the mystery kid, ain'tcha? You don't know who you are."

"I'm not afraid of you," said Joy, her lower lip trembling and tears welling up in her eyes.

"Why in tarnation should you be afraid of me? What kind of stories have you heard? What did Ara tell you? I could tell you stories about her. But damn! Why should we waste our time talkin'? Y'ever been on a mole hunt, honey?"

"Leave her alone!" said Steerforth, rising from his chair.

"Callin' me out, limey?"

"I'm asking you *politely* not to bother her anymore."

"What's *your* story?" asked Davenport. "Who are you really? What're you hiding from? If you're James Steerforth then I'm the Cisco Kid. I know my Dickens, limey. Who are you? Or are you afraid to—?"

"My name is William Ernest Albert Stubbs. Born in Bakewell, Derbyshire. Left there at the age of fifteen and entered the United States illegally. Changed my name to James Steerforth. Been living in this country legally for some time now and—as I've not had a chance to thank you properly till now, Robert—thank you kindly for what you did. But no more surprises, luv. Let me know the next time you do me a favor. My nerves can't take it." Steerforth turned back to Davenport and inquired: "Anything else, old son?"

The women in the saloon all stared at Steerforth with uncloaked adoration. Here was Rhett Butler come alive for them once more.

Davenport belted back another tequila and ripped open a can of beer.

"That was a good story, limey. Got to admit. But ain't it funny? With all your stories I get the feeling I'm the only person who really belongs here. Know what I mean? The only honest-to-God American. What do we got here? A bunch of Jews, wops, limeys. Ain't forgot the niggers neither." He pointed to Stu Jackson, who had arrived halfway through the meal having braved the fierce windstorm on the back of his Harley-Davidson.

"Thank you, Massuh Davenport," grinned Jackson, who turned to Rankoff and said: "Tell me when you want me to beat the shit out of him, Bobby."

"Now, now, you don't want to do that, Stu," said Steerforth in soothing tones, walking over to Jackson's chair and placing his hands reassuringly on the shoulders of the Black Adonis's whiter than white rodeo shirt. "Don't want to give Mister Rybnik the wrong impression of America. He seems so keen on fitting in here."

"Who's Mr. Rybnik?" asked Sabina.

"Didn't you know?" asked Steerforth with fake astonishment. Turning to the ashen Davenport, he questioned him with equally mock mystification: "What's the matter, Karel? Didn't you tell her?

About New Hope? And grandfather Stanislaus? A Polish hussar, wasn't he? That's what he told you anyhow. Got it all jumbled in your brain, old son. Well, Karel?"

"How—how did you find out?" gasped Davenport.

"Going to take your mask off, too?" asked Steerforth. "That's a good idea. Make ourselves nice and comfy. 'Real civilized,' I think you said."

"Who told you?" demanded Davenport. "Nobody knew—"

"That's where you made your mistake, Karel. Can't really erase your life. Pretend it never happened. You've got to come to grips with it. Want to know who told me? Your daughter."

"Don't have a daughter," said Davenport.

Joy turned her head sharply to stare at Ara but only saw as much amazement on the former Painted Lady's face as on everyone else's.

"Yes, you do," said Steerforth in an almost schoolmaster fashion. "Daughter Margaret born in Spotted Horse, Wyoming. 1949. Course you deserted her and her mother a year later and Margaret grew up very confused about you. Wanted to become an actress. Hitchhiked out here from Wyoming about twelve years ago. Her mother had remarried long before and she had dozens of stepbrothers and stepsisters. Didn't know you existed until she found some old poems you'd written her mother buried in a trunk in the attic. Made her mother tell her the truth. Came out here to track you down and become a star.

"Quite lovely, Margaret was. Maggie. Someone recommended her to me. Never forget the way she smelled when she walked into my office. Lily of the Valley. Forgive me, Louise. Can't help but remember such details."

"When you can't remember is when I'll get worried," smiled Wheezer.

"Maggie had no film," continued Steerforth, "no tape. No credits. But she had something special. Like poor Frances Farmer. Looked very much like her, too. Done her homework, Maggie did. Opened a copy of the trades that showed how Rees Davenport was looking for an unknown girl to star in his next picture. Seemed quite keen on meeting you, Karel. Something made me suspect there was more to it than a job. I set up an interview. Don't suppose you remember Maggie. So many girls auditioned for that part. Needless to say, she didn't get it.

"Maggie came back to the office later that evening. Worked much harder in those days than I do now. Heard sobbing from the corridor. It was Maggie. You hadn't been nice to her, Karel. One doesn't take one's daughter's hand and force it down one's trousers. Does one? Or try and rape her when she resisted your subtle overtures?"

"It's a lie!" Davenport looked at Sabina and Ara in the hopes of finding support. Neither woman would meet his gaze.

"Is it? Maggie told me the whole story. How you came to the Davenport ranch and met her mother. She didn't want to turn up and surprise you with anything as hackneyed as the long-lost daughter routine. Didn't want you forced to be nice. Decided to see what sort of a man you were first. She certainly found out. I gave her the money for air fare and sent her back to Wyoming the next morning."

There was a long and uncomfortable silence until Wheezer got up from her chair and kissed Steerforth.

"What's that for?"

"For being the only man I ever met who understood anything about women." She turned to Davenport, who appeared moments away from a slow agonizing death and asked: "Are we having that treasure hunt or not? I came here for a treasure hunt."

"Sure, sure," replied Davenport, slowly coming out of the ether. "Right! Okay. S'bina! Get out them maps from the box behind the bar."

Davenport was as meticulous about his games as he was about filmmaking. He'd personally supervised every detail; spent three days setting out different routes for each of the competitors, hiding clues for them, and planting booby traps.

The booby traps were all harmless. Except the one for Rankoff.

Davenport had designed Rankoff's map and clues so Bobby would end up at the old mining set used on almost every TV western in the Fifties. Outside the entrance to the mine was an ore car mounted on a track which ran inside along the darkness of the shaft.

The director had rigged up the old battery system for the ore car and marked instructions for Rankoff to take the car inside to the end of the track where the treasure was waiting.

The last part was a lie. There was no treasure.

The track ended abruptly in the darkness. The car would go right off the track into a pit fifteen feet below. Wouldn't be going fast enough to hurt Rankoff, but there was no way he'd be able to get out of the pit.

There was only one map per player so no one would know where Rankoff had gone. It would take a week to comb the hills of Agoura trying to find the lost agency boss.

Davenport hadn't planned to leave him there long. Maybe a day or two. Till he got hungry. And thirsty. And scared.

The director would finally go to the old mine and sit by the edge of the pit and make Rankoff beg—beg him till he wept—for mercy.

Davenport would tell him the story of the stagehand who begged for a chance, wept for a chance. Maybe then he'd let Rankoff live.

That had been the plan for days.

After Steerforth's life-shattering tale, the whole scheme had flown out of Davenport's mind. He was wandering in a daze of memories. Maggie. Her mother. His father. His grandfather. Past and present were swimming around his drink-soaked, embittered brain.

"This one is mine," said Sabina, continuing to pass out the maps.

"Don't like the sound of that," teased Big Stu.

"Oh, no! It's fair. Rees planned this on his own. I'm playing, too. Who else? Louise."

"Guarding the fort," smiled Wheezer, pointing to her bandaged foot. "Or the saloon. Or Mr. Davenport. Whatever needs the most guarding."

Although the ranch spread over three hundred acres of rolling hills, Rees had confined the treasure hunt to a ten-mile radius near the main street.

The players took their maps and started out of the saloon. The wind continued to blow with incredible force. Dust and tumbleweeds rushed up against them.

"Good luck!" said Ara jauntily, mounting one of the horses the players were to use. She set off on the trail marked on her map.

"Anyone mind if I use the jeep?" asked Joy. "Have enough trouble with people; don't ask me to cope with horses."

Joy took off in the jeep. Dwight, Steerforth, and Big Stu mounted the other horses and were away shortly afterward.

Rankoff stared warily at his horse when Matty approached him.

"I could get killed riding that thing," said Rankoff.

"Maybe not by the horse," said Matty. "But you're in real danger. Davenport's crazy. He might try to kill you. You don't have to do this." Matty quickly recounted what Yvonne had told him on the telephone about the radio broadcast years before.

Rankoff wasn't absorbing any of this startling information. No. He was back in Cleveland. At the railroad station with his father. Waiting for the honor corps from Washington who were to present them with Murray's personal affects and his medals. Murray Rankoff. The great hero. And his kid brother Bobby. The bum. *Maybe, thirty-six years later, I've got a chance to be a hero. Fight my own war. Maybe I can get rid of your ghost, Murray. And Pop's. Finally find some peace. And if not . . . ?*

"How many more times can I die?" asked Rankoff aloud as he mounted his horse.

Foley may have seemed his usual impassive hulk as he rode away from the ranch on his horse. Inside he was a seething network of short-circuited emotions. He'd been running scared, ever since Kislev vanished three nights earlier. Where the hell was Shmuel? What was all this Bornstein business? Who was he for real? Damn! Sounded like that maniac Davenport. Or Rybnik. Or whatever his name was. He'd rattled him as well. *How many men you kill?* He'd felt like going operative at that moment and showing him how easily he could kill. Want a tough Jew, Davenport? You got one!

Reaching into his shirt pocket, Foley lit a cigarette. He'd been smoking steadily for three days. First time in twenty years. Why? He was malfunctioning. Stop it. He hurled the cigarette from his lips to the ground, dug his heels into the horse's side, and rode like hell.

The cigarette continued burning on the trail. Within seconds, it erupted into flames. The Santa Ana winds carried on their deadly mission from there.

***

"Haven't you had enough?" Wheezer asked Davenport as the director broke the label on another bottle of tequila.

"Ain't never gonna be enough," he replied drunkenly and belted his drink back. "Never."

"Why are you destroying yourself? You're a great talent. You're out of the closet now. The only Polish cowboy in the business. What's eating you?"

"I like your man," said Davenport, pouring another shot. "He's got guts. Morty said I'd like him."

"Who's Morty?"

"Garber."

"His name is Matty," corrected Wheezer.

"Why do I keep callin' him Morty? You gonna marry that Englishman?"

"Got to get a divorce from Stanley first."

"Won't be hard. I'll kill him for you, if you like. Always wanted to see Rio."

"There really are two of you, aren't there, Rees? You and Ara. That why you two couldn't get along? Too alike? Tough exteriors and soft centers."

"I like you, too," grinned Davenport. "Always did. Just couldn't stand your husband. Or his partner."

"What have you got against Bobby?"

"He's a selfish prick. Wouldn't lift a finger to help—"

"Wait a minute, pardner!" Wheezer held her hand up like a traffic cop. "Bobby Rankoff is many things. But he is not ungenerous and he is not unkind. He's a goddamn philanthropist, if you must know."

"Oh, yeah?"

"Yeah. Just doesn't advertise. Stanley once told me that for the past twenty-five years he's been contributing thousands of dollars to the stagehands' fund. Widows and orphans of technicians in radio and television."

"How come?"

"That's what Stanley wondered. Every year he'd see Bobby give a check to the union rep. Finally Stan got him drunk one night and got the story. Bobby had a temper tantrum years ago and had a stagehand fired during his radio show. Next day he went looking for the guy—tried to get him his job back—but the guy had vanished.

"Bobby felt so badly about it he swore he'd never let anything like that ever happen to a stagehand or someone in his family again. Isn't that a wonderful story?"

"He . . . never did find out who the stagehand was?"

"Never."

"Jesus Christ!" Davenport picked up the bottle of tequila and threw it with violent force against the wall of the saloon.

"What's wrong?" asked an alarmed Wheezer.

"Got to find him! Goddamn! Before it's too late!"

Davenport stumbled toward the doors of the saloon and saw the great pillar of flame rising from the nearby hills.

"Call the fire department!" he shouted to Wheezer. "Tell 'em to send all the trucks and all the choppers they can."

"Jimmy's up there!"

"So's Sabina! And Ara! You can't do anything for them, Louise. Stay here. Understand?"

"Where are you going?" asked Wheezer, watching Davenport mount the horse tied to the hitching post.

"Get them out of that fire."

The only cowboy to ever come out of New Hope, Pennsylvania, rode off toward the rapidly blanketing flames.

***

Shmuel Kislev was terrified. He'd been so since the moment at Inez Sanchez's party when that voice from the dead had called out his name.

Bornstein.

The next few minutes had all passed like an acid experience.

Shomrim had hit him over and over again. Faces all staring at him with contempt and disgust. The sensation of flying through the air. Fortunately some of the old parachute training came back to him and he managed to land without breaking his neck.

Where could he go? Where could he hide? Only a matter of minutes before the police would be onto him. Would Dwight help him? Probably not.

He remembered the invitation Dwight had mentioned. The old movie ranch in Agoura. A whole town. Cabins. He could hide up there in the mountains. In one of the cabins. Perhaps Dwight would take pity on him. For old-times' sake.

There was some tinned food in the cabin so Kislev hadn't starved, although it had taken all his willpower to swallow that first spoonful of pork and beans. The tins had run out the night before and Kislev was beginning to—What was that?

The door swung open a second late. An enormous black man stood there in a Tom Mix white cowboy suit.

"Hey, man!" said Stu Jackson, who had entered in search of water and was astonished to find the place inhabited. "Ain't you seen the fire?"

"Fire?" repeated Kislev as if he was attempting to translate the word into Hebrew. "Where?"

"Down there!" screamed the ex-football star dragging the Israeli out onto the front porch. "It's comin' this way. We've got to split. Got any blankets or water we can take with?"

"Don't think I'll go with you right now—"

"Don't I know you? Sure. You're Dr. Kislev! Hey, ain't the Man looking for you?"

"You're mistaken. I'm not acquainted with—"

"Look, doc. Want to get fried here, that's your business. I just wanted to help you—"

"I misunderstood. Forgive me, Mister—"

"Jackson. Stu Jackson."

"Of course! Mr. Jackson. Dwight's mentioned you often."

"I'll bet he has."

"Why don't you wait here, Stu? I'll check on the blankets."

"Better make it fast."

Kislev slipped back inside the cabin, looked around, and picked up a shovel from a corner of the room. He crept up on Jackson and brought the shovel down on the back of his head.

Seconds later Shmuel Kislev was running like a crazed horse away from the fire, oblivious to the sound of the real crazed horses trapped within the inferno itself.

***

Rankoff pulled on the reins trying to control his horse. What the hell was wrong with it? He smelled the smoke. Jesus Christ! Looking toward the south, he saw the crimsons and scarlets rushing up toward him. No longer able to control the horse, he leaped down from it.

"No, Bobby!"

Rankoff looked up and saw Sabina coming toward him on horseback.

"Don't let it go!" she shrieked. "It'll go right into the flames!"

"I—I didn't know what to do," said Rankoff pathetically. "Didn't think. Horse's gone now."

"Get on!" said Sabina, nodding to the rear of her mount.

***

Matty was trying desperately to remember every bit of Boy Scout training he'd ever had as the flames continued to encircle him. Downwind or upwind? He couldn't remember. Had there been a badge for firefighting?

He heard the horse's hooves and looked up in time to see the image of Rees Davenport on horseback leaping through the flames.

Matty shuddered for a moment. It was like his fiery chariot nightmare come true. Unfortunately, this was reality.

"Rees! Rees!" The director had vanished back into the flames and Matty was alone once more.

"Matthew!"

Matty looked around frantically and saw Steerforth's dirt and smoke-begrimed face coming toward him then stopped by a ring of fire.

"Come on, lad. This way!"

"You okay, Jimmy?"

"Fine. It's you I'm worried about."

"Can't get out of here!"

"You can!" said Steerforth, removing his Doc Holliday jacket and holding it like a matador's cape. "Come on, old son. Run right toward this."

"I'll get burned!"

"You'll be a hot crossed bun if you stay in there another second. Come on! One—two—three—"

***

Joy was searching desperately for where she'd left the jeep. But for every path she turned down, she was greeted by flames trying to embrace her like anxious suitors.

"I don't want to die like this!" she cried aloud. "I want to die in my bed an old lady."

"With hundreds of grandchildren around you, I hope."

Joy looked up in astonishment to see Ara Whalen sitting on a rocky ledge above her.

"You scared me to death!"

"Once upon a time I'd have taken that for a compliment," smiled Ara, as she hoisted Joy up to join her on the ledge.

"What are you doing up there?"

"Thought it might be the entrance to a cave. Used to be one around here somewhere. Rees loved this ranch and used to bring me here a lot."

"He was really shitty to you back there," said Joy sympathetically.

"Grew immune to him years ago. Understood him for the first time today. His were probably the worst devils of us all."

"Worse than me?" asked Joy.

"Rose and Harry loved you so very much. You knew that."

"Still don't know who I am," said Joy, bursting into tears. "I thought—"

"I know. Wish I was. You're incredible."

"Really?"

"Wish I knew who your real parents were. But I don't"

"Thank you," said Joy. She impetuously hugged Ara. "Sorry for the pain I caused you. I stole your earrings!"

"What?"

"I broke into your house and stole your earrings."

"Thank God!" sighed Ara gratefully. "I'm not senile!"

"You're not mad at me? I'll give them back."

Ara looked at the tears running down the girl's doe like eyes and burst out laughing.

"Oh, Joy! Here we are sitting on a ledge in the middle of the most horrendous forest fire, our lives in jeopardy, and you're worried if I'm mad at you."

"I want a clean slate in heaven!"

"Oh, Joyous! Come on." Ara jumped down from the ledge. "Thank God for tennis! I could never have done that six months ago."

"Where are we going?" asked Joy, leaping down beside her.

"There's an old mine around here. If we go deep enough inside it, we should be safe from the flames."

***

Dwight Foley was in his element. Battle conditions again. He was operative now as he hadn't been for twenty years. Solo force! Just like the search and destroy missions in Nam. Flames everywhere. Pitiful cries. God! How he'd missed that sense of challenge. The sense of raw power. Just he, his gun and his knife. Sometimes just his bare hands. Against the Cong. The VC. Victor Charlie.

"Death to Victor Charlie!" he shouted aloud. He laughed heartily. It felt good. "Come on, you fucking gooks! I'm out here. Come on and get me—if you dare!"

Something was moving through the trees.

Foley could hear it

His body tensed up.

He flexed his palms.

His hands were weapons.

Then he saw the enemy coming at him.

He was ready.

"Dwight, no! You maniac!"

Foley brought the karate blow to a halt a micro-inch away from the bridge of Shmuel Kislev's hook nose.

"Shmuel! What the hell are you doing out here?'

"He's after me!" babbled Kislev. "That *shvartzer*! I should have killed him back there. He's after me!"

"What are you talking about? How did you get out here?"

"You've got to help me, Dwight. Get me out of here. Out of the country. The police are onto me. They'll tell Interpol."

"Good." Foley walked away from the grasp of his terrified former conspirator.

"You're not going to help me?" shrieked Kislev as he chased after Foley.

"Why should I?" asked Foley, who was staring at the entrance to an old mine that lay about three hundred yards north.

"Because I was your partner. Your friend. I know things about you, Dwight. Things you wouldn't want other people to know. I'll tell them. I swear! If you don't help me, I'll tell them how you killed Nolan and the girl."

"You'd tell them?"

"Yes!"

"No, you won't."

Before Kislev could contradict him, Foley dealt the phony guru three terminal karate chops to the nose, throat, and temple.

***

Ara and Joy were making their way through the dense smoke and flames when they heard the voices of two men quarreling.

It had been difficult for them to make out their identities through the pillar of fire but the wind shifted once again. They watched with shock and horror as Dwight dealt the three deadly blows to Kislev.

Joy gasped involuntarily. Foley's trained ear picked up on the sound. He raised his head and saw the two terrified women staring at him through the flames.

"You saw!"

"No, we didn't," lied Joy. "Honest, Dwight! We didn't see anything."

Foley pulled his snub-nosed .38 out of its holster and aimed it at Joy.

Ara rushed in front of Joy to protect her. The bullet ripped into Ara's chest and seconds later the front of her Annie Oakley costume was stained with blood. The Painted Lady emitted an agonized, gurgling sound and crumpled to the ground.

"Foley!"

Dwight wheeled around and saw a blood-soaked Stu Jackson racing toward him with hatred in his eyes.

"Stay away from me, nigger!"

Foley fired at him but the ex-football star dodged the bullets as if it was an offensive tackle and continued toward the ex-Green Beret. Foley looked around desperately and made for the mine.

Big Stu was hot on his heels all the way up the hill. He attempted a flying tackle but missed his prey by inches. Foley leaped into the ore car at the mouth of the mine and fumbled with the electrical apparatus that started the car up. Seconds later he was rolling along the track into the mine with Big Stu on foot following him.

Joy was oblivious to the chase and the distant sound of the fire department choppers on their rescue mission. Tears streamed down the baby barracuda's face as she clutched Ara's unconscious body and prayed with all her heart and soul that the Painted Lady would not die.

BOBCAYGEON

Davenport screeched his Lamborghini to a stop in front of the admissions entrance to Cedars-Sinai Hospital and raced inside the building. A security guard shouted that he couldn't park there. The director shouted a curse over his shoulder, grabbed the first nurse he could by the shoulders, and demanded to know where the victims of the Agoura fire were.

The elevator took forever to reach the ground floor, so Davenport sped up the emergency stairs.

He found Rankoff inside Foley's room staring at the mummified body of the unconscious ex-Green Beret.

"How is he?" asked Davenport.

"Not good," replied Rankoff. "He was badly burned in the fire. He and Big Stu almost killed each other at the mine."

"How did he break all them bones?"

"According to Stu, he jumped into an ore car and raced it inside the shaft to get away from the fire. When the firemen got there, they found the car and Dwight lying at the bottom of a pit. The track just stopped dead and the car must have tumbled over inside. Weird, huh?"

"Not really," growled Davenport. He stared up at Rankoff with the guilt of the ages on his face. "Rigged up that ore car. I'm responsible for the accident."

"Why would—?"

"Meant it for you. Didn't want to kill you. I was crazy, Bobby. Had this poison in me for years. Ever since the radio show."

"What radio show?" asked Rankoff, feeling the eeriest tingle to ever slither up his spine.

"When you had me fired. I was a stagehand at CBS and you—"

"That was you! My God! Rees, I didn't—"

"Found out this afternoon. How you gave all that money to the pension fund. You're a good man, Bobby. I . . . I apologize."

Davenport held his hand out to Rankoff, who took it gratefully.

"Been a helluva day for all of us," sighed Rankoff, who hadn't recovered from the image of a shaken Evelyn Shankman waiting for him in the lobby of the hospital with news that would set his world even more upside down.

"About Sabina . . ."

"Hey, man," grinned Rankoff. "She loves you. She's your old lady. I see that now. Just take care of her. I couldn't."

"Goddamn! I like you! Ain't it crazy? You remind me a helluva lot of me."

"Pretty good criterion for friendship. Can I finally take that dead chicken out of my freezer?"

Davenport let loose his wild stallion laugh, clapped Rankoff on the shoulder, and started out of the hospital room when he collided with a middle-aged nurse.

"What's the meaning of all this noise?" demanded the nurse. "Can't you see this patient is gravely ill?"

"Sorry, ma'am. Just havin' a word with my agent here. Want to be my agent?" The last question was a throwaway to Rankoff.

"Call my secretary and set up an appointment," replied the IAA boss with a straight face.

"Afraid you'll have to leave as well, Mr. Rankoff."

Rankoff walked out of the room and found a waiflike Joy Dworkin waiting for him in the corridor.

The two stared at each other in silence until he lit a cigarette and walked towards her.

"Hello, Joyous."

"Hi," she answered nervously. "Did Evelyn . . . . ?"

"Yeah," he nodded. "Want to sell it to 'Believe It or Not' or should I?"

"Pretty weird." Joy paused agonizingly then asked: "Would you prefer boss or Daddy from now on?"

Rankoff stared down into her face and saw tears sliding down her cheeks. He took her face in his hands.

"Sorry I never knew. Sorry I never sang you to sleep. Sorry you never had the chance to grow up with your sister. But you've got a family now, if you want it."

"I do!" she sobbed, wrapping her arms around him. "I do!"

She looked up and saw the two plainclothes policemen walking down the corridor.

"You'll have to come with us now, Mr. Rankoff. We can't wait any longer."

"Okay," he replied and attempted to remove Joy's arms.

"Where are you going?" she asked desperately.

"Have to go with these guys," he shrugged. "Not finished paying my dues, Joyous."

"Police? Are they police?"

"It's all right, kid." He brushed the tears away from his long-lost daughter's face. "I'll make some kind of deal. You know me."

"I don't want to lose you now! I've waited so long to find you."

"Go see Ara," said Rankoff as he headed down the hall with the two detectives. "Make sure she's all right"

"But—"

"Go on!"

A sea of flowers seemed to surround Ara as Joy stepped into the room on the same floor as Dwight Foley. The younger woman was pleased to see the Painted Lady sitting up in bed.

"How are you feeling?" asked Joy hesitantly.

"What hurts the most is my pride. Everyone knows now."

"Knows what?"

"Why I'm still alive."

"The doctor said it was a miracle," replied Joy.

"A Beverly Hills miracle. Nothing to do with divine intervention."

"I don't understand."

"Must I spell it out? The bullet shattered my saline implant and lost its impact."

"Saline implant? You mean . . . those aren't - weren't . . .?"

"No, Joyous. My boobs weren't real. They're what saved my life. There are no longer any mysteries left at IAA."

"Did Evelyn tell you? About me?"

"Yes. I was flabbergasted. Known her for thirty years and never suspected—well, her 'illness.' I really believed—"

"My mother was a great actress," said Joy proudly. "My mother. Wow! Going to have a little trouble with that for a while."

"Do you resent her?"

"For about a second. Until I realized what she must have gone through all those years. Having to carry on that charade. Making you all think she was some kind of invalid."

"Does Bobby know yet?"

Joy nodded then said: "They just arrested him. Goddamn Stan Feingold. Left him holding the bag, didn't he?"

"I'm sorry."

"Hey, Ara! That's my old man. The *capo* dealmaker. He'll get himself out of this. You know him."

"It's a serious charge, Joy."

"I know." Joy heaved a huge sigh and planted her lovely body onto a chair next to the bed. "Glad you're my friend now. I'm so screwed up."

"Everything's out in the open now."

"Yeah. Except everything's worse. I was in love with two men, Ara. Really hung up on them. One of them turns out to be my father and the other one's going to be my cousin through marriage."

"Who's that?"

"Jimmy!"

"Have you never heard of kissing cousins?" asked Ara, arching her eyebrow.

"Not the same anymore. He's going to marry Wheezer as soon as her divorce comes through. She's like family. Never stick my nose in there. I feel like Huck Finn. Got a feeling everyone's going to 'civilize' me."

"It'll be very flattering on you." Ara winced with pain and began massaging her right breast

"Gonna have them lifted again?" asked Joy.

"Haven't made up my mind," replied Ara. "Not planning on being shot in the near future, but it would look a bit strange walking around with one flat tire."

"What about those women in mythology, who used to cut off one breast so they'd be better archers. You know—"

"Yes, dear. I know. My Penthesilea, Queen of the Amazons, period is behind me. Opting out for a less rambunctious middle age. They're going to make fun of me, aren't they?"

"Who?"

"All the girls at the office. They were always guessing, weren't they? I can't handle any whispers in the Xerox room."

"They'll never find out, Ara. I swear. The secret stays in this hospital. You have my word as a baby barracuda."

Ara clutched Joy's hand gratefully and said, "Let's have lunch next week."

***

Steerforth pressed the doorbell in front of the mansion in Trousdale and confidently waited for Ames to open the door. Instead the Englishman was greeted by a beautiful woman in her late twenties with a haunting, childlike quality.

"Hi! Want to see my father?"

Steerforth was dumbstruck. His instinct was to go outside and check the front of the house. Yvonne appeared from the living room.

"Jimmy!" She hugged him warmly. "You remember Martine, don't you?"

"Martine!? Is it really—?"

"*Ma chere*, do you remember Mr. Steerforth?"

"Uh-huh. I had a terrible crush on him when I was little."

"Mr. Steerforth has that effect on women. As your mother, it's my place to warn you. After that, you're on your own."

"Nice seeing you again," said Martine, who bounced back towards the living room.

"How long has she—I mean—" Steerforth was speechless.

Yvonne clapped her hands together and laughed. "I've never seen you like this before! You're quite attractive when you're inarticulate."

"What did you do?" demanded Steerforth, recovering his self-composure. "Take her to Lourdes?"

437

"No. It was the strangest thing. We were watching the news on TV last week. The day of the fire. She knew Bobby had gone there. When the minicam showed the ranch going up in flames, she cried out: 'Daddy! No!' I fainted dead away. When I awoke, she was standing over me with a wet towel and asking, 'Are you all right, *maman?*' She hadn't called me that since she was a child."

"Are you . . . staying around for a while?"

"He's asked me to," replied Yvonne with delight.

"Where is he?"

"The library. Go ahead. He'll be furious I waylaid you."

Steerforth knocked at the library door, turned the handle and walked in when there was no reply.

Rankoff was wearing a dark-blue Italian-knit cardigan with a shawl collar and was engrossed in conversation with a tall, benign-looking man in his late fifties wearing an Eastern-cut suit

"Jimmy! Come in."

Rankoff rose from the ottoman and shook his colleague's hand.

"Just spoke to Martine in the hallway—"

"Fantastic, isn't it?' beamed Rankoff. "Oh, sorry. James Steerforth, this is Edward Marshak. Ted flew out from New York last night."

"You a producer, Mr. Marshak?" asked Steerforth, trying to get a measure of the man with the steel-rimmed glasses and firm handshake.

"An attorney," replied Marshak.

"He's married to my first wife," said Rankoff hastily as he moved toward the bar. "Want a drink?"

"Whiskey. Neat," replied Steerforth. "Out here for long, Mr. Marshak?"

"Call me Ted."

"Thank you, Ted."

"Ted's handling my, uh, problem for me," said Rankoff, passing Steerforth his scotch. "The best there is."

"Bet Phyllis told you that," smiled Marshak.

"I've been married to some fascinating women in my time, Jimmy. But his wife takes the cake. Haven't spoken to her in thirty years. She heard about my arrest and phoned me. Said there was nothing to worry about. Can you believe that?"

"That there's nothing to worry about?" asked Steerforth. "Or that she phoned you?"

"Don't give me any heat, you cynical limey!" warned Rankoff with a grin. "I'm just so touched Phyllis would do that."

"Robert, you happen to be one of those rare men women never fall out of love with . . . even after you've left them. It's a gift from God, old son. Wish I had it. Cheers." Steerforth brought his glass to his lips.

"Think he'll be here soon?" asked Marshak, gazing at his watch.

"Called from the hotel an hour ago," replied Rankoff. "Problem is he's always bumping into people—"

"Who's that?" asked Steerforth, wondering who they were all waiting for.

The doorbell rang. Ames's familiar footsteps could be heard crossing from the kitchen to the front door.

Seconds later the library door swung open. Abe Keller bounced into the room and immediately launched into a monologue.

"Can't walk across the lobby of the Beverly Wilshire without bumping into at least half a dozen people I thought were dead. How do these people stay alive so long out here? I take one breath of this smog, I'm ready for the undertaker. How can you live out here, Bobby? Hey, Jimmy, how are ya? What's all this Wheezer tells me about you two? I think it's terrific. I'm not losin' a daughter I'm gainin' a first-class agent. Between you and me, Feingold was a shmuck with earflaps. Greedy, greedy, greedy. But you know what I say: 'Once an actor, always an actor. A good agent stays that way till he drops'. Why I always liked you, Jimmy. Hey, Ted! Whadda you doin' here? Didn't know you knew Bobby. Small world, huh? What's the big *tsimmis*, Bobby? Why I have to fly out here?"

"Toochis auf dem tisch, Abe."

"Cards on the table?" asked Steerforth.

"A reasonable translation, James." Rankoff turned back to the glass-eyed Keller. "What the hell have you been up to. You're not sick. You haven't got cancer. And you have no intention of retiring. Right?"

"Really nice house you got here, Bobby—"

"Abe! I want answers. Not just for me. For Jimmy. He's going to be running the place for a while. I don't want any mysteries."

Steerforth stared in amazement at Rankoff.

"Bobby, what the devil are you—?"

"I'm going to jail. Jimmy. Need to know that this agency is in the best possible hands. You got million-dollar hands, kid. But I don't want your future father-in-law screwing you around anymore. So what's the story, Abe?"

"The business is dead in New York," whined Keller after an interminable pause. "There's nothing happening. You know me, Bobby. I need action. I'll die without it. The action's all out here now. You've been running this ship better than Sid ever did, *oliva shalom.* I couldn't just come out here and take over. So I figured I'd give you a little *zetz.* Nothin' serious. What do they say in England, Jimmy? 'Work a little mischief'? I got a phone call from Gilbert Bobcaygeon. That *shmigegge* wanted to get back in the agency business. Can you believe it? I didn't want him in the New York office. So I sent him to you. Figured he'd cause enough chaos here—"

"We'd be on our knees in six months and you'd fly out to pick up the pieces?" asked Steerforth, advancing on the forty-eight-inch-high Keller.

"Nah-nah!" warned Keller, shaking a finger up at him. "Going to be your father-in-law. Don't lift a hand to me."

"Merely offering you a seat, Daddy dear," said Steerforth. "Louise would never forgive me if any harm befell you . . . before the wedding."

"What about New York?" asked Rankoff.

"That's where it all went wrong!" wailed Keller. "My plan turned to rat shit. Rabaiotti's been waitin' years for me to retire. I been keepin' him waitin'. Never thought he'd quit!"

"Tony?" The name came out of Rankoff and Steerforth's mouths simultaneously. Rabaiotti had been the understood heir-apparent for years. How could he have given up everything after all that time?

"He divorced his wife," continued Keller. "Gone into the hotel business."

"Sylvia!" Again the duet of Rankoff and Steerforth.

"Yeah," nodded Keller. "Sylvia Nardino. He married her and he's the president of that whole hotel chain. The ungrateful wop! After everything I did for him. Bringin' him up from the mailroom over—"

"Yeah," interrupted Rankoff. "Over the heads of all the Jewish boys. I know the speech by heart, Abe." Rankoff burst out laughing, shook his head, and turned to Steerforth. "Nice to know somebody finally fucked Sylvia without getting fucked."

"We must send dear Tony a cable," suggested Steerforth.

"Think she'll let him out of the honeymoon suite once in a while?"

"This ain't funny, guys," whined Keller. "Means I gotta stay in New York."

"Well, Daddy, you can always phone me on the direct line," beamed Steerforth.

"Got nothin' to do in New York. I'm clippin' coupons."

"There's always the London office," suggested Rankoff.

"What am I gonna do there with a bunch of pippers? No offense, Jimmy."

"None taken, Daddy."

"Don't call me Daddy!"

"How long am I in charge out here?" asked Steerforth.

"Indefinitely," replied Rankoff.

"My God, Bobby! How long are you going up for?"

"Not long. Ted got me a terrific deal. Thirty days. Minimum security. First time in three decades somebody's made a deal for me!"

"What are you gonna do when you come out?" asked Keller. "You're not comin' back to the office?"

"Not for a long time, Abe. If ever. It's all yours, Jimmy. You should have been running it a long time ago."

Steerforth finished his whiskey, turned to Keller and said: "I'll take over on one condition."

"What's that?" asked the founding father.

"Mind stepping over to the side, Abe? Your bloody glass eye is blinding me. Thank you . . . Absolutely refuse to set foot inside the office again without a written guarantee Gilbert Bobcaygeon is off the payroll."

"No problem," said Keller with a wave of his hand. "The schmuck quit last week anyhow."

"Where's he gone?" asked Rankoff.

"Who cares? The guy was driving me nuts all the time with his vouchers for expenses. What the hell was he doing in Biloxi, Mississippi? And all those other places? I pray I never hear that Goofy laugh again!" He turned to Steerforth and trained his one good eye on him. "So, son-in-law? Are we partners?"

Abe Keller held his hand out to the man who had once been Willie Stubbs, a lifetime before in Bakewell.

Bobby Rankoff entered a minimum security prison near Palm Springs and was released the day before New Year's.

Stu Jackson recovered from his wounds and decided the agency business was even more dangerous than football. He accepted a lucrative offer from a Japanese automobile manufacturer to be their television spokesman and went from IAA agent to IAA client in one afternoon.

Dwight Foley remained in a coma for two months following his fall inside the mine shaft. The police waited patiently for him to regain consciousness, so he could be charged with three counts of murder. The ex-Green Beret escaped mortal justice when he finally succumbed to his wounds in late January. Despite the charges hanging over his head, Foley was given the military funeral he had asked for in his will and was buried with his uniform and medals.

Inez Sanchez embarked on a worldwide evangelical tour of the underdeveloped nations despite multimillion-dollar breach of contract suits filed against her by both the Scheherazade Hotel and the TV network she had left in the lurch.

Minden Prescott signed a six-figure publishing contract to write a biography of Lowell Sherman.

Rees Davenport left for Brazil to scout locations for a film starring Sabina Rankoff. He moved into a villa previously occupied by Stan Feingold, who—rumor had it—had fled to Paraguay under a false passport.

Martine Rankoff took a job at IAA as a secretary to her stepsister, Joy Dworkin.

On Valentine's Day, Evelyn Shankman married Ivor Manning in a simple ceremony at Robert Rankoff's home in Trousdale. Mr. Manning's best man was his nephew, James Steerforth, the head of the International Artists Agency in Beverly Hills. The maid of honor was the bride's daughter, Ms. Joy Dworkin, also an agent with IAA.

Matthew Garber and his fiancée, Lindsay Fairweather, missed the ceremony by seconds due to a delay in the arrival of their plane from St. Louis, where the senior IAA agent had taken Ms. Fairweather to meet his parents.

"So sorry," said Matty repeatedly as he kissed the bride and pumped the groom's hand. "That goddamn plane! Told the cab driver I'd pay the speeding tickets but he couldn't pull it off. I really wanted to be here."

"You're here now," smiled Evelyn. "That's what counts. We've all wasted a great deal of time and energy regretting things that didn't happen or things we should have done."

"Quite right, my darling," said Ivor, pecking her on the cheek. "The future is everything. I'm looking forward to the next seventy-five years . . . one day at a time."

The buffet lunch that followed the service was unanimously hailed as Ames's masterpiece. Champagne flowed endlessly as did the conversation.

They were all a family that afternoon. Matty had to pinch himself when he realized he'd known none of these people a year before. He watched in amazement as Steerforth and Wheezer held hands like two teen-agers discussing plans for their own upcoming wedding; smiled happily at the vision of Ara Whalen on the arm of her Italian textiles magnate; nodded gleefully at Evelyn and Ivor as they cut their wedding cake; and felt a special sense of pride at the picture of Bobby, Yvonne, Martine, and Joy together as a family.

"Admiring your handiwork?" asked Lindsay, carrying a dish of wedding cake over to him.

"What are you talking about?" he asked, opening his mouth to let her shovel in a spoonful of the delicious gateau.

"You're responsible for all this. The guardian angel."

"Lindsay, my love, there is only one angel in this room."

"Don't *schmooze* me, Matthew. Your mother warned me about you."

"What else did my mother tell you?"

"Not to let you get away with anything."

"She didn't! Did she? . . . Yvonne's waving to us. Come on."

They walked over to Yvonne, who introduced them to Martine. Lindsay and Martine began comparing stories about Bobby and the former agency head steered Matty off to a corner.

"Looking good, kid," observed Rankoff.

"Thanks."

"Got the twinkle back in your eyes. You lost it for a while there. How was St. Louis?"

"Terrific. Lindsay got enough lingerie for life."

"She's a terrific lady. You be good to her."

"I will. How does it feel having all these women in your life again?"

"That's a sensitive subject," laughed Rankoff. "I'm having a ball."

"How was it . . . ?"

"In the joint? Like a month in Palm Springs. They were very nice to me. Let me have a pianist three hours a day."

"What for?"

"Forgot. You're not writing my biography anymore. I'm out of the agency business for good. My daughter— you should pardon the expression—is carrying on the business. I'm going back to work."

"Singing?"

"Yeah. Bazzo got me a record deal in London. Apparently, I'm still a star over there. My old records are collectors' items. If this new album's any good, they're going to book me into Talk of the Town and the Palladium. Afterwards, Larry wants to bring me back to New York. The Carlyle. He's really into it."

"When do you leave?"

"Two weeks. Yvonne and I. Rees has given us his flat in London."

"Rees?"

"We're friends now," shrugged Rankoff. "I like him."

"Wow! How do you feel about it? Singing again."

"Scared shitless. But it's the right kind of fear. . . . Thanks, kid."

"For what?"

"All this."

"I didn't—"

"No, not you. A soaking wet kid from St Louis, who used to listen to 'Latin Lady' in his basement. Thank him for me."

Ames walked over to them at that moment and informed Matty there was an urgent long distance phone call for him.

"Take it in the library," said Rankoff.

Lindsay watched curiously as her future husband scurried out of the room and turned around to discover Joy Dworkin standing beside her.

"When are you two getting married?" asked Joy.

"Soon. Couple of months maybe. Want to get my new business set up first."

"What kind of business?"

"The time has come for me to leave IAA. Wouldn't be the same for me now that your father's left. Always wanted to be my own boss. That was my problem all along. Needed something of my own. I'm buying up old fifties cars. Wrecks. Going to redo and ship them to Germany. They'll pay a fortune over there for a '54 DeSoto."

"Are you serious?"

"About the prices?"

"No! The car business. Where did you—?"

"My grandfather was a car freak," shrugged Lindsay. "Guess it runs in the family."

"Don't you want any kids?" asked Joy.

"Not this week. Matty's not in any rush."

"Think he'll stay with the agency?" asked Joy.

"Why not? He loves it. I'm sure he'll end up running the place. No offense, Joy."

Matty returned to the living room at that point, looking all the world like a gunfighter marching down the main street of Dodge City. He paused in front of the two women.

"Who was on the phone?" asked Lindsay.

"Bobcaygeon."

"You're kidding! What did he want?"

"Offered me the chance of a lifetime."

"Again!"

"Exactly what I said," grinned Matty. "He finally explained why he's been traveling around the country so mysteriously all year. Setting up a fourth network. Linking independent TV stations across the States. That's what he was doing in St. Louis when I first met him. Finally got his deal together and wants me to come aboard as vice-president in charge of creative affairs."

"Fantastic!" squealed Joy. "What a coup!"

"Funny," said Matty. "He almost had me hooked again. Hundred thousand dollars a year. Car and chauffeur. Penthouse in New York. Beach house in Malibu. Shares in the company."

"When do you start?" asked Joy.

"I'm not taking it"

"You're crazy!" replied Joy. "You're blowing—"

"Almost said yes. Until he told me I wasn't his first choice. Wanted to be upfront with me. Said he'd offered it to someone else. But they didn't feel qualified. They said I'd be the perfect person for the job and he'd be a fool not to grab me. Guess who that wonderful person was?" He stared directly into Joy's eyes. "Are you that desperate to get rid of me, Joyous?"

"Of course not!" protested Joy in a futile attempt to cover her guilt "Thought it would be a terrific thing for you. What do I know about creative shit? I'm just a packager. Besides, we all know what a flake Gilbob is. What if the whole thing fell through?"

"Precisely!" shouted Matty. "I'd have walked away from my career and you're sitting in my office."

"Hey, calm down! You didn't do it, did you? We can still run this place, Matty. You don't mind me talking about this, do you, Lindsay? Now that you're going into business, you can really appreciate this. We can take over this agency on stock. Think of the proxy battle! Wheezer's got her father's shares and Jimmy's got his own. But I can get Bobby's shares and my mother's if I play my cards right. That'll give me controlling interest. I'm not greedy, Matty. I'll go partners with you."

"Who's going partners with whom?"

Joy spun around nervously to see an amused Steerforth towering over her.

"What are you up to now, Scheherazade? Flexing your little muscles? Testing your corporate clout?"

"Can't blame a girl for trying," she replied meekly.

"You are incorrigible," beamed Steerforth, wrapping a cousinly arm around her. "Which is one reason Matthew can never leave IAA. You were wise, old son, turning down Bobcaygeon."

"How did you know?" asked Matty.

"A little benign eavesdropping on the kitchen extension," replied Steerforth. "Learned that one from Scheherazade. See, Joyous? One can teach an old dog new tricks."

"I never—"

"Oh, sweet coz, methinks you do protest too much. Never mind. I'm creating a new position at the agency. Head of packaging. It's my wedding present to you, Matthew. You're going to keep tabs on us, lad. Make sure we don't unleash too many monsters on the world in the name of the Almighty Deal. My mind trembles at some of the potential packages Joyous may come up with in the years to come. What shall we call you, old son? Minister of Taste?"

"Jimmy!" It was Wheezer.

"What is it, my darling?"

"Bobby wants you to play for him. He's going to sing."

"My pleasure." He turned to Joy and whispered in her ear: "Expect you to have Mr. Rankoff signed by the end of the day."

"Signed him already," she shrugged.

"Cheeky bitch."

They all gathered around the piano, one large family, and listened to the golden tones of Bobby Rankoff as he sang of another time that really wasn't much different from this.

ABOUT THE AUTHOR

Charles Dennis was born in Toronto and began his performing career at the age of eight on the Canadian radio series, *Peter and the Dwarf*. He made his professional stage debut at 16 at the Red Barn Theatre. The following year he joined the staff of the Toronto Telegram as a second-string film and theatre critic. He received a Bachelor of Arts degree at the University of Toronto. The following year he moved to England where he remained for six years. During that period, he wrote his first novel, *Stoned Cold Soldier,* and created the television series, *Marked Personal.*

Dennis ended his sojourn in England and moved to Los Angeles where he has remained ever since. He resumed his acting career appearing as Sunad on *Star Trek* and other episodic TV series. He began a career as a voice artist supplying the voices for Rico in Disney's feature film, *Home on the Range,* TV's *American Dad,* as well as numerous video games including Odahving in *Skyrim* and Spock's father Surok in *Star Trek.*

He is an award-winning director, whose feature films include *Hard Four*, *Barking Mad* and *Deadly Draw.* He won the Best Actor award at the 2022 Studio City Film Festival for his performance as Franz Altman in *King Solomon's Treasure*, based on his play. His other plays include *Going On, The Alchemist of Cecil Street,* and *High Class Heel*.

Dennis resides at El Rancho Del Navitas in Shadow Hills, California with his wife, Ulrika Vingsbo, and their son, Greyson Nathaniel. Their household includes three horses, two Boston terriers, a turtle, and a bearded dragon.